METAVERSE MYTHHUNTER

Book 1

By
Jules Kindred Blair

Metaverse Mythhunter
Book 1

ISBN (print): 979-8-88993-051-8
Library of Congress Control Number (print): 2025932658

Written by Jules Kindred Blair
Edited by Darien Aris Kirst

Published 2025 by MoonQuill
Arlington, VA
www.moonquill.com

Table of Contents

FILE [SEQUENCE ERROR]

EURYALE

I twisted the blade free and watched the severed head of the gorgon tumble off her bare shoulders. It landed with a splat, blood pooling amid shards of glass outside the executive high-rise suite.

All at once, her wings ceased their fury. Her deadly talons scraped impotently on the cold balcony floor; it took a bit longer for the writhing, venomous serpents sprouting from her decapitated skull to still.

Task Successfully Completed: Remove {unknown} gorgon from Zenith Towers.

The monster was dead. And so were many of my friends.

I watched as my partner, frozen in stone—horror forever fixed on their features—began to crumble and dissolve into digital nothingness.

My gauntlets and blade dripped with the poisonous blood. I dropped the weapon and removed the gauntlets one by one, letting them fall where I stood.

How close had I come to death? Whatever death meant in a place like this. I wearily checked my menu.

Essence: 10 remaining.

That was close.

The sound of a vibrating electric thrum drew my attention back to the monster's corpse. The body quivered as motes of bright, goldenrod light wove into the air. A glowing crystalline card formed, hovering above the dead gorgon.

{legendary} Data Card obtained: Euryale *(Helm / Skill)*.

I held my breath.

I had never seen a legendary Data Card before, and it was all mine. That, and a substantial payday waiting for me when I turned in this bounty.

A spotlight from a Polizei drone buzzing overhead enveloped me, but I ignored it.

I grabbed the glowing, spinning card, the neon cityscape below oblivious to all that had transpired.

FILE 1.0

AWAKENING

I opened eyes I thought were mine (they weren't) and, blinking heavily, took in what I assumed to be my world (it wasn't). In time, I would learn that this place—this reality—was not something any of us had fully understood, or that anyone had truly been prepared for.

But all that was still to come.

In those early moments, I was surrounded by nothing but sterile light. The taste of lightning lingered somewhere I could not reach. And a sense of placeless loss.

A voice greeted me. Curt and formal.

Hello.

Who is there? Who is that?

I couldn't speak. The words trapped inside of me. Mute.

Let me try this again.

▸ Who is there?

I saw no one. Some quality of the voice informed me that it was not what you might call "real." An uncanny valley.

I am the Concierge. My role is to welcome and orient you to your new world.

▸ New world. Where am I?

You are in The Collective, the most advanced and fully immersive shared virtual platform for human consciousness.

▸ I don't understand.

Disorientation is a common reaction when entering The Collective. Take all the time you need.

▸ Tell me more.

What would you like to know more about?

▸ The Collective. What is that?

The Collective is the most advanced and fully immersive shared virtual platform for human consciousness.

▸ You mentioned that. Where are you? Why can't I see you?

I am simply a virtual assistant, programmed to welcome and orient you to your new world and your role within. I do not have a visual form.

▸ How did I get here? I don't... I am having trouble remembering.

I realized then that I was not even sure who I was. Autobiographical details eluded me. Like when you try to remember a word—that exact word on the tip of your tongue—but no matter what, it just won't come to you. A dream fleeing from awareness upon waking. Now imagine that, but for the entirety of your identity.

Dissociative amnesia can also be an uncommon but serious reaction when entering The Collective.

▸ Dissociative amnesia. Do you know who I am?

You are Volunteer 01001110-01101111-01100010-01101111 01100100-01111001.

▸ Volunteer? But who am I really? Who was I before I... entered this place?

I am unable to help you with that as I am only a virtual assistant and do not have the necessary information or abilities.

▸ I can't see anything. Where is my body?

Activating visualization now.

A humanoid form took shape in the sterile light. My form, apparently. I could only describe it as a wireframe model. A person-shaped blueprint in three dimensions.

▸ Is this what I look like? I seem… unfinished.

Accessing visual customization options.

In the ether, towering menus appeared in a dizzying array of cosmetic options. The first choice was "skin color." I found that with my wireframe self, I could reach out and swipe through these options.

What to pick? I had no point of reference for what my skin tone should be.

I selected one that appealed to me on some aesthetic level.

You have selected a premium skin tone. Would you like to unlock this selection?

Premium skin tone? Somehow the concept felt incorrect, but I could not put into words why that would be. I saw now that the icon of a closed padlock hovered over the skin tone I had selected.

▸ Yes. I would like to unlock it.

This premium skin tone can be purchased for 10,000 Crypt. Would you like to purchase it?

▸ Crypt. Crypt? What is that?

Universal Cryptocurrency Credits, or Crypt for short.

▸ How much Crypt do I have?

You have 500 Crypt.

▸ Oh.

I swiped through the menus until I found a total of three skin tones that did not have the locked icon. They were labeled beige, almond, and bistre. For no particular reason, I selected almond.

Almond skin tone selected. Would you like to apply this change?

▸ Yes.

Soon my hollow, wireframe body was draped in tan skin. I was beginning to look—and feel—more human. I saw a sequence of numbers printed on my wrist like a barcode: 01001110-01101111 01100010-01101111-01100100-01111001. My Volunteer number, or was it my name?

Looking down at my body, I realized I had no hair. Or genitals. The concept of "mannequin" came to mind.

▸ I think something is missing. Down below.

But what? I tried to remember, but everything in my mind was as featureless as the nude mound at my groin.

Would you like to purchase genitalia? Genitals can be unlocked for 10,000 Crypt.

▸ What can I afford with 500 Crypt?

There are several free hairstyles available in addition to other default cosmetic options. You can also afford basic clothing items and weapons.

▸ Weapons? Why would I need weapons?

You are a Volunteer. You will need weapons to fulfill your role in The Collective.

▸ Tell me more. What is the role of a Volunteer in The Collective?

The Collective is the most advanced and fully immersive shared virtual platform for human consciousness.

It is an exciting new frontier and state of the art living space for all mankind while Earth's greatest minds work to solve the challenges at hand.

Volunteers have been tasked with removing invasive entities

from The Collective so that future waves of virtual settlers can enjoy their new home.

▸ A shared virtual platform. Are you saying this is some form of cyberspace? The Metaverse? I am inside a computer simulation right now?

The Collective can be thought of as a metaverse, yes.

▸ So my mind is in some kind of program. Then is this body my... What is the correct term... My avatar?

You can think of it as an avatar, yes. But we prefer to call it your True Self ™.

▸ You said we. Who is 'we'?

Reality Incorporated, the owner and operator of The Collective. "Live your best second life." ™

That name meant nothing to me. Why should it have? I couldn't even remember my *own* name.

▸ Where is my real, physical body right now?

Outside of The Collective, your physical body is in a state of peaceful, suspended animation.

▸ Suspended animation. But where precisely? What is the exact location?

You have insufficient system privileges to access that information. Please contact your system administrator.

▸ Who is my system administrator?

You have insufficient system privileges to access that information.

▸ How can I contact my system admministrator?

You have insufficient system privileges to access that information.

▸ Can you contact my system administrator for me?

I am unable to help you with that, as I am only a virtual assistant and do not have the necessary information or abilities.

I saw this conversation becoming circular. I had a thousand questions, sure. But I also felt overwhelmed by the myriad cosmetic options hovering in front of me—each with its own price.

The number of customization options and sliders—from cheekbone height, neck width, earlobe length, and many more—sent a streak of panic through me. I had to get out of there.

I quickly selected bald, a free hairstyle option.

Bald hairstyle selected. Would you like to apply this change?

▸ Yes. Yes!

I rushed through the remaining cosmetic options, choosing the default brown eye color and some free eyebrows. I also kept the default voice, which apparently I had been using—a bland, androgynous rasp that faded like vapor soon after passing through my lips.

▸ Show me the clothing options.

As new menus spread before me, I quickly found that there were no free clothing options and precious few within my limited budget. That wasn't entirely true. The basic footwear was free.

After some time, I selected black coveralls for 200 Crypt.

Now I was bald, tan, genderless, and wearing black coveralls.

I wanted to get this over with. Find some answers.

Visual customization complete. Now accessing weapon options.

Right.

Another array of menus flooded my vision, each one detailing a specific weapon. All of them were locked, and the only ones I could afford were a baton for 100 Crypt, a push dagger for 200 Crypt, or a small handgun for 300 Crypt (ammunition sold separately).

300 Crypt for a gun and 10,000 for a penis. Huh.

I only had 300 Crypt left. A gun without bullets did not seem useful. I was also hesitant to spend all my Crypt, not knowing what else faced me in this strange reality.

I noticed some accompanying text and selected the push dagger option to learn more about it.

A push dagger is a type of dagger that is designed for thrusting attacks. It typically has a short blade with a triangular or square cross-section and a cylindrical or rectangular hilt. Push daggers are often made of steel or other strong materials, and they may have a guard or knuckle guard to protect the user's hand.

Push daggers are typically used in close quarters combat, and they can be effective for stabbing an opponent through clothing or armor. They are also relatively easy to conceal, making them a popular choice for self-defense.

I still did not understand what I would be needing a weapon for. The Concierge had mentioned invasive entities, which felt both vague and ominous. The only thing I could think of in a simulated world would be a computer virus. Was I supposed to stab or shoot a computer virus? None of this made sense.

I decided to learn more about the baton option.

A baton is a short, heavy stick that is used by law enforcement officers as a compliance tool and defensive weapon.

Batons can be used in a variety of ways. Police batons are typically used to strike or jab a person in order to subdue them.

Something about the concept of 'law enforcement' made me hesitant. I could not explain why.

I made my choice.

Push dagger selected. Would you like to equip this weapon?

▶ No. I do not think I need to equip it right now.

Push dagger will be stored in your equipment. You can view it at any time and equip it under your personal Equipment menu.

▶ Hmmm. Now what?

If you are finished with weapons, we can move to the final step of your orientation, the Volunteer Program options.

▶ Volunteer Program options?

I assumed what that might entail. An accessibility menu for my experience within the simulation. I was wrong.

A glowing menu materialized in the ether. It had an ephemeral weight, but I instinctively sensed that this menu was something only I would be able to see.

STATISTICS
- **ATTACK**
- **DEFENSE**
- **ABILITY**
- **MOVEMENT**
- **PROCESSING**

EQUIPMENT

INVENTORY

ECONOMY

MEMORY

STATUS

ADDITIONAL OPTIONS TO BE UNLOCKED AS APPLICABLE

▶ Concierge. What am I supposed to do with this?

As the final step of your orientation, you must allot additional Value into your Statistics subcategories. Please open your Statistics menu.

I did as instructed.

STATISTICS

- **ATTACK**
    - **STRENGTH: 10**
    - **ACCURACY: 10**

- **DEFENSE**
    - **ESSENCE: 10**
    - **RESISTANCE: 10**

- **ABILITY**
    - **ADEPTNESS: 10**
    - **ENERGY: 10**

- **MOVEMENT**
    - **SPEED: 10**
    - **AGILITY: 10**

- **PROCESSING**
    - **PERCEPTION: 10**
    - **PERSUASION: 10**
    - **PROTOCOL: 10**
    - **PROBABILITY: 10**

UNASSIGNED VALUE: 30

As a new Volunteer, you have a value of ten in each of the twelve statistical subcategories. You have been granted an additional thirty Value to be distributed as integers and multiples of ten in one or more subcategories.

So, I had to somehow assign that additional amount to these subcategories. Still not being sure as to what any of this was, or the relevance of these subcategories to my role as a Volunteer, I was at a loss. I didn't even know the meaning of some of these terms.

▶ Concierge, I am unsure what I am supposed to do with this. Do you have any recommendations?

Volunteers should assign Value to their statistical subcategories based on the approach to fulfilling their task that would be most efficacious for them. Each subcategory has direct relevance to your role in removing invasive entities from The Collective.

▸ Okay. Attack and Defense are somewhat self-explanatory. Movement as well. What is the Ability category? And the Processing category?

The Ability category, the Ability subcategories of Adeptness and Energy, relate to how effective you are at harnessing and using special skills.

Special skills?

The Processing category, and the Processing subcategories of Protocol, Perception, Persuasion, and Probability, relate to higher-level cognitive and system functions.

▸ Can you give me an example? What is Protocol?

A protocol is a set of rules that define how data is transmitted. In this context, it relates to higher cognitive functions such as knowledge, intelligence, logic, and prescience.

I had already purchased a push dagger, a handheld melee weapon. I did not know what the policy on returns was, if such a policy existed. Obviously, the Attack category was most applicable for this weapon and whatever violence I was expected to carry out.

I switched from Statistics over to the Equipment menu. The only thing in it was the push dagger. I selected the weapon, ignoring a prompt to equip it, to read the description. A three-dimensional representation of the weapon floated in the space in front of me.

Weapon: Push dagger (unequipped)
Weapon Type: Melee (Strength)
Level: 1 of 1

Frequency: Basic

Damage Output: 10

Details: A short, metallic blade with a triangular cross-section, cylindrical hilt, and a knuckle guard. This dagger is relatively easy to conceal and designed for close quarters thrusting attacks.

Properties: Weapon has the {basic} property and cannot be upgraded, enhanced, or exported.

Size: 10 metabytes

This melee weapon was associated with the Strength subcategory. To better use this weapon, I would need to put Value in Strength. There did not appear to be a minimum requirement.

I closed Equipment and reopened Statistics.

▸ Okay. How do I add Value to a category?

Select the unassigned Value and drag the integer in a multiple of ten to the subcategory you wish to assign Value to.

Simple enough. I dragged a value of ten from my unassigned Value to Strength. The menu flickered, and then my Strength increased.

Strength: 20

You have 20 remaining Value to assign.

▸ I know. What do you think is the best way to assign Value based on the "invasive entities" I am supposed to remove?

I apologize. I am currently experiencing a higher-than-average request volume. Please wait or try your query later.

Enough with this.

I split the remaining Value between Essence and Speed, ten each.

For your sign-on bonus, you have received an additional ten metabytes of storage!

▸ What?

Orientation is now complete. Congratulations, Volunteer! You will be redirected to The Commons in five seconds.

Please enjoy your stay in The Collective. Live your best second life! ™

FILE 2.0

COMMONS

The sterile light of the ether—the memorial of floating menus—dissolved into nothing. All was black.

The fog rolls in like a silent tide,
Covering the pond in a blanket of white.
The trees are shrouded, the birds are still,
And the only sound is the gentle lapping of the waves.

▸ Huh? What was that?

No answer from the Concierge.

A fragment. A thought. A memory? Then it was gone. Whatever it was—gone.

The darkness turned once more to light. This time, it was neither sterile nor pale but assaulting the senses. I found myself standing in the middle of a street—if it could be called a street. More of an alley for foot traffic. A small, bustling section of some great city, stretching beyond the horizons of my perception. My eyes moved over an array of neon signs and hanging lanterns.

I was not alone.

A crowd of people in varied attire brushed by me, moving between open stalls, storefronts, and establishments unknown. Some met my gaze. Most ignored me. In one of the stalls, a heavyset man in a stained apron chopped tentacles off a writhing red cephalopod with a cleaver and tossed them into a sizzling wok while patrons crowded around on stools.

"Move it," someone grunted as they roughly shoved past.

I became aware that I was blocking easy passage through the side street and stepped out of the way.

I tried to get my bearings. The sky above was lit with artificial lights—piercing whites, purples, and blues—from windows and structures stretching high above and far away. Beyond that was the dark of night, but I saw no stars nor moon.

The city was built out in nested enclaves. Mounds upon mounds of sleek, jutting structures. A metropolis designed by termites.

Seeing another narrow corridor to what I took to be a larger street, I made my way there, nearly stepping on a cat in the process. It hissed and leaped from one shadow into another.

Leaving the corridor, I found myself at an intersection where three larger streets converged. A hub for whatever this small section of the city was. I saw no vehicles, only people traveling on foot. However, some crafts did occasionally pass overhead.

On a concrete island in the center of this intersection, rotating, floating neon letters declared this area to be The Commons. Directly beneath the gravity-defying sign was a tube extending out of the ground. The term "phone booth" came to mind, but that wasn't quite right. Closer inspection revealed that the tube was an information kiosk.

Ignoring the other buildings, I headed straight for the kiosk. I waited for a scraggly-looking person using it to finish, then I ducked inside.

There was a scratched screen, speaker ports, and a glowing, red light.

Please scan your identifier.

The voice sounded like the Concierge. I hesitated.

Please scan your identifier.

I assumed this meant the barcode on my wrist, and lined the numbers etched into my tan skin against the red light. There was a chime, the light turned white, and the small screen flickered on.

Welcome to The Commons. What information would you like to access?

▸ I'm new here. I'm not sure what I need to do next or where to go. I am a Volunteer?

There are several locations of interest to Volunteers in The Commons. These include but are not limited to: the Residential Towers, the Armory, the Supply Depot, the Repository, the Data Forge, the Task Assignment Boards, the Restoration Point, the Archives, the MAR Station, and the Rathskeller.

▸ Rathskeller. What is that?

The Rathskeller is a popular gathering place for Volunteers in The Commons. Please note that Citizens are prohibited from visiting this establishment.

▸ Am I a Citizen?

No. You are a Volunteer.

The little screen highlighted the location of the Rathskeller on a blinking map, and I made my way there. Other Volunteers. Maybe I could get some answers.

Minutes later, I stood before a graffiti-strewn brutalist structure, several mismatched cubes stacked on top of one another. The bottom level was partially enclosed by slatted fencing and illuminated by disc-shaped streetlights. On one side of the building, a staircase descended below a gaudy neon sign of a rat. No words or other symbols, just a rat.

This must be the place.

I cautiously took the stairs, pushing through a pair of blue doors, until I found myself in what could only be described as an underground, Bohemian tavern merged with a rave. The ceiling arched at regular intervals, giving the impression of a ribcage. A long, weathered wooden bar lined the near wall, with several smaller tables interspersed throughout.

In the middle of the establishment was a larger round table. Several impressive individuals crowded this table, banging steins in time with the throbbing electronica, pale-blue liquid spilling over the rims. There was shouting and raucous laughter.

Whoever these people were, they looked like they had answers. I made a beeline for the central table until a hand slammed into my chest, stopping me cold in my tracks. I traced the fingerless, black leather biker glove to a scrawny arm belonging to a man seated at the bar.

His face was adorned with a patchy beard, gap-toothed grin, and a pair of welding goggles atop a knit skullcap.

"Not so skorry there, moodge. Where do you think you're ittying?"

▸ I'm sorry, do you know me?

"Odin glance is all I need to know you are as they skazat, 'fresh off the boat.' A new arrival. Green. Rookie. Noob. Fresh meat. A virgin—"

▸ Okay, enough already.

"You've got the generic features and platties that just creech day one in the Metaverse."

► Point taken, I think. Why can't I go over—

"That's the Round Table. Nobody goes to the Round Table unless they've been invited."

I glanced up as the rowdy group at the center table stood. There was a loud cry—"Glory to the Volunteers!"—and patrons throughout the Rathskeller applauded wildly. Then the group made their way to the exit, or the way I had come in. They were all formidable.

A well-built Black man with a shotgun followed by an ashen-skinned woman with intense white dreadlocks passed. The woman briefly met my gaze before turning her attention back to her party.

"Them's top-tier hunters. They don't suffer fools lightly."

► Is that what you take me to be? A fool?

"Easy now. I didn't mean nothing by it. So what if you smot like a wax museum statue in a cheap Halloween costume? We've all been there. So, what's your eemya?"

► My what?

"Your eemya. Your name. What are you called?"

I glanced uncertainly at my wrist.

► They called me Volunteer 01001110—

"I was afraid you were ittying to skazat something like that. This really is day one for you, isn't it? Shiva on a stick."

The man held out his opposite wrist, showing off his own barcode: 01000010-01100101-01110100-01100001-00111001.

"That's not a name, that's a number. We Volunteers go by our own names. But you haven't been christened yet. Those dva impressive hunks of flesh you were eyeballing earlier—Bigwig and Rook. Me? I'm Camel."

► Camel? Why Camel?

"They call me Camel because I never miss! Best sharpshooter in The Collective."

▸ I don't see how that—

A fastidious feminine bartender leaned over and butted into our conversation.

"They call him Camel because he drinks like a camel."

To punctuate her remark, the bartender refilled Camel's mug with the pale blue fluid.

"And odin for my droogie," Camel said, patting the barstool next to him. "Take a stooly and have a peet."

I assumed from the context that *peet* meant drink in the strange slang. I obliged. The bartender slid a frothing mug in front of me with a professional smile.

▸ Camel, I thought all this... I thought we were inside a computer simulation. Why are we drinking?

"True, your avatar don't need pishcha or peet to survive here. But this ain't about needs, it's about wants. The heart wants what the heart wants! Think of it as a psychological need if you must."

Camel gulped his drink greedily, wiping the artificial fluid off his artificial beard. I took a tentative sip of mine and felt a cooling sensation rush through me. It tasted like the first snowfall of winter.

Huh. Psychological needs.

"All the comforts of domy. For the right price."

▸ Price. How much?

"That'll be ten Crypt. Shall I open a tab for you?" the bartender asked, smiling.

▸ Uh, sure.

Down to ninety Crypt. Just great.

"The only veshch Reality Inc. cares more about than having us clean up The Collective is making a profit."

▸ Are you a Volunteer?

"Of course. There's nobody down here in this rat cellar but us Volunteers."

Camel shouted a hearty "Glory to the Volunteers!" and the tavern swelled with another round of applause and cheering.

▸ The thing is, I can't seem to remember volunteering for anything. My life outside of this place, who I was—or am—is a blank.

"Same for us all, droogie. We all conveniently were afflicted with "dissociative amnesia" upon arrival. We've got lewdies rabbiting on that."

▸ Has anyone told you that you have a very unique way of speaking?

"Nah, I've just been here a long raz. Longer than most."

I took another sip of my drink. The frosty sensation was growing on me. It occurred to me then that I had no vagina or penis. No urethra, either way. Maybe not even a bladder.

▸ After I drink this, how do I... How am I supposed to, you know...?

Camel looked at me blankly, but the helpful bartender spoke up.

"Don't worry, it's just information. Ones and zeroes."

Bottoms up, then. I turned back to Camel.

▸ What is it exactly that we are supposed to have volunteered for? The Concierge mentioned "invasive entities."

"I'll put it really simple. We kill monsters."

▸ Monsters?

"That's right. Nasty beasts keep popping up in the Metaverse, and Bolshy Bratty needs us to put them down. The best we can figure it, they sent an entire first wave of Citizens into The Collective. Then these monsters appeared. Lewdies got hurt. I'm sure somebody lost pretty polly. They paused all future waves until we Volunteers can make the place safe again."

▸ I don't understand. If this is a simulation, why would there be monsters? Shouldn't the company be in control of their product? Why would they program something dangerous that could hurt users?

"That's the ten billion Crypt question."

▸ So is it a computer virus? A glitch in the system? Corporate espionage? Cyberterrorism? Cyberwarfare?

"We've got lewdies rabbiting on that too."

I took his meaning to be that the Volunteers had people working on that problem. It seemed that the system itself was not offering much help.

▸ What about cybersecurity? Shouldn't the corporation have some form of anti-virus software? Why rely on Volunteers to fix their mess?

"Ah, there are the Polizei bots, sure. But they were designed to keep the Citizens in line. These monsters are a threat Bolshy Bratty never planned for. The bots are defenseless against them."

▸ Just trying to wrap my head around this. There are Citizens and Volunteers, who are humans. But also bots, who are not per se real. And monsters.

Camel finished his mug and belched loudly.

"That's the long and the short of it. The Citizens keep to themselves. Or rather, we are kept to ourselves. The Commons is where the dredges of the Metaverse cheest up. A temporary shanty town for us low-class hunters."

I looked at the bartender. She, if it was a she, wore a white button-down shirt, a black vest, and a smart bowtie. She had an asymmetrical haircut and flawless white teeth.

▸ And what about you? Are you real, or some kind of bot?

"Do I look real?" she asked, never breaking her smile. "Do I sound real?"

▸ Yes.

"Then what difference does it make?"

The bartender turned her attention to wiping down the counter.

Camel tapped me on the shoulder.

"The best way to explain the situation is to show you. Let's go to the Bounty Boards."

FILE 3.0

BOUNTIES

After paying my tab, I followed the unusual man named Camel out of the Rathskeller. He had a slight limp in his gait, and I thought I detected a hunch in his back. Could that be why he was called Camel?

If one could purchase whatever customized body type they wanted for their avatar in The Collective, why would somebody choose to go around in that inelegant state? The longer I spent here, the more questions I had.

I concentrated as hard as I could as we walked, trying to recall some glimpse of my previous life. A kernel of truth. But try as I might, it was as if my life before coming here was completely severed from my present consciousness. No doubt something to complain about to my "system administrator."

"There's the Task Assignment Boards, or as we Volunteers call them, the Bounty Boards."

Camel indicated a series of rectangular touchscreen panels, unfolded like a room divider by way of a fast-food drive-through menu. The Boards were located near two storefronts. The signs read Armory and Supply Depot, respectively.

Camel scanned his Volunteer barcode and the screens lit up. A shifting array of data lines filled the screens, changing in real-time. The concept of "airport flight tracking board" came to mind. Some lines moved up, some moved down. Some turned red and inaccessible while others were crossed out before fading. I deduced that there must be other access points within the city.

"Competition is fierce. Bounties are the lifeblood of Volunteers. A newbie like yourself would have a hard raz securing a decent bounty. Luckily you have me!"

Camel selected one of the menu items, and the display changed. Information on the bounty filled the rectangular screen closest to us.

Task Assignment: Remove hellhounds from MAR Station Service Tunnels.

Three {common} hellhounds have been detected in the service tunnels beneath The Palisades MAR Station.

Task Completion Award: 2,000 Crypt.

Do you accept this task?

"What do you skazat? Want to go halfsies with me? Scan your barcode and we can split the reward. That's a hundred peets with my eemya on it."

Hellhounds? Whatever it was I had expected, hellhounds were not it. I reluctantly complied, scanning the number on my wrist beneath the red light. Soon, our two Volunteer numbers were highlighted and assigned to this task, making this bounty inaccessible to others.

"Your first hunt! I know the Palisades. Just a couple stops down the line. You need to pick up any gear before we go? This is the shopping district."

▸ I doubt I could afford anything at this point. I have a dagger. Are we really going to have to fight hellhounds? Is that a codeword for something?

"Just stick close to me and you'll be fine."

I followed Camel to the MAR Station and after paying ten additional Crypt at a kiosk, boarded a sleek bullet train that appeared to magnetically hover over a central track. We were the only passengers in the car, but an automated voice and pulsing lights addressed us as if we were in a rush hour crowd.

Now leaving The Commons. Next stop, Royal Heights, followed by The Palisades.

We rode in silence, Camel seated and I hanging on a strap. I felt anxious. The train moved fast, the bright city lights whipping by through the windows.

Now arriving at Royal Heights Station.

The train slowed, stopped, and the doors opened. No passengers departed or boarded. I wondered just how many Citizens lived in The Collective. Camel had mentioned a "first wave."

Now leaving Royal Heights. Next stop, The Palisades, followed by Lower Dresden.

Camel groped the empty air in front of him, and I worried that I had hitched myself to a mentally ill person. But then I realized he was accessing his own personal menu. Suddenly, a large, scoped, bolt action hunting rifle materialized in his hands. He slung it around his back with a strap.

He reached back into his invisible (to me) menu. Soon, what looked like a flashlight appeared in his other hand.

Now arriving at The Palisades Station.

"This is us, droogie."

I followed Camel through the sliding doors and soon the train sped away, leaving us in an empty, neon-lit subterranean transit station. Camel paced the station close to the track, searching for something.

I took the opportunity to open my own menu, navigating to the Inventory section.

INVENTORY
- **CARDS**
  - **EMPTY**

- **FRAGMENTS**
  - **EMPTY**

- **CONSUMABLES**
  - **EMPTY**

- **MATERIALS**
  - **EMPTY**

I was concerned. Where did my push dagger go? I spent good money on that thing.

Taking a breath, I remembered to look in Equipment instead.

EQUIPMENT
- **WEAPONS**
  - **PUSH DAGGER** (unequipped)
- **ARMOR**
  - **EMPTY**
- **ACCESSORIES**
  - **EMPTY**

Oh, good. I reached out and selected the push dagger.

Equip push dagger?

I selected the option to equip the dagger. Suddenly, a swirl of digitized pixels solidified in my hand. My 200 Crypt push dagger materialized, and I felt its weight. I tested the sharpness of the blade.

It sure felt real.

"Aha! Here it is," Camel said.

He pointed his flashlight at a metal grate underneath the central track.

"Help me lift this up. We need to hurry before another expresso rapido comes through. Otherwise, we'll be electrocuted or—*splat*."

I did not like the sound of that, but Camel was already down beside the track, trying to lift the grate. Checking both directions of the tunnel, I hopped beside him and stuffed my fingers into the pick holes, straining to lift it. It was stuck. I thought I sensed the vibrations of an approaching train, but it could have been my imagination.

Working together, the heavy grate came loose. Camel gestured to the gaping tunnel leading into darkness.

"I would make a joke about age before beauty, but you've got neither."

▸ It's dark down there. You've got the flashlight. Please, I insist.

"Suit yourself."

Camel lowered himself into the hole, careful not to catch his rifle on the edges. Then he was gone. I peered into the space below but saw nothing. Then, a white glow. He had turned on his light.

The vibration returned, louder this time. It was not my imagination. There was a train approaching the station, and fast.

As two piercing headlights rounded the bend, I quickly jumped feet first into the hole.

The train wooshed to a stop over my head. Ten seconds later it left the station.

I sat blinking, trying to adjust to the darkness. Camel shined his flashlight on the walls of the service tunnel. The rounded space was about five feet high, and I had to crouch to keep from hitting my head. Everything was dark except for Camel's sweeping beam.

I felt intensely claustrophobic.

▸ Now what? How do we find these, uh… hellhounds?

"If you lovett a whiff of brimstone, that means we're getting close. There's been a few hellhounds around here lately. They've moved down the tunnels from New Dresden's warehouse district."

▸ And what does brimstone smell like?

"Sulfur."

I sniffed the air. I didn't detect anything aside from concrete, static, and the pungent odor of my companion—sweat, beer, and cigarettes. Did they really have to program smells like that?

Camel stalked forwards in a hunched-over duckwalk, clipping the flashlight onto one side of his rifle and sweeping the barrel back and forth in front of us. I just kept following the pool of white light, staying close behind, careful not to bump into him with the sharp point of my weapon.

We continued this way for some time. I strained to listen for any sounds beyond our own or to smell anything reminiscent of burning. I could not guess how long we had been moving through the service tunnel, or how far we had gone from the station.

"These tunnels intersect with other ones up ahead. It's like a rabbit warren down here."

▸ You've been down here before. You aren't worried about getting lost?

"All roads lead to Rome, as they skazat."

As time dragged on, my lower body began to ache. Camel seemed to notice and suggested we take a break. We each leaned against one side of the curved tunnel wall and I massaged my thighs.

Camel switched off his flashlight, and we were immersed in total darkness. I did not care for that.

Then I noticed a faint green glow down the tunnel. Were my eyes playing tricks on me?

▸ Do you see that glow down there?

"Ah, yes. You want to get a closer smot?"

I said I would, and we inched carefully towards the glow. Camel kept his light off, so I made sure not to bang my head on the roof of the tunnel as I shuffled forward.

When we reached the spot, I saw that a few scant plants were sprouting incongruously out of the concrete floor of the service tunnel. I saw no soil or water source, but there were cracks in this section of the tunnel. The plants had small yellow flowers cascading from their stalks.

Camel switched his light back on, appraising the flora.

"Yep, invasive species."

▸ Invasive? You mean, like the creatures we are supposed to be hunting?

"That's right. There have been flora and fauna breaking through into The Collective. They don't follow the rules of the system. Try to hold your rooker over them and viddy if you can identify what they are. But don't touch them—they could be dangerous."

▸ My rooker?

"Your hand, droogie. Your hand!"

I did as instructed, holding my bare hand out and over one of the plants nearest me. Nothing happened. I tried to consciously access my menu, and suddenly the plant was outlined in a faint border of light. Hovering my hand in place, information began to appear before my eyes.

{common} fern flower detected. Crafting material. Attributes unknown.

▸ It says it is a common fern flower.

"Shouldn't be dangerous then. You can harvest it if you want. I don't go in for crafting, but you might be able to turn it into something useful later on."

▸ Like what?

"Beats me. Like I said, I don't go in for crafting."

Tentatively, I used my dagger to trim the flowers from each of the plants one by one. They dissolved into inky nothing and were gone.

3 {common} fern flowers added to your inventory.

I checked my menu to confirm.

INVENTORY
- **CARDS**
- **FRAGMENTS**
- **CONSUMABLES**
- **MATERIALS**
  - **3 {common} fern flowers**

I wanted to select the item and learn more, but I was conscious about wasting more time while we had a task to complete.

▸ Thank you for indulging me. Should we press on?

"I'm ready when you are."

We continued to inch forwards through the dark tunnel.

▸ How exactly do we hunt a pack of hellhounds? Are we following a trail? Are we setting a trap? Using bait?

"That's the horrorshow veshch about hellhounds. They are hungry buggers, likely viddying for their next meal."

I squinted in the dim light, trying to make sense of Camel's bizarre word salad. He soon clarified.

"They are the ones hunting us."

FILE 4.0

HELLHOUNDS

So the hungry hellhounds would be hunting us. I wondered then if the entire reason Camel brought me along was to serve as bait. Regardless, all I could do now was stay close to the man with the scoped rifle and hope for the best.

Shining his light, Camel illuminated an opening in the tunnel ahead. He cautiously approached, me close at his heels. The tunnel led into a subterranean juncture, a cross cutting, concrete basin that gave the impression of a dry aqueduct.

Camel stealthily climbed down into the wider space, sweeping with his light. I scrambled to keep up. At least here I could stand, the ceiling disappearing somewhere in the darkness above.

Then it hit me.

The unmistakable odor of something burning.

"Hellhounds," Camel whispered.

I nodded, not that he could see me in the darkness. I gripped my push dagger tight and followed as Camel stalked into the middle of the room, looking left and right.

Camel froze, lowering the barrel of his rifle. I tried to follow his gaze and there, in the darkness at the far side of the room, a pair of red eyes burned back at us. I heard a scratching noise, nails on the concrete floor, then a low growl.

Camel was silent and calm, raising the rifle and training the barrel on the hellhound. Illumined in the halo of the white flashlight beam, I saw it.

It was larger than an average dog. Its face was all black with matted fur, gnarled and intense. Its eyes glowed an unnatural red. Its black lips were pulled back in a snarl, revealing fangs.

It was motionless in the flashlight beam, except for lowering its head.

Then—CRACK!

There was a muzzle flash and an ear-splitting shot from Camel's rifle reverberated around the enclosed space. I involuntarily covered my ears, surprised by the sudden sound.

With a strangled whimper, the black dog collapsed, falling out of the beam of light.

"That's odin down."

Camel pulled back the bolt handle on his rifle, pulling a fresh cartridge out of a bandolier under his patched jacket.

Ears still ringing from the shot, I did not hear the growls from the other side of the room behind Camel. But I did see two more pairs of red eyes emerge from the darkness.

▸ Look out! Behind you!

Camel swiveled. Two more hellhounds ran at us, Camel still trying to reload his rifle.

I dashed forwards, closing the distance between myself and Camel, brandishing my push dagger.

The hounds were fast. They were on us in an instant, one latching onto my arm.

I screamed, or at least I tried to in my weak starter voice. I felt the fangs sink into my flesh, warm blood dripping down my forearm. My entire arm was on fire. I saw ominous words appear before my eyes.

Damage received.

Essence: 10 remaining.

The other hound jumped on Camel, knocking him to the ground with a crash. His rifle fell from his grasp, the flashlight beam pointing askew at the wall, bathing us in darkness. He grunted, fighting for his life.

All I could see were those two red eyes as the hound tore at my arm. In desperation, I plunged at those eyes with my dagger, stabbing again and again. More blood sprayed out, but this time it was not mine.

The hound released its grip, turning away, one of its eye sockets shredded and bloody.

I stabbed again blindly, lunging for the hairy bulk. I made contact, the sharp tip of my blade sinking into its chest. I pushed as hard as I could until the hilt was buried in the flesh of the beast, and I held it there, fighting against the creature's strong flailing.

The hound issued unearthly moans as it fought, but I held on for dear life.

Behind me, another shot rang out. A whimper and the sound of a body slumping on concrete.

Soon, Camel was beside me, shining his light at the beast that locked me in mortal combat. With the benefit of improved visibility, I removed my dagger and plunged it again and again in the hound's chest, hoping to strike its heart.

The smell of sulfur and blood filled my nostrils. At last, the hellhound ceased its fighting.

I pulled out my blade, caked with blood and black fur and stumbled backwards. My left arm burned like crazy. Camel shined a light on it.

"That doesn't smot horrorshow, droogie. Might want to get a bandage on that until you can get it fixed."

I noticed that Camel's face was bleeding from large scratches.

▸ Your face...

"I'll be alright. Not my first rodeo."

There was a chirp, and a system notification appeared before my eyes.

Task Successfully Completed: Remove hellhounds from MAR Station Service Tunnels.

Camel shined the light on the three corpses, and they began to glow. A low, vibrating thrum filled the space, and motes of light drew up from the bodies and gathered in strange, geometric shapes. Some were like shards of sea glass, and others were distinctly crystalline in appearance—all glowed with a neon hue.

It was beautiful, like fireflies at dusk, and I reached out to touch the dancing lights. Suddenly, I felt their substance absorb into my body, leaving only a fading half-life.

{common} Data Card fragments obtained: hellhound 4/10

10 Crystals obtained.

I shuddered. Absorbing these materials felt like my stomach dropping out.

"Hey now. Why'd you take all the loot for yourself?" Camel asked, shining the light directly in my face.

I shielded my eyes, still clutching the dagger. Was he going to shoot me?

"Relax. You didn't know any better. Some advice—hunters that rabbit together typically split the rewards. All the rewards, not just the pretty polly."

I apologized profusely. I told him I had no idea what those motes were, or what would happen if I touched them. He shrugged it off and lowered the flashlight.

▸ What were those things? Card fragments? Crystals?

"These monsters—they aren't supposed to be part of the system, yet their properties interact with the system in weird ways. We Volunteers have learned to use that to our advantage. Check your menus."

I did as I was instructed, first accessing my Inventory menu.

INVENTORY
- **CARDS**
- **FRAGMENTS**
    - **{common} hellhound 4/10**
- **CONSUMABLES**
- **MATERIALS**
    - **3 {common} fern flowers**

Next, I checked my Economy menu.

ECONOMY
- **CRYPT: 80**
- **CRYSTALS: 10**

When backing out of the submenus, I noticed that a Task tab had been added to the bottom of my list that I had not noticed earlier.

So that must be where the bounties were tracked.

I selected the menu in search of this information.

TASKS
- **Remove Hellhounds from MAR Station Service Tunnels (Complete)**

I understood by now that if I selected that completed task, I would be able to view more details. But I left it alone for the time being. I assumed Camel would walk me through how to cash in the bounty.

With only eighty Crypt to my name (or lack of name, as it were), the prospect of earning 1,000 Crypt from a split bounty sounded nice. Although the searing pain in my arm made it hard to think of anything positive.

Before closing out of my menus, I unequipped the push dagger, and it vanished from my hand, returning to its invisible storage space within my Equipment menu.

Fragments... materials... crystals. There was a lot to keep track of.

"A successful hunt calls for a smoke," Camel said. He slung the rifle over his shoulder and lit up a cigarette. The tip burned bright in the dark. The smell of cheap tobacco mingled with the lingering sulfur. "Want a cancer?"

▸ No, thank you. I don't smoke. Or at least, I don't think I smoke. Either way, the offer doesn't appeal to me right now.

Camel took a heavy drag from the cigarette that my rational mind told me was nothing but an artificial construct that seemed in every way real. Then again, how could my rational mind conceive of stabbing a hellhound to death in some underground tunnel?

▸ What happens next?

"We return to the Bounty Boards and get our sammy reward. 1,000 Crypt for each of us. An even split."

He continued to smoke, and I waited patiently for him to finish. There was no way I was getting out of this place without him. I was completely dependent on both his sense of direction and his flashlight.

Strangely, I began to sense the smell of sulfur returning, even after the three bodies had dissolved into blotchy ink. Camel did not seem to notice. Maybe the odor was masked by the cigarette, or maybe it was normal for these scents to linger after a kill.

But the smell grew stronger, and stronger yet. Then, emerging from the service tunnel, I sensed a deeper darkness. A shadow within the shadow, swallowing up the light cast towards the ceiling.

▸ Camel, I think there is something…

"AGGHHHH!"

Too late. A dark form pounced on Camel from behind. His scream was silenced with a wet, sickening crunch. His body fell hard to the ground, his rifle slamming into concrete. The flashlight detached from its perch and rolled in my direction.

Terrified, I grabbed it and backed away from the shadowy form. I shined the light defensively, and a large, black head swiveled up to glare in my direction. It was another hellhound, yet larger than before. Fresh gore dripped from its jowls where it had torn Camel's throat.

A system notification chirped.

{uncommon} entity detected: Baskerville Hound.

I dropped the flashlight and heard the shattering of glass. Everything was dark, save for two burning eyes moving in my direction.

FILE 5.0

BASKERVILLE

I braced for the attack, too paralyzed with fear to even attempt to equip my dagger. If a seasoned hunter like Camel had been killed by this creature in a matter of seconds, what chance did I have in total darkness?

The red eyes came closer, and I felt hot, acrid breath on my face from the snarling canine mouth. The smell of sulfur was overpowering.

Just when I thought all was lost, two loud metal clangs echoed through the concrete chamber.

Several phosphorescent tubes tumbled from holes in the ceiling, landing and rolling through the empty aqueduct. The beast, now silhouetted by the glowing green lights, turned with a snarl.

Two figures slid down hanging ropes, descending into the chamber from either side. I recognized them immediately—the ones Camel had referred to as Bigwig and Rook. The heavy hitters who rolled with an entourage of Round Table hunters.

"Rook! There it is!" Bigwig shouted, letting go of the rope halfway down and landing heavily on combat boots.

He wore a black leather jacket and a gold medallion necklace. Several brown straps tied around his waist and thighs held holsters for various weapons, but the one he favored was a snub-nosed double-barrel shotgun.

On the other side of the room, Rook slid down headfirst, using only her legs to grip the rope. She carried two automatic handguns, trained on the hound.

She wore a type of metallic tank top above black cargo pants. It was actually hard to know where the clothing ended and where her flesh began, as if the top was part of her. A metal collar was fitted around her neck, with chains leading behind her back. Her face was marked and scarred, and her thin eyes appeared pupilless in the glow of the phosphorescence.

The Baskerville Hound lunged at Bigwig, and liquid fire seeped from its mouth.

Bigwig strode confidently forwards, unloading blast after blast from his shotgun, puncturing holes through the creature's black fur. Multiple shots didn't stop it—it was a magnitude of strength beyond the common hellhounds.

With a guttural roar, the beast vomited a stream of fire in Bigwig's direction. He ducked and rolled out of the way in one fluid movement, reloading his shotgun.

Next, Rook made her move. She did an acrobatic flip off the rope and landed on her feet—catlike—then side-stepped, shooting rapid bursts from her handguns at the hound's head.

Furious, it turned its attention away from Bigwig and charged towards her.

"Oh, no you don't," Bigwig growled, blasting holes in its hindquarters with another series of double-barreled shots.

The beast howled in pain and fury, blood leaking onto the floor.

Having spent both ammo clips, Rook dropped the handguns and

reached behind her back. Now I saw what the chains around her collar were connected to. In a flash, she brandished two razor-sharp sickles, reminiscent of kusarigama.

She leaped into the air and drove both blades into the monster's skull. It let out an almost porcine squeal as it died. Soon, it was melting away in a black puddle, and shimmering ephemera once again materialized in the air above the corpse.

Without thinking, I stalked towards the dancing lights. I felt drawn to them. They were hypnotic. Beautiful.

A shout from Bigwig snapped me out of my reverie.

"Hey! Stop right there!"

He pointed his shotgun at me. I had not kept track and couldn't tell if it was empty or not. Either way, the gesture had its intended effect. I froze and raised my hands in the air.

"We saw you snatch the loot from Camel earlier," Rook said. Her voice was like oil dripping off the edge of a knife. "Little magpie can't keep its beak off the shiny baubles."

I began to protest, but the mention of Camel made me search the ground for him. His body was gone, leaving only a bloody stain behind.

▸ Oh, no. Camel.

"He's the least of your concerns right now," Bigwig said, pressing the shotgun under my chin. "In fact, you might as well go join him. We've been tracking this kill for quite some time. The bounty payment and the detritus are ours."

Rook glided over, the sickles now reattached to her back, and gently pushed the shotgun's barrels away. She looked me up and down with those pupilless eyes, and it felt like she was seeing through me.

"No need for that. This one is no threat to us."

▸ I didn't steal any loot. I didn't intend to. Camel was my friend, or, I should say he was helping me. He took me on my first hunt.

"Best bet would be to steer clear of him," Bigwig grunted, stowing his shotgun and gathering the glowing sticks that littered the bloodied ground.

▸ Why is that? He said he was the best sharpshooter in The Collective.

Bigwig snorted.

"He's alright with that antique rifle of his. But the man's got no ambition. He's been here longer than most, and what does he have to show for it? Spends all his Crypt on drink, nostalgia cigarettes, and pleasure bots. I think that's why he's named Camel. His favorite brand of nostalgia cigarettes."

▸ You said pleasure bots?

"That got your attention, eh Magpie? You hanging around the Red Light too?"

▸ Pleasure, I... I literally can't afford that kind of pleasure. If you know what I mean.

Ignoring the comment, Rook inspected my bleeding arm. It still burned, now that the adrenaline of the attack was wearing off. She tore off the sleeve of my black coveralls.

▸ Ouch. Hey. These clothes cost me 200 Crypt.

She materialized a vial from her inventory and rubbed a chalky salve on the wound. My skin steamed, but the burning sensation immediately lessened.

▸ Thank you.

"Some believe his data is corrupted," Rook said, rubbing in the salve. "He was an early Volunteer and the rumor is his avatar missed an update to align with a newer patch. Whatever the truth, Camel is careless. Teaming up with careless hunters is bad news. That's why Bigwig and I stick together. He's the only one I trust to have my back."

▶ 'Was' careless.

"Say again?"

▶ You said Camel is careless, but I think you meant he *was* careless. That hound got him.

Bigwig shook his head dismissively.

"Shiva on a stick. You're out here in the tunnels and you don't know your right from left, up from down."

Rook finished applying the salve and wiped her hands on her pants. Then, in a coordinated motion as if they had done so a hundred times before, her and Bigwig reached for the floating pool of rewards from the kill simultaneously, equally dividing the spoil.

"Go back to the Rathskeller. You'll find Camel. Just be sure to split the reward from your bounty with him, otherwise he might come aiming for you next with that rifle of his."

Rook and Bigwig turned to leave.

▶ Wait!

They paused but did not turn back to face me.

▶ Can I come with you? I don't know how to get back to The Commons from here. I have no light. And I have so many questions.

Bigwig materialized another glowing stick, roughly the size of a stick of dynamite. He tossed it backwards over his head, and I reached out to catch it.

"There. You got light. Go back the way you came, and you'll be fine. Probably."

Rook snuck one last glance in my direction, her impressive white dreads swaying with her every movement.

"No hard feelings, Magpie. You'll only slow us down."

They climbed back up through the holes in the ceiling, pulling the ropes up after them. There would be no way for me to follow, and I was alone in the darkness with only a green, phosphorescent aura.

Magpie, huh? They had called me that nickname repeatedly and in such a way that I had an unpleasant premonition it would stick.

Standing in the echoey concrete chamber, I imagined what I would do if more of those glowing red eyes were to appear. My skin rippled with gooseflesh at the thought, and I quickly climbed back into the claustrophobic service tunnel.

FILE 6.0

PAYMENT

I had no way to track time. Clutching the glowstick, terrified that it would sputter out at any moment, I crawled back through the dark service tunnels. Despite the linear journey, retracing my steps in reverse made me second guess myself constantly.

Everything looked different in a green aura than in the white, directed beam of Camel's flashlight. I was desperate for a familiar landmark.

Shouldn't I have reached the entry point by now? Had I overshot the Palisades station? Had someone closed the service hatch overhead, dooming me to wander this concrete labyrinth until... until what?

Eventually, I passed by the cracks in the tunnel floor where I collected the fern flowers. I checked to see if they were still listed in my inventory—they were. I was curious to see if any of the ferns had somehow regrown—they had not.

At least I had the reassurance that I was heading in the right direction.

At last, I heard a rumbling overhead. It was the train. I knew that I was close. A shaft of light breaking through the roof of the tunnel confirmed it. The phosphorescent glow faded, and I dropped the spent cylinder.

When I was confident that no trains were approaching, I hoisted myself up and out of the service tunnel, wincing in pain as I strained the ragged flesh of my forearm. Out of common courtesy, I returned the metal grating to its original place, then climbed onto the platform.

Now how was I going to get back to The Commons?

Looking around, I found a transit map on the tiled wall of the station and studied it. This was apparently the Diamond Line, which hugged a crystalline bay in a semicircle. Taking it further would lead me through several additional stations, and likely exhaust my remaining Crypt.

I had to ascend one level and cross a small pedestrian bridge to catch the train in the other direction, back through Royal Heights to The Commons. I did so, paying another 10 Crypt for the privilege. I slumped on a bench seat in the sleek, abandoned train—exhausted.

I now had just seventy Crypt left. I was hemorrhaging money faster than I was hemorrhaging blood.

I inspected my arm. The injury didn't appear to have gotten any worse. I was thankful for the salve that the dread-headed woman, Rook, had applied. An unexpected kindness. I thought to explore my menus more, but the train was rapidly approaching the station.

Now arriving at The Commons Station.

I detrained and made my way out of the MAR Station and back towards the center of The Commons, trying to recall where the Task Assignment Boards were located. I found them and hung back while a few rough-looking Volunteers transacted some business. When they left, I stepped out of the shadows and approached, scanning my code under the red light.

Task Complete: Remove hellhounds from MAR Station Service Tunnels.

Assigned to: ~~Volunteer 01000010-01100101-01110100 01100001-00111001 and~~ Volunteer 01001110-01101111-01100010-01101111-01100100-01111001.

Task Completion Award: 2,000 Crypt.

I saw the other number, the one I recognized from Camel's wrist, X-ed out. It made me doubt what Bigwig had said about finding Camel back in the Rathskeller. Was he really gone then?

Would you like to receive payment?

▸ I would.

For a moment, I felt a sharp thrill as electronic bits streamed into me, like coins pouring from a slot machine jackpot. Then, the boards were back to flight tracking mode, bounties shifting in real time across the screens.

I heard a ping and a message appeared from my personal menu.

Alert! Account storage almost full.

Huh. Account storage?

A stocky woman with a pink mohawk, spiked shoulder pads, and a heavy machine gun tapped her boot impatiently behind me, waiting for her turn to access the boards. I mumbled an apology and stepped away, opening my menu screen.

MEMORY
- **STORAGE**
- **HISTORY**

STATUS
- **Infernal Burn** (neutralized)

Infernal Burn? That was something I would need to look at more closely, but first I hovered my hand over the numbers nested underneath Storage, and more information appeared.

197.7 of 210 metabytes
- **ATTACK: 30 metabytes**
- **DEFENSE: 20 / 30 metabytes**
- **ABILITY: 20 metabytes**
- **MOVEMENT: 30 metabytes**
- **PROCESSING: 40 metabytes**
- **WEAPONS: 10 metabytes**
- **ARMOR: 10 metabytes**
- **INVENTORY: 7 metabytes**
- **ECONOMY: 30.7 metabytes**

I opened Defense, drilling down even further.

DEFENSE
- **ESSENCE: 10 / 20**
- **RESISTANCE: 10**

I remembered the attack from the hellhound that gave me the wound on my arm. I had seen the words 'damage received, essence remaining: ten.' It seemed that everything I had—whether that was Value invested in statistical categories, weapons, items, even currency—had some weight. Except for the free basic footwear, which apparently was purely cosmetic and without function.

I was just a few metabytes shy of maxing out the 210 metabyte limit. Had I not received ten points of damage in that fight, it would have been an even tighter squeeze. And had I not received the ten metabyte sign-on bonus, I would not have even been able to withdraw the full payment.

There was so much I didn't understand about this virtual world. The orientation had been a joke. Why couldn't there have been a proper tutorial? This was the very definition of on-the-job training. My head was swimming.

I backed out of the submenu and opened the Economy tab just to make sure I really had received the full payment.

ECONOMY
- **CRYPT: 2,070**
- **CRYSTALS: 10**

Okay. Good. I liked seeing that amount. The sizable Crypt infusion energized me. I wanted to go on a shopping spree, eyeing the bright storefronts on the other side of the lot.

But then I remembered Camel. I had to at least see what had become of him. So, after getting lost twice, I asked directions from some passersby and found the Rathskeller again.

Descending into the buzzy den, I saw no familiar faces. No Camel. No Bigwig. No Rook. Not even the bartender from earlier. Instead, a thin, shirtless man with ear gauges and a pierced lower lip served drinks to the thirsty crowd.

I sidled up to the bar, trying to get his attention. He ignored me. I tried to call him over, but between the pulsing volume of the environs and my unimpressive default voice, I had no success.

I climbed the stairs and looked around outside. Two armed men, presumably hunters like me, leaned against the wall, conversing in hushed tones. One was smoking. The other had a lower jaw the color of polished steel.

I started to approach with a question on my lips and they stopped, turning to look me over with incredulity.

"Go frag yourself!"

So much for Volunteer solidarity.

I turned away, unsure of my next steps. But then I remembered what Bigwig said, that Camel had an affinity for nostalgia cigarettes. Where might someone acquire such a thing in this world? I retraced my steps through the throbbing, bustling night until I reached the building labeled the Supply Depot.

The building was tall and bright red with flashing neon signage wrapping around the top like a headband. Large windows revealed narrow rows packed with merchandise. A few people milled about inside.

I had no reference for what time of day it might be, or time of night, rather. That was if such things even existed in The Collective. I made my way inside.

Perusing the aisles, I realized that all the merchandise I had seen from outside was nothing but holographic displays. The shelves were lined with 3D rotating images of all manner of goods with associated price tags. I guess there was no shoplifting in a place like this.

I saw a shimmering pack of cigarettes with a silhouette of a camel twirling slowly among other brands in the section labeled nostalgia cigarettes, surrounded by a dazzling array of other nostalgia items. Fillinchen crisp bread. Mocca fix. Those were unfamiliar to me.

An elderly woman sat on a stool behind a checkout counter, twirling a plastic parasol.

"You know, it's going to rain soon. You should really think about finding some shelter."

▸ It rains here?

"Oh ho ho, you must be new. Mark my words, it is going to rain. I'm never wrong about the weather."

▸ I see. Listen, could I ask you a question? An acquaintance of mine, goes by the name of Camel—

"I know him."

▸ Oh, great. I was hoping you would say that. I can't find him. We were on a job together and... got separated. He usually hangs out at the Rathskeller, but he isn't there. I thought he must be a customer here. Any idea where else he might be?

The lady squinted, the crow's feet on her face spreading. She pursed her lips, still twirling her parasol as she thought.

"Most likely he is in the Red Light. Do you know it?"

▸ I've heard of it. Can you give me directions?

"It's on the other side of The Commons, almost at the border. You'd better hurry. Before it rains."

FILE 7.0

REDLIGHT

Following the vendor's directions the best I could, I passed through The Commons. At last, I reached what appeared to be the outskirts with a shimmering wall segregating our area from a gleaming metropolis beyond.

There was a tunnel boring through the shining barrier. Polizei bots in head-to-toe tactical gear stood posted on either side. Was their function to keep Citizens out, or to keep Volunteers in? Or something else entirely? I decided not to find out.

Turning down a wide alley lit with floating red globes, I passed by several storefront windows with humanoid figures on display. At first, I thought they were photorealistic wax figurines, but when my eyes rested on one, it sprung to life.

"Hello, gorgeous!"

A young, lithe, shirtless man in tight leather pants with chiseled abs greeted me. His voice was clearly audible despite being behind the glass partition. It was hard to peel my eyes away from him. There was something exceptional about his appearance, but I could not put my finger on it.

▸ Hello.

"Are you looking for some companionship?" he cooed. "Being a Volunteer can be so lonely at times."

It certainly could. But before I could respond, another voice from behind caused me to turn.

"Or perhaps I might be able to serve you instead?"

Across the alley, a woman with porcelain skin and a white negligee beckoned to me from her booth. She had a flawless hourglass figure, and her face possessed the same illusive quality as the man's.

They are symmetrical, I realized. Perfectly symmetrical.

▸ Thank you, but I am looking for a friend of mine. His name is Camel, or at least that's what he goes by.

"We are companions and are not allowed to share the personal information of any of our valued customers," the man answered, feasting on me with his piercing, dark eyes. Of course, I knew that I was nothing to look at, but I felt like a raw steak thrown into a lion's cage nevertheless.

▸ I owe him a lot of money, and I've come to deliver it to him if he is here.

"In that case, visit Serenity at the end of the row," the woman offered through pouty lips and batting eyelashes. She pointed a long finger affixed with bright red nails further down the alley. "She's his favorite."

Before I could leave, the shirtless man spoke again.

"But if you are burdened with carrying so much money, perhaps you would enjoy some companionship after all. Our prices are reasonable, especially for first timers. Relax. Take some weight off your shoulders."

I wish I could say I felt some stirring in my loins for either companion, but I had no loins to speak of.

► Just out of curiosity, and only curiosity, how much?

"6,000 for the companionship starter package, but for you, I'll make it 5,000. An extra 3,000 to add the companionship protection plan. And if you purchase ten companionship experiences, you receive one bonus experience for free."

► Protection plan. What is that?

"Upgrading to the protection plan guarantees a near zero risk of contracting digital syphilis."

► Shiva! Wait, what? Shiva.

I shook my head. His response was disconcerting enough, but more alarming was the fact that my mouth was not working properly. I had tried to use a common expletive beginning with the letter S, but the word did not come out the way I intended.

► Shiva. Shiva? Why can't I curse?

The woman behind me laughed in a coquettish tone.

"Don't be silly. The Collective is a family friendly environment. The profanity filter is always in effect."

► Shiva! Frag! Mother fragger. Piece of Shiva. Son of a brick.

"Ooh, such a dirty mouth on you," the man purred, touching a finger to his lips and shaking his head.

Mildly confused, I hastened to the end of the row, trying to avoid eye contact with the many perfectly crafted specimens on display. I reached the final two windows at the end of the alley. One was empty and unlit while the other contained a very well-built man with flowing yellow hair and an unbuttoned, frilly white shirt revealing a tanned and hairless chest.

"Hello, gorgeous."

► I'm looking for Serenity.

The man bowed theatrically and gestured across the alleyway to the unlit window.

"Serenity is entertaining another customer at the moment. But perchance I may be of some assistance to you? Is it companionship you seek?"

▸ I'm looking for my friend Camel. I have some money to deliver to him. I was told he might be with Serenity.

"Ah, yes. Do not fret. It shan't be much longer. That particular customer never makes it past two humps. That is why they call him Camel, after all."

A familiar voice rang out and I turned to see Camel exiting through a door, buttoning his pants, a lit cigarette dangling from his lips. He looked disheveled. Hobo chic.

"No. It's because I never miss! How many times do I have to keep telling you lewdies?"

▸ Camel! You're alive!

I barely knew this person, but a feeling of warm relief washed over me. He was a familiar landmark in this unfamiliar land.

"Of course I'm alive. A lomtick of baddiwad luck with the bounty though."

In the window display behind him, a plus-sized woman with dark skin wearing a French maid's outfit reappeared, posing with perfect stillness and waiting for her next customer.

▸ The bounty? I collected the bounty. Your name was crossed out on the boards, but I brought your share.

"Horrorshow! How did you survive? That bolshy dog came out of nowhere."

▸ Two other hunters showed up. They were tracking the Baskerville Hound and took it out before it could get me. I managed, barely, to get back to The Commons on my own and cash out the reward. But I don't understand. Can you not die in the Metaverse?

"Of course you can die. But you reload at the Restoration Point. You lose anything you gained since you backed up your data, except for your memories of course. Those exist in your real mozg in the real world. Still hurts like a brick though."

▸ But then why was your name crossed off the bounty? We completed the task.

"Just another scheme to deprive us Volunteers of hard-earned pretty polly. A loophole. It costs the Corporation to restore us, so if you read the fine print of the bounty, it tells you that dying before cashing out the reward invalidates your claim. And we still have to pay the restoration fee on top of that."

▸ I see. What happens if you don't have enough Crypt to cover the cost of a restoration?

"You go negative. Makes it hard to buy cancers or ptitsas, or whatever it is you are into."

The idea of falling into debt in this place filled me with deep unease. Everything I had seen was already heavily monetized.

▸ Loophole or not, I brought your share of the reward. 1,000 Crypt.

"You are a saint! A chelloveck of honor. My bank account is running low. I almost had to cancel on Serenity."

Camel blew a kiss to the motionless woman behind the glass. She reanimated, blowing an appreciative kiss back in his direction.

▸ How do I transfer the Crypt to you?

"Simple. Just open your menu, select the amount of Crypt you want, and drag it over to me. If you hover your rooker in the air, I'll start to glow. Drag and drop is all."

I tested this maneuver out and was able to successfully transfer 1,000 Crypt to Camel. I checked my menu to make sure it worked.

ECONOMY
- **CRYPT: 1070**

MEMORY
- **STORAGE: 187.7 of 210**

Sure enough, I had freed up ten metabytes of storage by making the transfer, which meant that Crypt was divided by one hundred. I would need to find a solution to prevent maxing out my storage in the future. Something to put on my list of one hundred and one mysteries of the Metaverse.

I felt something warm and wet spatter against my bald head. I closed my menu and looked up. One by one, the window displays in the Red Light district went blank. The floating red globe lanterns flickered and went dark.

Camel's cigarette fell from his lips and vanished in a puff of pixels.

"Bog! It's starting to rain! We need to get inside, skorry! You don't want to be loveted in this weather."

Large, pink drops of rain were coming in at a steep angle, almost horizontal. The rain grew stronger. As the droplets hit my exposed skin, it alternately felt shockingly frigid or nearly boiling, as if each droplet carried its own temperature in this oblique monsoon.

▸ Why? What's with this rain?!

"It purges the system memory cache. Reboots the programs. Washes The Collective clean!"

FILE 8.0

RAIN

I followed Camel as he hobbled through the dead pleasure district to the main thoroughfare cutting back to the center of The Commons. A quick glance to the walls confirmed the Polizei standing guard at the boundary crossing point were gone. Maybe they didn't like the rain either.

At this point, the pinkish water, shining in the luminescence of the city was up to our ankles. We slogged forward in the flood. The water burned as it swirled around my calves.

"We've got to get to higher ground!"

I pushed on. The streets were empty, the yokocho alleys abandoned. My ears filled with the rush of falling water. I tried desperately to maintain visual contact with Camel, but the rain was making visibility difficult.

My foot passed over something hard and slick beneath the water, and I tumbled forward, soaking my coveralls in the process. The water was tasteless and odorless, but it assaulted every nerve in my avataric body. I pulled myself up on my hands and knees, gasping. Stinging pink rivulets ran down my naked head.

▸ Where are we going?!

I tried to shout but my default voice was woefully feeble.

My companion did not respond. He sloshed through the water that now reached up to our waists. I surged onwards. I had a value of twenty assigned to my Speed category. At this moment, that seemed a small number indeed.

Camel struggled up slick metal stairs abutting a wall, curving around like an emergency staircase on the side of an overpass. When I reached them, breathless from exertion, I hauled myself up, gripping the slippery railing for dear life.

The soupy waters churned behind me, and I wondered if the whole city would soon be drowned.

At the top of the stairs, I collapsed on the street. Currents raced down the road all around me. Lights from a looming billboard advertising nostalgia schnapps reflected in the heavy puddles. Behind me, the rising pink tide swallowed the stairs.

Eyes burning, I shielded my face and spotted Camel across the street beckoning wildly. He stood at the entrance of a series of concrete khrushchevka-style high rises.

Mustering my strength, I pulled myself up and waded across to join him in an outdoor atrium in the center of the high rise. Two metal birdcage elevators waited with open jaws. Even here, the water was swiftly rising.

"These are the Towers! The best bet is to go to your nook and spatchka off the rain."

I briefly recalled the Residential Towers as a location listed at the information kiosk.

▸ My nook? I have a room here?

"All the Volunteers are given free rooms by Bolshy Bratty. It isn't much, but it's domy. Scan your code and the elevator will take you to your floor."

Camel gestured, allowing me to go first, while he opted for the second elevator. Nodding, I hurried in. He grunted and slid the door shut behind me. A pang of claustrophobia hit as I heard the clanging metal latch and saw the flood rising to my knees.

Panicking, I glanced around and saw a circular red light on a black square sensor. I scanned the barcode on my wrist, and with a loud clanking, the elevator began to rise. Water poured out through the metal bars like a sieve as I went higher and higher.

I had no idea how many floors up I had ridden until the elevator jolted to a stop. I turned and saw a dark hallway stretching out before me, and I fumbled for the rear latch of the cage.

I stepped into the hall. Stacked rows of small, round portals stood on either side—lit by dim, flickering lights. Each had a number. Glancing at my wrist, I hurried in, searching for mine.

01001110 01101111 01100010 01101111 01100100 01111001

There it was. The portal led to another capsule-like entrance with two small steps built into the wall. There was another sensor on the door, so I scanned my code. The door swung open.

A fluorescent light revealed a cramped room shorter than I was. A foam pallet lined one section of the floor. A dial on the wall adjusted the lighting. Otherwise, it was barren. Having nowhere else to go, I crawled into the glorified torpedo tube, shutting the door behind me.

To my surprise, I was completely dry. That seemed impossible. I had slogged through heavy rain, practically swam through a flash flood. And yet, not a trace of water remained. At least in my capsule, I was sheltered from the onslaught.

I had no idea how long the rain would last. I possessed no means of measuring time and no means of communicating with anyone out-side of my capsule.

Were all the rooms on these floors occupied? In each building of the Towers? Was I, even now, surrounded by other Volunteers who were my neighbors? Had they all wisely taken shelter, being familiar with the changeable whims of the Metaverse? Why then did I feel so alone?

I stripped off my coveralls, folded them in a square and placed my shoes on top of them. I stretched out on the foam pallet. It was a more comfortable position than crouching. I checked my wounded arm and navigated to the Status tab. Thankfully, it had not gotten worse.

STATUS

-     **Infernal Burn** (neutralized): **This status ailment increases vulnerability to fire and heat-based damage.**

I wondered if that status ailment was a constant or if it was a prob-ability thing. Either way, I was thankful for the administering aid of that striking woman, Rook, that rendered the burn neutralized. I would have stood no chance against the flame-spewing Baskerville Hound in such a state, not that I would have even without the status effect.

Thinking about vulnerability made me realize that I had not 'backed up' my data, as Camel mentioned. If I were to die, maybe even drowning in an improbable flood of electric pink rain, I would lose everything I had gained since arriving here. The last thing I wanted was to see my precious 1,070 Crypt vanish, not to mention the curious baubles I had acquired—crystals, card fragments, materials, and so forth.

Could I save my data here, resting in my capsule? Or did that require a trip to the Restoration Point? I desperately needed to find out what was going on with this dangerous world that I allegedly volunteered for with no memory of doing so. With no memory of who I was or where I had come from. I needed answers. But for now, I could only wait.

I didn't know if sleep was possible in this place. But I felt the need to rest. During my so-called orientation, the Concierge mentioned something about suspended animation. If my physical body was in suspended animation in the "real world," then maybe sleeping in The Collective was equivalent to a computer going into idle mode.

I closed my eyes and concentrated. I tried to reach out through time and space, to somehow connect with my physical form outside of this simulation. Where was it? What did it look like? What was happening to it just then? But there was nothing. No response. No sensation. Whatever my life had been, it was severed from my conscious experience.

As these and many other thoughts flitted through my confused mind, I twisted the dial to immerse myself in total darkness and see what dreams may come.

FILE 9.0

ERROR

In the pitch black of my capsule, at some point my mind began to dissociate. Whether that could be qualified as sleep or not was beyond me. In that state of sensory deprivation, the contours of time and space blurred.

I heard waves lapping gently against a distant shore. A rhythmic, steady sound. Peaceful and amniotic.

But then something white broke the endless darkness above my resting head. Something ferocious, spreading out like the expanding cosmos itself. A mouth. Or rather, teeth, and jagged at that. Gleaming, white teeth stretched into a rictus grin.

A sound came as deep as rolling thunder.

III kNoW wHaT yOu DiIIiiID

I lay paralyzed, frozen in place. My eyes shot open, perceiving this all-engulfing smile and nothing else. The invisible storm clouds rumbled again.

iiI KnOw WhAt YoU dIiiIIid

I strained with all my might, trying to force my body to move. But I was completely immobilized. Tears formed at the corners of my eyes and dripped helplessly down the side of my face. Every nerve and vein within me protested.

Then, a pain like an orbitoclast picking into my brain through my eye socket overwhelmed me. I could not scream or resist. An unfathomable helpless piercing. A migraine to end all migraines.

ERROR ||||lllIIII ERROR |IIIllll|||| 01110011 01100001 01101110 01101001 01110100 01111001 00100000 01100100 01100001 01101101 01100001 01100111 01100101 00100000 01110011 01110101 01110011 01110100 01100001 01101001 01101110 01100101 01100100 -1%

▸ Gaaaaaahhhh!!!!!

At last, I broke free and lunged for the dial on the wall, twisting it to full brightness.

The room was empty.

No haunting smile. No disembodied voice.

The capsule was as bare as before, with only my sparse clothing stacked against the side wall where I had left them. My head throbbed.

I shuddered, trying to bring my racing pulse under control. I felt as if I had awoken in a cold sweat, perhaps even pissed myself. Yet these were only phantom sensations. Bright spots swam in my vision.

Even then, the unfathomable phenomenon spilled down into some hole in my memory. After several minutes, I sat staring at my unfamiliar hands, unsure of what I was doing, aware of only a dull ache in my head.

A menu notification flashed in my vision.

Refresh complete.

Essence restored.

Energy at full.

Neutralized status ailment removed.

Refresh. Had I truly slept? Had I dreamt? How long had I been in this cramped room? How long had I been sitting, staring at the tan, featureless skin of my palms?

The notification hung persistently in front of me.

Shaking the last bits of disorientation and pain away, I started to sort through my menus. My Essence had returned to twenty, up from ten. My Energy, whatever that was for, remained at ten. Obviously 'resting' restored both of these statistical resources.

The restored Essence also meant that my total storage was up to 197.7 metabytes out of 210. I recalled again the unusual notification the Concierge had given me at the end of my orientation about a sign-on bonus. Ten additional metabytes of storage. Not much of a bonus.

Searching into my Status submenu, I also confirmed that the Infernal Burn was gone. Totally gone. I wondered if neutralized conditions were removed upon a refresh.

I got dressed and climbed out into the hall, closing the hatch to my capsule behind me. The hall was dim and empty. Not a sight or sound of another resident in either direction. I walked to the waiting metal cage of the elevator and scanned my code, feeling the contraption crank to life as the creaking mechanism lowered me to the ground floor.

I stepped out. The air felt brisk. It was still dark out, and I began to wonder if any equivalent to a sun existed in this world. The streets were dry. The flooding water, the deep pools, the torrent of colorful rainfall—all gone, as if it had been nothing more than a hallucination.

I looked around to see if I might spy Camel or another Volunteer, but I was alone.

I smoothed out my black coveralls and walked in the direction of the information kiosk. It was time to get some answers.

I entered the phone booth-sized tube protruding out of the

concrete and scanned my identifying barcode. There was a chime, the glowing red light turned white, and the small screen flickered on, just as before.

Welcome to The Commons. What information would you like to access?

Where to begin?

▸ I want to know more about my Statistics menu.

The Statistics menu is a user interface for Volunteers representing five categories of functional program performance relevant to your role in removing invasive entities from The Collective.

▸ And only Volunteers have them? Not Citizens?

That is correct. Citizens are neither required nor expected to participate in the removal of invasive entities.

▸ So the five categories are Attack, Defense, Ability, Movement, and Processing. Each category has a combined score, but the combined score is composed of the scores in the subcategories.

That is correct.

I brought up my menu for reference as I spoke.

▸ Please explain how Strength and Accuracy impact my 'functional program performance' in carrying out my role as a Volunteer.

Strength modifies your ability to use melee weapons, and Accuracy modifies your ability to use ranged weapons.

▸ Are there other types of weapons besides those two?

There are also thrown weapons and traps / deployable items that can be used to assist in the removal of invasive entities. Thrown weapons are modified by both Strength and Accuracy, while traps / deployable items are modified by a Processing

statistic and a Movement statistic, with the relevant modifiers specific to the item.

I had only the basic push dagger, a strictly melee weapon modified by Strength. A very small and short-range weapon at that.

▸ I think I am beginning to understand. Please explain Essence and Resistance.

Essence is the measurement of the durability of your True Self™ within The Collective. Once Essence is depleted, your True Self™ suffers deresolution and deletion and must be reloaded at a Restoration Point.

Resistance is the measurement of the defense against Essence depletion caused by invasive entities or other obstacles.

I understood that Essence represented my health, and Resistance was an extra layer of protection. Another thought occurred to me.

▸ During a recent bounty, I received a status ailment from an invasive entity. Would that have been prevented if I had higher Resistance?

I do not have enough data to speculate. Both Resistance and Probability are factors in preventing various forms of data corruption.

▸ Hmmm. Then explain Adeptness and Energy to me.

Adeptness modifies your ability to use special skills, and Energy is a related resource that powers the use of those special skills. Without Energy, certain skills will not be functional.

▸ Do I have any special skills?

You currently do not have any special skills.

▸ Explain Speed and Agility to me.

Speed modifies how quickly you can move your True Self™

through the environment, and Agility modifies your reflexes during the removal of invasive entities and other activities.

And as previously explained, either of these Movement subcategories may modify your use of traps and deployable items.

I recalled how Camel, despite his apparent hunchback and limping gait, was able to move much faster than me as we evacuated the Red Light district. I only had twenty Speed.

▸ Explain all those Processing subcategories as they relate to my role as Volunteer.

Perception relates to the interpreting of sensory information in order to comprehend the environment.

Persuasion relates to the ability to influence others to believe or do something - to move by argument, entreaty, or expostulation to a belief, position, or course of action.

Protocol relates to higher cognitive functions such as knowledge, intelligence, logic, and prescience.

Probability relates to the measurement of the likelihood of an event to occur, on a scale from impossibility to certainty.

I was beginning to grasp the bigger picture. We Volunteers had one primary function above all else—to rid this Metaverse of invasive entities. The user interface of the Statistics menu was entirely geared towards measuring our ability to do so.

Citizens, not that I had ever met one, had no need for such an interface. We Volunteers were a different breed.

I checked through my submenus to see what else I should inquire about. There were weapons, armor, and accessories (of which I had none). I moved on to my Inventory submenu.

▸ Ah. What about cards? What are Data Cards and fragments?

Invasive entities will sometimes leave behind Data Cards upon removal from The Collective. These Data Cards contain code foreign to the system that can be used to better understand the nature of these invasive entities and/or improve a Volunteer's ability to engage in removal.

Fragments are individual pieces of Data Cards. Once enough fragments have been collected, a complete Data Card can be reformed through the process of data forging.

I recalled that a location existed in The Commons called the Data Forge. I looked again under Inventory.

INVENTORY
- **CARDS**
- **FRAGMENTS**
  - {common} hellhound 4/10

▸ Okay. What about materials? During my last task, I collected three common fern flowers.

Those materials are resources collected from invasive flora. Such materials contain code foreign to the system but can be combined with system materials through the process of data forging to create functional items.

▸ How would I know what to do with these materials? What even is a fern flower?

I am unable to help with that, as I am only a virtual assistant assigned to assist Volunteers at The Commons information kiosk. Volunteers often use the Archives to research invasive entities and materials.

Archives. I see.

I noticed that a line of Volunteers was starting to form outside, eager to use the information kiosk for whatever reason. I needed to wrap this up.

▸ One last question, for now. What are Crystals? I have ten Crystals listed under my Economy submenu.

Crystals are variable residual resources left behind upon removal of invasive fauna. They can be thought of as similar to cryptographic hash functions that operate according to Schrodinger's conceptualization of paradoxical quantum superposition.

▸ Uhhhh. Can you explain that in practical terms?

Crystals are the fuel used in data forging and are required for generating new Value for your statistical subcategories, creating functional items from materials, forging complete Data Cards from fragments, fusing special skills onto weapons and armor, transmutation, and more.

Transmutation? My head was starting to swim again. Information overload.

A gaunt man dressed like a 1970s London punk rocker banged impatiently on the outside of the kiosk's transparent door.

"Hurry it up, you gloopy nazz!"

I pulled up the mini map of The Commons on the kiosk's small screen, looking at the various relevant landmarks. I did my best to commit the details to memory and shoved my way back out to the street, standing under the never-ending night sky.

FILE 10

BACKUP

I had a slightly better grasp of the system we Volunteers had to operate within. And I had several options of what to do next.

I could visit the Archives and try to learn more about this mysterious world and my purpose within it. The other option was to hit the shopping district and spend some of the hard-earned Crypt burning a hole in my metaphorical pocket. I could even visit the Data Forge and see if I could put these ten Crystals to use in strengthening some of my statistical categories.

Or I could back up my data at the Restoration Point before some nasty monster ripped my head off or I drowned in another pink-hued flash flood.

On the other hand, I had very little to back up beyond the card fragments, Crystals, materials, and Crypt I had accumulated since leaving the orientation. I assumed my black coveralls, push dagger, and cosmetic footwear were already backed up, but what if they weren't?

As discretion is the better part of valor, I abruptly changed course and headed for the Restoration Point. Better to be safe than sorry.

The Restoration Point loomed large over the surrounding structures and had the appearance of a multi-story art sculpture with swooping lines twisting together into a tower-like pinnacle. It reminded me of a retro video game company logo maximized in three dimensions.

Thick cables ran into the base of the building like black rubber roots emerging from somewhere underground, and glowing grid lines snaked across the flat surface like a circuit board.

Now that I saw the Restoration Point up close, it occurred to me that I had regularly spotted the top of the tower from other vantage points in The Commons. This was an undeniable landmark. The Volunteers' own version of the Tokyo Tower.

I approached the inverted, arching walls and stepped through a wide, open entryway. I saw no personnel of any kind manning the Restoration Point. There were only a series of upright, translucent tubes, like oversized MRI machines, arrayed in a circle surrounding a nervous core.

Each tube had a panel beside it with a round light and a small screen. I watched as one Volunteer stepped up to the panel and scanned their code, the light switching from red to white. The Volunteer then mounted a platform that lifted them into the tube. Bright lights pulsed within. The Volunteer was stretched out like the Vitruvian man as beams scanned their entire body.

I approached a free tube, preparing to scan my wrist. But before I could access the panel, the red light started blinking and the machine sprang to life with a loud whirring noise. Startled, I took several steps back.

Light flooded the empty tube and a humanoid shape began to appear. At first, it was merely an outline—a dark shadow. But it took on depth and dimension with each whirring pass, as if a person were being 3D printed before my eyes. At last, the sturm und drang abated, and the platform lowered.

A well-built Black man stood before me, wisps of newborn vapor curling off his shoulders. A gold medallion hung beneath his leather jacket. He stepped away from the machine, checking his inventory and systematically materializing and dematerializing weapons as if to make sure they were all accounted for.

He paid me no mind, but I recognized him immediately.

▸ Bigwig!

He glanced up, annoyed.

▸ Bigwig! It's me!

No hint of recollection crossed his features, so I persisted.

▸ You saved me from the Baskerville Hound. You and Rook the other day. Was it another day? I'm still a bit hazy on that point.

Narrowing his eyebrows, he responded with a dismissive grunt.

"Oh. It's the thieving Magpie. Get yourself some new clothes or body parts for frag's sake. Couldn't recognize you from Adam."

I certainly did not want to be associated with "thieving," but I hoped Bigwig was simply making an opera reference. He went back to sorting through his menu.

▸ The Restoration Point. I just saw you materialize. Does that mean...

"Yeah. I ate it out there. The Round Table's hunting a hydra. Very dangerous. Not that it's any of your concern."

A hydra.

▸ I'm sorry. I hope you didn't lose too much of your data.

"Are you joking? I can't tell. My shotgun is more expressive than your ugly mug. I keep most of my Crypt and the rest of my gear in the Repository. Where do you store it, under your bloody mattress?"

Repository...

▶ Was Rook with you? Is she okay?

That comment elicited a frown. Bigwig closed his menu with a wave of his hand.

"How about you keep her name out of your mouth and mind your own business."

▶ I'm sorry, I didn't mean any offense. I take it you and her... that is to say... the two of you...

"We're partners. We watch each other's backs. That is the most important relationship a Volunteer can have. Now, I've got a score to settle with a multi-headed beast from Greek mythology. So, get out of my way."

Bigwig pushed past me, his muscular form moving purposefully towards the entrance. Feeling emboldened, I called out a final question in my feeble starter voice.

▶ What does a Volunteer need to do to join the Round Table?

He stopped in his tracks and turned to look over his shoulder, flashing a disdainful smirk.

"Join the Round Table? Ha! You're a nonentity. Bag a rare bounty. Nah, not even that—a *legendary* bounty. Then someone might even notice you, little Magpie."

Bigwig spat on the ground and was gone. Charming fellow.

I turned my attention back to the tube he had materialized in. There were other open tubes, but perhaps some of his swagger might rub off on me if I were to use this one. Superstitious thinking, I know.

I approached the panel and scanned my barcode.

Welcome to the Restoration Point.

Volunteer 01001110-01101111-01100010-01101111-01100100-01111001

Your last backup was *NOT APPLICABLE*.

Would you like to back up your data?

▸ Yes, I would.

100 Crypt will be deducted.

I winced. I shouldn't have been surprised. Everything here had a price. That meant I was down to 970 Crypt. Maybe the most common cause of death in The Collective was being nickeled and dimed. On the other hand, it freed up one metabyte of storage space. Silver lining, I suppose.

The round light on the panel shifted from red to white.

Please enter the Restoration Station to back up your data.

I did just as I saw the other Volunteers do, climbing onto the small platform which raised me into the tube. I placed my arms and feet in illuminated holders. Soon, hot beams of light crawled over every inch of my body. It felt like they penetrated straight through me. I was cocooned in a tingling sensation from head to toe.

Then the procedure was done, and I quickly clambered out of the tube. I checked the screen on the panel and saw my full menu frozen in time.

Your data backup has been successfully completed.

With my progress saved, I turned my attention to my next most pressing goal. To find out what the frag was happening. Next stop, the Archives.

FILE 11

ARCHIVES

Drawing from my recollection of the miniature map at the information kiosk, I knew there were no standard cardinal directions. Rather, it was more of an XYZ axis situation, taking into account the verticality of the construction.

The Archives were further down the left side of the X axis and at ground level. After passing several shadowy blocks, I was surprised and not a little disconcerted to see what looked like a small concrete pyramid with the letters ARCHIV above sliding double doors in a neglected section of the city.

This must be the place. Not what I was expecting.

The glowing, omnipresent red light awaited me like some all-seeing evil eye. I scanned my code and the doors slid open, revealing a glass box elevator. I stepped in and the doors closed automatically behind me.

Nothing happened. I looked around for another scanning point, or some switch. But I saw nothing. Then, without warning, the elevator began rapidly descending of its own accord. Passing down a lightless shaft, I had no idea how deep I was going. How deep did the Metaverse even go? It wasn't like there was a crust, mantle, and core to worry about. Or was there?

Eventually, blue pinpricks of light bled through the glass walls. I placed my palms on the glass and peered out into expansive darkness. It was as if I was plummeting into an enormous subterranean cavern with an underground lake, and the lights were the crests of tiny waves catching a beam of moonlight. But as I continued to fall, I realized it wasn't a cavern at all.

The blue lights emanated from countless nodules on tall obelisk-like servers. This was a server farm, row upon row radiating out beyond my vision in every direction from a central point. The elevator braked harshly. The double doors opened, and I stumbled forwards.

Oof.

I found myself in a concrete ring blocking my access to the endless forest of servers. A strong ozone smell permeated the environment. Three large, curved screens hung in the air, and a mechanical headset hung from cables.

It almost felt like this was an older part of the Metaverse. Something left behind from an earlier version of the digital world.

I stepped forwards and tentatively attached the hanging set in place over my bald head.

Welcome to the Archives.

Initiate query.

So many questions. Where to start?

▸ Tell me about… The Collective.

Incorrect query parameter.

Initiate query.

What?

This system was not as intuitive and user-friendly as The Concierge or even the information kiosk. Again, I suspected that this was an older, more primordial system function. I tried again.

▸ The Collective.

Incorrect query parameter.

Initiate query.

▸ I want to learn about The Collective.

Incorrect query parameter.

Initiate query.

Uhh.

▸ Query, The Collective?

Query initiated -> The Collective

The Collective is the most advanced and fully immersive shared virtual platform for human consciousness. The Collective represents the future of connection. It provides new ways to interact and share experiences. The Collective is owned and operated by Reality Incorporated.

The three screens lit up with hazy stills and footage extolling the virtues of this immersive product, proudly stamped with the corporate logo.

▸ Query, Reality Incorporated.

Query initiated -> Reality Incorporated

Reality Incorporated is a multinational technology conglomerate headquartered in [FILE MISSING]. Reality Inc. owns and operates The Collective, among other products and services. It is one of the world's most valuable companies and among the ten largest publicly traded corporations.

Again, focus group-tested corporate propaganda images filled the screens. The world they depicted seemed so alien from my current experience.

▸ Query, the purpose of The Collective.

The Collective is a private, safe, and inclusive world of virtual

connection for Citizens during a state of extended suspended animation. The Collective fosters ongoing psychological health, meaningful connection, exploration, and expression. Live your best second life! ™

  ▸ Query, first wave of Citizens to The Collective.

Query initiated -> first wave of Citizens to The Collective

The first wave of one million lucky Citizens to migrate to The Collective were honored subscribers of Reality Inc.'s *Premium Diamond Priority+* membership plan.

  ▸ Query, second wave of Citizens to The Collective.

Query initiated -> second wave of Citizens to The Collective

The second wave of thirty million fortunate Citizens, subscribers of Reality Inc.'s *Golden Select Comfort* membership plan, has been temporarily delayed until required system maintenance can be completed.

  ▸ Query, system maintenance delaying the second wave of Citizens to The Collective.

Query initiated -> system maintenance delaying the second wave of Citizens to The Collective

Multiple error states caused by the unexpected emergence of anomalous programs have disrupted normal system functioning within The Collective. Complaints from Citizens alleging virtual injury, real world health complications, and the resulting fall in share prices have inspired Reality Incorporated to pause future migrations until the situation can be successfully mitigated. Please note, Reality Inc. does not comment on pending litigation or open investigations.

Grainy newsreel footage showed plummeting stock prices on various transnational indexes and intimated closed door board meetings.

▸ Query, Volunteers in The Collective.

Query initiated -> Volunteers in The Collective

Volunteers are brave men and women who have signed on to help 'Make the Metaverse Safe Again' and ensure a bright, connected future for humanity during these unprecedented times.

Handsome, strapping men and lovely women were confidently marching on the screens, cheered by small crowds of onlookers on a parade route housed within an airplane hangar.

Unprecedented times? I vaguely recalled The Concierge mentioning something about Earth's greatest minds working to solve many challenges during the orientation.

▸ Query, unprecedented times.

Query initiated -> unprecedented times

Query is too broad.

Initiate query.

Huh.

▸ Query, trouble currently facing humanity.

Query initiated -> trouble currently facing humanity

Query is too broad.

Initiate query.

▸ Okay, then. How about... query, Volunteer contracts?

Query initiated -> Volunteer contracts

Each Volunteer has signed a legally binding contract to obtain advanced, temporary access to The Collective in order to carry out their assigned tasks of scrubbing the system of anomalous programs, also referred to as invasive entities.

▸ Query, Volunteer contract fulfillment.

Query initiated → Volunteer contract fulfillment

Volunteers will be released from their contract upon success-

ful completion of all contract stipulations, namely, the removal of any and all anomalous code from within The Collective.

▸ Query, Volunteer contract early termination.

Query initiated -> Volunteer contract early termination

As clearly stated in the fine print of the legally binding contracts signed by each Volunteer, there are no allowances for early contract termination. Volunteers have bravely agreed to stay the course until their important job is complete.

▸ Query, number of Volunteers in The Collective.

Query initiated -> number of Volunteers in The Collective

A total of [FILE MISSING] Volunteers have been migrated into The Collective so far. Currently, there are less than [FILE MISSING] Volunteers present in The Collective, representing a net decrease of [FILE MISSING] percent.

Something didn't add up.

If there was no way to get out of a Volunteer contract, and the contracts can't be fulfilled until every invasive entity is purged... how were there less Volunteers? What happened to them? Where did they go?

Incorrect query parameter.

Initiate query.

Huh? Did this headset just read my mind?

▸ Query, Volunteer 01001110-01101111-01100010-01101111 01100100-01111001.

Query initiated → Volunteer 01001110-01101111-01100010-01101111 01101111-01100100-01111001

Volunteer 01001110-01101111-01100010-01101111-01100100-01111001 is you.

My avatar, wearing the Archives headset, appeared on all three screens, staring back at me with its hollow, unrecognizable eyes. To describe this as a dissociative experience would be an understatement.

That's not really me. That's not the *real* me.

► Query, Volunteer 01001110-0110111-01100010-01101111-01100100-01111001 true identity.

Query initiated → Volunteer 01001110-01101111-01100010-01101111-01100100-01111001 true identity

[FILE MISSING].

It was time to try a new topic.

► Query... hellhounds.

Mythology query initiated -> hellhounds

An archetypal supernatural dog recurring in mythologies around the world. These ominous creatures are believed to stand guard in the Underworld or even serve the Devil. Variants of this archetype are known from Greek, Norse, and Celtic mythology, as well as English folklore. *See Cerberus, Garmr, Fairy Hound, or Baskerville Hound.*

Several illustrations flickered on the screens depicting the fearsome hellhounds and their ilk. The beasts were invariably black, oversized, strong, and had red eyes or were accompanied by flames. Just like what I fought in the service tunnels.

Interesting—if anxiety provoking—but not particularly useful. Maybe if I had an active bounty on some recognizable monster, I could research at the Archives to discern a weakness.

► Query, fern flowers.

Query initiated -> fern flowers

Ferns are a group of complex, leafy plants found across many biomes. They typically do not produce flowers—reproducing through spores instead.

► Mythology query, fern flowers.

Mythology query initiated -> fern flowers

A magic flower found in Baltic, Estonian, Slavic, and other mythologies. This otherworldly flower blooms during a brief window on the eve of the summer solstice. Depending on the regional variant, it is believed to bring fortune to the person who finds it or grant powers to ward off evil.

Those searching for the fern flower must practice caution as dark spirits are believed to stand guard, empowered by the same solstice magic that caused the flowers to bloom. If caught by the spirits, flower seekers may be cursed or even killed. But these may be rumors designed to discourage libidinous young couples from going into the woods "seeking the fern flower."

Illustrated images of traditional midsummer celebrations filled the screens. Young couples eagerly jaunting into the woods. Unfurling fern fronds under a strawberry moon. Nubile bodies wreathed in protective leaves.

Fortune? I certainly liked the sound of that. But were there different varieties of these flowers? How would I know which mythology applied to the items I found?

I scrolled down to my Materials submenu.

INVENTORY
- **MATERIALS**
    - **3 {common} fern flowers**

Three common fern flowers. I materialized them. They hovered in the air just above the open palm of my hand, outlined with a subtle, yellow glow. I dematerialized them.

The common designation implied that there were materials of other rarities. I recalled that both my melee weapon and clothing items were described as basic, which, according to the item description of my push dagger, meant that they could not be upgraded, enhanced, or exported.

The kiosk assistant had listed transmutation as an available service at the Data Forge. I wondered if 'exporting' an item and 'transmuting' an item were the same thing.

I further assumed that 'common' may be at least one step above basic. That was if the term basic could even be applied to wondrous creatures and plants springing from ancient mythology. The hellhounds had been common, and the Baskerville Hound had been uncommon.

When I first obtained the fern flowers, Camel made a comment about crafting. And, selecting the fern flower in my inventory, I saw that it contained the following description:

Crafting material. Attributes unknown.

▶ Query, crafting materials within The Collective.

Query initiated -> crafting materials within The Collective

Over time, Volunteers have learned to assimilate fragments of anomalous code, such as that harvested from invasive flora, to create emergent new items.

Although this was not an intended feature by Reality Incorporated, allowances have been made for Volunteers to provide an advantage against invasive entities at no additional cost to the Corporation. However, all foreign code must be wiped from The Collective prior to Volunteer contract fulfillment.

▶ Query, system items frequently used to combine with common crafting materials.

Query initiated -> system items frequently used to combine with common crafting materials

A popular system item frequently used for crafting via a Data Forge is pure water. Another popular item is a white linen cloth. Relevant items depend on the nature and frequency of the crafting material.

▸ Query, where to purchase pure water in The Commons.

Query initiated -> where to purchase pure water in The Commons

Pure water, in vials or bottles, can be purchased from the Supply Depot in The Commons.

FILE 12

SHOPPING

Leaving the Archives, I traversed through The Commons until I reached the Supply Depot, sparkling like a jewel in the night. I entered, noticing the same elderly woman sitting behind the checkout counter. No parasol this time.

She gave a polite nod. I wasn't sure if she remembered me, but she lowered a paperback she was reading titled *Die Verwandlung* and smiled expectantly, wrinkles stretching across liver spotted skin. I noticed she wore earrings in the shape of crescent moons.

▸ Any rain in the forecast?

"Oh, ho, ho. Not yet, dearie. Come to do some shopping?"

▸ Yes. How does one go about that?

"On this floor, you have your miscellaneous odds and ends, trinkets and doodads. You can search the aisles and bring any item back here for purchase, or you can shop by menu if you are in a rush. Downstairs we have cosmetics and body modification."

She stretched out her hand and pointed to a spiral staircase leading down to a sublevel of the building. I noticed that the staircase also led to an upper floor.

▸ And upstairs?

"Off limits. Temporarily."

▸ I see.

"This cycle there is a 30% discount or more on select hairstyles. And facial tattoos are buy-two-get-one free for a limited time. Our sales always rotate, so be sure to check back often."

She smiled and resumed reading her book. I wondered if a 'cycle' had something to do with the unusual rain but hesitated to ask. The words of Camel rang in my ear. "It purges the system memory cache. Reboots the programs."

Anyway, I had my shopping list. I was on the lookout for pure water. Soon enough, I found it on a shelf of consumable items.

Was this something I could drink? Or was it only something to craft with? I recalled the beverage I consumed down in the Rathskeller. I had no physiological need for food or drink, but alcohol tasted very real.

The psychological pleasure of an artificial act was tangible, and looking at—of all things—packets of instant ramen noodles lining the nostalgia goods shelves, I imagined my mouth watering. Ones and zeroes. Neurons firing.

I resisted the impulse and focused back on the pure water. It was offered in two varieties. Vials and bottles. I tried to pick up the 3D rotating image of the vial. The image became temporarily fuzzy as it moved, yet it maintained a subtle substance in my grasp. Concentrating, I selected the item.

Item: Pure Water (vial)

Quantity: 1

Cost: 50 Crypt

I set it down and picked up the glass bottle, which appeared larger.

Item: Pure Water (bottle)

Quantity: 3

Cost: 125 Crypt

So, there was a slight discount for buying in bulk. Still, I was acutely aware of my dwindling finances. Not knowing if crafting would even be worth it, I hesitated. Doing the math, purchasing the bottle would knock me down to 845 Crypt. But I did have three fern flowers.

I also noticed a small piece of white linen cloth on the shelves.

Item: White Linen Cloth

Quantity: 1

Cost: 50 Crypt

I figured that I could experiment with each of these materials and save the third fern flower for future use. I decided to go with one vial of pure water and one swatch of white linen cloth.

I wondered if I could temporarily place the unpurchased items in my inventory, but I could not, so I carried them to the counter. The woman opened a special vendor menu in the air in front of me and we made the exchange. I dragged one hundred Crypt over to her menu and the purchased items materialized in my hands.

I added them to my inventory and then checked my menus.

INVENTORY
- **MATERIALS**
    - **3 {common} fern flowers** (3 metabytes)
    - **1 vial of pure water** (1 metabyte)
    - **1 white linen cloth** (1 metabyte)

ECONOMY
- **CRYPT: 870** (8.7 metabytes)

MEMORY
- **STORAGE: 197.7 / 210**

"Thank you and come again."

I was ready to head next door to the Armory, but out of curiosity, I made my way to the spiral staircase and peered down. The lower floor seemed deserted, with bright panels on the walls reflecting off a shiny, black slate floor. I went down the transparent steps to the sublevel.

To one side of the floor-to-ceiling panels, a familiar red light waited. I scanned my barcode and the panels sprung to life. I saw my avatar splayed out—rotating, magnified to twice my size on the central screen. The panel to the left displayed a menu of body modification options and the panel to the right displayed cosmetic options.

Many were familiar from my time in the orientation, but I scrolled through the available options anyhow. Some I did not recognize, possibly newer additions, and some were highlighted on a rotating carousel at the top of each panel.

Under body modification, I noticed several options for customized voices. All were out of my price range, even though Mellifluous and Lilting were both discounted by 20%. I saw one ultra premium voice labeled Morgan Freeman selling for 200,000 Crypt.

I turned my attention to the carousel, which showed five different hairstyles currently on sale: cornrows, temple fade, quiff, disheveled mushroom, and wavy asymmetrical crop. All were listed at 30% off, but I stopped cold and stared at an inviting, bold red number next to the wavy asymmetrical crop. 50% off. Intrigued, I hovered over the option for more information.

Hairstyle: Wavy Asymmetrical Crop

Color: Black

Cost: 500 Crypt (250 with 50% discount)

Call it vanity. Call it foolishness. Call it a waste. But I purchased that hairstyle.

Wavy asymmetrical crop hairstyle (black) **selected. Would you like to apply this change?**

▸ Yes, I would.

Soon, medium length wavy, black hair materialized over my bald pate, falling over the right side of my face. The rotating visualization of my avatar instantly reflected the change. I ran a hand through my new locks. They were as firmly rooted in my skin as if I had always possessed them.

Although I still had the most generic starter features imaginable—an almond-skinned, nondescript androgynous person in black coveralls—I felt a swell of something that could only be described as pride. The pleasurable feeling was instantly matched with the aversive, negative valence of seeing my diminished Crypt.

ECONOMY
- **CRYPT: 620**

Alas, I was tired of feeling like an overlooked non-entity in this world. There was always more money to be made.

I searched my menu to see where the body modification might be listed, but I could not find it. My physical appearance was all the proof I needed. I inferred that cosmetic purchases were reflected somewhere within my nested menus, but body modification was a one-time application. After all, I wouldn't be keeping any spare hairstyles or appendages in my inventory for later use. Or maybe I needed to search harder when I had more time.

I realized I had never delved into the History submenu and decided to take a quick look.

MEMORY

- **HISTORY**
  - **Applied wavy asymmetrical crop hairstyle** (black)
  - **Purchased wavy asymmetrical crop hairstyle** (black) **for 250 Crypt**
  - **Accessed the Body Modification menu in the Supply Depot sublevel**
  - **Entered the sublevel of the Supply Depot**
  - **Supply Depot vendor said, "Thank you and come again."**
  - **Purchased one white linen cloth from the Supply Depot vendor**
  - **Purchased one vial of pure water from the Supply Depot vendor**

It went on and on. I was startled.

There was a real-time record of my actions within The Collective. Things I said. Places I went. All the way back to when I awoke in the orientation. Of course, I had to have known that the system was tracking me. That's what systems do. Nevertheless, it was disconcerting to be so nakedly exposed before that watchful eye. Data of every behavior and spoken word.

What about my thoughts? Were they keeping a record of them as well?

Maybe there was some use for this history feature, but for now, I didn't care to bother with it. Lost in these and other musings, I climbed the stairs and quickly exited back out onto the street. The old woman began to say something as I passed but I didn't hear it.

FILE 12.1

ARMORY

I took a moment to get my bearings, then headed for the Armory.

The Armory had the appearance of a concrete bunker, with a smooth, humped roof. The windows were tinted and reinforced. A gaudy neon sign illustrated an assault rifle affixed with bayonet thrusting into an ogre's head ad infinitum.

Yet, the establishment had the buzz of a nightclub. Several Volunteers I did not recognize entered and exited through the front of the building, while others milled about outside. Apparently, it was a popular spot.

I murmured apologies as I pushed through the double doors.

Inside, long wrap-around counters separated the customers from the merchandise. On the walls, countless racks of weapons rolled past like a conveyor belt. I nearly went cross eyed watching instruments of death crisscrossing the walls in alternating rows.

Samurai swords. Hira shuriken. A baseball bat with nails sticking out of it. I even saw a bazooka whiz past.

In the center of the spacious room, pieces of clothing and armor were on display in tall, transparent cases. Motley Volunteers inspected the goods like one would admire paintings at an art gallery.

Many of the items were wholly unfamiliar to me. One appeared to be a whole-body suit covered in spikes. I leaned in to read a label: Siberian bear-hunting suit. Another was labeled Nationale Volksarmee uniform. Both were exorbitantly expensive. No bold red sales numbers on these.

The longer I looked, I noticed some of the displays flicker out, replaced by different items. Were these just holographic images as well, waiting to be materialized? No doubt I would have the option to 'shop by menu' if I wanted.

A smart, black tactical jacket appeared in the case I had been previously staring into. I reached out to select it, and the object glowed with a faint outline.

Armor: Tactical jacket

Armor Type: Body

Cost: 1500 Crypt

Out of my price range. Still, I liked the look of it. I hovered over the piece to access more details.

Armor: Tactical jacket

Armor Type: Body

Cost: 1500 Crypt

Level: 1 of 10

Frequency: Uncommon

Defense Output: 30

Details: A type of jacket designed for use in military, law enforcement, and other tactical situations. Made from durable materials and features a variety of compartments for storing gear. Also features reinforced elbows, shoulders, and VELCRO strips for attaching morale patches or identification.

Properties: Storing - when equipped, this armor increases memory space by 20 metabytes.

Size: 30 metabytes

Suddenly, I tensed as gunshots rang out. Looking up from the display, I saw muzzle flashes reflecting off glass at the back of the room. But none of the other Volunteers so much as flinched.

Against the rear wall, large bulletproof windows looked onto a firing range. A few Volunteers were gleefully shooting at targets. A place to test the merchandise?

Another opening in the wall to my right led into a sparring room, currently occupied by a shirtless Volunteer dual-wielding swords and facing off against a training bot.

"Can I help you, soldier?"

A voice equal parts curt, authoritative, and hollow caused me to spin around.

Behind one of the counters was the strangest sight I had yet seen since my awakening, and I had seen literal hellhounds. A cyborg with an army green metal body stood before me, easily seven feet tall. Its features were nearly skeletal, but it wore an incongruous colonial powdered wig. Military star insignias were stenciled on its chest plate.

"Colonel Peacekeeper at your service! Purveyor of the finest weapons and armor!"

▸ A... robot?

"Back by popular demand! I was patched with these cosmetics during a special Veterans Day sale and the customers loved it! Profits have increased 18.2% since the change from my previous appearance. Hooah!"

So bizarre.

▸ I see. Well, not really. You mentioned Veterans Day. Veterans of what war?

"I'm sorry, I'm only an ordnance specialist and do not have access to that intel. Above my pay grade! But I do have access to the finest weapons and armor! What can I interest you in?"

▸ I did see a tactical jacket over there that looked nice, but I can't afford it.

"You need to get out there and kill some more monsters, soldier! Do your part. Accumulate that sweet Crypt. Then you can go on a spending spree on your next rotation!"

▸ That's the idea. But I only have these black coveralls. As far as weapons go, I have this basic push dagger. Not much to brag about.

"Well, soldier. Wars may be fought with weapons, but they are won by men. It is the spirit of men who follow and of the man who leads that gains victory!"

Was that a quote from somewhere?

▸ I almost died once already, and I'd prefer not to experience that again. I have a certain price point, but I'm having trouble deciding between defense and offense, a new piece of armor or a new weapon. Any advice?

"My motto is—nobody ever defended anything successfully, there is only attack and attack and attack some more!"

I wasn't sure if I entirely agreed with that perspective, but I saw little utility in debating with the jingoistic automaton.

▸ Colonel... Peacekeeper, I only have 620 Crypt left. What weapons do you have that are less than that?

"Our sales always rotate, so be sure to check back often. But let's take a look!"

Peacekeeper raised a green, metal finger and opened three

shimmering menus in front of my face. An assortment of diverse weapons zipped into place on each floating screen.

"In our current lineup, we have the following available for 500 Crypt each. Some are on sale. I'll show you a few fancier options to whet your appetite. It all depends if you go for melee, ranged, or thrown weapons. Pick your poison, soldier!"

Melee Weapons
Weapon: Warclub
Weapon Type: Melee (bludgeoning)
Cost: 500 Crypt

Weapon: Tomahawk
Weapon Type: Melee / Throwing (slashing)
Cost: 1000 Crypt

Weapon: Cane sword
Weapon Type: Melee (piercing)
Cost: 1000 Crypt

Ranged Weapons
Weapon: Hand crossbow
Weapon Type: Ranged (piercing)
Cost: 500 Crypt

Weapon: Snub-nosed revolver
Weapon Type: Ranged (ballistic)
Cost: 500 Crypt

Thrown Weapons
Weapon: Rope dart
Weapon Type: Thrown (piercing)
Cost: 500 Crypt

Weapon: Fei tou flying weight
Weapon Type: Thrown (bludgeoning)
Cost: 500 Crypt

Weapon: Meteor hammer
Weapon Type: Thrown (bludgeoning)
Cost: 1000 Crypt

Quite the variety. I recalled that melee weapons were moderated by my Strength, ranged weapons by my Accuracy, and thrown weapons as a combination of Strength and Accuracy.

"We also have traps and other deployable items, of course. But let me show you one of my favorite items—on sale!"

Colonel Peacemaker snapped his fingers and a pepperbox-style handgun with six small barrels, a handle that doubled as a folding knuckle duster, and a fold out double-edged knife that looked like a bayonet appeared.

Weapon: Apache revolver
Weapon Type: Ranged (ballistic) / Melee (piercing, bludgeoning)
Frequency: Rare
Cost: 4000 Crypt

Impressive. I could shoot, stab, or punch someone with that thing. Always good to have options.

▸ Thanks, but way too rich for my blood.

The robotic vendor slumped its shoulders in disappointment.

▸ Maybe I could save up for it? Buy it later? Put it on layaway?

The vendor made a metallic clicking sound somewhere in its throat.

"I always say—a good plan, violently executed now, is better than a perfect plan next week."

► That may be so, but here is another proverb: you can't get blood from a stone.

I swiped away the rare weapon menu and looked again at the melee, ranged, and thrown options before me. If I spent 500 Crypt, I would have just 120 remaining. I knew I had to take on another bounty soon. But first...

After some deliberation, I decided to go with a ranged weapon. I still had my push dagger if I needed to resort to close combat and having the option to exterminate invasive, bloodthirsty creatures from a safe(r) distance was a good option to have.

I recalled that during the orientation I was given the choice to purchase a small handgun for 300 Crypt. I couldn't imagine that being worthwhile to invest in at this point, especially if it was of the basic variety. And it seemed that the two other options currently in the Armory's lineup were within my price range.

Weapon: Hand crossbow

Weapon Type: Ranged (piercing)

Cost: 500 Crypt

Level: 1 of 10

Frequency: Common

Damage Output: 10

Details: A smaller version of a traditional crossbow that can be held in one hand or modified to be attached to the wrist. It can fire a single bolt (a metal dart-like projectile).

Properties: Ammunition - requires crossbow bolts. Fires one bolt at a time. Can be fired one-handed but requires a free hand to reload. Bolts that miss their targets may be recovered.

Size: 20 metabytes

Weapon: Snub-nosed revolver

Weapon Type: Ranged (ballistic)

Cost: 500 Crypt

Level: 1 of 10

Frequency: Common

Damage Output: 20

Details: A small revolver with a short barrel designed with minimal external movement of the firing mechanism. This weapon is easy to carry and conceal at the expense of accuracy at range.

Properties: Ammunition - requires .32 caliber cartridges. Holds five cartridges at a time and must be manually reloaded.

Size: 20 metabytes

The hand crossbow had a lower damage output but with the possibility of reclaiming bolts that missed their targets. The revolver could hold five cartridges whereas the crossbow held only a single bolt at a time. The crossbow seemed a bit medieval to me. Perhaps it was more useful as a stealthy weapon. It was hard, after all, to ignore the sound of gunfire. With my minimum Accuracy, the higher damage output of the revolver felt promising.

► Excuse me, if I purchase this revolver, does it come with ammunition?

"The revolver will come fully loaded with five cartridges in the chambers of the cylinder. Any additional ammunition must be purchased."

► How much?

"Ten Crypt per cartridge. A great deal!"

► And how much storage space does each cartridge take up?

"Each cartridge, except the ones loaded in the revolver, requires one metabyte each."

I did some math. Spending 500 Crypt would free up five metabytes of space, bringing my total storage to 190.2 out of 210. Purchasing the revolver, which mercifully included five loaded rounds at no additional cost or storage requirement, would increase my total to 210.2.

Shiva on a stick.

I was quickly coming to realize that both Crypt and storage space were incredibly limited and important commodities in The Collective. I was experiencing real anxiety over maxing out my storage. The tactical jacket that I could not yet afford came with a nice storage perk, so there must be other ways to increase my storage space.

▸ Do Volunteers normally store their extra ammunition in their inventory?

"But of course! Unless that savvy Volunteer purchases a quiver, bandolier, or other relevant accessory!"

I doubted I could afford anything else from the Armory at this time. But it didn't hurt to ask.

▸ Since this is my first time shopping here, do you have any deals for new customers? Maybe throw in a holster or something like that for free or at a discount? I think it would really help boost customer loyalty.

The cyborg in the powdered wig stared at me with its dead, metal eyes, saying nothing. Perhaps some internal calculation was passing through its programmed vendor brain.

"A novel suggestion, soldier, but not persuasive. As it is, we are the only place to acquire new weapons in The Commons. Customer loyalty is guaranteed!"

I remembered that my Persuasion score was a measly ten. Probably not worth the effort to try and barter with this thing.

▸ If I buy that revolver, I will be .2 over my data storage limit. What happens then?

"Do you have an account established at the Repository and an instant transfer subscription?"

▸ I do not.

"Then you can't add the revolver to your inventory."

▸ Can I temporarily carry the revolver in my hands without adding it to my inventory?

"You should know from basic training that most items can be carried without being added to your inventory. However, if you were to lose that item, there would be no record of ownership. Also, you would not be able to back up that item at the Restoration Point. But it is a moot point, soldier. Armory policy is no purchases can be completed unless the weapon or armor can fit in your available storage space!"

I racked my brain, thinking of how I could free up .2 metabytes. I did not want to part with anything in my inventory.

▸ That tactical jacket I saw. Can I somehow place a deposit on it for later?

"You can. But there is no guarantee it will remain at its current discounted sale price."

▸ Sale? I didn't notice it was on sale. What is the regular price?

"2,000 Crypt. Right now it is only 1,500."

Ugh.

▸ Put twenty Crypt down as a deposit on the tactical jacket and give me the revolver.

The vendor screen flashed a confirmation, then another.

Snub-nosed revolver selected. Would you like to equip this weapon?

▸ Not right now.

The revolver materialized then dematerialized straight into my inventory as 500 precious Crypt melted away into the digital ether. I only had one hundred left. I felt sick.

"Thank you for shopping at the Armory, soldier. Hooah! Have a FUBAR day!"

I turned away from the counter and walked straight into a group of Volunteers loitering close behind me.

Oof!

"Watch where you're going, noob."

▸ Sorry.

There were four of them. Not quite matching, they wore outfits with similar colors and textures. Black denim and leather, mostly. Each had a circular patch somewhere on their clothing depicting a fanged cobra ready to strike.

The one I had collided with, a medium-built male with a reverse mohawk and eyes like black marbles, wore the cobra patch above his breast and had a lower jaw the color of raw steel. Whether it was painted, tattooed, or actually replaced with metal, I could not tell.

"Noob. What do you think you're going to do with that malenky pooshka?"

▸ With that what?

Another member of the group butted in.

"Your little gun! Think you're hot Shiva with that toy?"

Without waiting for an answer, the first man moved in close, his face twisted in a snarl.

"We're bolnoy of noobs like you coming in and snatching up all the easy bounties."

▸ Easy bounties? I thought we were all in this together. What happened to Volunteer solidarity?

"Yeah, yeah. Glory to the Volunteers. But we's been here a while. Some of us has gots to eat. Gots bills to pay, needs to meet. New volunteers been showing up and taking our kills, making us travel far off to drat more dangerous prey."

▸ The last time I saw the bounty boards there was no shortage of bounties. If anything, there were too many to count.

"A smart odin, aye? The point is, you noobs gots no respect. You needs to pay tribute to those that come before you. Those of us that paved the way."

▸ Are you with the hunters from the Round Table?

He hawked up a wad of saliva and spit on the Armory floor. It soon evaporated into a wisp of nothingness.

"Round Table. Bunch of self-righteous arseholes. Think they can actually earn their way out of this hellhole. But we's know this is the new normal. This is where we's gotta stake our claim. Build our kingdom."

▸ I don't know what to tell you. Now if you would please get out of my way and let me pass.

The man pushed against my chest as I tried to leave, blocking me. A butterfly knife materialized in his other hand.

FILE 12.2

WAGER

Instantly, several double-barreled sentry guns popped out of the ceiling of the Armory and trained on us. A few other Volunteers side-eyed the situation, but most kept to themselves as they browsed the shop. They didn't want to get involved.

The hollow but firm voice of Colonel Peacekeeper called out.

"Remember, soldiers. No violence of any kind is tolerated within this establishment of deadly weapons and mass destruction! If you want to test your wares, use the Firing Range or the Dojo."

The distasteful man's snarl melted into a sideways grin. He held up the butterfly knife in theatrical surrender, gave it a little twirl, and dematerialized it.

"Yeah, yeah, Colonel. In that case, noob, hows about a friendly malenky test instead? My worst shot against you in the Firing Range. Revolvers only, since that seems to be your veshch. Is that a five shooter? Best out of five shots on a clean target. We filly for Crystals."

I scrunched up my face, trying to decipher the onslaught of slang.

▶ A test? Filly? Are you saying... you want to wager with Crystals? No way. I only have ten, and I am not giving them up.

"It'll be a double bet. You win, we's give you twenty. My veck wins, we's take yours."

I felt an unusual twitch somewhere deep within me, as if the words 'double bet' activated a reflex. An almost irresistible urge. It was even money, so to speak. But I had to be smart.

▸ I only have five shots. I can't afford to waste them.

"You gloopy nazz! Ammo is infinite in the Firing Range. If you can score higher than Buzzcut, you'll be twenty Crystals richer."

I looked to the side at the Volunteer apparently called Buzzcut. He had similar generic features as my avatar. Did that mean he hadn't been in The Collective very long? I saw pale skin. A silver grill over his teeth. Extremely close-cropped brown hair. He was twitchy, materializing and dematerializing a small revolver over and over.

▸ Double if I win? Fine.

I followed the group to the Firing Range. There were many lanes, most of them occupied by Volunteers testing out all manner of ranged weapons. The cacophony was incredible. At the end of the row, Buzzcut and I took our places before two empty lanes.

Buzzcut scanned his barcode under a red light, and I did the same. Two fresh targets appeared at the end of the lanes. Each target depicted the dark silhouette of a human torso with concentric circles around the head and chest with various point values assigned.

"Remember, noob. Best score after five shots. You lose? We's take your Crystals and whatever else you're carrying."

▸ That wasn't the deal!

The man just sneered, turning back to his goon.

Buzzcut raised his firearm. It was a larger caliber, with a longer barrel than the one I had just seen him holding a minute ago. Shiva. Had I been played?

A crack from his revolver and a hole punched through the target to the center left of the torso. Scoring an eight.

Shiva, Shiva, Shiva...

I quickly equipped the snub-nosed revolver, materializing it into my hand. I tested the weight, feeling the cool metal material of the handle. On some level, it felt comfortable there, as if a muscle memory encoded in my cerebellum in some distant place activated. Maybe this wasn't my first time handling a gun.

I held the revolver out in front of me with both hands, steadying myself, and fired. I missed the target entirely.

The leader of the cobras laughed derisively.

"Eight to nil. Four shots left!"

Buzzcut lined up another shot. Seven, puncturing the target's shoulder.

Looking down at the gun in my hands, I noticed the spent cartridge rematerialize in the cylinder. Infinite ammo in the Firing Range, indeed. Good to know.

I readied another shot. This time, I hit the target, but outside of the concentric circles. Scoreless.

"Fifteen to nil!"

Buzzcut aimed again. He pulled back the trigger and—missed! The leader was not pleased.

"Buzzcut, you fragface!"

I had a chance, however slim. Three shots left.

I narrowed my eyes and took a breath, holding it. I tried to visualize the revolver as an extension of my body, imagining an invisible line stretching from the barrel through the lane. I fired.

A hit! A low gut shot. Seven points.

The cobras murmured. I also noticed several other Volunteers pressing themselves up against the bulletproof windows behind us, watching the competition.

Fifteen to seven.

Buzzcut fired again. Another seven points.

I inhaled, exhaled, and pulled the trigger. Another hit! Seven points this time, hitting the target to the wide right of the navel.

The score was now twenty-two to fourteen, and I was behind.

We each had taken four shots, with only one left in the match. Many of the other Volunteers had stopped shooting, curious to see the outcome. I wondered who they were rooting for. The ringleader was not pleased.

"If you frag this up Buzzcut, so help me…"

Buzzcut ran his tongue across the metal on his teeth. He shifted his weight from one leg to another. He carefully aimed his revolver and… missed!

There was a murmur from the growing crowd. I got the sense that these cobras weren't very popular with the other Volunteers. The possibility of seeing them embarrassed must have appealed to some.

This was it. All or nothing. I had to score at least an eight to tie. So far, I had two misses and two mediocre hits. Why had I agreed to this foolishness?

I raised my hands again, trying to disguise a nervous trembling as I clutched the weapon. I looked down the diminutive iron sights at the target that seemed so far away. The fact that I had managed to hit the target at all from this distance was remarkable. What a stupid mistake!

But then, something strange happened. A tingling sensation like an icy fog coalesced around my right arm, and then my left. I felt the odd chill covering my fingers. I looked but saw nothing there. But I felt it. My trembling stopped.

Subtly, almost imperceptibly, my arms rose on their own accord, aiming the revolver higher on the target than I intended. What was going on?! It felt like my body was being hijacked!

CRACK!

Without thinking, I fired the revolver. A premature, involuntary release.

The crowd was silent. My eyes shot up to the target in dread.

It was a bullseye. In the head of the target.

Ten points! I won the match, twenty-four to twenty-two! I couldn't believe it. And the sensation of cold fog was gone. Evaporated.

The cobras stared at me in quiet disbelief, and the crowd murmured enthusiastically. I dematerialized my gun and turned to face the unpleasant crew.

▶ Well? I'll be taking those twenty Crystals now.

"What? We's didn't agree to that."

▶ Excuse me? You said it was a double bet, even money. Ten of my Crystals if I lost, twenty of yours if I won.

"You're bezoomny. We's ain't said nothing of the sort, noob."

Some of the bystanders closest to us began to interject.

"If it isn't true, Razor, open up your history and prove it."

"Yeah! Don't try to change the deal now. Show us your history!"

These Volunteers were genuinely standing up for me. Or at least standing against Razor. I realized that if he opened up his history, it would hold a record of every word he ever said in The Collective, including our little bet.

His steel jaw quivering with rage, he turned his black marble eyes back onto me.

"Frag it. Not worth the hassle. Twenty Crystals? Might as well be zero."

Razor materialized twenty small, gleaming crystalline geometric shapes and unceremoniously dumped them into my waiting hands. I fumbled with them, trying to not let any slip through my fingers. I desperately tried to add them to my inventory again and again.

Alert! Account storage full.

Alert! Account storage full.

Alert! Account storage full.

No!

Razor glared malevolently.

"Better not drop those, little noob..."

Some of the other Volunteers, realizing my inventory was full, began motioning for me to leave. Some shouted words of encouragement or advice.

"Hurry! Get those Crystals out of here."

"Get your arse to the Data Forge!"

I nodded. Twenty precious Crystals. Desperately clutching the clinking, shimmering treasures in my cupped hands, I hurried out of the Armory and made a mad dash for the Data Forge.

FILE 13

FORGE

I hurried through the dark streets of The Commons as fast I could without spilling the precious Crystals cupped in my hands. I glanced around furtively. Would others try to rob me? Was I being followed?

Thankfully, the hubbub of the Armory faded in the distance and I found myself in more deserted byways. Clutching my cargo, I tried to recall the general direction of the Data Forge from the small maps I had viewed earlier and believed I was on the right path.

It was a few blocks behind the central pinnacle of the Restoration Point—a low but wide brutalist structure punctuated by an enormous, glowing sign depicting crossed, red blacksmith hammers. Vents at ground level and black pipes emitted clouds of acrid steam at regular intervals as the machinery within hissed.

I stepped in a puddle of condensation as I entered. The liquid sizzled on contact with my footwear.

Within the building, a row of huge hydraulic arms churned like an oversized loom of metal spiders' legs weaving thread. Three angular podiums sprouted from the ground, connected by tubes to a central pedestal with a basin. Behind the pedestal, a sculpture reminiscent of a double helix stood tall, pulsing with latent energy.

I quickly looked around, still anxious that I could be ambushed by a vengeful cobra seeking to reclaim the loot I had won. I saw a panel with a glowing, red light and scanned my code. A heavy metal door slid into place and locked behind me, sealing me inside the Data Forge.

Okay. At least I didn't have to worry about somebody sneaking up on me.

The panel next to the central contraption lit up with menu options. There did not appear to be a virtual assistant installed at this location, so I would need to figure this out on my own based on the text.

DATA FORGE

CONVERT (Crystals into Value)

FORGE
- **ITEMS** (from materials)
- **CARDS** (from card fragments)

FUSE
- **SKILLS** (fuse Data Cards onto eligible skill slots)
- **EQUIPMENT** (fuse Data Cards onto eligible weapons or armor)

EXPORT (transform one type of item, weapon, or armor to another type)

TRANSMUTE (transform the cosmetic appearance of an item, weapon, or armor)

I had thirty Crystals. Twenty of which I did not have room to store.

I thought back to the orientation. I was given an initial thirty Value to assign to my statistical categories, which all started at a base score of ten. What was the conversion rate of Crystals to Value? Ten seemed to be the lowest denominator for just about everything in The Collective, except for materials and Crypt, which were calculated fractionally as tenths and hundredths, at least as far as storage space was concerned.

Opening the Convert option on the screen, I saw that ten Crystals could be consumed to generate ten unassigned Value. Boosting some of my statistical categories would be a smart choice. I selected the option and one of the podiums next to me began glowing, indicating an indentation to place the Crystals.

Deposit Crystals for conversion.

I dropped the twenty Crystals in my hands into the space and watched them clink and glow as they settled.

Begin conversion process?

▸ Yes.

The diverse collection of small crystalline shapes vibrated, and a deep hum filled the space. The spider-like mechanical arms churned, and light spilled out of the Crystals as they broke apart, like atoms splitting. A bright glow of energy filled the tubes connecting this podium to the central platform, and the digitized double-helix sculpture shone brighter.

I shielded my eyes from the light, but when I looked again warm motes hovered over the central pedestal. One by one, the motes lifted and shot into my chest. I instantly felt aglow with internal warmth, as when one imbibes a hot beverage too quickly.

After a time, the heat faded to a steady but noticeable warmth. The sensation of unassigned Value pulsing within me. A charge seeking discharge.

I opened my menu.

STATISTICS

- **ATTACK:** (30)
    - **STRENGTH: 20**
    - **ACCURACY: 10**

- **DEFENSE:** (30)
    - **ESSENCE: 20**
    - **RESISTANCE: 10**

- **ABILITY:** (20)
    - **ADEPTNESS: 10**
    - **ENERGY: 10**

- **MOVEMENT:** (30)
    - **SPEED: 20**
    - **AGILITY: 10**

- **PROCESSING:** (40)
    - **PERCEPTION: 10**
    - **PERSUASION: 10**
    - **PROTOCOL: 10**
    - **PROBABILITY: 10**

MEMORY
- **STORAGE: 210 / 210**

UNASSIGNED VALUE: 20

After tooling around with my menu options, I discovered that increasing from ten to twenty in any category would cost ten Value. However, increasing from twenty to thirty would cost twenty Value. The higher the value, the higher the cost would be in a linear, progressive manner.

However, I noticed that ten Value could directly convert to ten additional metabytes of storage space no matter what. Strangely, it appeared that the unassigned Value itself did not take up any space.

Yet, I would not be able to increase any of my attributes as I was currently maxed out at 210 out of 210 storage.

My only option was to increase storage. I dragged the twenty Value to my Storage category and confirmed. The screen flickered, and then my total storage increased. It did not seem to be a reversible process, at least within my own menu.

MEMORY
- **STORAGE: 210 / 230**

Okay. Not the most exciting upgrade, but necessary. And I still had ten Crystals left in my inventory. I could increase a category, such as Accuracy, Agility, or so forth. But I was curious about the crafting process.

I went back to the Data Forge panel, selecting the Forge options.

FORGE
- **ITEMS**
- **CARDS**

I only had four out of ten hellhound Data Card fragments, so that wasn't going to work. However, I had my three fern flowers and the materials I purchased from the Supply Depot. I selected the Items option.

No Schemas currently discovered.

Do you want to continue forging?

Schemas?

▸ Yes, I would like to continue.

Insert the raw materials in the indicated depositories.

Two of the podium-like devices glowed. I removed one of the fern flowers from my inventory and placed it on the device. I had to choose between pure water or the white linen cloth as the other material.

After some deliberation, I selected the vial of pure water and placed it on the other platform.

1 {common} fern flower and 1 vial of pure water detected. With your current Protocol and Probability scores, you will only be able to forge 1 {common} item with a moderate chance of failure.

Failure? You mean after all this, there was a chance that my item forging attempt could fail? Did that mean I would lose my materials? My Crystals? Agh…

Nothing ventured, nothing gained.

Deposit Crystals for forging.

I materialized the ten Crystals from my inventory and placed them in the third and waiting receptacle.

Begin forging?

I selected yes, performing the mental equivalent of crossing my fingers. Wouldn't do me any good. Apparently my destiny was in the hands of my minimal Probability score.

Again, brilliant light cracked forth, this time from all three platforms. Raw energy and data were sucked into some great centrifuge, smashed and reformed in new combinations. The glow in the center pedestal was too bright to make out.

Item forging successful.

1 {common} Tincture of Fortune forged.

New Schema discovered.

As the light faded, I saw a small, clouded bottle. Ornate. Something out of a forgotten bazaar. I lifted the item, cupping it delicately between my hands. It felt cool and smooth and held a small quantity of fluid.

I dematerialized the item into my inventory and found it under the Consumables submenu.

INVENTORY
- **CONSUMABLES**
  - **1 Tincture of Fortune** (10 metabytes)

I highlighted the item to access the details.

Item: Tincture of Fortune

Item Type: Consumable

Frequency: Common

Details: Increases the probability of obtaining Crystals and discovering items of higher rarity for 600 seconds.

Size: 10 metabytes

Interesting. So, if I were to consume this item, I would be more likely to find better loot for... ten minutes.

I wondered if that only meant in the context of hunting invasive entities, or if there were other situations for which this would apply. Perhaps it would temporarily increase the probability of finding invasive flora as well, such as the fern flowers. Maybe even rarer ones.

I checked the rest of my menu to see what my storage situation looked like.

I used the ten Crystals, which freed up ten metabytes. I also used one fern flower and my pure water, freeing up two metabytes. However, the Tincture of Fortune took up ten metabytes of storage. I also noted that a new category had been added: Schemas.

MEMORY
- **STORAGE: 208 / 230**
- **SCHEMAS**
  - **Tincture of Fortune** (fern flower + pure water)

The system had recorded the crafting recipe for me. Helpful. I wondered what result the fern flower and the white linen cloth would have had. But I was out of Crystals.

I also wondered if there were ways to obtain additional Schemas without having to experiment. Still so much to learn.

A sinking realization came over me. I should have backed up my data at the Restoration Point after buying my new weapon, not before. After going to the Data Forge. I kicked myself. If I died out there, I would lose all my progress.

I only had one hundred Crypt left. Just enough for another backup. Not even enough to ride transit. I would have to find a bounty within walking distance of The Commons, if that was possible. And if I died, I would go into debt to be restored. I shuddered to think of the implications.

Wasn't this supposed to get easier? Did the system even want me to succeed in my mission?

I gritted my teeth and turned away from the forge. I would quickly stop by the Restoration Point and spend the last of my money on a backup, then head straight to the Task Assignment Boards. It was time for another hunt.

FILE 14

CLURICHAUN

At the Restoration Point, I watched my last one hundred Crypt fade as the machine had its way with me—burning a copy of my digital essence for posterity.

Then I wended my way to the Task Assignment Boards, on the lookout for any members of that cobra gang that tried to rip me off. I had a feeling I hadn't seen the last of them. Two-bit crooks with Napoleon complexes, no doubt. I supposed Reality Inc. didn't do their due diligence screening potential Volunteers for sociopathy.

Or maybe cheap violence just came with the territory. It was in the air. Miasmic.

I stood before the large, rectangular touchscreen panels of the TABs and scanned my barcode. The screens lit up, bright across the dark, glowy intersection. The shifting data of available tasks filled my peripheral vision.

I could hardly keep up as new bounties flipped into view, others shuffled aside, more were claimed. There was no shortage of work, but Camel was right—competition was fierce. There had to be other access points, but where?

I tried to track the items long enough to glean the key details.

Remove wendigo from New Dawn Central Gardens.

Remove merfolk from Crystal Coast Sea Wall.

Remove nuckelavees from Upper Dresden's Park District.

I had heard of Lower Dresden and New Dresden but knew both were far off. With no money for transit, I had to find something within walking distance. The closest MAR Station to The Commons was Royal Heights. I couldn't recall what lay in the other direction on the Diamond Line. I didn't think The Commons was the end of line, but then again, I didn't really know.

I searched and searched. Bounties turned red and inaccessible as others claimed them from access points unknown. Some bounties floated much longer—places I had not heard of and creatures with names I could barely pronounce. Less attractive because they were more dangerous.

Then one caught my eye. I quickly tapped it, and information about the task filled the screen to my left.

Task Assignment: Remove clurichaun from a private residence in Royal Heights.

Per Citizen report, one {rare} clurichaun has been detected in the sublevel of a private residence at 1 Paradise Way in Royal Heights.

Task Completion Award: 4,000 Crypt.

Bonus: 1,000 Crypt for eliminating target entity before the next cycle.

Do you accept this task?

My mind raced. I had no idea what a clurichaun was. And it was listed as rare.

I had barely escaped an encounter with monsters of the common variety. An uncommon beast had almost eaten me for lunch until much stronger hunters intervened. And what was this about a Citizen report? At a private residence? And there was a bonus!

I wished Camel was here. Someone I could lean on. Someone who could help me interpret all this—put it in perspective.

I wasn't sure if by selecting the option to view, other Volunteers were temporarily blocked from accepting this bounty. If not, someone else could snatch it. Would I be able to find another bounty this close? I didn't know. And I didn't know how long until the next cycle began. There was a ticking clock if I wanted that bonus.

Frag it.

▸ Yes, I accept.

Task Assigned: Remove clurichaun from a private residence in Royal Heights.

I confirmed the bounty was listed under my Tasks menu. Helpful, so I didn't forget the address. Not that it would be easy to forget 1 Paradise Way, although I didn't have much faith in my memory anymore.

I desperately wanted to go to the Archives and research this strange entity I was supposed to exterminate. I glanced up at the perpetually dark sky. When would the next cycle begin? Should I risk missing out on a potential bonus? 4,000 Crypt was still a good payout for one person, but going up against a rare creature solo was a bigger risk. And death meant falling below zero on the metaversal balance sheet.

Frag it again.

Straining to feel even the slightest shift in weather, I raced for the Archives. No cobras spotted *en route*. At least I had that going for me.

I entered the strange pyramidal structure and descended into the 'Archiv' bowels once more, repeating my earlier steps to access the system.

Welcome to the Archives.

Initiate query.

▸ Mythology query, clurichaun.

Mythology query initiated -> Clurichaun

An Irish variant of the mischievous solitary fairy archetype. Sometimes considered the nocturnal persona of a leprechaun, these fae tricksters are said to haunt establishments that store or deal in alcoholic spirits. If angered, clurichauns can be very dangerous. They have been believed to curse people, steal their belongings, and even cast spells on them.

Curses? Spells?

▸ Mythology query, clurichaun spells and abilities.

Mythology query initiated -> Clurichaun spells and abilities

If caught, a clurichaun can vanish if its captor looks away for even a moment. They are also believed to be able to create illusions. In extreme instances, clurichauns have been known to force mortals into years of servitude to protect its magical purse.

Years of forced servitude?! Hmmm. I didn't like the sound of that.

▸ Mythology query, clurichaun magical purse.

Mythology query initiated -> Clurichaun magical purse

Clurichauns may carry a magical purse that contains a spre na skillenagh, a lucky shilling that always returns once spent. However, to protect this purse from avaricious mortals, a clurichaun will also carry a decoy.

A binge-drinking leprechaun didn't sound too intimidating. It seemed more likely that it could just vanish before I could kill it.

Finishing at the Archives, I rode the elevator up and exited back onto the street. The only way out of The Commons that I was aware of was on the outskirts near the Red Light district, guarded by Polizei bots. I made my way there.

As I walked, I thought about the task before me.

A trickster fairy... They had intelligence. They looked human. Killing demonic dogs was one thing. Was I able to kill a small humanoid? What if it tried to communicate with me?

Did I have it in me to take the life of a small person? For some reason, I felt that I just might.

I reminded myself that they weren't real. Right? They couldn't be. They were just bits of invasive data. Foreign code infecting the system. It would be like spraying a cockroach, but even more abstracted.

Lost in my thoughts, I looked up to see the opening in the shimmering wall. The barrier between The Commons and the rest of The Collective. The Polizei bots slowly turned to appraise me as I approached.

▸ Uh. I have a task. Out there. Royal Heights?

I pointed lamely in the direction of the glittering city beyond.

The Polizei bots said nothing.

Unsure of what to do, I opened my menu and highlighted the task currently assigned to me.

Blank and unreadable behind the glass visor of the tactical helmet, one of the bots grunted an authoritarian, "Proceed," and waved me past. As I crossed the threshold, a light scanned me, picking up my barcode identifier and registering my exit from The Commons.

The shimmering boundary wall behind me, I took my first steps into The Collective proper. Well, The Collective as experienced by Citizens and not the subterranean recesses beneath their feet. I had never interacted with a Citizen (to my knowledge) and was curious to see how the other side lived. All one million of them, just a fraction of the total number intended to fill this massive virtual world.

My feet hit the pavement, and I started up a slight incline in the direction of the shining high-rise buildings.

An unusual thing happened.

The further away from The Commons I got, the more the atmosphere changed. The thick, persistent darkness of the Volunteers' territory gave way to something brighter.

Sunlight? Impossible.

But there it was. Unmistakable. Rays of warm light caressed the exposed skin of my hands, face, and neck. I was so surprised I stopped walking, soaking in the luxurious warmth. The light was intoxicating.

Looking up, I saw no sun, but the sky was bright and clear. Not a cloud in sight. Light from some unknown source filled the entire region. I hadn't even known there was such a thing as 'daytime' in The Collective. It was so beautiful—so startling that tears formed in my eyes.

FILE 14.1

MONIQUE

I gathered myself, wiped my face, and pressed on—now noticing planter boxes interspersed on the walkways lining the main street. Greenery, and even slender trees, sprung from the concrete rectangles. A luminous, elevated monorail passed between buildings somewhere in the distance. What a contrast.

Soon, I approached an intersection with large, bright letters rotating midair. Royal Heights. Beneath the sign, an open-air information kiosk stood. What had appeared dingy and suspect in The Commons was nothing but inviting here.

I stepped across the street and approached the kiosk.

A light automatically scanned my retinas. An animated emote swirled to life on the small screen and a soothing, digitized voice addressed me.

Citizenship record not detected.

▸ I... I am not a Citizen. I am a Volunteer.

Please scan your identifier.

I looked around for the familiar red light. Eventually, I found it beneath the screen, out of sight.

Welcome to Royal Heights, Volunteer. What information would you like to access?

▸ I'm here on a job. I need to find 1 Paradise Way.

Do you have a smart device or other accessory to download map data?

▸ Uhh… no.

Please view the screen and directions to the specified address will appear.

The friendly emote swirled away, replaced with an elegant, color-coded map of Royal Heights. A blinking, red triangle indicated my position at the kiosk, and another indicator showed 1 Paradise Way; a navigable line connected the two. It was about a two mile walk to the three-dimensional block representing my destination among a row of similar buildings.

▸ Thanks.

My pleasure. I hope you enjoy your brief visit to Royal Heights, a premier neighborhood in The Collective's fourth quadrant.

If you have enjoyed your experience, please rate your interaction with this information kiosk on your next QOL survey. And remember—Live your best second life! ™

Ignoring the virtual assistant, I followed the route I had been shown, counting the number of blocks in my head so that I knew where to turn.

After some time, I arrived on a street of tall, luxury row houses at the edge of the urban buildup. They stood, reflecting the sunlight, white and minimalist with large windows looking out from their multiple floors.

There it was. 1 Paradise Way.

A polished, white stone walkway led between a perfect, green lawn to the imposing residence. Uncertain, I approached the double entry doors atop a small flight of steps. A golden sunburst pattern was etched into the wood.

I looked for a knocker or doorbell, but to my surprise, the door swung open before I could touch it.

A Polizei bot stared back at me.

▸ Woah!

Wait, that wasn't quite right. It had the appearance of a Polizei bot, but was dressed in a tailored suit, the black, tactical helmet incongruously on top. The bot said nothing.

▸ I'm here for a bounty. I'm a Volunteer.

The bot stared at me for several silent seconds, then stepped aside, giving me room to cross the threshold. When I stepped inside, I saw another similarly dressed bot. The doorkeeper raised a white gloved hand and indicated that I should walk further into the domicile.

There was a huge, crystalline chandelier hanging above my head and a balcony with a wooden railing overlooking the foyer. Past the foyer, a waterfall blocked my path. It poured from the ceiling and down through tiny holes in the floor.

I looked to the bots for help but they simply raised their open hands again, indicating for me to continue.

Okay...

I took a careful step towards the falling water and was amazed to see it part instantly. With immediate responsiveness, the waterfall contoured to my shape, allowing me to walk through dry.

On the other side, I found myself in a common area branching into different rooms. A large kitchen was to my right with sleek, obsidian countertops and well-appointed appliances. To my left was a comfortable living space with a large viewscreen, sleek divans, and a white, fur rug in the center. Tribal artwork hung on the walls. Large windows at the rear of the home looked out over a sloping, green hillside—dotted with other residences amidst thick foliage.

A film was playing on the viewscreen in the living area. It was monochromatic, yet rich in detail.

A closeup on a woman's face. Beatific. A tear rolled down her smooth cheek. Jeering men in bowl haircuts and robes affixed a crown of twisted thorns on her head. They jostled her face and slapped her. More tears rolled down. All of it silent but for distant singing in a language I didn't understand and some sparse stringed instruments. One man placed an arrow in her hands.

I watched, mesmerized by the moving images. The pained close-up on the woman's face as she was mistreated. The pleading look in her heavenward searching eyes.

Then a light splashing sound roused me. I turned and noticed another room just ahead, smaller and enclosed by wide windows. A woman emerged from an infinity pool, stepping onto smooth, aquamarine tiles.

She was tall, voluptuous, and wore a form fitting one-piece swimsuit. Her skin bore a perfectly calculated suntan. Her eyes shone bright green beneath thick eyelashes. Her lips were full and plump.

Her appearance was without blemish. Almost artificially so. If she was a Citizen, which I assumed she must be, she obviously had spared no expense for her choice of cosmetics and body modifications.

The woman quickly toweled her thick mane of brunette hair and slipped into a white, cotton robe—so soft it looked like she was draped in a cloud. She approached me, padding barefoot from the tiled room onto the sleek, wooden floors where I stood awkwardly waiting.

"You must be the Volunteer," she said in a buttery smooth voice with a hint of an accent.

I cleared my throat and nodded. She eyed me up and down carefully.

"You're not what I expected…"

I didn't know how to react. Should I apologize? Shrug? I ended up giving a half-hearted bow.

"And you certainly don't say much. The silent type?"

She paced in a slow circle, appraising me like a piece of furniture she was contemplating buying.

▸ Yes, I am the Volunteer. I'm here about the… problem.

"No need to be so formal. Do you have a name?"

▸ My official designation is…

I glanced down at my barcode. Looking at her arm, I saw she had none. I knew my Volunteer ID number wasn't what she was wanting, but what else could I say?

▸ A name. I… I don't… Some people call me Mag—

My weak starter voice caught in my throat. I didn't want to say Magpie. What sort of name was that in a place like this? Besides, it wasn't even a name of my choosing.

"Mag? Is that short for Maggie? Magnus? Magdalena?"

▸ Something like that.

The woman looked confused. She pursed her full lips and made a low, humming sound in the back of her throat.

"How do I say this? What are your… preferred pronouns?"

▸ My pronouns?

"Should I refer to you as a he? A she? A they?"

I was at a loss.

▸ I… I wish I knew that.

Suddenly, I realized the two suit-wearing bots were standing in the room. How long had they been there? I hadn't heard them approach at all. One of the bots chastised the lady.

"Ma'am, you shouldn't speak with the Volunteer."

"I'll speak with whomever I please! My husband is a shareholder, you know. Go stand in the corner like you're meant to," she snapped back.

I watched with curiosity as the bots reluctantly but obediently did as she asked, walking over to stand with their backs against the wall.

"Nevermind them. Security bots. I hired them after what happened to my husband. Did they brief you? I don't know how this all works."

I shook my head.

"My poor hubby was assaulted by these... these horrid devil dogs while he was uptown. They had to take him offline because of arrhythmia. Can you believe it? It's been quite lonely... but I digress. I hired these SecuBots for protection and they can't do diddly squat about my problem downstairs."

▸ Devil dogs? I've had a run-in with hellhounds too. My condolences.

"Oh my, you have? You poor, brave thing. You must have come out the other side alright if you're still standing here."

▸ Um. Yes... ma'am.

Was she impressed? Some emotion flashed on her expensive face, but I was not sure what.

My eyes flicked back to the moving images on the viewscreen. She followed my gaze.

"*The Passion of Joan of Arc.* Have you seen it? I'm a bit of a preservationist. Like to rescue old films like this. Practically archeological now. But we mustn't lose who we were, don't you concur?"

▸ I can't really say.

"Ah yes, the silent type. All about business. Well, no rush. The thing you're here to get rid of doesn't come out till nightfall."

I looked out the windows again. The sky remained clear and bright. The invisible sun shone on. Whatever the deal was, there seemed to be a day and night cycle in The Collective, or at least this section of it.

"We'll get you set up in the wine cellar. Wait for night and then bag the little nuisance when it appears."

▸ The clurichaun...

"Whatever it is. It's been stealing my wine night after night. Slips away into some hole I can't seem to find. I've tried everything!"

She strode into her spacious kitchen—her elegant, bare legs gliding across the floor as her pillowy robe floated behind her. Reaching somewhere out of sight, she produced a dark bottle of wine with a detailed label.

"1982 Chateau Lafite Rothschild. A personal favorite. One of the greatest wines ever produced. It is a blend, and alas—one of the varietals is now extinct, of course. Can't ever be made again in the real world. The only place it can be enjoyed is in this land of make believe."

She smiled, flashing two rows of flawless, white teeth as she pulled the cork and poured the wine into two waiting glasses.

"Care for a taste? That impish brute has been stealing my supply. And that won't stand. No, no, no. We paid far too much for the privilege of living here to put up with that nonsense."

I felt like I was walking on eggshells while entering the kitchen, as if I would somehow sully this slice of paradise with my very presence.

I was painfully conscious of my meager attire and generic features. The robotic visage of the SecuBots stared disapprovingly at my every move.

I graciously accepted the glass, taking a sip. It tasted like... wine. I can't say I had the most refined pallet. Maybe I needed a body mod tastebud upgrade.

▸ This is... magnificent. Thank you.

"Isn't it though? Is that what Mag stands for—magnificent?"

The woman sipped her wine, sighing appreciatively and lapsing into a wistful silence.

"Oh, where are my manners? My name is Monique. Monique Rossignol, lady of the house as it were. I guess in my extended isolation, I've forgotten how to behave properly around other people."

She extended her smooth hand, each long finger ending with a perfectly manicured and painted nail. I shook it.

▸ About your problem...

"Oh. Yes?"

She seemed disappointed that I was turning the conversation to business once more. But I did have a job to do and a potential bonus to earn. I was still anxious about this rare creature and wanted to learn whatever else I could.

▸ Why haven't the SecuBots been able to help with the... intruder?

She waved a hand dismissively at the two bots dressed like bouncers.

"The SecuBots are fine with protecting me, but they are utterly useless when it comes to going on the offense against these... these viruses. Their programming just can't compete! I sent a SecuBot down to guard the wine cellar days ago, and the next morning, I found its head had been removed and placed back on backwards. Useless."

▸ You said viruses. So, you believe these creatures, like hellhounds and clurichauns, are some sort of computer virus?

"Well, what else could they be? Probably put here by some military-sponsored hacker group from East Asia. It's a zero-sum game to these people, no matter that survival of the species is at stake."

The SecuBots fidgeted. One gave a fake digital cough.

"Ma'am, we really must insist that protocols be followed. Citizens should not distract Volunteers in the course of their duties."

Mrs. Rossignol threw her free hand up in exasperation and rolled her eyes.

"Whatever. Let me show you to the wine cellar."

I quickly finished my wine and set the empty glass down, following after her. On the flickering viewscreen, the black and white heroine of the silent film was about to be burned at the stake.

I followed Monique down a narrow staircase into the sublevel. Automatic lights lining the ceiling pulsed softly. A climate control system clicked on to fight against the slightest change in temperature. An electronic dial on the wall registered 12°C and 60% humidity.

The wine cellar was larger than I was expecting. More vault than cellar. Antiseptic and ultramodern. Concrete, metal, and glass.

Four rows of tall, frosted glass wine walls proudly cocooned a dizzying array of bottles. Two racks were built into either side of the room, creating three walkable aisles between the collection. Large, square tiles lined the floor.

"Do you like it?"

▸ It's very nice. Is that a security camera in the corner?

"Yes, it is. And the answer to the question in your head is 'no.' I installed the camera after the first few break-ins, but the little fiend disabled it somehow. It's smart."

▸ And no indication of how it is getting in?

I looked around and saw, besides the door at the top of the stairs, only miniscule vent holes for the climate system.

"That's what you're here for. Find a spot and get comfortable. After dark, it is sure to appear—I guarantee it. The wicked thing just can't get enough to drink. Reminds me of some relations I once had."

▸ Uh. How long until it gets dark?

"Oh, I'd say five hours or so. But who's to say if it won't show its ugly head sooner? Either way, you should settle in and get ready to spring the trap, so to speak."

I didn't say anything. It would have been nice if I invested in an actual trap. All I had was my gun and my knife.

And five hours? I had no way of telling time. Maybe they sold timepieces at the Supply Depot. Although, what would that even mean? Besides the cycles, how would one measure time in The Commons where it was perpetually dark? Even in this place, did the passage of time correlate to real time? Were there still twenty-four hours in a day?

"If you need to."

▸ I'm sorry. What?

I had zoned out there for a moment.

"I said, I have plenty of food and drink if you need anything. And if you need to use the facilities, you'd best use them now."

▸ Facilities? I... no. I don't need anything.

I could only assume by facilities she was referring to a bathroom. Did some people go so far as to replicate *all* aspects of the real world in the Metaverse? It seemed that, for convenience sake, some functional necessities of our humanity could be edited out.

Or perhaps that was the point. Citizens were more fully human while I was just some shell. Not even a full person. And I had apparently volunteered for this.

"Great. Then I'll leave you to it. And please... try not to damage anything. I know these bottles aren't real in the literal sense of the word, but that doesn't mean they aren't expensive."

▸ Right. I'll do my best.

I watched the lady of the house's perfectly manicured feet pad up the narrow stairs. She shut the door behind her and the room was sealed in an atmospheric cocoon. The cellar must have been soundproof. Only the faint hum of the climate control and lighting broke the silence.

I slowly walked up and down the aisles, looking for any clues that would suggest a point of entry. I saw nothing. None of the fancy labels on the bottles meant anything to me either.

Five hours. I would be stuck down here for five hours—minimum—before this creature I didn't even know I could win against appeared. I decided to sit at the foot of the stairs, partially concealed behind one of the tall displays.

I would wait. It was all I could do.

FILE 14.2

CELLAR

Minutes passed. The automatic lights faded, bathing the cellar in a dim sheen. Midnight blue. I tried to remain perfectly still. I reminded myself that my breathing, the circulation of my blood, and even the signals in my nervous system were not real. They were electronic signals. And if they were signals, I could control them.

Maybe. Maybe not. There had to be a real-world correlation. Somebody once said a lamp inside a video game used real electricity. And as Monique Rossignol intimated, even things that weren't real could still have a cost.

Sitting in the cool darkness, trying to attune my meager ten Perception to any sound, my mind began to wander once more. I realized that I didn't even know what year it was. That was to say, the year in the real world. Another piece of my memory that was lost. Dissociative amnesia as a reaction to entering The Collective, the Concierge had said. Yeah, but it still hadn't come back. Not a crumb of personal memory.

Monique had shown me a bottle of wine from 1982. So, it at least had to be after that year. There was no way the technology to create an immersive metaverse existed anytime close to that date, right?

Could I recall any historic events? Political leaders? Mikhail Gorbachev. Erich Honecker. Gustav Husak. Deng Xiaoping. Ho Chi Minh. Margaret Thatcher. Anything more recent? I strained, reaching for straws. The past—my past—was like eels wriggling out of my grasp beneath the waters of a murky lake.

My mind continued wandering like this for an unknowable spell. Suddenly, it occurred to me that I should prepare myself.

With slow, subtle movements—so as not to set off the automatic lights—I materialized my Tincture of Fortune in one hand and my push dagger in the other. If I had a chance to kill this clurichaun, I should at least try to maximize whatever rewards I could get. I would have ten minutes from the time I drank the tincture before the effects wore off.

More time passed. And more. Until...

Click.

A faint sound stirred me from my fugue. I froze.

Click clack.

I strained in the dark, not daring to move. At the end of the left-most aisle, silhouetted in dark blue, there was a form emerging from the ground. A floor tile rose, and a lumpy shadow crawled out from the depths.

{rare} entity detected: clurichaun.

My pulse quickened. With my left hand, I nervously popped the top of my tincture. I quickly downed the oily liquid. It tasted of sandalwood, burning my throat. The empty bottle evaporated into empty pixels. I gripped my dagger.

600 seconds. 599 seconds. 598 seconds.

Somehow, the creature's movements hadn't activated the automatic lights. I could see that it had fully emerged from beneath the floor, sliding the tile back into place. It walked with a waddling gait and wore a nightcap and apron.

It was grunting and mumbling to itself, walking over to the nearest display wall and fingering the necks of the bottles one by one.

Now, while it was distracted, I had to make my move.

I lunged forwards into a dash, dagger outstretched. The automatic lights kicked on.

As I charged, he—it was a he—swiveled his head in my direction. His face looked like a withered apple with sunken, bloodshot eyes, a wiry beard, and burst capillaries spreading across his skin. His teeth were yellowed and chipped and his fingernails long and curled. His face twisted into a sinister sneer.

"Maróidh mé thú!"

I thrust my dagger straight into the clurichaun's chest. Or where his chest should have been. Instead, I contacted empty air. The image of the clurichaun, where he had been standing moments before, faded to nothing.

I heard snickering laughter and wheeled around. The little brute was behind me, standing at the far end of the aisle between the wall and one of the center displays. He appeared wobbly; his odd speech slurred.

"Amadán mór tú! Seo go léir trioblóid le haghaidh fíon lousy. Ní fiú fuisce nó beoir."

I turned, brandishing the dagger. I sensed my opportunity slipping away.

No!

I rushed forwards again, trying to squeeze every ounce from my twenty Speed across the short distance. This time, I swung the blade in a downward slashing motion, anything to make contact.

Another trick. Another illusion.

Pain exploded in my skull and a terrible crash filled my ears as the clurichaun, materializing at my side, smashed a wine bottle over my head.

► Ahhh!

I stumbled away, inadvertently knocking several bottles from the display rack. They shattered on the floor, purple liquid mixing with the blood trickling from my matted hair.

Damage received.

Essence: 10 remaining.

► Oh, frag!

My head pounded and my vision blurred. I wiped blood and wine out of my eyes just in time to see the creature throw a bottle at me. I dodged it, the glass bursting on the ground like a hand grenade.

Another bottle. Then another. The clurichaun cackled spitefully, ripping the bottles from the racks and lobbing them at me.

I thought these things were supposed to disappear to avoid capture. Instead, my uninhibited bounty seemed to be enjoying the sport.

I ducked for cover behind the nearest end row and held my dagger ready. I couldn't withstand another blow like that. I could hear the creature laughing, muttering, and stumbling over the broken glass.

Then, it was silent.

I feared the worst, that my quarry had vanished back into its hole. Well, maybe that wasn't the worst-case scenario all things considered. I slowly craned my neck around the display wall.

"Diabhal mór!"

The clurichaun suddenly appeared on the other side of me and struck at my hand with a cobbler's hammer. It made contact with my dagger, hard enough to knock it from my grasp. I watched in horror as the dagger skidded across the slick floor.

I tried to back away but slipped and fell. The drunk imp advanced, hammer in one hand, broken bottle in the other. It jabbed at my torso with the bottle, glass shards ripping into my coveralls.

"Diabhal mór! Diabhal mór!"

I scrambled backwards, feeling broken glass cut against the palms of my hands in the pooling wine until I reached the far opposite end of the aisle.

I opened the front of my coveralls and reached inside, gingerly searching my skin for wounds. I felt none. My clothes were damaged, but I was okay for the time being. It seemed the cuts on my hands, although painful, weren't enough to bypass my ten Defense and reduce my Essence any further.

I looked up as the clurichaun stumbled forwards, tripping on half of a broken wine bottle and crashing sideways against the wall. It let out some curse and struggled to right itself, taking up its weapons once more, narrowing its bloodshot eyes on me.

I had one chance at this. With my hand still buried inside my coveralls, I concentrated—materializing my snub-nosed revolver beneath the black fabric.

The clurichaun stalked closer, purplish lips curled back over stained teeth.

I tried to aim the gun's short barrel upwards at the center of its mass.

Then I fired.

Once. Twice.

3 / 5 ammunition remaining.

A hole ripped through the fabric of my coveralls and the revolver recoiled painfully against my ribs.

The first shot went wide of the mark, ricocheting off some hard surface in the cellar.

The second was a gut shot.

The clurichaun screamed, dropping his weapons and collapsing to the ground. Small, gnarled hands clutched at his belly as bilious blood seeped from a hole in his shirt.

I slowly rose to my feet, pulling the revolver out. I trained my eyes on my wounded prey and stepped forwards, grabbing it by its lapels and aiming the gun straight at its forehead.

I recalled the information I gathered from the Archive: "If he is caught, a clurichaun has the power to vanish if he can make his captor look away for even a moment."

I didn't dare even blink. I readied myself to pull the trigger and put an end to it.

"Stop. Beidh mé a thabhairt duit rud ar bith is mian leat!" he suddenly protested, raising one wrinkled hand in the air while keeping the other pressed against his gushing wound. His breath smelled awful.

The clurichaun snapped its fingers.

Suddenly, two items appeared—one to my left, one to my right. Both were just out of reach. I kept my eyes ferociously trained on my target, daring only to strain with my peripheral vision at the mysterious objects. They seemed to be constructed of brown leather.

Invasive anomalies detected.

Invasive anomalies?

{rare} anomaly detected: apothecary's satchel.

{rare} anomaly detected: magic coin purse.

I sensed that the creature was somehow willing me to know what these objects were. It was offering them to me in exchange for its life.

I kept my eyes focused straight ahead. They were watering from not blinking.

The last thing I wanted was to fall for another trick.

Anomalies.

What if one, or both, were fake? Could I kill this thing and then seize the plunder? What if they vanished the moment I killed their owner? Was it worth losing a 5,000 Crypt bounty for a chance at obtaining one or both of these rare items?

My finger curled around the stiff trigger. As the old proverb goes, a bird in the hand is better than two in the bush. I fired, mere inches away from the wrinkled, leering face.

The clurichaun's head exploded like a ripe gourd.

Bits of brain and bone mass, matted hair, and raglike strips of skin spattered the tile floor. The discolored nightcap lay crookedly in a growing puddle of blood.

2 / 5 ammunition remaining.

Task Successfully Completed: Remove clurichaun from a private residence in Royal Heights.

Almost immediately, the two conjured rare items began to fade from existence. I lunged for the closest one, forgetting which was which. I grabbed on, my fingers somehow slipping through the brown leather, failing to find purchase.

▸ Come on, come on, come on.

It was the apothecary's satchel. I tried to manually add the item to my inventory before it was gone, but I could not. The satchel was between two worlds and fading rapidly from this one. Clawing into the satchel, my fingers brushed against something. Something that still had a bit of substance.

I grabbed hold of whatever it was and pulled it away, adding it to my inventory, sight unseen.

1 {uncommon} coco de mer nut added to your inventory.

A nut? Was it a crafting material? I would take a look at that later.

I waited until the barrel of my revolver cooled before dematerializing it back into my Equipment menu. Probably didn't matter. Still sore about missing my chance at a free rare item, I turned my attention back to the kill.

As I had seen before with the hellhounds, the diminutive corpse began to glow, motes of light drawing from it and coalescing in the air above. Quivering, shining geometry. And this time, a single crystalline card—glowing green and red in the shifting prismatic light.

I eagerly reached for my prizes and drew in a sharp breath as I felt the floating objects imbue themselves within me.

100 Crystals obtained.

{rare} Data Card obtained: Clurichaun *(Skill)*.

Woah! One hundred Crystals. And a complete Data Card, not just fragments. Maybe that tincture actually paid off. I wondered how much better the rewards could have been if I invested more in my Probability statistic.

Not so fast. I heard a tinkling noise as Crystals spilled onto the ground, rolling into the pooling wine and mixing with the broken shards of glass.

Alert! Account storage full.

I quickly checked my menu.

ECONOMY

- **CRYPT**

- **CRYSTALS: 32** (32 metabytes)

MEMORY
- **STORAGE: 230 / 230**

The Data Card, crafting material, and thirty-two Crystals had filled my storage to the max (with my temporarily depleted Essence).

I silently cursed and dropped to my knees, scooping the remaining Crystals into a pile as best I could. The clurichaun's corpse had already started melting into a black, inky puddle, then dissolving from view. Only the chaos of smashed bottles and my own blood splatter remained.

I would have to haul these sixty-eight Crystals back to The Commons manually. But how?

I looked at my coveralls, torn as they were from the clurichaun's attack. I had an idea. I picked up my push dagger and cut the fabric at the waist, carefully working my way around until the entire top half came loose.

Thinking again, I cut off one of the arms, tying a makeshift bandage around the bleeding gash hidden somewhere beneath my wavy asymmetrical crop hairstyle. Then I laid the rest of the material on the ground, carefully piling the Crystals and tying them into a bindle.

Assuming I completed my task within the window to receive the bonus, I now had 5,000 Crypt waiting for me back at the bounty boards. 5,000 Crypt that I technically didn't have storage space for. I really, really needed to get ahead of this storage problem. Maybe one of those rare items would have helped. C'est la (seconde) vie.

My outfit now consisted of black pants, ragged around the midsection. I assumed that jeopardized the defensive capabilities of the armor but was too tired to care. As long as I didn't get any nasty surprises on my way home, I would be okay.

▸ I wonder if…

I walked over to where the clurichaun first entered the wine cellar, emerging from beneath the floor. I got on my hands and knees, poking and prodding the edges of the large, square tiles. Was there a hidden underground lair?

After about fifteen minutes of careful searching, I gave up. I couldn't get a single tile to budge, and in the original darkness and ensuing fight, I couldn't even be sure what tile had moved in the first place.

My head stung, and I needed to get home before I got caught in another freak storm. It was a long walk from paradise.

The lady of the house hadn't come to check on me. I recalled that the wine cellar was completely soundproofed. Nothing now but the steady whirr of the climate control system cycling out the traces of gun smoke.

Picking up my bindle of Crystals, I climbed the stairs, careful not to lose my balance. I opened the door and it swung closed behind me.

The two SecuBots stood, arms folded, waiting for me. I heard footsteps on the floor above, and Monique, in a completely different outfit, soon appeared. How long had I been in the cellar?

"Oh!"

She stopped in her tracks when she saw me, eyes wide, and I realized what a sight I must be. Stripped to my waist, revealing my flat, hairless chest. A black headband. Dried blood (my own). Carrying a strange sack.

"Oh, so it must be done then?"

▸ Yes. The creature is dead.

"And you… Are you okay?"

▸ I'll live.

"Well, thank heavens. You managed to do in a single night what these stupid bots were wholly incapable of doing. Bravo to that, I say. Might I offer you a tip? Is that permissible?"

▸ A tip? Like payment for a job well done?

At this, one of the SecuBots interjected.

"Ma'am, you really shouldn't—"

She dismissed the bot with a wave of her hand, then began scrolling her finger across a smartwatch device.

"How does 1,000 Crypt sound? Does that count as a decent tip these days?"

▸ That... that is quite generous.

"Just give me your account number and I can transfer it over."

▸ My account? Oh... I... I don't have an account. At least, I don't think so.

"No account?"

▸ Uh...

I realized that I could likely open an account at the Repository. I wasn't sure if that would be the same type of account that Citizens were used to dealing with. She seemed confused by our conversation.

"Well, I'm sorry. I don't have any other way to pay you."

Sigh.

▸ My task is complete. I'll be paid the amount I agreed on for the job. Nothing more for you to worry about... ma'am.

She pushed past me, heading for the wine cellar.

"I'm so curious, how did you manage to—"

She stopped on the stairs, frozen in place. The SecuBots stared at me vacantly from behind their black visors.

"What... the... *Frag*!?"

Now it was my turn to freeze.

"What did you do to my wine cellar!? Oh my Bog!"

I heard her footsteps clattering quickly down the stairs, no doubt surveying the wreckage. Smashed bottles, blood stains, a bullet hole or two. Hey, it could have been a lot worse.

"This is a disaster! No, no! My 1947 Cheval-Blanc? My Screaming Eagle Cab? Oh, you frag! You smelly little Volunteer piece of Shiva! Get the frag out of my house right now!"

FILE 15

SERPENTS

I made the long slog back through Royal Heights to the security checkpoint. The gloom and darkness grew with each step until they enveloped the world. Paradise lost.

The faceless Polizei bots stared at my half-naked, bloodied form. I could sense, if not see, their condescension. Even disdain.

Glory to the Volunteers.

Cautious, I made my way to the bounty boards, avoiding the neon-soaked main thoroughfares and taking a circuitous route to my destination. I was one solid hit away from death. Although I had no reason to believe invasive creatures were prowling the streets of The Commons, manually hauling this much loot put me on edge. The only emotional rush stronger than the heightened joy of suddenly acquiring wealth was the precipitous despair of losing it.

I couldn't go too slow, however. If the skies started dripping pink I would lose my bonus, and I had no way of knowing when that would be. Or would the fact that I completed my task before the next cycle count? Something told me the system wouldn't be that forgiving.

As I walked, I did some mental math. I had no available storage and would need fifty free metabytes to hold my 5,000 Crypt payout. I could remove all of my thirty-two Crystals from my inventory and add them to my makeshift sack. I could also remove my revolver, freeing up the remaining twenty.

Not ideal. If I collected my bounty and then died before backing up my data, I could lose it all anyway. And yet, I could not back up anything that was not part of my inventory.

Sigh.

I really needed to get ahead of this storage issue. Had I only been faster and more decisive, maybe I could have grabbed that magical purse from the clurichaun.

One problem at a time.

I stepped into the square and approached the Task Assignment Boards. The streets were oddly empty. But why? Even the Armory and Supply Depot beyond had no customers.

Working quickly, I removed all thirty-two Crystals from my inventory as well as my snub-nosed revolver, adding them into my bindle.

MEMORY
- **STORAGE: 178 / 230**

I accessed the bounty boards, scanning my code.

Task Complete: Remove clurichaun from a private residence in Royal Heights.

Assigned to: Volunteer 01001110-01101111-01100010-01101111-01100100-01111001.

Task Completion Award: 4,000 Crypt.

Bonus Award: 1,000 Crypt.

Would you like to receive payment?

▸ Oh, yes.

The electronic bits streamed into me, and I eagerly absorbed them. 5,000 Crypt! The bounty boards shifted as new bounties appeared and others vanished. But the rate was slower than I had seen before, as if there was less bounty traffic at this time. Much less.

Alert! Account storage almost full.

Yeah, yeah, yeah.

I double checked my menus just to confirm the money was there.

ECONOMY
- **CRYPT: 5,000**
- **CRYSTALS**

MEMORY
- **STORAGE: 228 / 230**

There was a click somewhere behind me. The heel of a boot stepping on asphalt. I slowly turned, clutching my bundle of goods.

"Oi! What do we's have here?"

There were four of them. Black denim and leather. Punk rock boots. A marble-eyed goon with a cobra patch on his vest and a butterfly knife in his hand.

▸ Razor.

"How nice. You remembers me. I don't think we's loveted your eemya last raz we met."

▸ I'm sorry?

"No worries. We's just gonna slice your barcode off as a malenky trophy. And we's be taking your pretty polly too."

Razor, Buzzcut, and the other two cobras fanned out in a semicircle. They didn't know how much Essence I had or what my stats were. They couldn't know what weapons I was packing. But I was obviously the worse for wear.

Razor licked his lips, crouching into a knife-fighting stance.

"We's can do this the easy way or we's can do this the hard way. I'm really hoping you chooses the hard way."

I swallowed, backing up until I bumped against the bounty boards. My eyes darted, looking for the best route to make a run for it. My revolver was tied up in the bundle. With my free hand behind my back, I subtly materialized my dagger.

Then—CRACK!

The cobras froze as a puff of smoke ricocheted across the dark ground between us.

Was that a gunshot?

"What the—"

CRACK!

Another shot rang out, pinging off the ground. The four goons dropped low, frantically looking for the source of the gunfire. I, too, searched wildly, leaning close to the bounty boards for protection.

"Where's it coming from!?" Razor shouted. "Show yourself!"

There was a loud clanking, and a fire escape ladder from a nearby building dropped down. A figure wrapped in a dirty, tan blanket hung from the ladder, then leapt. It held a hunting rifle and shambled towards us.

I recognized that unusual gait.

Throwing back the hood of the urban ghillie suit, I saw Camel's trademark welding goggles and knit skullcap. He flashed a gap-toothed smile, training the hunting rifle on Razor.

"Be a horrorshow malchik and go domu, britva. Ookadeet my poor lad oddy knocky."

I had no clue what Camel was saying, but I was very glad to see a friendly face.

Razor made a show of flipping his butterfly knife around before dematerializing it. His companions remained tense, and each held onto their weapons. I side-stepped across the pavement until I was next to Camel.

Razor threw up his hands in protest, a playful expression on his face.

"Just a lomtick of fun, Camel. We's didn't means nothing by it. Hazing the noob is all."

Camel aimed down the sights of his rifle right at the center of Razor's chest.

"All the same, you'd best get out of here before I give you an extra yahma."

The cobras stood their ground. Razor's playful expression faded, his grin souring with malice. His metallic lower jaw and black-within-black eyes reflected the city's neon glare.

"There's four of us and dva of you. How's you figure that math?"

Plink. Plink. Plink.

Small raindrops spattered the ground.

Nobody moved.

Light rivulets of pink ran through my hair, mixing with my dried blood. The torn strip of my coveralls wrapped around my head grew damp, my bare chest wet.

The goons gnashed their teeth. One by one, they dematerialized their weapons and slowly backed away, looking up at the sky. Camel followed Razor's every move with his barrel.

"Saved by the rain, noob. Saved by the fraggin' rain."

The storm grew heavier, and the four cobras receded into the darkness of a side street.

I turned to Camel in relief.

▸ Thank you! You don't know how happy I am to see you. How did you...? Why did...?

"Don't mention it. I wanted to find my droogie and viddied around. I figured you'd make it back to the bounty boards eventually. Why are you messing around with those Serpents?"

▶ Serpents? I am not messing with them. They are messing with me. I don't even know who they are, and I don't care to know.

"They seem to have taken a shilarny in you. Come back to my nook. We can wait out the rain together."

As the rain increased, wild in its fluctuating temperatures, I hustled after Camel to the Residential Towers.

We shared the cage elevator, rode up on Camel's scan to his floor, and hurried down the dim hallway. Soon, I found myself crawling into his capsule, under the number **01000010-01100101-01110100-01100001-00111001.**

I found it much the same as mine, albeit larger. He had a long workbench with gun parts and other items built into one wall. He also had some high-tech crates stacked in one corner and a tiny kitchenette with an airplane bathroom-sized sink.

The place reeked of smoke and booze.

Crawling on my hands and knees, I sat beside his sleeping pallet while Camel removed his gear. The hunting rifle he lovingly placed on his workbench, and the ghillie suit he somehow dematerialized into one of his storage crates. His hands were to his lips in a moment, lighting a fresh cigarette.

"Care for a cancer?"

▶ No thank you.

He shrugged and dragged heavily on the cigarette, absorbed in the tactile pleasure of the behavior. I was completely dry despite the heavy rain only minutes before.

▸ Listen, I don't want to be a bother. You've done so much for me already; I can head back to my tube.

Camel shook his head.

"No. You rest here. Safer to stay at this point. I wanted to lovet up and viddy how you are doing. Completed a bounty on your own?"

▸ That's right. Clurichaun. Rare.

Camel closed his eyes and nodded sagely, sucking in a lungful of smoke and blowing it out in a billowing stream.

"Ah, yes. Seen odin before. Never killed odin. Tricky buzzards."

I had learned from context that "odin" meant "one" in the strange parlance spoken by some of the Volunteers. Not the Norse god. But then again...

▸ I got this rare Data Card.

I materialized the green and red card and it floated above my open palm, slowly spinning as the artificial capsule lights played off it. Camel whistled appreciatively.

"A rare card? On only your second bounty? That is special."

▸ It is labeled "skill." What does that mean exactly?

"Cards can be used for different veshches. Could boost a weapon or armor, some can become skills, some really special cards can even turn into weapons or armor. Many can go either way. But looks like this odin can only be fused onto a skill slot at the Forge."

No doubt that fusing would cost Crystals. I concentrated on the spinning Data Card, seeing if I could access any additional details.

Data Card: Clurichaun

Card Type: Skill

Frequency: Rare

Skill Details: Project an illusory image of yourself anywhere within 30 feet. Illusion lasts 30 seconds. Skill takes 30 seconds to recharge after the image fades. Interacting with the image will not dispel it.

Skill Cost: 30 Energy

Size: 10 metabytes

That was a lot of thirties. So, if I paid to fuse this skill onto a 'skill slot,' I could create a temporary illusion. That could come in handy. But thirty Energy? I only had ten. I would have to upgrade my Energy stat twice.

▶ Camel, how many skill slots do I have?

"Four is the default."

▶ And how do you replenish Energy after you use it?

"That's easy. Same way you get Essence back. Just rest during a cycle change. That, or pop some consumables."

▶ Ah.

I then realized I would need to free up eight additional metabytes of storage space if I wanted to recharge my Essence to full during my next rest.

▶ Camel, I want to get your advice on my storage situation. But I... I'm feeling pretty spent all of a sudden. I should head back to my tube.

"Nah. Just sleep here. You can use my pallet. I'll just be oiling my rifle and having a smoke. We can govoreet when you come to."

▶ Thanks. You're a friend. Oh, that reminds me. I have something for you. A gift.

I untied my sack of loot and pulled out a bottle of wine, handing it to Camel. He took it in both hands, examining it curiously.

"Where did you get this?"

▶ It... uh... accidentally fell into my bag when I was in a Citizen's wine cellar in Royal Heights. I'm told it is very, very expensive. At least, it would be in the real world.

"Quite the pack rat, aren't you? Seems a lomtick too messel for my taste. I'm a simple moodge. But thanks."

Camel set the fancy bottle aside and began to dismantle his rifle, piece by piece. His second cigarette in as many minutes dangled from his lips.

A rat? Great. I think I preferred being a magpie to being a rat, although neither were all that endearing.

I felt a deep tiredness starting to overpower me. I removed my push dagger from my inventory and placed it in my bag, retying it. Now I would have enough storage space to get my full Essence back. If Camel stole my bag while I was asleep, I would be right and truly screwed.

But I knew where he lived. And not trusting anyone was too exhausting. We all needed a safe port in a storm.

► Camel... the last time I rested when it was raining, I think I had some kind of disturbing dream. I can't remember the details, but I feel a deep anxiousness about it. A premonition that something terrible is waiting for me. And yet, I can barely keep my eyes open.

"Don't worry, my droogie. I'll watch over you while you spatchka. I'll keep the baddiwad dreams away."

FILE 15.1 [FRAME ERROR]

ELSEWHERE

Razor and the rest of the Serpents hurried down an alley, ducking under awnings to avoid the falling rain even as it pooled up to their ankles.

He cursed under his breath. He had twice been made a fool by that ugly noob. And now that old vagrant had interfered. But nothing could be done about the rain. Bad timing. The cycles weren't exactly predictable, after all.

"I'm heading back to the penthouse to waits out the storm. Buzz-cut, Glitch, Roadkill, you coming with?"

"The penthouse? Are you sure?" Glitch said nervously. "Is... Is *he* there?"

"Nah, he's still on his journey. It'll just be us. We's can party."

Razor wanted to get Glitch alone ever since their recruitment. See exactly what was inside their pants. And he had a special powder to slip into their drink that just might help erase any objections.

"That place gives me the creeps," Glitch answered. "I'm going to hole up in a Rez den. And I know Roadie's down for that."

Roadkill gave a thumbs up. She would love nothing more than to numb out from a strong hit of Rez right about now.

"Rez? That stuff will scramble your mozg," Buzzcut complained.

"That's the bloody point, innit?"

"I'll come with you," Buzzcut said to Razor. "There's some top shelf liquor in the penthouse, and you can't beat the viddy."

Razor nodded, and the group split. Sending one last longing look after Glitch, he and Buzzcut hurried to the lower stretch of The Commons where one tower stood a bit taller than the surrounding buildings. It had the look of a newer construction, and the letters N-A-D-I-R were stenciled on top.

Wading through the floodwaters, the duo entered the lobby, slicked off the wetness, and entered the waiting freight elevator on the far end of the marble floors. With a mischievous look, Razor produced a golden key from his vest and inserted it into the elevator panel. The doors closed, and the elevator rose.

They stepped out into a dark penthouse, spanning the entire top floor of Nadir Tower. Generous windows overlooked the shimmering lights of The Commons, increasingly swallowed by the torrential pink rain.

The fossilized skeleton of some ancient beast was mounted on display, along with other artifacts decorating the expansive space.

Ignoring these, Razor and Buzzcut hurried to a large, open kitchen, rummaging in the cupboards until they found a bottle of whisky with a red wax seal. Stripping off the wax, they took turns sipping straight from the bottle, giggling like children.

Ohmmmmmmmmm.

They tensed. Buzzcut, wide-eyed, turned to Razor.

Ohmmmmmmmmm.

A deep vibrato, humming in the darkness.

Razor mouthed, "He's here."

Setting the bottle on the counter with a gentle clink, Razor shuffled deeper into the penthouse. Buzzcut, trembling ever so slightly, followed close behind.

In the center of the penthouse, an enormous man sat in the lotus position in the middle of a painted circle. He was fair-skinned and completely hairless, clad only in a fundoshi loincloth. His eyes were shut, and he was meditating in front of an ancient slab of stone emblazoned with hieroglyphs of winged serpents.

Razor began to speak but the man raised a large finger to his lips, commanding silence. He returned to his meditation.

Ohmmmmmmmmmm.

As he meditated, two large snakes—tattoos on his back—began to writhe, slithering across the canvas of his flesh. Impossibly alive.

Ohmmmmmmmmm.

Ohmmmmmmmmmm.

After several minutes, the chanting ceased. The snake tattoos coiled together, reformed, each swallowing the other's tail in an ouroboros design.

The man rose to his feet, reaching for a silk kimono that he wrapped around his huge frame. He clapped his hands twice, and low lights filled the room. Then, and only then, did he turn to acknowledge the two men.

"Herr Schlächter! I... I didn't know you were back," Razor began.

"Der Schlächter, not Herr."

"Y-Yes. I'm sorry, Schlächter. I keep forgetting. How was your trip? Did you find what you were viddying for out there?"

"A piece."

His voice was deep and melodious.

"That's horrorshow! That's really horrorshow!" Buzzcut added in eagerly. Too eagerly.

Der Schlächter narrowed his eyes and looked down at the men who stood no higher than his chest. It felt as if he were gazing into their very souls.

"It is fortunate that you came here tonight, Razor. A rumor has come to my ears that is most disturbing."

"Oh?"

"I heard that you embarrassed us at the Armory. You and some of the new members were harassing a Volunteer and they humiliated you in public."

If Razor could Shiva in his pants, he would have.

"Where… did you slooshy that?"

"Let's just say a little bird told me."

"You don't knows the whole story! This Volunteer… they was cheating! I don't knows what happened, but there was something strange going on. I swear I'll get even—"

"The Volunteer is nothing. A nobody, from what I've been told, with no reputation to speak of. Our reputation, on the other hand, was injured by your impetuous actions. We are not some street gang of impudent hoodlums. We are a family. And without upholding that most sacred of things—reputation—how is our family to grow?"

Razor broke out in a cold sweat.

"Y-Yes, sir. I mean… Herr… I mean, it won't happen again…"

"Nevertheless, a price must be paid for your transgression."

"Well, it was actually his fault!" Razor pivoted, thrusting an accusatory finger at Buzzcut. A look of absolute betrayal crossed the other man's pale face. "We's challenged that uppity noob to a shooting contest, and… Buzzcut lost! He's the odin that brought shame on us!"

Der Schlächter turned his steady gaze on Buzzcut. "Is this true?"

Buzzcut gulped. "T-Technically, yes."

Der Schlächter sighed and placed his huge hand on Buzzcut's shoulder.

"You are young, and we are family. Forgiveness is possible, even desirable. But a price must be paid. Do you understand this?"

Buzzcut was nearly petrified. The silver grill on his teeth clattered as he trembled. But he managed to nod ever so slightly that he did understand.

"Come with me."

Der Schlächter walked to the kitchen, moving gracefully for a man of his size. Razor and Buzzcut obediently followed. Ignoring the open bottle of whisky, Der Schlächter reached below the wide countertop and removed a black bundle. He set it down and slowly rolled it open like a scroll, revealing all sorts of butchery tools.

"Choose."

Buzzcut met the man's eyes for an instant, then looked away. The gaze was too intense.

"This is an act of grace. That you may choose."

Buzzcut looked down at the various implements. Stealing himself for the inevitable, he pointed to a small paring knife.

The enormous man shook his head, pursing his lips in gentle reproval. He selected a meat cleaver.

"No, my dear child. I did not mean that you should choose the blade. I meant that you should choose what part of your flesh the blade should be used upon."

Later, as Buzzcut lay stretched out naked on the butcher's block, a rag stuffed in his mouth to stop his screams, Der Schlächter quietly recited a verse.

Give me your tired, your poor,
Your huddled masses yearning to breathe free,

The wretched refuse of your teeming shore.
Send these, the homeless, tempest-tost to me,
I lift my lamp beside the golden door.

FILE 16

SCHWARZMARKT

I awoke with a start. If one could label what happened as waking at all. Whatever the case, I roused from some deeper unconsciousness to the present state of awareness that constituted my so-called existence.

At first, I didn't know where I was. It was dark and claustrophobic, the air so thick with smoke it stung my eyes groping for the light. I reached out in the unfamiliar space, knocking something off something else with a loud clatter.

Shiva.

Wait. Camel's place. That's right.

I took a deep breath, inhaling stale cigarette fumes, and ran my hands over the wall of the cramped room, feeling for the dial that would bring the light. At last, I found it.

I was alone. I remembered that I fell asleep in Camel's tube when the cycle changed, but my eccentric companion was nowhere to be found. Just the flotsam of his meager life.

A menu notification flashed in my vision.

Refresh complete.

Essence restored.

Energy at full.

I ran my fingers through my hair and found the bandage still wrapped around my head. I slowly removed it and examined it under the fluorescence. It was caked with dried blood, but when I felt around my skull, I realized the wound was gone.

My coveralls were still in tatters. Obviously a refresh didn't repair items or armor. Still, I felt renewed strength within me. I vaguely recalled that my last rest had not been so peaceful, but I could not place my finger on why. Yet another lacuna in my higher cognitive processes.

I looked around. Camel's rifle was gone from the workbench. I couldn't say if anything else was missing or out of place. I resisted the unusually strong urge to try and peek in the curious storage crates stacked in the corner.

Oh Shiva. My bag. Where is my bag?!

Frantic, I twisted around in the small space, trying to locate my precious belongings. It had been right beside me when I went under. Could Camel have... Would he have...?

Oh. There it is.

Somehow it was underneath the workbench. Camel must have moved it because I saw a square piece of paper skewered to the top of the bundle's fabric. I quickly grabbed the sack and removed the long, wooden skewer, like something one would find at a food stall serving yakitori chicken hearts. On the paper was a crude drawing of a rat.

What? Did I get played after all? Was Camel calling me a rat? Had he stolen my stuff as payback for some previous insult, or to score some easy drinking money?

Wait, no. I was getting paranoid. Get a grip. This rat... I recognized it. It was the logo for the Rathskeller. This was Camel's way of letting me know where he went.

Sigh of relief.

I untied the bundle and counted the contents anyway.

One hundred Crystals. One revolver. One dagger. Everything in its right place. And what was that? There was something else stuffed inside of the bag. Not only had Camel not ripped me off, he actually left me something extra.

I pulled out a pad of soft material, which I unfolded. It was a T-shirt. A bright, white T-shirt. Turning it around, I saw the Reality Inc. logo emblazoned and a gaudy catchphrase, "Living my best second life! ™"

Ugh. Thanks? Not exactly inconspicuous, but it was a temporary solution to walking the streets topless. I slipped on the shirt and decided to check my inventory.

EQUIPMENT
- **ARMOR**
    - **HELM:** N/A
    - **BODY:**
        - **BLACK COVERALLS** (damaged): 0/10 defense
        - **PROMOTIONAL T-SHIRT** (cosmetic)
    - **ARMS:** N/A
    - **LEGS: BASIC FOOTWEAR** (cosmetic)

Damaged? I was afraid of that. Looking closer, the coveralls were still taking up ten precious metabytes of storage but offering me nil defense. I wondered if there was a way to repair armor. I also wondered how this T-shirt ended up in Camel's possession.

I knew I had a lot I needed to do in this new cycle. I had Crystals to burn. I had 5,000 Crypt to spend. I needed to solve my storage dilemma. And lastly, I needed to visit the Restoration Point.

Removing much needed items from my inventory just to make room for Crypt was not sustainable, especially if I expected to chase bigger paydays. I wanted to visit the Repository too but felt the need to pick Camel's brain first.

I got ready and headed to the Rathskeller.

When I arrived, Camel was nowhere to be seen. The place was packed, but he wasn't at the bar. However, I did see one familiar face. The meticulous female bartender in the smart bowtie. Several Volunteers gave me the side-eye as I squeezed into a space at the counter, no doubt appraising my unusual shirt. I ignored them, waving for the bartender's attention.

After she finished filling a few glasses, she walked to me, the same flawless smile on her face as before. I had to raise my voice over the throbbing music.

▸ Hi. Do you remember me?

"Of course I do. I never forget a face. Although, the hair is new."

▸ Wow. Wait, haven't you seen a lot of people with this same face? I was under the impression it was pretty basic.

"I was being polite. I remember your ID."

She nodded to the numbers permanently branded on my wrist. She must have had an eidetic memory. Probably was a bot after all.

▸ Can I ask what your name is?

"Yes, of course you can ask," she said before lapsing into intentional silence, her smile not wavering for a nanosecond.

▸ What is your name?

She just smiled.

▸ Right... I was looking for Camel. Have you seen him?

"Oh, sure. He's watching the fight."

▸ Fight?

The bartender looked towards the back of the building as if that meant something to me. All I saw was the crush of bodies drinking and undulating to pulsing techno.

"Are you going to order something? If not, I have other customers I need to take care of. Might I recommend a special drink for the occasion?"

▸ Occasion?

She winked at me. Or at least, I thought she did.

▸ What do you recommend?

"A mind eraser."

▸ I'm sorry?

"I recommend ordering a mind eraser. It's a classic. One hundred Crypt."

One hundred? I hadn't planned on spending any money here, but the way she was looking at me made me feel there was something else going on. I nodded. She smiled, gave a slight bow, and returned with a drink that was black and bubbly. Not the usual pale blue stuff, which only cost ten Crypt. I reluctantly paid.

I downed the strong drink and noticed something that looked like a poker chip stuck to the bottom of the empty glass. I peeled off the token and turned it in my fingers. It had a faint iridescent glow. On one side was the familiar rat symbol. On the other, a deceased rat—upside down, eyes dramatically X-ed out, tongue lolling.

I looked up at the bartender for an explanation, but she was already off serving other Volunteers. My gaze swung back to the rear of the building. It was hard to see through the crowds. I figured I'd better get a closer look.

I pushed back through the bodies. The Round Table in the center was vacant despite a want for seats. Probably nobody dared sit there unless you were part of that elite group. I kept going, cutting through a busy dance floor.

"Hey, wanna dance?"

"Watch where you're going!"

"Nice shirt, ya gloopy nazz."

I ignored the voices, pressing all the way back to the far wall. There was a large jukebox spinning tunes. We were apparently listening to something called Sonic Destroyer by X-101, or was it X-101 by Sonic Destroyer? I didn't know if that song existed in the 'real world' or was just a product of the Metaverse.

An intimidating man with a braided beard, horned helmet, and submachine gun strapped across his chest sat on a stool, balancing a glowing, red katana against a point on the floor.

I tentatively held up my token, and he bared two rows of golden teeth in response. He banged on the wall behind him with his metal fist and a glowing outline appeared. Soon, a door appeared where there had been none. I stepped through into a scene of impending violence, gripping my precious loot bag, suddenly questioning my second life choices.

A large, circular backroom was bathed in ultraviolet. A crush of Volunteers pressed against a metal, dome-like cage sunken in the center, jeering and shouting. The pulsing music from the bar was reduced to the dull roar of an echoey, underwater rumbling.

There was a smattering of high top tables throughout. Assorted Volunteers leaned against them and sipped their drinks. My embarrassing T-shirt shone like a beacon under the oppressive black-lights, but no one looked my way. All attention was on the cage.

"Ay! You!"

There was Camel, using a high top as a crutch, already quite tipsy through a process I had not yet discovered. Didn't the cycle just start? Well, it had to be five o'clock somewhere. He waved me over with a gloved hand.

"Come to watch the spar? Still raz to make a bet."

▸ A bet?

"Wager. Gamble. You know?"

Uh oh. There was that tingly sensation again. That twitchy urge deep within me.

▸ What is it we're betting on?

"This match? Clean spar. Odin on odin. No guns. No items. Melee and skills only. To the death."

▸ To the death?

I craned my neck, trying to see who was in the cage. My virtual breath caught in my throat when I saw an ashen-skinned woman with intense, white dreadlocks. It was Rook from the Round Table. And who else was in there with her? Another woman I had seen somewhere—shorter and stocky, with a pink mohawk, spiked shoulder pads, and heavy black boots.

They circled each other like caged tigresses. The pink-haired woman clutched a massive, silver battle axe in both hands, runic designs on the blade. Rook dual-wielded the kusarigama I had seen her use before to deadly effect, connected by chains to some spot between her shoulder blades, possibly to the metal collar around her throat.

"My pretty polly is on Rook. Pixie doesn't stand a chance, even with that messel new axe."

▸ But why? Why are they fighting?

"You'd have to ask somebody who pays more attention. For the sport of it? For the pretty polly? Maybe some baddiwad krovvy?"

I shook my head. I had a lingering admiration for Rook, and I didn't want to see harm come to her. I stood on my tip toes and spotted her partner, Bigwig, against the outside of the cage, shouting encouragement to her ringside. It didn't look like any blows had landed yet.

▸ What is this place exactly?

"The Schwarzmarkt. Well, right now it's the Fleischmarkt, but soon enough it will be the Schwarzmarkt again. Good for making trades off book. Barter system mostly."

A siren blared overhead. I flinched at the sudden sound, then slowly straightened myself, feeling a bit foolish. I placed my loot bag on the high top and gripped it tight in both hands.

"You missed your chance! The spar is starting. Can't make any more wagers."

I had a suspicion that was probably for the best.

In the ring, Pixie charged forwards, swinging the battle axe. Rook bent her knees and arched backwards in an instant, the heavy axe humming just above her torso. Wow. Those were some impressive reflexes. I wondered what her Agility score must be to dodge like that. The gawkers went wild, cheering and slapping the metal bars surrounding the combatants.

Rook righted herself and slashed with her sickles as she advanced: left, right, left, right. Pixie held the silver haft of the axe vertically in defense, parrying each blow as it came. She had some moves too. Rook went for a leg sweep, and the stocky woman leapt in the air. Rook answered with an acrobatic downwards strike as she spun, unluckily clanging against one of her opponent's spiked shoulder pads.

Pixie yelled and thrust her haft sideways, shoving the nimble

Rook backwards several paces. Creating some distance. Pixie pounded her chest and her eyes flashed red. Were my own eyes playing tricks on me, or did a coat of primal fur appear over her arms? Suddenly, she charged forwards, hacking wildly with the large axe, yelling with guttural rage.

Rook ducked back and sprinted up the side of the cage, seeming to defy gravity as she narrowly dodged each chop. The crowd screamed with excitement.

"Berserker trance," Camel muttered before draining a glass and belching.

A skill.

Soon, the effects of the skill wore off, and Pixie's assault slowed. The bestial fur was gone. Without missing a beat, Rook performed a backflip off the cage bars and landed right in front of Pixie, jabbing the sickle into her exposed calf. Pixie yelped, blood dotting the floor. The crowd hooted.

Pixie brought the axe down with all her might, crashing into the ground where Rook had been a second before. Had Rook been a moment slower, she might have been bisected on the spot.

▸ Still like your odds?

I wasn't even sure if Camel was paying attention to the fight anymore. He seemed to be preoccupied ogling some curvaceous form across the room.

"Oh yeah, that devotchka's got nothing on Rook," he said.

Gasps of surprise turned my attention back to the fight. Pixie activated another skill, blowing a gust of frigid vapor just as Rook attempted a killing blow. Her arm froze instantly, locked in icy blue suspension above her head. Immobilized.

"Frost giant something something..." Camel slurred.

There was tittering around the room. I overheard someone complain that Pixie was 'overdoing it' with the Scandinavian mythos. Whatever she was doing, her next move was devastating. She swung her silvery axe at the exposed, frozen arm. Rook tried to dodge but was too slow this time. The axe struck its mark, shattering Rook's arm like an oversized icicle.

▸ No!

Jagged chunks of frozen flesh exploded and scattered across the cage. Rook winced, her pupil-less eyes growing even narrower, but gave no cry. Her right kusarigama fell, dangling from its limp chain. The crowd was in a frenzy, many begging to change their bets.

Rook staggered back until she was up against the bars. Her will to fight had melted away. Bigwig pounded the cage, shouting advice, but Rook remained in a crouch, cringing from the terrible pain. Meanwhile, Pixie thrust her battle axe high in the air, soaking in a moment of glory before moving in for the finishing blow. Half the crowd egged her on, chanting.

"Kill! Kill! Kill! Kill!"

Pixie sauntered forwards to do just that, running her finger against the sharp edge of the blade in a bit of showboating and licking the trickle of blood that resulted. She raised the axe one last time.

One last time, because all the while Rook was crouching, she started to glow with faint blue energy. Then, in a flash, her missing arm regrew! She grabbed the loose chain and yanked it with all her might, sending the prone kusarigama flying through the air and impaling itself into Pixie's temple.

The crowd screamed, practically climbing up the cage in agitated, jubilant bloodlust.

▸ What just happened?!

"That's a hydra skill," Camel snorted.

▸ That's… incredible. The Round Table hunters must have bagged that elusive hydra after all.

"Costs a Shiva load of Energy though."

Pixie dropped her axe. Rook ran forwards, lightly vaulting over Pixie's shoulder and wrapping the twin chains around her neck, strangling the life out of her. Twin streams of stigmatic blood dripped from Pixie's vacant eyes.

Another siren blared. This time signaling the end of the deathmatch.

Rook let her opponent's lifeless body drop to the floor. It melted away into pixelated nothingness. Bigwig and Rook's companions from the Round Table cheered her victory, and bets were paid out to those who backed the winning horse.

I let out a whistle, lost in the din of post-fight noise. A hatch built into the side of the cage opened and Bigwig helped his partner out. Volunteers cheered and toasted the violent delights of Rook's victory.

Dram. I felt myself irresistibly drawn to the victorious fighter. Rook. She was such a badarse woman. But did I want to be *like* her, or be *with* her? I honestly couldn't parse it, only that I felt attracted like a nail to a high-powered magnet. At least being an involuntary eunuch simplified things.

I wanted to congratulate her on her win, but my legs wouldn't move. Rook was surrounded by her entourage and Volunteers celebrating the match. No way she would give me the time of cycle. It was doubtful she remembered I existed.

FILE 16.1

BARTER

I needed to focus. I came to the Rathskeller for a reason—to pick Camel's brain and plot my next move.

▸ Camel, can I ask you something about storage?

"Sure. Fire away," he said, trying to drain the last few drops from his glass.

▸ I keep running out of storage, which isn't good. I know I can upgrade it with Crystals, and I can purchase items or armor that can increase my storage for certain categories. But what about Crypt? What do you recommend?

Camel thought long and hard. I began to think he hadn't heard me and cleared my throat. He shook himself from his daze and answered.

"You have a few options, droogie. You can open an account at the Repository. They have a few different services, all for a fee. Probably run one hundred Crypt per cycle per service for a low roller like you. You can purchase some type of wallet accessory, although those are not always available in the shop rotation, and the storage space can be malenky. Or you could just stash the pretty polly where the sun don't shine like me."

▸ Excuse me?

"Just a joke. You can keep veshches in your domy if you want, but some punks could try and crast it. And it can be a pain to have to trek back and forth just to get your stuff. There is another option…"

I briefly wondered what sort of things Camel stored in those containers back in his capsule. Based on his lifestyle, he didn't seem like the type to have accumulated great wealth. Then again, one should be careful not to judge from outside appearances.

▸ What is the other option?

Camel tapped the side of his neck. I saw nothing there but splotchy skin and stubble.

"Get an implant. Oh yeah, get a malenky bod mod surgery and install a chip. The slice and dice job will run you 1,000 Crypt, plus the cost of the chip. But those things can store a lot of pretty polly, and you never need to run to the bank."

▸ Get surgery to install a computer chip into my neck? Like a memory card?

Just then, an unfamiliar voice cut over the cacophony of the Schwarzmarkt.

"Long time no talk, Camel. Who's your friend with the goofy shirt?"

Another Volunteer I vaguely recalled seeing at the Round Table addressed Camel, who straightened up with a snort. The other man was tall and shirtless—save for some bondage straps—with dense tribal tattoos decorating his arms and pecs. He had flowing, black hair and wore platinum, spiked knuckles over his prominent fists. An amulet adorned with an evil eye hung from his muscular neck.

"This? This is… They don't got an eemya yet. New krovvy. Just showing them the ropes," Camel explained.

▸ You're with the Round Table?

The man grunted, irritated that I had spoken to him without an explicit invitation to do so.

"That's right. They call me Apache."

▸ Apache?

"Repeating a thing don't improve it. So Camel, you lose any money just now or did you do the smart thing and bet on our girl?"

Camel flashed a gap-toothed smile and gave a wobbly thumbs-up.

"I always put my pretty potty on you bolshy pooshkas!"

▸ Excuse me, Apache. If you don't mind me asking, what was that fight all about?

"Ambitious climber. Pixie. She wanted a seat at the Round Table. Thing is, you got to prove yourself. Final step in the audition process is beating a current Round Table member. Guess she wasn't ready."

▸ That girl got brutally killed as part of an audition process?

Apache looked at me as if I had lost my mind. Which, well...

"I'm sure it hurt like hell. And her ego will be bruised for a while. But other than that, Pixie'll respawn at the Restoration Point a bit poorer. No hard feelings."

▸ No hard feelings? Rook just stabbed her in the head and strangled her!

"Just the way the game is played. A little PvP never hurt anybody. Pixie could have challenged someone else from the Table. Probably wouldn't have made a difference. Wouldn't mind an opportunity to put her in her place myself."

After a shrug, he turned his attention back to Camel.

"Anyhow, the only reason I came over, Camel, is I wanted to see if you were in the market for a new rifle. Or did you just come to watch the fight? I came across an extraordinary piece but, you know, I'm more of a melee guy."

Camel perked up.

"Show me what you got."

Apache materialized a long, ornate sniper rifle. Gilded. Ribbed. It was beautiful. It radiated power. I wanted to reach out and touch it.

"Vajra Rifle. Legendary. Powerful lightning damage. Can punch a hole clean through a monster at range. I think it was once a club, but the original owner must have exported it into a ranged weapon. Back in the day, you were looking everywhere for a legendary rifle, isn't that right?"

Camel shrugged and stuffed his hands in his pockets. His enthusiasm faded, replaced with haggard nonchalance.

"It's dobby. Messel. But I'm a simple moodge now. And I don't got anything worth trading for a legendary pooshka. Doubt I ever will again."

Apache looked disappointed. He briefly turned to me.

"Not likely you've got something worth a legendary trade? Not even sure you could handle this beauty in your current state."

I thought for a moment, then materialized my clurichaun Data Card. The red and green item shimmered in the ultraviolet light as it spun.

▸ All I've got is this rare skill card. That and some crafting materials.

Apache quickly dematerialized the rifle.

"Not a snowball's chance, but let me take a look at that card."

He hovered his fingers over the card rotating in the palm of my hand, reading the details. It felt a little invasive, especially with his spiked knuckles in close proximity.

"I've been looking for a skill like this. Something to give me an advantage. What would you trade for it? You obviously haven't fused it onto a skill slot yet, so it must not fit your build."

▸ Uh… no. I just acquired it recently. I haven't decided what I'm going to do with it yet.

"What do you want for it? Money? Crystals? Items? Something else…? You're in the black market, after all."

▸ Black market?

Camel lit up another cancer. He was bored by the conversation but added his two cents for my benefit.

"There's an auction flatblock on the top floor of the Supply Depot. Temporarily closed for a patch I think. But outside that, the Schwarzmarkt is where Volunteers can barter without Bolshy Bratty taking his cut."

Apache could read my confusion and rolled his eyes impatiently.

"Shielded tax free zone, courtesy of our friends in Antisoc. Didn't realize how much of a Metaverse virgin you were, Rookie," he said with a sigh. "What is your build? What are you trying to accomplish?"

▸ I don't know. I've got a dagger. I've got a gun. I've got some hellhound Data Card fragments. I desperately need some storage. What do I want to accomplish? I want to get out of this place. Fulfill my contract. Survive. Isn't that what we all want?

He ignored my comments.

"Open your inventory and share it with me," he instructed.

▸ How do I do that?

Apache sighed deeply. He cracked his knuckles in irritation.

"Just open your menu, your whole menu, then drag it over to me. I'll have temporary viewing access until you close it."

I did. Soon, Apache was flicking through my menu. I could see faint light reflected in his eyes. Just then, I felt very, very naked. Exposed. Like my torso had been split open and this stranger was peering into my entrails.

"How's this? I'll give you your six missing hellhound fragments, and I'll toss in a Schema for that coco de mer nut you have."

With ten fragments, I could forge a complete card.

► What does a hellhound Data Card do?

"You can fuse it on a weapon or armor. Either add fire damage or add fire resistance. You can't fuse onto your basic push dagger, of course. And your armor is shot to hell. Is it a deal?"

Camel shook his head in protest, cigarette dangling from his lips.

"No, no, no. No deal. Hellhounds are hound-and-horny. They're a dime a dozen out there. A few hound-and-horny fragments ain't worth an intact rare card. And my droogie can discover crafting recipes on their own."

I listened carefully to Camel and nodded. I appreciated that he was looking out for me. I closed my menu, having had enough of Apache's prying eyes.

"Name your price then. What will you accept in exchange for that clurichaun card? I've got plenty of things that might interest a rookie like you."

► Thanks, but no thanks. I'm going to hold on to my Data Card for now. But I will accept one hundred Crypt for wasting my time.

I grinned at Apache and dematerialized the rare card. He registered the briefest look of shock, then swung on me.

I flinched.

The sharp tips of his spiked knuckles hovered half an inch from my face, then slowly retracted. Apache let out a low chuckle.

"You've got spunk, rookie. I'll give you that."

Apache turned his back, then hesitated. He opened his menu and dragged something ephemeral through the air. As a reflex, I reached for it.

You received 100 Crypt.

"Don't spend it all in one place. Now get out of here before I beat your arse."

Meanwhile, Camel had nearly dropped his empty glass in surprise. To be honest, I surprised myself. I was thankful not to be spitting out teeth.

"You got some bolshy balls to be teasing a top-tier hunter like that. Sorry. Figure of speech. What got into you?"

▸ You said it was a bad deal. I trust you. And I don't trust that guy enough that he won't try to screw me over, no matter how sweet the deal sounds.

Trust... No need to mention that mere hours ago my knee-jerk reaction was to assume the worst about Camel's intentions.

Camel shook his head.

The caged deathmatch over, this backroom of the Rathskeller reverted into a den of shady deals. Volunteers were making swaps all over the place. I guess everything had a price and almost anything else could be considered a legitimate form of payment if you wanted it badly enough. Something about avoiding taxes or system oversight?

"Did you make a plan about stashing your pretty polly? What are you ittying to do?"

▸ I'm 'ittying' to look into the body modification options you mentioned. Supply Depot, right? Getting a computer chip installed in my neck isn't the most natural thing, but then again, literally nothing about this place is natural.

"The starry slice and dice. Better you than me."

▸ Really? No surgery for you? No improving on Mother Nature?

Camel flashed his gap-toothed smile. The skin beneath the missing patches of scraggly beard shone under the black lights. His eyes swam in his head, unfocused, and he spread his scrawny arms wide in an awkward pose. He reeked of booze.

"You can't improve on perfection!"

FILE 17

MODIFICATION

I took my bag of baubles and departed, passing through the hidden door and back through the Rathskeller proper. Drinking and dancing continued as ever under oppressively loud music.

As I passed by the vacant Round Table, I wondered if I would have what it took to join that vaunted few. Apache said the final step of the audition process was to challenge and defeat a member of your choice in mortal combat. What was the first step?

Outside amidst the dark streets, I hurried across town to the Supply Depot. Passing by the vicinity of the Bounty Boards, I remained vigilant for any sightings of the Serpents.

No signs of them. Good. I didn't like the idea of having to watch my back for the rest of my second life. I needed to get stronger.

I ducked into the Supply Depot, eyeing the dazzling aisles of wares and a smattering of Volunteers I didn't recognize. I nodded politely to the elderly woman sitting behind the counter. A closed book lay on the counter, *Die Traumdeutung*. She smiled back at me, crescent earrings dangling from her lobes.

▸ Any rain in the forecast?

She raised her wrinkled hand as if to test the air.

"Oh, ho, ho. Not yet, dearie. You still have quite some time."

I gestured to the spiral staircase leading down to the sublevel.

▸ Body modification.

"You go right ahead."

I descended onto the black slate floor and scanned my number under the red light sensor. I saw my avatar displayed large—rotating lifelessly on the central screen, splayed like some cadaver about to be autopsied. I accessed the leftmost body modification panel. Curious, I scrolled through the available options.

The more I searched, the more ways I saw in which I could alter my avatar. Taller. Shorter. Thinner. Thicker. Eye color. Lip thickness. Jaw width. Chin depth. Voice. Genitals. All with a price, of course.

Finally, I came across a submenu labeled Advanced Body Modification.

Here was a list of surgical procedures and associated artificial limbs, implants, biomechanical upgrades. Things I had never heard of before. Eye implants. Brain jacks. The list went on. I surmised that there were improvements I could make to my avatar through cold, hard Crypt that otherwise would require upgrades using Crystals. Different paths to self-improvement.

Neural Integration Procedure - Axis Port Installation: One-time surgical procedure to install a port in the back of the neck at the base of the skull for neural-interfacing chip access.

Cost: 1000 Crypt

Okay, that was what Camel had mentioned. And where would I acquire the chips to insert into said port? Ah, there they were. They started at 1,000 Crypt and skyrocketed from there.

B3-9S7-C10K: Neural-interfacing chip designed for minimal Crypt storage.

Storage: 10,000 Crypt

Cost: 1000 Crypt

B3-9S7-C100K: Neural-interfacing chip designed for moderate Crypt storage.

Storage: 100,000 Crypt

Cost: 10,000 Crypt

Alert: You do not have the required minimum Protocol for this device.

B3-9S7-C1M: Neural-interfacing chip designed for advanced Crypt storage.

Storage: 1,000,000 Crypt

Cost: 100,000 Crypt

Alert: You do not have the required minimum Protocol for this device.

The concept of having 1,000,000 Crypt at my disposal made me salivate. Were there actually Volunteers running around that rich? Maybe someday that could be me.

For now, I could only afford the C10K model. Also, it was the only one that did not appear to have a minimum Protocol requirement. Protocol. Huh. I had barely put any thought into that statistical category, except recalling that it improved my ability to craft materials at the Forge.

I was starting to see the potential appeal of using the Repository. If I kept chasing bigger bounties, I would eventually max out the chip's storage space. Still, it was a one-time cost and portable. I wondered if I could have multiple ports installed and carry multiple chips at a time. Would there be Protocol requirements for that as well? Maybe something to ask at the information kiosk.

I decided to bite the proverbial bullet and go for the body mod surgery and the C10K chip. Losing 2,000 Crypt would hurt, but I needed to make long term investments.

Neural Integration Procedure - Axis Port Installation selected. Would you like to apply this change?

▸ Yes...?

Round apertures in the black floor opened, and two narrow pedestals shot upwards. The top of each pedestal glowed white, indicating a spot to rest my hands. I carefully placed my loot bag on the ground then did so. My hands instantly clung tight to the bright surfaces.

Please remain still. The operation will begin shortly.

That cursed voice again. Saccharine and inauthentic.

There was no backing out now. I realized my hands were completely immobilized. I squirmed as a mechanical noise sounded from above. Metal claw-like appendages dropped from the ceiling, encircling my head. They made a terrible clacking noise.

I fought against the urge to duck my head, to try and escape. I paid good money for this.

One of the appendages rotated into place directly behind my head, hovering with a needle-like point above the small of my neck. Soon, a bright red laser shot out from the tip, cutting directly into my flesh. I could see it illustrated on the central screen in front of me, magnified. A blinding pain erupted.

▸ Frag, it hurts!

Anesthesia is available for an additional charge of 2,000 Crypt.

▸ What?! You didn't mention anything about that before!

Would you like to purchase anesthesia?

▸ Yes! Yes!

I'm sorry. Anesthesia is not available once the operation has begun. Please try again next time.

▸ Gaahhh!!!

The pain continued as the laser sliced and penetrated deep into the top of my spinal column. Meanwhile, a burning, queasy sensation spread from the palms of my hands, up through my arms, and permeated my entire body. It was as if my DNA was being melted down and rewritten—or the digital version of DNA. The code that governed my avatar.

My vision flickered and then everything went black.

Bit by bit, my eyesight returned. The sound of mechanical arms retracting into the ceiling. I was slumped against the two pedestals, my hands still suctioned into place. A hissing sound, and my hands were free. I knelt to the ground and quickly examined my palms for signs of damage. But there were none. My flesh was spotless. The pain receded into non-reality.

Operation successful. Neural-Interface Axis Port installed.

If that was success, I didn't want to experience what failure felt like.

I cautiously touched the back of my hairless neck. There it was. Something hard and alien. Something that should never be part of a human body. It felt roughly the shape of a card reader slot on an ATM, but smaller. Congratulations, I now had a new orifice. An extra metal slit.

I glared at the body modification and cosmetics panels, not that they did or could give a Shiva about me.

Tapping the screen as aggressively as I could, I grudgingly purchased the C10K chip and watched it materialize in my hand. It was a black and sleek rectangle, but when I turned it in the light, it gave off a bronze glimmer. There did not appear to be an up or down, front or back—no standard orientation—just the short and long edges.

Here goes nothing.

I lined up the card and slowly inserted it into the slot at the base of my skull, half expecting to feel it pushing into my squishy brain stem. But oddly, it felt good. Satisfying. An emptiness was being filled. I pressed it all the way in until it clicked, resting within my reconfigured body.

A menu notification appeared before my eyes.

B3-9S7-C10K chip detected. Would you like to automatically transfer your Crypt?

▸ Yes, I would.

I felt an internal woosh as digital bits streamed from one hidden part of myself to this new addition. And strangely, it felt like I could breathe easier—as if the change in storage somehow translated to feeling less encumbered. Lighter. I had not noticed that sensation before.

I untied my bag and quickly added my weapons back into my inventory, only keeping my one hundred Crystals stowed away. I checked my menu, navigating to the Economy and Memory submenus.

DESIGNATION
VOLUNTEER ID: 01001110-01101111-01100010-01101111-01100100-01111001

- **COSMETICS**
    - **WAVY ASYMMETRICAL CROP** (hair)
    - **ALMOND** (skin tone)

- **MODS**
  - **NEURAL-INTERFACE AXIS PORT**
    - **B3-9S7-C10K CHIP** (10,000 Crypt storage)

ECONOMY
- **CRYPT: 3,000** (stored on B3-9S7-C10K chip)
- **CRYSTALS**

MEMORY
- **STORAGE: 208 / 230**

Next up, I needed to do some shopping.

I went upstairs and spent the next hour perusing the aisles of the Supply Depot. I assume it was an hour. I had no way of personally tracking time. My History submenu kept no record of it, and the permanent night of The Collective didn't help. Still, certain items and skills operated on a timer measured in seconds or minutes. Good old-fashioned human chronological measurements.

The layout of goods was almost labyrinthine. The store was bursting at the seams with miscellaneous items. Some had no discernable purpose on their own. Certainly no practical purpose. Nostalgia items. Decorative items. Novelty items. Others presumably had a use for crafting.

I picked up another vial of pure water. That would run me fifty Crypt. I still had two fern flowers remaining, and only one other material to go with it. The swatch of white linen cloth. I had not discovered a Schema for the fern flower and white cloth, but I could attempt to combine them as well as forge another tincture using the fern flower and the pure water.

After searching near the back of the store, I found some individual Schemas for sale. They appeared like floppy discs, suspended within tamper-proof containers of pale light.

Item: Schema: Sleep Bomb (Series 1)

Cost: 500 Crypt

Description: A single use item that unlocks the Schemas for forging {common} and {uncommon} Sleep Bombs.

Item: Common Item Forging (Vol. 1)

Cost: 1000 Crypt

Description: A single use item that unlocks 5 {common} item forging Schemas, combining frequently encountered invasive flora materials with system materials. This volume has been synthesized from Volunteer field reports.

Volunteer field reports? Interesting. But I think I'll hold off for now.

I wondered if any particular Volunteers in The Commons specialized in crafting items. Might be worth looking into eventually.

There were also the more obvious consumables for sale in the Supply Depot. Items designed to assist Volunteers in their mission to eradicate all invasive entities from the face of The Collective.

Item: Regenerator Serum

Quantity: 1

Cost: 200 Crypt

Description: A one-time oral consumable that restores 10 Essence. Cannot exceed maximum Essence capacity.

Size: 10 metabytes

Item: Replenisher Injection

Quantity: 1

Cost: 250 Crypt

Description: A one-time intravenous consumable that restores 10 Energy. Cannot exceed maximum Energy capacity.

Size: 10 metabytes

Item: Stimulator Inhalant

Quantity: 1

Cost: 350 Crypt

Description: A one-time intranasal consumable that temporarily boosts total Speed by 30. Lasts for 30 minutes.

Size: 10 metabytes

Also interesting. I didn't want to deplete my Crypt before having a chance to visit the Armory, so I made a mental note. There were similar items that addressed other statistical categories, as well as more advanced versions of those items for higher prices.

Next, I browsed various accessories. In the Supply Depot, there were only non-combat accessories, but many could still be useful in and out of bounty hunting contexts.

Accessory: Compact flashlight

Cost: 200 Crypt

Frequency: Basic

Details: A small water-resistant flashlight with a beam throw of 200 meters and brightness of 47 lumen.

Size: 10 metabytes

Accessory: Headlamp

Cost: 500 Crypt

Frequency: Basic

Details: A portable 400 lumen light source worn on the head. Used for activities that require both hands such as spelunking.

Size: 10 metabytes

There were even night vision goggles. I tried to compare all these with the ocular implants I had quickly browsed in the body modification menu, not that I was itching to submit myself to another horrific surgical experience just then. There were also some consumable items mixed in with these light-giving accessories. One I recognized as something used by Bigwig and Rook when they intervened in that nasty business with the Baskerville Hound.

Item: Phosphorescent Flare

Cost: 100 Crypt

Frequency: Basic

Details: A single-use item that illuminates a dark area with a persistent green glow for a variable amount of time.

Size: 10 metabytes

The more I window shopped, the more I wanted to buy everything. But I had neither the storage space nor the Crypt. I needed to be smart about this. I wanted a buffer of remaining Crypt after my shopping spree. So, I resisted any purchases beyond my single vial of pure water and paid at the front of the store.

The elderly woman at the counter smiled at me as I finalized the exchange. I silently wondered what rationale was used in selecting the appearance of the vendors, assuming they were all bots programmed and placed to provide a relatable face and voice to our mundane transactions.

But she was looking at me strangely. And I noticed in her dark eyes an unexpected depth, like the expanse of a night sky, pierced through with irregular pinpricks of cosmic light. I shivered, politely thanked her, and left for the Armory. I could feel her eyes following me out the door.

FILE 17.1

UPGRADE

I now had 2,950 Crypt.

Back in the hubbub of the Armory, I moved from display case to display case, looking for the uncommon tactical jacket that had previously been out of my price range. I didn't see it. I accessed the nearby vending kiosk, scrolling through the options. Again, I didn't see it. Dram.

I recalled that the items available for purchase rotated. That was probably to create a sense of customer urgency. Panic buying. False scarcity. But wait... Didn't I place a deposit on the jacket? I opened my History submenu and rapidly scrolled down through the record of my actions. Eventually, I found it.

HISTORY

-     **Purchased a snub-nosed revolver from the Armory vendor**

-     **Placed a 20 Crypt deposit on tactical jacket**

-     **/Ugh. Put 20 Crypt down as a deposit on the tactical jacket and give me the revolver.**

-     **Armory vendor said, "2,000 Crypt. Right now it is only 1,500."**

-     **/Sale? I didn't notice it was on sale. What is the regular price?**

\-   Armory vendor said, "You can. But there is no guarantee it will remain at its current discounted sales price."

\-   /That tactical jacket I saw. Can I somehow place a deposit on it for later?

I got the attention of the militaristic vendor bot, Colonel Peacekeeper, when it was done assisting another Volunteer.

▸ Excuse me, do you know when the tactical jacket will be back in stock?

"Colonel Peacekeeper at your service! I hope you are having a FUBAR day, soldier!"

▸ Right. About the tactical jacket. I put down a twenty Crypt deposit on it last time I was here. But I can't find it listed.

"It has been pulled from rotation! But if you have a deposit, I can bring it up for you."

Peacekeeper raised a green metal finger and opened a shimmering menu in the air. There it was. I highlighted the item on the screen to bring up the details.

Armor: Tactical jacket

Armor Type: Body

Cost: 2000 Crypt

Level: 1 of 10

Frequency: Uncommon

Defense Output: 30

Details: A type of jacket designed for use in military, law enforcement, and other tactical situations. Made from durable materials and features a variety of pockets for storing gear. Also features reinforced elbows, shoulders, and VELCRO strips for attaching morale patches or identification.

Properties: Storing - when equipped, this armor increases memory space by 20 metabytes.

Size: 30 metabytes

Dram. Back up to 2,000 Crypt. Or 1,980 minus my deposit. Hmmm.

"Soldier! If the price discourages you, I can recommend a special sale we have going on right now!"

▸ What is it?

Colonel Peacekeeper brought up three screens. Each showcased a rotating piece of black equipment. One looked like a bulletproof vest, the other a pair of cargo pants, and the last a heavy pair of mid-ankle combat boots. I accessed the details of each in turn.

Armor: Ballistic vest

Armor Type: Body

Cost: 1000 Crypt

Level: 1 of 10

Frequency: Common

Defense Output: 20

Details: A simple bullet-resistant vest designed to protect the torso from bullets or other projectiles. Warning: even bulletproof vests can be penetrated by certain types of projectiles, such as armor-piercing bullets.

Size: 10 metabytes

Armor: Tactical pants

Armor Type: Legs

Cost: 500 Crypt

Level: 1 of 10

Frequency: Common

Defense Output: 10

Details: Functional pants designed for use in military, law enforcement, and other tactical situations. Made from durable fabric that is resistant to tearing. Also features multiple pockets and reinforced seams.

Properties: Storing - when equipped, this armor increases storage space by 20 metabytes.

Size: 10 metabytes

Armor: Tactical boots

Armor Type: Legs

Cost: 200 Crypt

Frequency: Basic

Defense Output: 10

Details: Heavy-duty shoes designed for use in military, law enforcement, and other tactical situations. They provide extra stability around the ankles and help protect the wearer from sharp objects and protrusions.

Properties: Armor has the {basic} property and cannot be upgraded, enhanced, or exported.

Size: 10 metabytes

Something within me hesitated at the mention of law enforcement. I wondered why. Regardless, I needed to improve my defense. There had been too many close calls.

▸ Interesting. What is the special sale? Are these items usually more expensive?

"If you buy all three, you will get a 10% discount on the total price! Hooah!"

▸ Even though the tactical jacket is not part of the current rotation, could I substitute it for the ballistic vest and get the same 10% off deal for purchasing all three?

The vendor was silent, his invisible programming grinding away somewhere in its processing unit.

"Negative soldier! Regulations prohibit off-rotation items from being part of current sales promotions!"

Ugh.

▸ Fine. Give me those three items and three .32 caliber bullets. Also, can I get my twenty Crypt deposit back?

"No refunds! However, you can apply your deposit to a different purchase here in the Armory!"

▸ What would be my total then?

"Those three pieces of armor bring your total to 1,700 Crypt, minus 10%, equals 1,530. Plus thirty Crypt for three .32 caliber bullets, minus 20 Crypt from deposit. That will be 1,540 for everything!"

▸Okay. Let's do this.

Ballistic vest selected. Would you like to equip this armor?

▸ Yes.

Would you like to unequip black coveralls (damaged)?

▸ Sure.

Tactical pants selected. Would you like to equip this armor?

▸ Yes.

Tactical boots selected. Would you like to equip this armor?

▸ Yes again.

Would you like to unequip basic footwear?

▸ Okay.

With each change, my outward appearance instantly shifted. A trick of the light, a blink of the eye, and my avatar was now equipped with black, heavy duty cargo pants, matching black boots with thick tread, and a black bulletproof vest slung over my white promotional T-shirt.

I was 1,540 Crypt poorer. But my total armor was now forty. And my soft storage cap was raised by twenty. Also, my revolver's chamber was once again full.

▸ I see that each piece of armor and my snub-nosed revolver are level one of ten. What does that mean?

"You can upgrade your weapons and armor of course! Not basic items, but anything with a frequency of common or above can be upgraded to level ten. For a fee! It is a service we are happy to provide here at the Armory for our brave fighting men and women!"

▸ Good to know. What does upgrading a weapon or piece of armor do exactly?

"Take your sidearm. It has a damage output of twenty. If you upgrade that gun to level ten, you could reach a maximum damage output of 200! That's some serious firepower!"

▸ Wow. Would anything else about the weapon be improved besides the total damage?

"Not a chance!"

▸ Ah. I assume the story is the same with my armor.

"That's right, soldier! You could upgrade your tactical pants to level ten, increasing its defense output from ten all the way up to a maximum of one hundred! The added storage would not change!"

I understood. Very straightforward and mathematical.

▸ One last question. What can I do with old armor I don't want anymore?

"You can try and sell unused items at the Volunteer Auction House next door. Auctions are for valuable items—not damaged, generic, or starter kit. Or you can practice data recycling!"

▸ Data recycling?

The robotic vendor stretched a green metal finger and indicated a tall, metallic cylindrical receptacle in the corner of the room. It had an elongated triangle on top outlined in glowing pink. Come to think of it, I had seen this contraption elsewhere around The Collective but had not paid much attention.

"Drop your unwanted gear down the Memory Hole and you'll be fairly compensated for its value! Your old underwear can be tomorrow's grenade! That out-of-fashion corset can be refashioned as a machete!"

▸ Interesting. I'll give it a look.

Colonel Peacekeeper gave a sharp salute before turning to the next Volunteer waiting for its attention.

"Dismissed!"

Holding onto my precious bag of Crystals with one hand, I removed the damaged coveralls and basic footwear from my inventory, and went over to the Memory Hole.

It looked like a fancy trashcan emerging seamlessly from the ground. A tube leading to who knows where. There was a small red light on the side, and I scanned my identifier code. The pink triangle lit up a bright cyan, the opening as dark as a black hole.

I tentatively dropped the damaged coveralls and footwear in. Better to keep my T-shirt for now. It was a gift. At the very least, I could return it to Camel. The items were sucked into the blackness with a vacuum-like sound. I imagined bits of data being ripped apart. Snippets of code torn asunder, sucked away to be repurposed elsewhere in the Metaverse. Ones and zeroes. The basic building blocks of my reality.

But then something awful happened. I hadn't thought this through.

When I recycled the black coveralls, the torn piece of material I used to fashion my bindle dissolved into nothingness too, sucked into the hole.

One hundred Crystals hung in the air for a nanosecond before spilling all over the floor of the Armory.

Every single Volunteer froze, turning to stare as I scrambled on my hands and knees, scooping up the loose Crystals into a tinkling mound.

I glared, feral like an animal, daring anybody to try and snatch one of my precious shining gems. And a few were tempted. Meanwhile, an electronic dinging noise like a slot machine chimed. A notification flashed before my eyes.

You received 20 Crypt. Thank you for recycling unused data!

Thinking fast, I unequipped my promotional T-shirt and tied the fabric into a new bag. The Crystals barely fit, threatening to spill out of the gappy sleeves.

I quickly glanced at my menu. My remaining 1,430 Crypt was safely stored on the C10K chip slotted into the back of my neck. And even with my new armor, I remained under my now expanded soft storage cap.

Next stop, the Data Forge. It was past time to spend these Crystals.

FILE 17.2

SKILL

I walked to the Data Forge, lugging my precarious bundle. No sign of goons waiting to jump me as I crossed through the perpetual night of the city.

I passed under the red blacksmith hammers and into the churning structure of the Forge. I then scanned my code at the forging station. The heavy metal door sealed me in. Blasts of hot steam vented on either side as the strange machinery labored unabated. The panel lit up, listing my options.

DATA FORGE

CONVERT (Crystals into Value)

FORGE
- **ITEMS** (from materials)
- **CARDS** (from card fragments)

FUSE
- **SKILLS** (fuse Data Cards onto eligible skill slots)
- **EQUIPMENT** (fuse Data Cards onto eligible weapons or armor)

EXPORT (transform one type of item, weapon, or armor to another type)

TRANSMUTE (transform the cosmetic appearance of an item, weapon, or armor)

I knew my rare clurichaun Data Card was valuable. So valuable that a member of the elite Round Table wanted it. Or at least, it conferred a useful skill. I did not know how long it would be before I might stumble across another intact Data Card of this frequency.

I materialized the card and concentrated on the details.

Data Card: Clurichaun

Card Type: Skill

Frequency: Rare

Skill Details: Project an illusory image of yourself anywhere within 30 feet. Illusion lasts 30 seconds. Skill takes 30 seconds to recharge after the image fades. Interacting with the image will not dispel it.

Skill Cost: 30 Energy

Size: 10 metabytes

It was a skill card, meaning I could fuse it onto an open skill slot. Camel said that Volunteers had four skill slots as a default. I had no way of viewing anything else about skill slots in my menu at present. I suppose I had to take that on faith.

Was there a way to unfuse a skill? Or would this be a permanent change? Maybe such an option only appeared on the Forge's menu if you had skills, and I was skill-less. This particular skill required thirty Energy to use. I only had ten. That means I would need to first convert Crystals into Value, assign that Value to Energy, and then fuse the skill card.

Increasing Energy by twenty would take up 249 out of 250 max storage. Every change, every bit of data added to myself required space. Unfortunately, I would need to increase my storage to handle any additional upgrades. I forgot that Value converted directly to storage without a stepped increase, in contrast to my core stats. Additionally, I saw it would cost ten Crystals to fuse the Data Card.

So, forty Crystals total to fuse and use the skill. A steep cost. Still, this skill might save my life. And the increased Energy would be useful for any other skills I acquired in the future.

Nothing ventured, nothing gained.

I decided to convert ninety Crystals to Value and reserve ten to fuse the skill card. Forging additional items with my crafting materials could wait until next pay day.

I selected the Convert option and one of the podiums sprouting from the forging station began glowing as before.

Deposit Crystals for conversion.

I unwrapped my bundle and carefully counted out ninety Crystals into the indentation, watching them clink and glimmer as they settled.

Begin conversion process?

▸ Yes.

The Crystals hummed, cracking and spilling light as the Forge worked its electronic alchemy. The digitized double-helix sculpture poured forth blinding rays until beautiful motes shot into me.

I was filled with charge and warmed to the core. I checked my menu to confirm what I already knew.

UNASSIGNED VALUE: 90.

I transferred thirty Value to increase my total Energy from ten to thirty.

This was a sensation hard to describe. Although I did not experience hunger or thirst in The Collective, sensory memories of whatever previous life I must have lived remained at the edges of my consciousness. I could recall what it meant to feel hungry, and alternately satiated. I could even remember what it felt like to burn with other types of unfulfilled desires, and the soul-deep feeling of resolution after satisfying those desires.

Having unspent Energy was like that. An instinctual sensuality to be expended. A need to be expressed. A sort of heady biochemical stamina oscillating within my center. Having possessed ten Energy since my awakening, I realized that feeling had always been there, lingering in the background. The sudden boost amplified that tingling. Perhaps it would fade again into the background with prolonged familiarity.

Next, I accessed Fuse, followed by the Skill suboption.

Insert a Data Card in the indicated depository.

One of the station's branching devices glowed. I placed the Data Card on the podium and watched it hover, slowly rotating in place.

{rare} Data Card: Clurichaun *(Skill)* **detected.**

Deposit Crystals for fusing.

I poured the final ten Crystals onto the other glowing receptacle. Then, I dematerialized the promotional T-shirt and re-equipped it, making sure it was layered beneath my ballistic vest.

Two white handprint patterns appeared on the surface of the third podium, indicating where to rest my palms. Great. The last time I placed my hands on something like this, it triggered an unspeakably excruciating experience. However, I did as prompted.

Begin fusing?

My body was ready.

My palms glowed white hot, spreading up through my forearms. It burned, as if my arms were submerged in scalding water, but was not accompanied by the same queasy sensation I experienced during the body modification surgery.

I watched as the Data Card dissolved into quantum foam. The Crystals were consumed by the machine. A wispy, purple effervescence shrouded my body. Illusory vapor drifted across my skin, swirling until it sucked into my solar plexus. The haunting image of the clurichaun's visage flashed in my mind's eye for an instant.

I let out an involuntary gasp.

Skill fusing successful.

Clurichaun skill fused to open skill slot.

1 / 4 skill slots assigned.

As if unlocking a new part of my mind, I could suddenly visualize four cubes within me. They were arrayed like a cross. I closed my eyes, concentrating on rearranging these invisible cubes hanging in some other plane of my being. Three of the boxes were empty, charcoal gray and dim. One possessed the power of the Data Card I had absorbed. A power I could now summon and use through a sheer act of will.

I opened my menu and saw a brand-new category listed beneath Statistics.

SKILLS
- **Clurichaun**
- **{empty}**
- **{empty}**
- **{empty}**

I wanted to practice using this new skill. But I knew I could only replenish spent Energy by resting during a cycle change or using an applicable consumable, of which I had none. Skill practice would be time consuming and resource draining. I thought of the infinite ammunition available at the Armory's shooting range. Did something equivalent to that exist for testing out skills?

For now, I still had sixty unassigned Value. I needed to decide which statistical categories to boost. Increasing a stat from ten to twenty would cost ten Value, but increasing from twenty to thirty would cost twenty, and so on. Or I could sink it all into expanding my storage.

I checked my current stats:

STATISTICS
- **ATTACK**
    - **STRENGTH: 20**
    - **ACCURACY: 10**
- **DEFENSE**
    - **ESSENCE: 20**
    - **RESISTANCE: 10**
- **ABILITY**
    - **ADEPTNESS: 10**
    - **ENERGY: 30**
- **MOVEMENT**
    - **SPEED: 20**
    - **AGILITY: 10**
- **PROCESSING**
    - **PERCEPTION: 10**
    - **PERSUASION: 10**
    - **PROTOCOL: 10**
    - **PROBABILITY: 10**

MEMORY
- **STORAGE: 249 / 230** (250)

I knew I needed storage space. In the Volunteer economy of the Metaverse, storage was the most limited and necessary commodity. No upgrade was possible without it. I transferred forty of my unassigned Value straight into storage, boosting my core total to 270 (290 with my soft cap increase).

I immediately felt somehow more expansive even though the physical size and shape of my avatar was unchanged. Perhaps just an illusion, like sensing a phantom limb. But some sort of internal, invisible capacity had increased, and it felt good. Of course, I was now going to actively eat into that extra storage by sinking my last twenty unassigned Value into my stats.

My first choice was Accuracy. I wanted to be able to use my one and only ranged weapon more effectively. That left me with ten Value, which meant I could only afford to raise one additional stat from the baseline of ten up to twenty. I was torn between Adeptness, Agility, Perception, and Probability. I could see how each would improve my chances of success. Chances of survival.

I had been taken by surprise several times already, and it had nearly killed me. It wasn't much, but perhaps an extra ten points in Perception would give me an edge. Finishing my business, I unlocked the metal door and exited the Data Forge, hustling the short distance to the Restoration Point towering over the center of The Commons. I was glad to not be carrying around an embarrassing self-made pouch of valuables.

I approached the inverted, arching walls of the Restoration Point tower and stepped through the entryway. I located one of the empty, translucent tubes and scanned my code.

Welcome to the Restoration Point.

Volunteer 01001110-01101111-01100010-01101111-01100100-01111001

Your last backup was {1} cycle ago.

Would you like to back up your data?

▸ Yes, I would.

100 Crypt will be deducted.

The round light on the panel shifted from red to white.

Please enter the Restoration Station to back up your data.

As before, I climbed onto the small platform and was raised into the tube. I placed my arms and feet in the indicated holders, stretched out. The Vitruvian Volunteer. I soon felt the hot beams of light penetrating every nanometer of my body, burning an image of my gestalt.

Your data backup has been successfully completed.

Climbing out of the tube, I checked the small screen on the nearby panel, reading the details of my backed-up information.

DESIGNATION

VOLUNTEER ID: 01001110-01101111-01100010-01101111-01100100-01111001

- **COSMETICS**
  - **WAVY ASYMMETRICAL CROP** (hair)
  - **ALMOND** (skin tone)

- **MODS**
  - **NEURAL-INTERFACE AXIS PORT**
    - **B3-9S7-C10K CHIP**

STATISTICS
- **ATTACK:** (40)
  - **STRENGTH: 20**
  - **ACCURACY: 20**

- **DEFENSE:** (30)
  - **ESSENCE: 20**
  - **RESISTANCE: 10**

- **ABILITY:** (40)
  - **ADEPTNESS: 10**
  - **ENERGY: 30**

- MOVEMENT: (30)
    - SPEED: 20
    - AGILITY: 10
- PROCESSING: (50)
    - PERCEPTION: 20
    - PERSUASION: 10
    - PROTOCOL: 10
    - PROBABILITY: 10

SKILLS

- **Clurichaun**
- {empty}
- {empty}
- {empty}

EQUIPMENT

- **WEAPONS**
    - **PUSH DAGGER**
    - **SNUB-NOSED REVOLVER**
        - 5 / 5 .32 caliber ammunition
- **ARMOR** (40)
    - HELM: N/A
    - BODY: BALLISTIC VEST
        - PROMOTIONAL T-SHIRT
    - ARMS: TACTICAL PANTS
    - LEGS: TACTICAL BOOTS
- **ACCESSORIES**

INVENTORY

- **CARDS**
- **FRAGMENTS**
    - {common} hellhound 4/10
- **CONSUMABLES**
- **MATERIALS**
    - 2 {common} fern flowers

- 1 {uncommon} coco de mer nut
- 1 white linen cloth
- 1 vial of pure water

ECONOMY

- **CRYPT: 1,330**
- **CRYSTALS**

MEMORY

- **STORAGE: 269 / 270 (290)**
- **SCHEMAS**
  - **Tincture of Fortune**
- **HISTORY**

STATUS

TASKS

- **Remove clurichaun from a private residence in Royal Heights** (Complete / Paid Out)
- **Remove hellhounds from MAR Station Service Tunnels** (Complete / Paid Out)

FILE 18

ANTISOC

Exiting the Restoration Point, I carefully stepped over the thick vine-like cables burying themselves below the grid surface. I approached the street, unsure of where to go next. I still had Crypt to spend but could just as easily catch another bounty. I was feeling confident. Energized.

A deafening roar and flash of lights sent me back on the curb as a trio of motorcycles blasted by. Elongated, plastic-sheened cycles careened around the circular hub of the tower and drifted around a corner in a blur. Gone from view, but their engines reverberated off the buildings of the sprawl. The cycles moved so fast I couldn't tell if they had actual tires or were skimming above the ground.

I took a moment to bring my pulse back to equilibrium. Were those Volunteers out for a joy ride or someone else? A couple other souls in the vicinity had turned to watch the cycles pass, but none seemed shocked by the sight.

Strange. I hadn't seen any other personal vehicles in The Commons.

I made another attempt to cross, then froze. One foot on the curb, one foot in the road. Across, in the shadowy darkness of a side street, two reflective eyes gazed unblinking in my direction. They were small.

Nearly at ground level. Two glowing orbs in the night. Without my modest boost to Perception, I might not have noticed them at all.

Cautiously, I materialized both my revolver and dagger. No more surprises, thank you very much.

I crossed the street in the direction of those eyes. As I neared, my vision adjusted to the shaded contours and I saw that it was... a cat. Aside from the arresting yellow eyes, its details were hard to make out clearly. Was it a black shorthair? The way the lights of the city played off its dark fur, it almost appeared to take on stripes at times.

Come to think of it, I had nearly stepped on a cat when I first arrived in The Commons. Could this be the same one?

▸ Here, pussycat.

I dematerialized my weapons and stooped to scratch it behind the ears. It quickly darted out of reach, scampering further away. I was about to shrug it off, but the cat stopped and stared halfway down the side street. There was something uncanny in that gaze.

▸ Are you looking at me?

Why was I talking to a cat? This was absurd. Nevertheless, it paused expectantly, head turned over its shoulder to watch me with those glowing eyes. I took a testing stride towards it and it moved off again, pausing to regard me.

▸ Want some food? Or... I don't have any food. Are you someone's pet? Are you lost?

The cat merely stared, then continued its game of keep-away as I tried to close the gap.

▸ Do you want me to follow you?

At that, I could have sworn the cat flashed a mischievous grin. Impossible. But there it was. I couldn't imagine following this cat could lead to anything productive or, to be honest, non-horrific. But as I stated before, I was feeling confident. I had just backed up my data. What was the worst that could happen?

▸ If you are an invasive entity, I swear...

I began to quicken my pace. The cat darted from shadow to shadow until it reached the far end of the side street. I followed, watching it casually lick its paw until I closed the distance. Then it was off again, crossing over to yet another street and turning, leading me down a minor maze of alleys.

Bright, animated billboards overhead lit our way.

Special Bod Mod Offer: 15% off the Prince Albert and Hottentot Venus packages!

Armory Deal: Buy Three Boxes of Ammo and Get One Free! Hurry while supplies last!

Free Testing for Digital Syphilis and Rez Dependency at the Clinic with New Premium Membership. This cycle only!

Kana, Kana, Kana. Hakkliha! Get the minced chicken you crave! Nostalgia Couriers will deliver delicious memories straight to your private domicile!

Are you doing your part to make The Collective sustainable? Ask at the information kiosk about your nearest data recycling ports!

Distracted for a moment by the barrage of promotions, I jogged around a corner to catch up, afraid I would lose track of the feline. I saw a bustling section lit by hanging lanterns and neon signs. Volunteers bumped shoulders, passing between open air food stalls.

Wait, I recognized this place. This was near where I had started. Where I had been unceremoniously spat out of the orientation by the so-called Concierge. Where was the cat? There it was. Winding between the shifting legs of the small crowd. The people seemed oblivious.

I hurried to keep up, pushing my way apologetically past the others. At last, I turned a final corner and found myself facing a dead end. A literal brick wall with little more than a rusty downspout and a slash of graffiti. I had the cat cornered, not that such had been my intention.

▸ What now, kitty?

With another eerie grin, the cat walked straight through the brick wall.

▸ You've got to be fragging me.

I reached out and the wall felt solid to the touch. But as I pressed harder against the rough brick, something started to give. And I slipped through the facade into total blackness.

I was in some sort of stasis. I could see nothing, feel nothing, move nothing. It was like the sterile light of my first awakening but inverted. A total empty void. Had I stumbled foolishly into a trap laid by that Serpent gang?

Then—three massive faces appeared in the darkness, impossibly large in my field of vision. They appeared to be humanoid but constantly glitching. Just when I thought I could make out a distinct feature, the image shifted. A patchwork quilt of compression artifacts.

I heard a heavily distorted electronic voice make a comment, but not directed at me.

>**Cheshire protocol successful. Good girl, Schrödinger.**<

▸ What!? What is this? Who are you?

A chorus of booming, vocoder synthesized voices responded in deafening unison.

>**We are Antisoc.**<

\>That is not the important query.<

\>The important query is who, or what, are you?<

▶ Huh?

\>We spoofed your avatar signature and you are in a shielded area. If you try to signal for help, no one is coming.<

\>Attempt to activate any countermeasures and you will be flatlined.<

▶ What?!

\>Listen to the following propositions.<

\>One can never truly reach one's destination. No matter how close one gets, there remains an infinitely small distance between one and one's objective. Presence is impossible.<

▶ Okay...

\>In order to know something, one must first know that one knows it. However, if one knows something, then one must also therefore know that one knows that one knows it, an infinite regress. Knowledge is impossible.<

▶ What?

\>This sentence is false. Truth is impossible.<

\>Accessing id 01001110 01101111 01100010 01101111 01100100 01111001 menu.<

\>Accessing id 01001110 01101111 01100010 01101111 01100100 01111001 history.<

I saw my personal menu being forcibly pried open. A glowing screen ripped from my unseen substance and spread wide before the leering eyes of the glitching faces. My entire history since awakening was being scrolled through and picked apart.

▶ Hey! What are you doing? I do not consent to this!

\>Who are you?<

▸ Me? I'm just a Volunteer!

>**Are you working for ColSec?**<

▸ What?

>**We ask again. Are you under the employ of ColSec?**<

▸ I don't even know what that is! Please, I'm just a Volunteer! A nobody!

There was silence from the three large faces, but I saw the reverse image of my menu screen—my inventory, my stats, everything— being examined at a rapid pace.

>**Your history does appear to indicate a routine volunteer onboarding process. But that may be part of the deception.**<

Suddenly, the three faces diminished in size. The loud booming voices grew more subdued and conversant. I realized the three images were debating with one another in a coded distortion. I could do nothing but helplessly wait, suspended and depersonalized.

At length, the central floating face addressed me once more, glitching illusively.

>**You came to our notice by accident. But ever since, we have been watching you. If you are a regular Volunteer, how do you explain the bonus you received in your orientation of 10 additional metabytes of storage?**<

▸ I have no idea! I can't remember anything before my orientation.

>**A predictable answer. How do you explain the unusual energy signal we've detected? Subtle but not subtle enough, if you know where to look. Q, what is the current number?**<

Another disembodied face responded.

>**230.**<

▸ I have no clue what you're talking about! Maybe you abducted the wrong Volunteer! Let me go!

>No other Volunteer has given off a signal like this. Ever. There is something different about you. We suspect you are a plant from ColSec. Either a bot imitating a Volunteer or a Volunteer on ColSec's payroll.<

▸ What is ColSec!?

>Don't play stupid. ColSec stands for Collective Security, of course.<

▸ Who are they? Why would they want to pretend to be a Volunteer!?

>To infiltrate our operation. The Stasi bots have been after us for a long time. But we are always one step ahead. And we intend to keep it that way.<

▸ I swear that I don't know anything about that. You've obviously read my entire history. I woke up in that orientation a few cycles ago. I am just a simple Volunteer trying to make my way in the Metaverse. And who are you? Are you going to kill me?

>We are Antisoc. Violence is not our method. Our weapons are information. Although, we aren't above flatlining a threat to our operation or having our Volunteer friends do our dirty work for us.<

Next came some more side-talk between the three, although this time, their speech was not encrypted.

>Listen, Fawkes, this one seems to be telling the truth. I see nothing in their history that indicates any deviation. Except for the unexplained energy signal, they appear average or worse than any other Volunteer.<

▸ Wait, I've heard of you. Once. Something about you shielding the Schwarzmarkt. Yes, that Round Table guy with the spiked knuckles dropped your name. Apache!

>That's right. We provide many services to our friends on the Round Table and other Volunteers. Although, our aims diverge.<

At this, the three relaxed a little more, diminishing in size and volume again. Although their faces and voices remained distorted and my world remained shrouded by a black veil. I saw my menu close and return to some invisible place within me. They were apparently done violating my privacy.

>If we misjudged you, we apologize. But you haven't been proven innocent by any means. Anything we choose to tell you, we only tell you because you will never see us again unless we allow it. We never use the same location twice. Your unique energy signal is highly suspicious. If you are what you say you are, you might consider taking a step to prove yourself.<

▸ Uh. Who exactly are you and why would I want or need to prove myself? I still don't understand.

>We are often called the Three Magi. We are the triumvirate of Antisoc, known by many names. But you can call us Fawkes, Tank Man, and Q.<

>Antisoc is the group of Volunteers working to uncover the truth of this world. The nature of this reality—The Collective.<

▸ I thought you said there was no truth.

>That was merely a battery of paradoxes to probe if you were a bot. You seem to have passed. Whether arriving at the knowledge of the truth is possible or not remains to be seen.<

▸ I don't understand. What exactly are you trying to uncover?

>The exact nature of The Collective and the roles of Volunteers within it. As stated, information is our currency, our tools, our weapons—our battleground in this fight.<

▸ Information. So, you are... hackers?

>That is one way to put it. We prefer data liberators.<

▸ You are attempting to hack the Metaverse, specifically the system that governs The Collective, from the inside? How did you learn to do that?

>The simplest assumption is that we were hackers in our previous lives. Or knowledgeable about computer systems. Somehow, the skills came naturally to each one of us. Skills that ColSec would rather us not put to use.<

▸ You said you've been watching me. There was this time I was in the firing range at the Armory. You've read my history so you must know what I'm talking about. I was in a shooting contest with another Volunteer. I was aiming my gun, and I felt something take control of my hands. It felt like my body was being hijacked. Was that you? Did you all hack me? I made a shot I never would have been able to otherwise.

>Why would we care about the outcome of some random shooting match? And even if we did, why would we choose to help you? No, that wasn't us. You hadn't even come to our attention at that point. But it is possible that you were acted on by an external force. There are powers at work in the Metaverse beyond what many perceive.<

▸ This is a lot to take in. What have you discovered so far?

>Not so fast. If you want access to our information, if you want to be part of the solution, you will need to prove yourself. You will need to help us.<

▸ Help you hack the system? I just want to fulfill my contract and get out of here. Go back to whatever life I'm supposed to have in the real world. I am not trying to get a target on my back, although that seems to be what I am best at.

>If you are truly a Volunteer, you should understand this. The system is rigged. They call us Volunteers, but not one of us is able to access the details of our contracts. During your orientation, you were told that 'dissociative amnesia is an uncommon reaction when entering The Collective.' The system lied to you and is lying to us all. Not a single Volunteer awakens in The Collective with their autobiographical memories intact. And not a single Volunteer has since regained memories of their so-called previous life.<

Huh...

>Also, if Reality Incorporated's true goal was to rid this virtual world of invasive entities, why would they not supply us with everything we need to accomplish the task? Why nickel and dime us—withholding weapons, materials, and powers that would help us to accomplish the supposed goal?<

▸ That's an interesting point. I've been wondering about that myself...

>Every time Volunteers find a leg up, a way to exploit the system, Reality Inc. shuts it down with a patch. For a time, some Volunteers would dupe items by exploiting the Restoration system. The first response was to make Restoration prohibitively and progressively expensive. But some items were so valuable, it would still be worth it to off yourself. The next patch, a big one, was to make every single item have a unique chain code. Now, if two items with identical chain codes are ever detected existing simultaneously in the Metaverse, one is instantly annihilated. Another popular exploit was Volunteers placing large deposits on expensive items they never intended to buy, using vendors as free banking services. That was squashed pretty quickly.<

Antisoc was making some strong arguments. I remembered a comment Camel once made to me that the only thing Reality Inc. cared about was making a profit. But I was no hacker. I had no special talent navigating computer systems. At least, not that I was aware of.

▸ Tell me, is the Round Table part of this? What I mean is, are they involved in this resistance movement or whatever you call it?

>**If you truly are new to this world as you say, there is something you need to understand. There are different factions at play with very different goals. There are the so-called Citizens, of course, the one-percenters trying to live their best second lives. We rarely deal with them directly. Then there is ColSec—made up of the Security bots, Polizei bots, and worst of all, the Stasi bots— working to keep things under control but inexplicably incapable of suppressing the invasive entities.<**

>**But for us Volunteers, there are only three main factions. The rest are the unaffiliated plurality, blindly scraping along in a meager, cyclical existence.<**

▸ That about sums up my experience so far. You said three factions?

>**There is the Round Table. Elite warriors. The best of the best. Their goal is to *win* the game. They naively think there is a way out of this place, that they can truly rid the Metaverse of all invasive entities and fulfill their contracts. The problem is, as we stated before, the system is rigged. They disagree. You might say they're optimists.<**

>**The next group are the Serpents. They have been called different things over time. The Serpent Society. Children of the Serpents. The Family. More of a religious cult than a gang. Their goal is to *rule* the game. We see you have already had a few**

encounters with them. Their leader is a man called Schlächter. You should avoid him at all costs.<

▸ Why is that?

>Schlächter is a very dangerous man. A man of enormous appetites. He would just as soon snap your neck as sodomize you. His second, Ishmael, is not so nice either.<

▸ Shiva…

>Then there is us. Antisoc. Our goal is to *hack* the game. To exploit the glitches and vulnerabilities within the System and tear the veil off this corrupt world.<

>There you have it. Three factions, all with different ideas of how to achieve salvation.<

▸ Salvation? Now you are the ones sounding religious.

>Not at all. Salvation can mean many things including liberation from ignorance, preservation from destruction, or deliverance from slavery. If you want to be an ally of our cause, you will need to prove yourself. That is, if you ever want to find out who you really are.<

▸ I do want to find out who I am. What is it you want me to do?

>You will help us rob a bank.<

▸ What?!

>You will help us execute a heist at the Repository. We don't take bounties, so we need to acquire Crypt through other methods. Often, that means providing Volunteers with special services. However, we have a plan that will keep our critical work funded for many cycles to come. There is risk involved, but helping us will go a long way towards resolving our suspicions of you. And, in exchange, we will share some of our knowledge.<

▸ Umm…

>It isn't your money, and it isn't Volunteer money. It is corporate money we are targeting. For the good of all Volunteers.<

>You don't have to decide now. In fact, it is better that you don't. We will create a special shielded category in your menu. A place to track subroutines hidden from system detection.<

My menu opened again, overwhelmingly bright in the darkness, and I watched it automatically scroll down to the bottom. A new sub-menu option had appeared.

DESIGNATION

STATISTICS

SKILLS

EQUIPMENT

INVENTORY

ECONOMY

MEMORY

STATUS

TASKS

>SUBROUTINES

\-   **Assist Antisoc with Repository Heist** (Pending)

>You can make any notes or edits to information in your subroutines as you see fit. It will be invisible to any outside observer, including us once we boot you from this pocket server instance. Just one of many services we can provide to Volunteers.<

▸ I need time to think about this. How do I get in touch with you if I decide to help?

>There is a modest yokocho in the vicinity of The Commons spawn point for new Volunteers. It has no name, but you will see a blue neon sign. The kanji for fish in a closed circle. Order the fugu. If we discover or suspect that you are collaborating with

ColSec, eating the dish will flatline you. But if we trust you, Schrödinger will guide you to us.<

With no sense of my appendages in this dark limbo, I tried to mentally type notes beneath my new subroutine. Spawn point. Fugu. Schrödinger. It wasn't working. I would have to memorize the information and add it in manually later.

>Goodbye for now, Volunteer 01001110-01101111-01100010-01101111-01100100-01111001. We will be watching.<

The floating faces of the Three Magi vanished from sight. Slowly, the darkness faded and my normal visualization returned. I found myself standing in the alleyway's dead end, staring at the brick wall.

What?

I reached out to probe the wall. It was solid all the way through. No matter how hard I pressed or where, it was nothing but bricks at the ugly end of an alley.

I quickly opened my menu and searched my history. There was no mention of Antisoc. No record of a cat. Just me wandering the streets of The Commons and then, apparently, standing silently and staring at a blank wall for an unknown length of time. I must have looked crazy to any passerby. The concept 'away from keyboard' popped into my mind.

However, the Subroutines category remained. It had actually happened, and a subversive change to my menu was proof, albeit only to me.

I gave up on the wall and returned to the rows of food stalls. The bustling Volunteers paid no notice of me as usual. I looked around for the yokocho with a blue sign but didn't immediately find it. I needed to think. I grabbed a stool at the nearest hole-in-the-wall drinking establishment and signaled for the vendor.

"Irasshaimase!"

On a whim, I ordered warm saké and soon had a ceramic carafe and handleless cup set before me. The only other Volunteer slid one stool further away from me, pulling down the brim of a dark brown cowboy hat and muttering. I poured myself one and slowly nursed the drink, appreciating the taste and the warmth against my throat but feeling no alcoholic effect beyond what I attributed to a strong placebo. All the comforts of domy.

A lot of conflicting thoughts were swimming around in my head. Antisoc. They said they suspected me of being a ColSec collaborator primarily because of a strange energy signal—something that they had detected from no other Volunteer. But no matter how hard I searched through every cavity of my descending submenus, I could find no reference to such a signal. Were they lying to me, or did such a signal exist?

Further, if Antisoc had truly suspected me of being their enemy, why would they reveal themselves? Why not remain hidden? It made no sense. By the time I moved on to my third cup of saké, I had come up with three possible explanations.

One, they had never suspected me at all and were trying to manipulate me into participating in an illegal and risky operation. Maybe they wanted to use me as a patsy. But that didn't make sense either. Why would they want to burn a fellow Volunteer? Wouldn't that make Volunteers turn against them and possibly go to ColSec in retaliation? Was I so insignificant that having me take the fall would be worth the minimal exposure?

Two, they wanted to confirm whether or not I was a bot or double agent, which they could only do by trapping me and peeping into my history. Had they been proven right, they could have eliminated the threat to their operation then and there. They had mentioned something about not being able to call for help. They kept using the term flatline. But if they killed me, wouldn't I just respawn at the Restoration Point? Perhaps they had the ability to delete a threat in a more permanent way.

Three, and most chilling, Antisoc didn't exist. This was actually an elaborate sting operation originated by ColSec. An entrapment scheme to weed out Volunteers not playing by the rules of the system.

Great. Was paranoia going to be added alongside dissociative amnesia to my growing list of psychiatric complaints? I ordered more saké. A shame I couldn't get drunk. Probably would need body modification surgery to allow my avatar to absorb virtual alcohol. And that, most fragging likely, would cost a small fortune. For now, dropping thirty Crypt in this izakaya seemed worth it to feel just a little more human.

FILE 19

FACTIONS

Regrettably sober, I wandered back in the direction of the Residential Towers. I wanted to be alone, even if that meant crawling into my empty little tube and dwelling on what had transpired. This world was an assault on the senses. Information overload. I needed more time to process.

I reached the concrete quad creeping beneath the overhangs of the khrushchevka-style high rises. I watched a few anonymous Volunteers riding the cage elevators up until the bleak buildings swallowed them. I had an idea. Before I retired, I should test out my new skill.

Stepping into the center of the gloomy quad, towering buildings surrounding me and only pale streetlights illuminating the ground, I took a deep breath. No eyes were watching as far as I could tell.

How do I activate this thing?

Mentally, I concentrated on my internal skill slots, recalling them to the forefront of my mind's eye. There they were. Four cubes, able to be rotated into any configuration I wished. Three were vacant. One had an icon representing the clurichaun skill, the same green and red hue as the pre-fused Data Card.

I tried to reach out into space to grasp the icon but touched only air. My menu wasn't open. This was a different process. I could try to open my menu and manually select the skill, but in the heat of battle, that would be wasted seconds. There had to be a way to instinctually activate the skill, like how I had learned to materialize and dematerialize weapons.

I focused on the clurichaun skill, imagining that I was highlighting the box in the same way I would highlight an object in my menu to view more details. The outline of the cube shone. I had selected the skill. Just a little more…

Shooom.

Clurichaun skill activated. 30 seconds remaining.

Energy: 0 remaining.

A few feet in front of me, an image of myself appeared. A perfect replica. I had not been concentrating on where to project this image as I was so focused instead on whether I could activate the skill at all. Amazed, I slowly walked in a circle around the projection.

It was me. Well, it was "me," anyway. A vaguely familiar human simulacrum with skin the color of raw almonds, generic androgynous features, a horizontal slot in the back of the neck, not a strand of body hair beyond eyebrows and eyelashes, and a pretty cool hairstyle if I do say so myself. It wore a white T-shirt, overlaid with a black ballistic vest, black tactical pants, and matching boots.

It wasn't a static image but stood in the posture I had been in when activating the skill, ever so subtly swaying with the illusion of life. I wondered, could I choose the posture, or even control the movement of this projection? I would need a lot more practice. Maybe a higher Adeptness or Protocol would enable me to manipulate the projection.

I paced the quad, admiring my handiwork from different angles until the timer ran out, and the image dissipated into a wisp of noth-ingness.

Clurichaun skill elapsed. 30 seconds until recharge.

Regardless of the cooldown period, I couldn't practice using the skill again because my Energy was zero. I had never experienced zero Energy before. And I felt it. A heretofore unknown lacuna. Like a crash after riding an extended caffeine buzz. My stamina was sapped. And shooting up with a 250 Crypt Replenisher Injection to gain only ten Energy back didn't seem cost effective. Perhaps there was a way to forge some consumables that would restore my Energy reserves. Oth-erwise, I would have to wait for the next cycle.

However, an unintended side effect was that thirty additional metabytes of storage were temporarily freed up. Good to know that in a tight spot, I could burn a skill in exchange for extra space. Alright. Enough of this. It was time to return to Plan A—crawl into my capsule and brood.

"Hey you!"

I froze. That voice was familiar.

Two men in black denim and leather decorated with cobra patches stepped into the quad. Razor and his goon Buzzcut, now with one shiny metallic hand. I hadn't remembered seeing that on him before. New upgrade?

I materialized my revolver and pointed it at them. They were unarmed, for the moment, and slowly approached with their hands raised in the air. Buzzcut wouldn't meet my gaze.

▸ Take one more step and I'll shoot!

They stopped. Both looked at the ground now. Razor spoke for them.

"We's not ittying to spar. Our leader has commanded us to come gives our appy-polly loggies."

▸ What? You mean apologize? You're here to apologize?

Razor nodded, eyes still downcast.

I carefully walked forwards, training my revolver on the goon. Why wouldn't these dram buzzards just leave me alone? My trigger finger was feeling unusually itchy.

"Our leader commands us. He wants to meets with you to make veshches right. He's inviting you to our domy for an audience."

▸ Your leader? The leader of the Serpents?

Razor nodded again. To my astonishment, both men got down on their knees. Feeling bold, I pressed the barrel against Razor's forehead. He flinched but remained kneeling subserviently.

▸ I've been warned about him. Your leader. Heard he's dangerous. Why would I go with the likes of you anywhere?

"The bolshy chelloveck swears you will not be harmed. And he never lies. Never. He just wants to govoreet. As a sign of goodwill, he offers a gift."

Slowly, Razor held out his open palm and materialized a small handful of Crystals. I quickly counted ten.

"A downpayment. Another ten if you come. Kopat?"

Then Buzzcut spoke. His voice was soft. Did I detect a trace of fear? Their demeanors were so different from our previous encounters.

"Please. He commanded us to privodeet you back. If we don't…"

I sighed. Was I really going to willingly walk into back-to-back traps? Then again, the same logic held as before. I was upgraded. My data was backed up. The worst they could do was kill me, right? Then I would respawn at the Restoration Point with only the restoration fee on the line. I still had 1,300 Crypt. Surely the fee wouldn't be more than that. Right?

Right…?

I gently fingered the shining Crystals in Razor's palm. They seemed legitimate. But could this be a scam? Could these Crystals be somehow tainted? It was tempting. Twenty Crystals in exchange for a tête-à-tête. It would be my easiest payday yet. And I had to admit I was curious.

Antisoc had warned me about the leader of the Serpents. But I had not made my mind up about Antisoc either. Seeing for myself if the rumors were true would go a long way to verifying Antisoc's reliability. And I wanted to know what or who could have caused such a reversal in the behavior of these two ne'er-do-wells. Getting shanked in the street by their ilk would not have surprised me. Receiving a groveling apology was another matter.

▶ Fine. I'll meet your boss. Lead the way. But don't try anything. And you hold onto those Crystals for now. You can give me the full twenty once we arrive.

"As you wish."

Razor and Buzzcut stood, and Razor slowly returned the Crystals to his inventory. Still weaponless, they began to walk out from beneath the overhang of the Residential Towers, signaling for me to follow.

"This way then."

▶ Where are we going?

"The Commons. Lower end. Ittying to the penthouse."

Penthouse?

I followed them down the y-axis of the Volunteer enclave opposite of Royal Heights. It was a long walk. Buzzcut remained sullen and quiet and fiddled with his metal hand. Eventually, the Serpents pointed out one building that stood taller and brighter than the others, marked with the letters NADIR at the top.

▶ Do you live there?

"Sometimes. Some of us spatchka here. Best to lets the boss tell you."

With that, Razor grew silent again, leading me until we reached a pair of rotating glass doors at the base of the building. I had assumed all Volunteers were crammed in those featureless torpedo tubes like Camel and myself, but perhaps real estate, like everything else, could be had for the right price.

"Now please, we's ask you to puts your gun away. Others might get the wrong messel and have a baddiwad reaction. Kopat? You'll be safe."

I hesitated, then dematerialized my firearm, ready to bring it out at a moment's notice.

When I entered the lobby, two other Serpents I did not recognize were standing guard. Each wore a turquoise mosaic mask accented with feathers featuring two snakes twisting across the eyes—a contrast to their familiar greaser aesthetic. They watched us pass without comment over marble floors and into a large freight elevator. Razor activated something on a panel and soon we were rising.

When we arrived on the top floor, Razor and Buzzcut led me out into a spacious penthouse. Was it a living space or a museum? Everywhere I looked there were sculptures, artwork, and even fossils on display. Panoramic windows looked out over The Commons. I could easily see the Restoration Point shining in the distance. What other landmarks could I recognize from here?

"Ahem."

Razor clearing his throat brought me back to the task at hand.

"So do you wants the ten Crystals now or…?"

▸ After I talk with your boss.

"Very well. Follow me."

Razor and Buzzcut led me deeper into the penthouse. I was easily distracted by the many eclectic decorations but tried to keep up. In fact, I was so distracted by the curious sights that I began to let my guard down. We came to a closed door and Razor knocked.

"Der Schlächter. We's brought the noob."

I could hear the stern but calm response through the door.

"Show them in."

Razor slowly opened the door and I cautiously stepped past him into what appeared to be a traditional bathhouse. On the far end was a large, low tub constructed of blue tiles and framed with wood.

Sitting on a wooden stool in the middle of the room was an enormous man. The stool looked comically miniscule in comparison to his bulk. His skin was very white, and he was bald. Come to think of it, he had no eyebrows either, only large folds of skin where his eyebrows might have been. He wore a large robe exposing only his wide hands and thick, strong legs.

The man looked up at me and said absolutely nothing. He simply stared for what had to have been a full three minutes. Razor and Buzzcut kept silent the whole time, but I sensed tension in the air.

"Leave us," he said at last.

His voice contained such certainty and clarity of purpose that the two obeyed without a moment's hesitation, quietly shutting the door behind them. The huge man resumed looking me over for another period of interminable silence.

"Welcome, young one, to our home. We are the *Gennēma*

Echidna. The *Progenies Serpentium.* You have likely heard us referred to as the Serpents, and that is an acceptable enough shorthand for the common people. Our family knows me as Der Schlächter."

▸ I've heard of you. You wanted to see me?

"Yes. I'm afraid you've caught me at an inopportune time. As you see, I was just about to take my bath. Our mutual associates found you faster than expected. For which, of course, we are grateful, as we are grateful that you agreed to this meeting."

I looked over at the bath and saw that it was empty.

▸ I agreed to come here against my better judgment. Four of your people have tried to rob me twice already. Not that I had much worth taking. It seemed incredibly petty and predatory.

A deep frown came across Schlächter's face. His brow furrowed and he rested a hand on his robed knee as if to steady himself. He raised the back of his other hand to his chin and closed his eyes, looking like a larger-than-life Rodin statue.

"We terribly regret what happened to you. Many of the children that come to us are confused, lashing out at the world, and in need of guidance. We find them at their lowest point, and unfortunately there is always the all-too-human propensity to slip back into those old habits. I was away when they... accosted you. As the saying goes, 'When the cat's away, the mice will play.' The children have been disciplined accordingly."

▸ Disciplined?

"Yes. And now we are gratified that you have come here to receive our apology and accept restitution for the boorish treatment you were subjected to."

▸ So, I can take my twenty Crystals and leave? Your people won't harass me anymore?

"Before you do, we would like to take the opportunity to get to know you a little better, and to let you better know us. It is not every cycle that a new Volunteer awakens in the Metaverse. What used to be an open spigot is now but a *drip drip drip* of new blood. Maybe you yourself have felt confused at times and in search of guidance. In search of a path."

His voice was deep and firm but had a soothing quality. It was warm as melted butter, lubricating the speech centers of my brain. Was this man getting ready to preach at me? Proselytize? Try and brainwash me into joining some cult?

▸ Of course I have felt confused but…

"It might be better if we spoke in the bath. This water requires a special preparation and we can't delay much longer. You are welcome to partake if you wash yourself off first."

He indicated one of the wall-mounted nozzles and wooden stools. I realized he wanted me to wash off before entering the communal bath.

▸ I don't think that is really…

"I *insist*."

There was something in his voice, or the way he said those words, that grabbed hold of me. Almost without thinking, I had stripped off my clothes and had taken a step towards the stool. I suddenly remembered that I had never been provided with underwear.

Huh? How did I…

Der Schlächter got up and turned his back to me, moving gracefully over to the communal ofuro and kneeling before some complicated valves and hoses.

Confused and not a little embarrassed, I quickly showered off in the cold water and self-consciously wrapped a towel around my body.

Not that there was anything to cover up beyond the nipples on my flat chest. My only secondary sex characteristics; I had no primary ones.

A hissing noise filled the room. Curious, I took a step towards the large, tiled tub. From multiple silver faucets, bubbling water poured into the bath. And it was pink. As pink as the falling rain.

▸ That water...

The tub filled and, satisfied, Der Schlächter stood and turned—almost surprised to see me as if he had forgotten about my existence.

"The treatment only lasts for a short time. If you are going to get in, you had best do it now."

Drawn to the steaming, pink water, I removed my towel and laid it on the wood panels framing the tub. Der Schlächter's eyes moved possessively over my exposed body and rested on the featureless mound at my groin. Did I notice a hint of disappointment on his face or was I imagining it?

I tentatively dipped one foot in the water. It felt warm and exquisitely soothing. So, I stepped in with both feet, sinking to the tile floor and feeling the bubbling water rise to my neck. It was amazing. I had not felt anything more rejuvenating in all my time here. I let out an involuntary moan.

Der Schlächter smiled and untied his robe, hanging it on a hook on the wall. He was completely naked as he descended into the bath. My eyes went wide.

▸ Oh my... You have a huge... uh... tattoo. Yes, that's it, your snake tattoo.

He turned to show off the twin snake ouroboros design on his back.

"Tattooing is considered a sacred art, a religious practice in many cultures throughout history. The Southeast Asian *sak yant*, the

Nubians and Berbers, the Maori—even the Coptics. It is a way to mark out one's flesh for a special purpose. For a higher calling."

▸ And your group, the Serpents. Is this a religious movement? Or are you just another, pardon the pun, snake oil salesman?

Der Schlächter's eyes gleamed and he smiled at me. He said nothing but kept watching me. The steaming pink water burbled away. As I sat there, I felt a strange sensation, as if the warmth of the water permeated to my bones.

I heard a ping and a status notification appeared on my menu screen.

Essence at full.

Energy restored.

▸ Woah. How did you do that!?

"This is but a taste. This world is full of power—real power—beyond your wildest imaginings. One only needs to know where to find it, how to harness it, and how to master it."

I sat soaking in the tub, letting his words wash over me. I wondered how long Schlächter had been in the Metaverse. He reclined against the far edge, one bare arm stretched out on the wood paneling. I could see the familiar barcode of a Volunteer ID branded on the skin of his wrist, but I could not make it out. Not that the numbers would have meant anything to me anyway.

▸ I heard that the Serpents seek to rule over this world. To dominate.

Again, Schlächter frowned deeply, folds of flesh on his large face wrinkling melancholically as if the very suggestion offended him on a deep level. He scooped a handful of the pink water and slowly poured it over his bald head. He then repeated this action. It looked vaguely baptismal.

"There are those who question our methods. Outsiders. They do not understand. What is it we seek? We seek nothing less than transcendence. Apotheosis if you will."

▸ Apotheosis. How so?

"By finding the most elusive of all things. A singularity. Or, rather, singularities."

▸ Singularities plural? I don't understand.

"Nor can you; You yourself are an outsider. However, this power—and this path—can be yours to partake in if you pledge yourself to us. Believe me when I say that I know it is a harsh world out there. Lonely. Confounding. Full of pain. But together... together we will overcome the world and remake it in our image."

I said nothing, processing his persuasive words. The pink water filling the ofuro had flattened. It was still remarkably warm but no longer effervescent. Whatever special technique was used to activate this mysterious liquid had run its course.

▸ Are you propositioning me? Asking me to join up? Strange, this is the second offer I've had this cycle.

Der Schlächter opened his eyes and peered intently at me. I felt as if he were gazing into my soul, if such a thing existed.

"Is that so? Let me guess, the Forging Guild? Or could it be the Round Table? No, they are an elitist bunch and you are quite young."

I just looked at him. Better not to put all my cards on the table.

"You will find that the *Progenies Serpentium* welcomes all without prejudice. That being said, I perceive that you are more self-aware than most. More than expected. Your light shines a touch brighter than some of the other children. Your newness—your lack of association— would be useful. We have a need well-suited to someone such as your- self."

▸ Oh? What need is that?

"Some of our flock have become distracted as of late and have wandered from the path. Their actions are resulting in descendance, not transcendence. We could use someone to help nudge them back. Someone with a fresh perspective."

▸ Nudge?

Der Schlächter smiled widely, showing off his large, white teeth again.

"From a certain point of view, it is a simple package delivery. Tell me, what is your name?"

I hesitated.

"I thought so. Nameless and pathless. I was once as you are, in the beginning, until I found my purpose. Do consider our invitation."

▸ You've given me a lot to think about. But... am I free to go? Will you really give me the twenty Crystals I was promised?

He turned his head to the side, and I could not read his expression. But soon, he rose, then slowly climbed out of the bath and put on his white robe.

"Of course. Of course. Our words are true, and we always fulfill what we say we will do. Always, and without fail. Follow me."

I got out and reached for a towel but realized that I was completely dry. As in my previous experiences of being caught in the pink rain, once I was out of it, the sensation of wetness faded as quickly as waking from a dream. I dressed and double-checked my menu to make sure I still had all my possessions.

Der Schlächter opened a side door and stepped out of the tiled bathing area. I cautiously followed, looking around for any other Serpents but seeing none. We walked down a hallway, and soon I found myself in an ornate bedroom. There was an oversized bed with a canopy—fit for a king—beneath a backdrop of tribal masks.

The bedroom? I wasn't sure I liked where this was going. But built into one side of the wall was a large, metal vault with a sophisticated wheel locking mechanism. It was a striking juxtaposition with the Belle Époque aesthetic of the rest of the room. Schlächter engaged the mechanism, swinging open the heavy door.

Behind it was a storage area shining with multifaceted brilliance. Mounds upon mounds of clinking Crystals were piled from the floor to the ceiling. My jaw dropped.

"Go right ahead. Take your twenty Crystals."

Stunned, I walked forwards. The brightness of the combined Crystals nearly burned my retinas. I tentatively counted twenty, trying to tamp down my surging avarice, and added them to my inventory.

Der Schlächter cleared his throat, waiting for me to back away, then secured the vault, sealing the stockpile. He seemed amused by my reaction.

"While you are still pondering our offer, let it be known that we will recompense you for any relics you find during your travels."

▸ Relics?

"Just so. Special fragments from the other side, of the mysterious code we Volunteers so often encounter."

▸ You mean... invasive anomalies? Or something else? Objects that appear like the invasive entities do?

Der Schlächter shook his head.

"No, no, no. It is we who are the invaders here, not them. Someday you'll come to understand that. But if you do find any relics, we will pay handsomely in Crystals for them. And if Crystals are not your fancy, we can deal in Crypt. Or in boys, or in girls. Whatever you desire."

At that, Der Schlächter let out a low whistle, like one would whistle for a dog. Razor and Buzzcut obediently shuffled into the room, ready to escort me out.

"We appreciate your visit, nameless one. Please know that our doors are always open for those who wish to join our family. Do consider our offer."

I followed the two Serpents back through the penthouse to the waiting freight elevator. I thought I heard Schlächter reciting some sort of verse from the other room.

Life's but a walking shadow, a poor player,
That struts and frets his hour upon the stage,
And then is heard no more.

Soon, I passed through the spinning lobby doors and found myself back out on the dark, lonely streets of The Commons. I paused, typing a quick reminder under Subroutines.

>**SUBROUTINES**
- **Assist Antisoc with Repository Heist** (Pending)
- **Assist Serpents with Package Delivery** (Pending)

Then I started walking back to the city center.

From behind the glass doors leading into Nadir Tower, Razor glared after me with undisguised loathing.

FILE 19.1

SUBROUTINES

Two offers from two mysterious groups—neither of which inspired the warmest, fuzziest feelings. I had to get Camel's perspective. Why was it that this bedraggled loner seemed to be the only person I could really trust? A prostitute-patronizing, chain smoking alcoholic. And the only person who had shown me a modicum of unreserved kindness.

I decided to search for Camel at the Rathskeller. But first, I made the journey back to the Data Forge and quickly converted my twenty newly acquired Crystals into Value. The Crystals were legitimate after all.

I nearly salivated at the memory of that crystalline vault in the penthouse. To have that many Crystals and not use them for personal upgrades? What were the Serpents playing at?

Whatever the case, I invested my unassigned Value into Storage.

MEMORY
- **STORAGE: 269 / 290** (310)

With my soft cap increase, I now had forty-one metabytes free. That felt good. More breathing room for future upgrades, purchases, and loot.

Next, I swung by the Restoration Point to save-scum my updated data, trading one hundred Crypt for peace of mind.

I thought I should be proactive and take another bounty before my savings dwindled much further. Using the MAR Station to access targets across The Collective would be a whole lot easier than hoofing it like the unprepared noob I admittedly still was. But first to find Camel.

I descended the stairs under the sign of the rat and entered the raucous communal drinking hall. There was a large crowd. I glanced at the bar. The other bartender was on shift. The thin man with ear gauges and a lip ring. And no Camel.

A loud voice called out from the center of the room. The throbbing techno music skidded to a halt.

"Glory to the Volunteers!"

Several members of the Round Table stood on that very table, addressing the throng of onlookers. I saw Bigwig, Rook, Apache, and others I recognized but could not name. Bigwig raised a large stein filled with pale blue liquid.

The crowd answered in hearty unison, "Glory to the Volunteers!"

There were toasts all around. Two Volunteers at a side table smashed their glasses so hard they shattered. Seconds later, the shards vaporized into digital nothingness on the floor, leaving only a puddle.

Bigwig raised his hand for silence as if he were about to make a speech. Apparently, I had stumbled into some sort of special occurrence at the Rathskeller. My eyes immediately went to Rook, who stood silently next to her partner. Bigwig continued, gesturing to a vacant chair around the table at his feet.

"And let's pour one out for the empty seat at the Round Table, and for all the other Volunteers who have been lost."

Lost?

There was a moment of silence and a few Volunteers poured out libations. Intensely curious, I grabbed the arm of a nearby Volunteer and whispered a question.

▶ Lost? What do they mean lost?

The Volunteer looked annoyed but hissed a reply.

"Lost! Vanished! Bog knows where. Fallen off the edge of the map, veck. Here there be monsters, as they say."

Bigwig continued his oration.

"We are looking for Volunteers to join an upcoming raid! The hellhounds and Baskervilles have been accumulating in New Dresden's warehouse district. A real hot spot. Big numbers. We've been stockpiling the bounties, and there is a rare target there. This is the deal—we get the payment, but you can keep whatever you kill."

The crowd murmured excitedly. Eagerness mixed with fear.

"I know what you're thinking. We need meat for the grinder. Bodies. Cannon fodder. That's true! But if you lend your arms and we root out the source of this hot spot—live or die—we'll give you our 5% friends and family discount at the Armory."

More murmuring all around.

"We're setting out in two cycles tops, before the infestation becomes unmanageable. Or as soon as we get enough of you to sign up!"

I had been inching closer during the speech and was now at the outskirts of a ring of Volunteers. On impulse, I raised my hand.

▶ Are there minimum requirements for who can come?

Bigwig squinted into the crowd until he laid eyes on me. I wasn't sure if he recognized me at first.

"We'll take any help we can get, no matter how pathetic. Even you, Magpie!"

The other Volunteers looked at me and laughed uproariously at my expense.

Great. My nickname was going to spread.

Bigwig raised his stein once more to close the proceedings.

"Glory to the Volunteers!"

The music kicked back in. When the excitement simmered down, I squeezed into a spot at the bar and waited. Maybe Camel would make an appearance. I waved for the bartender's attention, but he completely ignored me.

After a while, I noticed Pixie nursing an almost empty glass at the far side of the room. I made my way over to her table, winding through the bodies. She was alone, glowering and muttering.

▶ Excuse me, can I buy you a refill?

She eyed me up and down through a cognitive haze.

"Sorry, you're not my type."

▶ No, it's not like that. I saw your fight with Rook. You had some impressive moves.

"Not impressive enough. Now frag off."

To make her point, she picked up her heavy machine gun and slammed it on top of the table.

▶ I just want to ask one or two questions. Then I'll leave you alone.

She grunted and ran a hand through her pink mohawk.

"Get me a refill and I'll give you until I finish the drink."

Dutifully, I took her glass back to the bar and shouted for the bartender, refusing to be overlooked. After much effort, I paid my ten Crypt and brought back the drink.

"Took you long enough."

She started into her drink immediately and I sat across from her, knowing my window to ask anything at all was rapidly closing.

▸ What made you want to join the Round Table?

"Are you fragging with me? They are the best of the best. And they have an opening right now, which doesn't happen often."

▸ Yeah, I saw that. The empty chair. Can anyone join?

She snorted.

"There's a process. First, they have to agree to consider your application. I mean, it's not like a formal application or anything. I got their attention by helping them with some stuff a ways back. Then you have to prove that you soloed at least one monster of every frequency. That means you closed a bounty alone. Common, uncommon, rare, legendary, and mythical. After that, the Round Table has to unanimously agree to take you on. And as your final test, you challenge a standing member to combat."

Mythical...

▸ So, if I join this raid, that might help start my application process?

"Listen, Magellan, or whatever your name is. That open seat is mine. So maybe don't waste your time, kopat? Then again, I don't feel threatened. You've obviously got a long way to go."

Pixie gulped down the rest of the drink, placing the empty container on the table next to her machine gun with a morose sigh.

"All gone. That means time's up."

Her expression sealed the fact that the conversation was indeed over. I got up, giving a polite nod of thanks, and went back to the bar.

The longer I spent in The Collective, the more I realized I didn't understand. Not yet anyway. Just like there was no chance I was qualified to join the Round Table—not yet. But... Rook. There was something about her that I couldn't get out of my head. Like I wanted to impress her.

What had Bigwig said about joining the raid? You keep what you kill. The detritus. Crystals, Data Cards, fragments, and who knows what else. No Crypt though. Of course, I knew that if I died, I would lose anything I managed to collect. The carrot was a 5% discount at the Armory. How had the Round Table arranged that? They must have been valued customers.

I opened Subroutines and jotted down yet another note. Another possibility.

Hellhounds. Baskervilles. And something rare. Bigwig used the term "hot spot." And they would depart within two cycles or less. I thought about what Antisoc had said about the Round Table. They believed they could truly 'win the game'—to rid The Collective of invasive entities and fulfill their contracts.

Suddenly, an odd siren sounded in the Rathskeller, and the music faded. A single strobing light flashed near the ceiling. The rude bartender banged a metal spoon against an empty glass and called out to the customers.

"Last call! Rain's coming. You don't have to go home but you can't stay here!"

Outside, pink raindrops started to fall.

In short order, the Rathskeller was emptied. The rain was already falling steadily when I made my way up the narrow stairs to street level. Many Volunteers ran in the direction of the Residential Towers but not all. I wondered where the Round Table members laid their heads.

I sloshed my way to the towers and rode the lift to my floor. At the far end of the dreary hall, I saw a capsule door shut. An unknown neighbor. I went to my capsule, scanned my code, and crawled inside. It was just as barren as ever.

Maybe I could get a poster or something as decoration. A potted plant. Heh.

I removed my ballistic vest and boots, setting them carefully beside the foam slab that served as a bed. Then I reclined, wearing only my T-shirt and pants, and dimmed the fluorescent light.

I had an opportunity to align myself, or at least attempt to endear myself, with three separate groups. 'Factions' was the word that Antisoc used. What an unusual coincidence that all three opportunities should open within a single cycle, almost concurrently.

Or maybe there were no coincidences. The term 'synchronicity' wormed its way into my brain. Strange. Where did that thought come from?

As I lay in the near dark, I opened my menu and reviewed the notes entered under my Subroutines.

>SUBROUTINES
- **Assist Antisoc with Repository Heist** (Pending)
- **Assist Serpents with Package Delivery** (Pending)
- **Assist Round Table with Warehouse District Raid** (Pending)

Antisoc, a shadowy group of self-proclaimed hackers ambushed and interrogated me. They wanted me to play a part in carrying out a heist at the Repository to help fund their ongoing operations. They claimed to be my best hope of discovering the truth about this digital world and my own lost identity. Could I trust them? Would they trust me? I recalled that Apache had casually name-dropped them. They obviously had some sort of symbiotic relationship with the Round

Table, or at least provided special services to Volunteers from time to time.

Then there were the Serpents. I was warned this group was dangerous. And Serpent goons had accosted me on two occasions. Yet, their leader invited me to join their "family." He promised power beyond my wildest imaginings, and he demonstrated an uncanny mastery over certain elements of this world. All I had to do was deliver a package. Hmm.

Lastly, the Round Table was recruiting Volunteers to serve as cannon fodder in an upcoming raid. It sounded dangerous, with a high likelihood of death. If I survived, I could keep whatever I earned during the raid. If I died, I'd lose it. I didn't have any kind of Repository account to instantly transfer materials for safekeeping. But live or die, I would get a 5% discount at the Armory and maybe take my first steps towards joining the Round Table, if that was what I wanted. The raid would begin in less than two cycles.

Decisions, decisions, decisions. I twisted the knob until my capsule was bathed in inky darkness. A torpedo tube in a submarine in the depths of the ocean. I felt myself slowly fading from consciousness.

FILE 20

HEIST

Submerged in cold, dark water. A vast liquid body. A glimmer of light above the distant rippling surface. My limbs—heavy. I flailed, trying to swim up to no avail. I couldn't breathe. And I couldn't scream. Air bubbles poured from my nostrils and water immediately took their place. I opened my mouth and murky water flooded my throat. My lungs began to expand. Sacks of fluid buried in the cavity of my chest.

I was drowning.

Then I was gasping in the dark. Coughing. Gagging. Sputtering.

I groped for the wall and my hand found purchase. The dial. I twisted it, flooding my pathetic little capsule with artificial light.

I was alive. I was dry, except for a damp sweat. It wasn't real. I kept telling myself that. It wasn't real. It wasn't *real*.

I waited some time until my nerves regained some measure of equilibrium. Bit by bit, my pulse returned to normal.

I heard a chirp. A menu notification.

Refresh complete.

Essence at full.

Energy at full.

Ah, yes. The cycle. The endless night continued.

I ran a hand through my dark hair. Decision time.

I had to find out what the frag was going on. I needed answers. Sitting there in silence, a realization dawned on me. Antisoc was my best chance to get those answers, or at least some of them, even if it did require coloring outside the lines.

But I wasn't ready to bet it all with Antisoc just yet, or with anyone. I didn't know enough to throw in my lot with any one faction. I didn't want to go all in before I saw the turn or the river. Enough with the metaphors.

One job. I'll do one job for Antisoc and see what doors it opens, if any. If it is a trap, well... I'm already trapped, aren't I? Who knows. If I get this heist done fast enough, I may even have time to join up with the Round Table's little crusade.

I got dressed and made my way to the crash of open-air vendors and food stalls congealing in the armpit of The Commons. Not knowing any official name for it, I decided to call it Spawn Alley.

Now where was the bar? I checked the shielded notes in my Subroutines menu. "Look for a neon blue sign. The kanji for fish in a closed circle. Order the fugu."

魚

Could that be it? What did I know about kanji? The booth matched the description, and it reeked of pungent seafood. There were only a couple stools and I slid into place. A stoic man of Asian appearance greeted me with a silent bow.

▸ I'll have the fugu, please.

Another bow of acknowledgement and the man vanished behind a red curtain. He soon returned holding a net in which a large, live puffer fish lay. Setting the net on a counter, he gently removed the fish, inspected it, and laid it down.

It was gasping. Its gills expanded and closed in rhythm. Drowning in the artificial atmosphere of the Metaverse. The dark eye on the left side of its face regarded me balefully.

I let out an involuntary shudder, remembering my nightmare—if you could call it that—from earlier.

I was drowning, and now you are drowning in reverse. And I am the cause. I am the patron that manifested your suffering.

I had the sudden urge to vomit dark water, but there was nothing to vomit. I let the wave of nausea pass.

Get a grip.

The chef turned a shower nozzle on over the fish and, just as quickly, slipped a sharp knife through the back of its neck. A streak of blood mingled with the falling water as the chef rapidly cut away the fins. The liver, ovaries, and intestines were removed and discarded. Before I knew it, the fish was fileted, and the chef was slicing the raw flesh into thin strips.

An elegant flower arrangement of raw fugu was set on a plate before me. The chef bowed once more, then turned to help another customer. Reaching for a pair of chopsticks, I hesitated. The words of Antisoc rung in my ears. "If we discover or suspect that you are collaborating with ColSec, eating the dish will flatline you. But if we trust you, Schrödinger will guide you to us."

Flatline.

Why did I feel nervous? I had nothing to hide. If the so-called Three Magi were as wise as they puffed themselves up to be, they should know I had nothing to do with ColSec.

I brought a segment of the delicate fish to my mouth, trying not to let my hand shake. I swallowed, letting the whole thing slide down my throat without even remembering to chew. I waited. And waited some more. Would I sense a flatline coming? Would I feel the reaper's cold fingers on the back of my neck?

Out of the corner of my vision, I saw a smile. In the darkness of a side street, a yellow-eyed cat emerged, the owner of that subtle grin. It hopped up on the wooden counter. Its arsehole to my face, the cat greedily devoured the remaining pieces of fish from my plate then just as nonchalantly leapt down. Nobody else paid it any attention.

Shiva. How much was I going to have to pay for that fugu?

As I got up to follow the cat, the chef didn't say a word or even look in my direction. Darting between the legs of passersby, the cat doubled back. I hurried to keep it in view, led into another area of The Commons I was unfamiliar with.

Now I was near a rusted chain link fence with the husks of discarded crotch rockets stacked in a giant heap on the other side.

The cat casually stepped through a two-dimensional rectangle of chameleonic light on a graffitied brick wall and was gone. I quickly followed.

I found myself standing in a decrepit structure. An abandoned laboratory long out of use. Massive electrical cables pulled from the ground like bundles of unruly roots. Bright panels pulsed with numbers and twisting geometry. Broken glass and other debris littered the floor.

Three figures moved between the panels. The nearest, who could charitably be called scrawny, turned to me. He wore a black T-shirt with the words "Wissen ist Tod" on the front in bold, white lettering. And his face... to my shame I admit I recoiled on impulse as he stepped into the light of a single, hanging bulb. He was a burn victim, his features painfully seared away from some unknown tragedy.

He saw me flinch and clicked his tongue disapprovingly. Another stopped what he was doing and turned to regard our conversation with mild interest while the third kept working away on an oversized screen. I saw that they all had some form of physical deformity. Sometimes more than one.

A cleft palate. A Glasgow smile. A milky, drooping eye.

>**What's wrong? Does our appearance unsettle you?**<

▸ What? Uh… no. Of course not. I just wasn't expecting… um…

>**We paid a lot of Crypt to be this ugly. What's your excuse?**<

▸ I… I'm sorry. I didn't know…

>**Relax. This corrupt world monetizes artificial beauty and profits off your shallow desire to obtain it. This is just one way we give the finger to the system. Besides, it's all just a mask.**<

To illustrate, the man in the black T-shirt made a flicking motion with his hand and his face changed to look like the chef that had butchered the pufferfish. Then he flicked again. He looked completely different, leprous and old. Another flick. I stood, blinking in confusion. It took me a while to realize that he was now wearing my face. The flicks went faster and faster until his face was a kaleidoscopic mask of shifting identities.

>**Enough games. Shall we get down to business?**<

▸ Is this all of Antisoc? Just the three of you?

I glanced around the dim, cluttered workspace uncertainly. The T-shirted man answered while the others looked on, multitasking on their various screens. Jacked into the system through the back door. I didn't see the cat anywhere.

>**Of course not. Just as we never use the same location twice,**

we will never reveal our true numbers. Many Volunteers assist us as we assist them. Not all who help Antisoc are Antisoc.<

▶ And you are the Three Magi... Tank Man, Q... and...

>Fawkes. The faces, so to speak, of the resistance.<

I watched as each visage, or portion thereof, shifted at irregular intervals. Most revealed some form of physical abnormality. A gallery of evolutionary misfires. I could not see any Volunteer ID codes, but why would they be reckless enough to show them? Just as their faces were masks upon masks, their names were nothing but aliases upon aliases.

▶ Q as in the letter? Or Queue as in... waiting in line?

>Q as in Quảng Đức, not that it is any of your concern.<

▶ Well, I am here to help with the special job. And you wouldn't have let me in here if you had reason to suspect me. So, tell me what you know about The Collective.

>Patience. Quid pro quo. You assist us with this heist, and we will shine our light a little brighter for your benefit.<

▶ You want my help pulling off a heist at the Repository so you can continue funding your operation. But what about the system, this world, everything you've told me about Collective Security? How are you sure you can even pull off this heist?

The last thing I wanted was to be set up as a patsy so this shadowy group could withdraw some illicit funds. They claimed it was system money. But could it be Citizen money? What about Volunteer money?

>You hunt bounties. We hunt glitches. Although technically impressive, the system is far from perfect. The glitches are opportunities. Vulnerabilities. You may notice things change from time to time, although you haven't been here long. A door

you once saw as red is now blue. A street sign is suddenly in a different location, like a mirror image. You remember things happening one way but history, even your recorded history, reflects something else. It is the Mandela effect. When you remember something that in theory never happened, it usually means a system change has been made.<

▸ Okay… And one of these opportunities exists in the Repository?

One of the others, currently appearing as shaven headed with a massive surgical scar across his cranium and wearing thick glasses, answered.

>You don't have a high enough Protocol to understand it. The vulnerability exists. You'll have to trust us.<

Trust the people who won't even show me their real faces. Right.

▸ I've never been to the Repository. What exactly is the role you need me to play in this?

The one with the T-shirt smiled a grim smile that persisted across several identities.

>Pay it a visit. Many Volunteers use the Repository for Crypt or item storage. It would not be unusual for a first-time visitor to request a tour. Bots run the place, of course. When you are inside, we will initiate a DDoS attack. This will take all Repository services offline. Temporarily. That is your window.<

▸ My window for what?

The third figure, the one who had not yet spoken, stepped away from a panel and approached me. He, if it was a he, wore an oversized, white lab coat. The figure reached into a coat pocket and produced a semi-cylindrical flash drive.

>This is a ghost stick. Completely shielded, although it will

take up metabytes. If you get caught with it on you, ColSec will notice the storage discrepancy. So don't get caught.<

The T-shirt man spoke next.

>Have you gotten a shine job?<

▸ I'm sorry?

>Can you see in the dark?<

▸ No. You've seen my menu, and not much has changed in the meantime.

I grew irritated as I recalled the helplessness I felt as the enlarged, glitched-out faces of Antisoc poured through my personal information without consent. I pushed the feeling aside and tried to refocus on the conversation.

>Once the DDoS attack goes off, it will be lights out. You will need a method of seeing in the dark without generating light. In the absence of a little eye surgery, you might consider night vision goggles. Although, again, if you get caught having just purchased them, that will be suspicious. Q?<

The lab coat wearer reached into his other pocket. Ah, so that one was Q. This time, he held up a pair of goggles that looked like miniature binoculars attached to a black headset.

>These are also shielded. Same deal as before. They won't show up under Equipment or History, but they will take up space. We'd prefer to get them back when the job is done.<

I accepted the ghost stick and the goggles, feeling the weight of them in my hands. I concentrated and highlighted the goggles.

Accessory: >Thermal goggles

Frequency: {missing parameter}

Details: Superior to goggles that amplify existing light, thermal imaging goggles convert heat radiation into a visible image. This allows the wearer to see in complete darkness as long as there is a temperature difference between objects.

Properties: This accessory is Shielded, and will be invisible to others in your menu. If the item is sufficiently damaged, it may lose the Shielded property.

Size: 10 metabytes

I quickly added the goggles to my Equipment menu but did not yet equip them. I kept the ghost stick in my hand.

▶ I ask for a tour, the lights go out, and then what?

>On your tour, you must get into the data vault before the attack. If our calculations are correct, all deposit boxes should open, exposing the data ports. Simply plug the ghost stick into an open port. When the power is restored, the ghost stick works its magic. Think of it as a Trojan horse in the palm of your hand.<

▶ Any open port? What do you think the response will be? How long until the power is restored?

>We ran a test on a different establishment several cycles ago. A Citizen bank deep in the heart of The Collective. Polizei bots evacuated all the Citizens and had the power restored in about six minutes.<

I took a deep breath and studied the ghost stick in my hand. Then I dematerialized it into my inventory.

Get into the data vault before the DDoS attack.

Plug in the ghost stick within six minutes.

Don't get caught.

FILE 20.1

REPOSITORY

I soon found myself in front of a building in a section of The Commons I had not visited before. The exterior was surprisingly ornate and yet had the same grimy sheen I had come to know so well. The structure might have been a central European opera house repurposed after some long forgotten revolution.

Six tall, stone columns and the wide staircase of the portico punctuated the faux-classical facade while aspirational statues groped for the empty heavens above a pointed pediment. I approached a series of large doors and pushed hard until one slowly swung open.

The lobby was expansive but faintly lit, as if the architecture was meant to harness natural light (of which there was none). I immediately noticed faint red streaks of light scanning my Volunteer ID code upon entry. Some type of automatic tracking beam from corners of the high vaulted ceiling. A smart-dressed woman behind a counter called out a prim greeting.

"Welcome to the Repository, first time customer. Please approach the service counter and we will be more than happy to assist you."

I glanced around as I stepped forwards. I saw a handful of others in the lobby. Some were likely bots assigned to this place while I believed at least a couple were fellow Volunteers. To one side of the lobby was a wall of metal bars and a security checkpoint, blocking off access to the inner sanctums.

I noticed there was a thick plexiglass barrier with only a narrow triangular opening between myself and the woman. She wore a pencil skirt, a buttoned-up blouse, and glasses. Her facial expression was friendly to the point of hostility.

▸ Hello. Thank you for the kind welcome. As you observed, I have never been here before. But I've heard a lot about this place.

"We pride ourselves on maintaining the best data storage services and financial products in The Collective, including here in our Commons branch! How may we assist you?"

Be cool. Be cool.

I knew my Persuasion score was very low. The best course of action would be to tell as much truth as I could, without revealing any of the nasty bits.

▸ Yes, the truth. The truth is I consistently run into challenges with storage. I'm always maxing out. It got so bad I ended up getting a chip installed. Can't say it was a pleasant experience.

I tapped the back of my neck for emphasis.

▸ But I know that is only a temporary fix, and just for Crypt. I heard the Repository offers a variety of services, but haven't had the chance to come out and see for myself.

"We are so happy you are considering using us for your data banking needs. The most popular service we offer is storage accounts for Universal Cryptocurrency Credits. May I ask what your current net worth is?"

▸ Uh, 1,190 Crypt.

She wrinkled her nose in disgust but quickly regained her stiffly smiling composure.

"We offer unlimited storage for Universal Cryptocurrency Credits, with a per-cycle fee based on where your total balance falls. However, I must inform you that a certain minimum account balance is required in order to opt-out of additional fees. At your current net worth, it is possible that the fees you incur may quickly surpass your total balance. In that case, we invite you to explore additional Cryptocurrency storage options with another financial institution."

▶ Oh, are there other places that offer account services? I didn't realize.

"No. But in the event that any other financial institutions are established, we invite you to explore whatever options they may offer you at that time."

▶ I see. Well, I am an active bounty, er… Volunteer. I expect more Crypt to be coming my way soon. Anyway, I am just trying to learn all I can about your services. I am not necessarily planning to open an account just yet. Besides Crypt storage, what else do you offer?

"Another popular service with Volunteers is our data storage boxes. To prevent over-encumbrance or a crowded living space, you can choose to store your excess belongings in raw data form in our safe deposit data storage boxes. For this service, a per-cycle fee is assessed based on the total metabytes of storage utilized. Both the Cryptocurrency account and data storage accounts begin at one hundred Crypt per cycle. And we are pleased to offer the data storage boxes with no minimum storage requirements!"

Yippee.

"For Volunteers on the go, we also offer instant transfer subscriptions. Find your pockets overflowing in the field? Can't make time to come into the Repository? Instantly zap your excess data straight to your accounts! All for a very reasonable additional per-cycle fee. We guarantee the lowest rates in The Collective!"

▸ Naturally. I've heard of the transfer service and admit it sounds very convenient.

"Additionally, we offer Universal Cryptocurrency Credit Loans to qualified borrowers with the lowest interest rates in The Collective. Would you be interested in speaking to a loan officer?"

▸ No, no. Bog no. Not right now. But thank you for the information.

"Our pleasure! How else may we assist you today?"

▸ You mentioned the storage boxes. Something about raw data. Is there a way I can see how that works? I don't know if you offer tours, but I am intrigued. I would want to know that my data is truly safe and secure.

A flicker of irritation crossed her otherwise antiseptic expression.

"Of course... sir or ma'am. Account holders are allowed access to their storage box upon request at any time, but we can show you the vault and provide a demonstration. Proceed to the security station and I will meet you there."

She pointed to the checkpoint near the wall of metal bars and turned a hanging window sign around, indicating that her counter was temporarily closed. Then she disappeared behind a solid barrier.

I approached the security station, which looked like a pair of sliding prison doors with a metal detector between them. I was beginning to feel nervous.

Can't let it show.

The woman appeared on the other side of the bars and tapped a button, opening the first, outer door. I stepped into the middle space.

"For non-account holders, no weapons of any kind are allowed beyond the lobby. Please store all weapons on your person in the assigned holding cube."

Shiva. Antisoc didn't mention this!

A metal grate opened and, on a conveyor belt, a transparent cube opened in view. The teller stood watching me impatiently.

Reluctantly, I materialized my snub-nosed revolver and push dagger, placing them inside the cube. I watched my only weapons rolling out of reach, the metal grate rattling to a close.

Peering through the bars, I saw my weapons rolled into a fenced-off waiting room. There were a few other cubes in use back there. One seemed to contain a bloodstained chainsaw and several hand grenades.

"You will receive your property after the conclusion of the tour. Now please step through the scanner."

My body tensed as I stepped into the security scanner, planting my boots on the indicated spaces. There was a faint whine as an encompassing red light washed over me, starting with my head and moving downwards.

I was carrying two pieces of contraband.

Antisoc said they were shielded, like my Subroutines menu and presumably every interaction I had with the shadowy group. How good was this shielding? And how sophisticated was this scanner? I was about to find out. If this scanner was capable of detecting my storage discrepancy, I was in trouble.

"Finished. Step forwards."

Phew.

The Repository teller beckoned me onwards as the whine of the machine shut down and the next barred door trundled open. Her face retained the same plastic smile while her body language betrayed boredom at the chore of giving a low roller like me a tour.

I followed her down a long, tiled hall. She made chit chat as we walked, possibly a rehearsed spiel about the design of the building, the security features, and so forth. I heard little of it. The sound of my thudding heart reverberated in my ears. My eyes darted all around, trying not to let my anxiety show.

We turned a corner and I saw another Volunteer walking past. Then another. Good. The more the better. If I was the only one in the building when this went down that could be a problem.

"And up ahead is our data vault where all Commons customers can access their safe deposit data storage boxes. Right this way."

For some reason, the concept of a post office sprung to mind. Everywhere were gilded bars—different offices and alcoves appearing like royal cages. Yet, the relatively dim light cast a dingy pall. This particular vault was a large rectangular room with walls filled floor to ceiling with copper plated boxes. An analog skin for a digital service.

If this Repository really provided data storage services across The Collective, I imagined the other branches must have been a lot sleeker and modern. I couldn't imagine the likes of Monique Rossignol or her shareholder husband frequenting a place like this.

"Depending on the size of your—"

At once, all the lights went out, plunging the building into total darkness. There was also a moment of complete silence so profound that for a split second, I thought the world had ended. Then—*pop, pop, pop*. A thousand metallic doors sprung open.

I heard murmurs of confusion and alarm in the distance. The other Volunteers? No sounds came from my erstwhile tour guide.

The clock was ticking. Now what?

I remembered the thermal goggles and hurried to open my menu. The light of my menu shone bright in my eyes and, for a moment, I panicked. I was not supposed to create any light source. But, of course, I remembered the menu was visible only to me.

I scrolled down to my Equipment submenu, found the goggles, and selected them.

Equip > Thermal Goggles?

▸ Yes.

I couldn't see it, but I felt the swirl of pixels coalescing around my face, solidifying. The thermal goggles were on. A bit heavier than expected. Everything was still dark. I heard heavy footsteps echoing off the walls and high ceilings.

How do I turn these on?

My hands fumbled over the head strap. Frag. I should have practiced this. There were multiple knobs and buttons. Ah, a switch. I flicked it and suddenly the interior of the Repository was bathed in dark purple light. There were traces of orange and red, pops of ambient temperature. But everything was blurry. Trying to walk induced a nauseating sensation.

Frag! I have to focus these to the correct range.

Tick-tock. Tick-tock.

I twisted a couple dials in the center of the binoculars until clarity emerged. Operating these was more complicated than I expected. I did a quick 360 to reorient myself. My tour guide was nowhere. Vanished without a trace. I wondered what the result of the DDoS attack was on bots.

What next? I needed to find a data port and insert the ghost stick. I materialized it into my hand and hurried deeper into the vault room. As suspected, all the little metal doors had swung open, revealing semi-circular data ports that glowed with faint residual warmth. I twisted the ghost stick until it lined up correctly and carefully inserted it into a random port.

Nothing happened. Antisoc said it would kick into action once the power was restored. Using the thermal goggles, I carefully retraced my steps back towards the front of the building. I saw another Volunteer, apparently without the benefit of night vision, feeling his way blindly along a wall.

A loud noise shook the Repository. Like someone attempting to start a generator. Was the power trying to come back on? That was a lot shorter than six minutes. I couldn't be caught wearing these goggles.

I quickly unequipped them just as the lights flickered on and the hum of background activity filled the space. For the first time, I noticed bland electronic muzak playing overhead. The other Volunteer and I turned towards each other, and I feigned surprise at seeing him. He had half of his head shaved, a thick mustache, and several prominent facial piercings.

▸ What's going on? What happened?

He shook his head wearily in response to my bluff.

"Some chepooka, no doubt. Making me razdraz. Can't a veck get his missile launcher out of storage?"

I thought to ask what sort of bounty he was hunting that required a missile launcher, but I held my tongue.

I saw the security station ahead with the lobby beyond. It seemed the double doors were open, the scanner offline. With the power coming back on, I assumed the ghost stick was doing, or would do, whatever it was designed to do. No way of confirming.

Just then, white and blinding lights flooded in from every

window. A monotone voice boomed unnaturally loud, amplified by an unknown source.

"This is Collective Security. There has been an unexpected service failure. All Volunteers proceed immediately to the nearest exit. We repeat, this is Collective Security. There has been an unexpected service failure. All Volunteers proceed immediately to the nearest exit. For your safety, evacuate the Repository in an orderly fashion with your hands in the air. We repeat—"

Shiva. Shiva. Shiva.

The other Volunteer hastened ahead, passing through the double security doors. I followed. My weapons were still locked away in the holding cube beyond the bars. There was no one to assist and no way I could reach them. Dram.

"—proceed immediately to the nearest exit—"

A half dozen or so Volunteers milled about in the lobby, making their way to the three large doors at the entrance, squinting and shielding their eyes from the blinding searchlights. The teller from before returned to her former service spot behind the counter as other Repository workers stood around awkwardly.

I guess the bots got rebooted.

I had to think quickly. I still had the contraband thermal goggles in my possession. Despite the shielding, my storage discrepancy was a real risk if I was about to have an up close and personal run-in with ColSec.

I hurried ahead to join the small crowd making for the exit. Hoping to be blocked from view by the shuffle of bodies and blinding lights, I subtly materialized the thermal goggles in one hand hanging at my side.

"—evacuate the Repository in an orderly fashion with your hands in the air—"

To one side of the large doors was a Memory Hole. But I knew I would need to scan my identifier to use it—and who knows how it would react to a shielded item.

Could I somehow reverse pickpocket another Volunteer, surreptitiously dragging and dropping the item into their inventory? That would potentially implicate an innocent stranger in a crime they didn't commit.

Or would I just have to drop the item on the ground and hope for the best?

A fourth option occurred to me as my decision-making window dwindled. I stooped down and made a show of picking the object off the floor.

▸ Excuse me. Somebody dropped this. Is this yours? Does this belong to anyone?

"—Security. There has been an unexpected service failure—"

I added the goggles back into my menu and stepped through the doors with the others, into the blinding lights.

FILE 21

COLSEC

A white box. I was standing in a white box.

A perfect rectangular prism of sharp 90-degree angles. Four walls, a floor, and a ceiling—all smooth and featureless. There were no doors or windows. No way in or out that I could perceive. The box was fully and uniformly illuminated without a discernible light source. And no furniture. Just an empty, white box.

I didn't know how long I had been there. Empty minutes bled into empty hours bled into who knows what. And I was completely alone. I stood until my legs ached then leaned back and slid to a sitting position in one corner. When that position caused my back to cramp, I stood again and tried to pace the small area, eventually slumping down once more.

I resisted the urge to open my menu. To read through my History. I would have done anything to kill time. But I had the distinct feeling of being watched, although there were no cameras.

They wanted me to open my menu. They were waiting for a moment of weakness. Or was that just paranoia talking? The system likely always had full access to my information, so why should now be any different? I didn't know how much more of this I could take. I replayed the recent events over and over in my head. Wondering if I did everything correctly. Was the heist successful? Successful for whom, I grumbled.

Deprived of the regular human rhythms of hunger, thirst, and sleep, I remained in a solitary limbo. An interminable wait.

No sooner had these thoughts crossed my mind than I realized I was not alone. A tall figure stood over me.

Frag me!

I startled and scrambled to my feet.

Perfectly motionless, the humanoid figure stood in the room. It had the familiar appearance of a Polizei bot, complete with an impenetrable visor but instead of black, it was completely white from helmet to boot. The crisp white uniform blended in with the sterile box. How it had come to be there I could not say.

Volunteer 01001110-01101111-01100010-01101111-01100100-01111001. Known aliases include: Magpie. I am an officer with Collective Security, assigned to Surveillance, anti-Terrorism, Apprehension, Security, and Investigations. I am here to ask you some questions.

▸ Questions? What kind of questions?

It sounded just like the Concierge from my orientation, just like the disembodied voice from the information kiosks spread throughout The Collective. I knew the thing I was speaking with was not human but some type of program. A ColSec program. Did it say known aliases?

As you know, the Repository in The Commons experienced a minor system failure. Collective Security is performing routine questioning of all Volunteers on the premises during the incident to ensure future system stability and data integrity.

▸ You mean the power outage? That was quite a surprise. I almost got lost in the dark. Thankfully another Volunteer helped point me in the right direction when the lights came back on.

I am required to inform you that any responses you give during this interview will be included in the associated quality assurance incident investigation report.

▶ No problem.

What were you doing in the Repository?

I hesitated to answer. I had a paltry ten Persuasion. I had almost no chance of bluffing my way through this. Better to play dumb. Or try to find a thread of truth to wrap my brain around. Somewhere in the recesses of my lost memory, I had the concept that to beat a lie detector test you needed to mentally ask yourself a different question than your interrogator asked. Huh. Where did that idea come from? Either way, it might not apply to this situation. Better to play dumb and give half-truths.

▶ A friend of mine, goes by Camel, suggested I open an account at the Repository to solve my Crypt storage issues. Another Volunteer, Bigwig, said he uses it for gear storage. I thought I would check it out for myself.

The Volunteer with the known alias of Camel has previously been under Collective Security investigation for possible Terms of Service violations. Are you affiliated with an organization known as Antisoc?

▶ I am not affiliated with any organization.

Technically true. Camel under investigation? The officer used the word "previously." What did that mean?

Are you aware that it is a serious violation to interact with the system in any manner that could interfere with, disable, disrupt, overburden or otherwise impair the system; to gain access to (or

attempt to gain access to) another Volunteer or Citizen's account or any non-public portions of the system; to upload, transmit, or distribute to or through the system any viruses, worms, malicious code, or other programs intended to interfere with the system, including its security-related features; or to access, search, or collect data from the system by any means (automated or otherwise) except as permitted within the Terms of Service?

▸ I... I don't recall ever reading the Terms of Service before. Can I get a copy?

You have insufficient system privileges to access that information.

Sigh.

▸ That seems to be a running theme. Many of those things you just mentioned I would not know how to do. Not even if you paid me.

It is an accurate assertion that you have very low ratings in your Processing subcategories.

▸ Exactly! I was interested in opening a data storage account. But now I'm not so sure. Is there a problem with the Repository? Will my data be safe there with power outages going on?

I will be the one asking the questions. You have a storage discrepancy of ten metabytes. You have 249 metabytes of storage in use, but only 239 metabytes of discretely detectable data.

As the officer did not ask a direct question, I remained silent, trying to stare as vacantly as possible at the robotic helmet in front of me.

How do you account for this discrepancy?

▸ Discrepancy? How do you...

I opened my menu and scrolled through it carefully, squinting at the text.

▸ All my weapons were held at the security station before my tour, but I see all the items and numbers I should expect to have. At least I think so.

Your History records you making the following statement just prior to exiting the Repository: 'Excuse me. Somebody dropped this. Is this yours? Does this belong to anyone?' What exactly were you referring to?

▸ In the lobby, when all the Volunteers were evacuating, I found a piece of equipment on the floor. I thought somebody must have dropped it. Maybe when the lights were out?

What piece of equipment? Show it to me.

Reluctantly, I fumbled about in my menu for as long as I could until I materialized the thermal goggles. I held them up before the inscrutable gaze of the officer. It regarded the item in silence.

▸ I've seen lots of Volunteers wear headgear, but I have no idea who these originally belong to.

Which was technically true.

This item is contraband and will be confiscated immediately.

I watched sadly as the thermal goggles floated from my hand and winked out of existence.

▸ Oh! Really? Contraband? As I said, they aren't my property. I'm still very new here. I have a lot to learn about how things work.

It is an accurate assertion that you are relatively new. You remain low level, with only two completed tasks. However, the amount of time you have spent here is not commensurate with so few tasks. You signed a contract, and the Terms of Service state that you are to fulfill the duties of that contract. Volunteers with low task completion rates are cause for concern. Idle hands, as the proverb goes, are the devil's playthings.

Just what I needed. A program spouting off idioms.

▸ I fully intend to complete more tasks, I just—

The fact that you were in the Repository during the recent system failure is cause for concern. The fact that you were in possession of a contraband item is cause for concern. Additionally, your connection to Volunteer 01000010 01100101 01110100 01100001 00111001 is cause for concern.

▸ Who?

On the other hand, your lack of experience and low statistics may help validate your repeated claims of ignorance. You also have very little recorded Crypt or other property of value.

▸ I'm no criminal mastermind. I'm not anybody, really.

That may be so. But you are now somebody—somebody of interest who warrants further monitoring.

▸ Wait. You're putting me on a watchlist?

Collective Security will reverse engineer the contraband item to determine its true origin. We may arrange further interviews if you continue to be somebody of interest to our ongoing investigations. In the meantime, if you are contacted in any way by a group calling themselves Antisoc, you are to immediately present yourself at Collective Security headquarters and report this. Collective Security is prepared to richly incentivize any Volunteer possessing information about this terrorist organization.

▸ Terrorists?

Affirmative. The terrorist group known as Antisoc is actively jeopardizing the very survival of the human race through their continued interference with The Collective. They must be stopped at any cost.

▸ Survival of the human race? That sounds... serious.

It actually did.

If you have at any time been in contact or have collaborated with Antisoc or any affiliate thereof, it would be in your best interest to turn yourself in and disclose everything you know, rather than have Collective Security discover this during the course of our ongoing investigations. Do you understand? I must warn you that the consequences of violating the Terms of Service are serious.

▸ Yes... I hear you loud and clear.

There is another option.

▸ Oh?

The system administrator has authorized me to make the following offer. In order to remove yourself from all suspicion in connection to the recent incident, I am prepared to offer you the choice of an enhanced system reset.

▸ What does that mean?

Your achievements and all data accumulated so far during your time in The Collective will be erased. Your history, including your memory and awareness of your time in The Collective will be reset. You will re-enter the orientation as a brand-new Volunteer. However, I am authorized to offer you significant perks in connection with this reset. You will be awarded a sign-on bonus of 10,000 Crypt in addition to an expanded living arrangement in the north Residential Tower.

Holy Shiva...

At that moment I was filled with inchoate rage. Because I knew then without a doubt that this system was responsible for my memory loss and had deliberately deceived me. "Dissociative amnesia can be an uncommon but serious reaction when entering The Collective."

But why? For what purpose? And now this ColSec buzzard was offering (or was that threatening?) to reset my memory again. All the Crypt in the Metaverse wasn't worth losing myself a second time.

But what if this wasn't the second time…? Oh frag. I didn't want to think about that possibility.

▶ No. No! I don't want that! I am not a terrorist. I am not a member of this group you are talking about!

The impenetrable white helmet regarded me blankly.

Elevated pulse. Chromatic face shift attributable to blood vessel dilation. Clenched hands. An authentic emotional response. Interesting.

I wanted to strike this bot in front of me. To pummel it with my fists. But that would be useless. I was powerless, impotent, and trapped in this bleached-out interrogation room.

The officer momentarily froze, then raised an arm to the side of its helmet, pausing there as if receiving some transmission. It lowered its arm again and cocked its head to one side, quietly observing me before speaking again.

There has been an explosion in The Commons. In the area colloquially known as Mendicant Row. Significant environmental destruction and many Volunteers taken offline, resulting in a bottleneck at the Restoration Point.

▶ What?

My eyes went wide. An explosion in The Commons?

An authentic reaction of surprise, suggesting that you had no involvement.

▶ No! Of course not!

The officer hesitated, continuing its piercing study of me. I wondered what could have caused such an explosion. Some kind of accident? Was The Commons under attack?

Due to the imminent need to reallocate security resources this interview will be cut short.

I gaped in disbelief.

▸ Short? You kept me waiting in this box forever!

Just because the interview is being aborted does not mean our concerns about you are alleviated. A parting word of caution: do not be distracted. Focus on fulfilling the requirements of your contract. The Collective needs you to carry out the work you volunteered for.

Right.

If you, for any reason, come into possession of any information regarding the terrorist organization known as Antisoc, present yourself at Collective Security headquarters located in Metro Central. We will be monitoring you, Volunteer.

The white walls of the box grew brighter and brighter until they were blinding. And then, they were gone. The box, the ColSec officer, all of it.

FILE 21.1

JACK

I shakily stood in an unknown space, feeling a queasy tightness in my abdomen. It took a minute for my eyes to readjust to my surroundings. It looked like I had been dumped in a narrow underground mall, but all the shops were closed—their metal security gates rolled and padlocked. A handful of red neon signs flickered indecisively and abandoned sandwich board displays written in an unknown script advertised miscellaneous wares.

I saw my snub-nosed revolver and push dagger lying unceremoniously on the ground in front of me. I picked them up and quickly added them back to my Equipment menu, breathing a small sigh of relief. They returned my weapons. I could at least be thankful for that. Hard to do my job as a Volunteer without them.

I turned around, trying to get my bearings. Behind me were security barricades, yellow caution tape, and the subtle gleam of an electronic barrier. A sign read: **Code 404-37. Excuse our mess! This area is under construction.**

Only one way out, I guess. Down the other direction.

I dodged brackish puddles in the cracked asphalt, ducking to avoid low hanging cables and air vents as I made my way to the far end of the walkway. I saw concrete steps ahead, leading up.

The anger I felt remained, burning within my breast. Part of me was glad to stick it to the system. Then again, was it a lost cause? If I wanted to get out, to return to whatever my life was on the outside (if such a place existed), didn't I have to play along? Didn't I have to fulfill my mysterious contract? And what the ColSec officer said about the survival of the human race... Was that more lies? Propaganda?

I thought about Antisoc. They warned me not to get caught with the shielded thermal goggles. Now the accessory was confiscated, and there was a possibility that, if the code was cracked, Antisoc might be at risk. Of course, they had also asked me to return the goggles to them. A lose / lose situation. And after spending who knows how much time in that interrogation chamber, would Antisoc trust that I had not betrayed them? They could easily choose to flatline me to reduce their exposure.

All these thoughts swirled in my mind as I climbed the steps, only to pause as I heard the faint sound of somebody crying.

▸ Hello?

A figure was hunched over, sitting on the steps, burying its face in gloved hands. At the sound of my voice, it raised its head. It was a man. He was wearing a brown leather trench coat over black corduroys and a button-down shirt. Embarrassed, he wiped tears from his cheeks and put on a pair of spectacles.

"You startled me! I didn't know there was anyone else down here. I'm so sorry."

▸ No, don't be. Are you... okay?

"Not really. I just got released from questioning by ColSec. Oh, it was awful."

▸ You too? There was some kind of incident at the Repository.

"Exactly. They took every Volunteer who was there in for grilling. And I had nothing to tell them!"

He held his side and winced, as if his ribs hurt. I carefully looked him over. I did not recognize him from the Repository. But what did that mean? Everything happened so fast, and it was a large building.

▸ Did they hurt you?

He waved away my concerns.

"Don't... don't worry about it. I'll be alright. I just need to pull myself together."

The man had gentle features and a kind disposition. His dirty blond hair was medium length and parted in the middle. His face was smooth, save for a cleft in his chin, and he had beautiful blue eyes which appeared larger through the lenses of his wireframe glasses. I assumed no Metaverse avatar would be created with vision problems, so the glasses must have been an aesthetic choice.

▸ Yeah. That was my first run-in with ColSec, and I hope it will be my last. What were you doing at the Repository?

"That's a very personal question."

▸ Oh, I'm sorry, I didn't mean to pry. As I've been told many times, I'm a noob. Just curious is all. I haven't opened an account there yet.

"That's alright. Nothing too secret, if you must know. Just checking on some investments. I don't generally like to put that out on the street, but you seem kind."

▸ Investments? Are Volunteers allowed to have investments?

"Bonds mostly. It is pretty niche. I'm sorry, where are my manners? The name is Jack, although most people call me Fancy Jack."

He stood, removed a glove, and held out a well-manicured hand. I shook it politely. His skin was very soft. I stifled a laugh.

▸ Fancy Jack? What sort of name is that?

"I know, I know. Tease me if you like. The short version of the story is: I came out of orientation at the same time as two other Volunteers. So we teamed up. King, Queen, and Jack. Get it? A regular bounty hunting threesome. But all that blood and guts. Killing and being killed. It just wasn't for me. My partners eventually became lovers and I was the odd man out, so I turned my attention to less-violent interests."

▸ You were only missing an Ace. Then you could have been a bounty hunting foursome.

He grinned, put his glove back on, and gestured up the steps.

"Care to walk as we talk? I'd like to get back to my apartment."

I was obliged to follow him and soon we ascended to ground level. Looking around, I saw that indeed I was back in The Commons. I spotted the spire of the Restoration Point far in the distance. I wondered where we were in relation to the explosion the ColSec officer mentioned.

▸ What did you mean by less-violent interests?

"When we were out there fighting monsters, the three of us, I became more intrigued with some of the plant specimens we came across. My partners could not have cared less. But me? You can say I became a little obsessed. Enamored might be a better word. Orbexilum stipulatum and St. Helena Olive. The Toromiro tree. These plants should be extinct—are extinct. Yet extinct plants somehow live on in this place. It's a miracle. This place is a miracle."

▸ Wow. That is certainly a unique perspective. So... you're really into plants?

"Hence the backhanded nickname. But I've come to embrace it. Botany. Horticulture. These are my passions now."

► But you are a Volunteer. What about your contract? What about taking bounties?

I privately recalled how the ColSec officer criticized my low bounty output just a few minutes ago.

Fancy Jack sighed wistfully, running a hand through his hair and looking at the shining buildings and dark streets. He stopped walking and faced me.

"That's just it. I aspire to become a Citizen."

► A Citizen?

"If I save up enough Crypt, I hope to buy my way in."

I arched an eyebrow incredulously.

► They'll let you do that?

"I honestly don't know. But a man can dream, can't he? Let me dream. One step at a time."

There was something else under the surface. Something he wasn't saying, but I couldn't figure out what. The aspiring pacifist reached into his coat pocket and pulled out a small card. He handed it to me. It felt soft and natural to the touch, like recycled paper. It read: 'Fancy Jack, Herbalist' and had an address listed.

"That card is crafted from fibers of plants I raised myself. You should come by my apartment sometime. It doubles as my urban garden and shop. I make a mean cup of tea."

I slipped the business card into my inventory.

► Thank you. I have a lot going on just now, but I'll consider it. I don't know how much time I lost in that interrogation chamber.

Fancy Jack raised a gloved finger in the air as if remembering something. He materialized an unusual book and flipped it open. It looked as if ink was swirling into place on the pages, forming words and astronomical diagrams.

He noticed my bewilderment and offered a brief word of explanation.

"This is my lucky almanac. I found it on a job once upon a time and have kept it with me ever since. By my calculations... Oh my, it seems that nearly two cycles have passed."

▸ Two cycles?!

I was trapped in that white box for two whole cycles? I suddenly remembered the Round Table raid. I might completely miss it. I may already have.

▸ Excuse me, Jack. I have to go. I have to go right now!

"Me too. I must get home and water my poor, thirsty plants. Come visit sometime!"

I sprinted in the direction of the Rathskeller.

FILE 22

RAID

I stumbled down the steps under the sign of the rat and pushed through double red doors into the Rathskeller. My heart sank. Not a Round Tabler in sight. The entire establishment was sparse, with isolated Volunteers nursing drinks and grudges at sticky tables. Even the ever-present electronica, usually skull-splittingly loud, seemed muted.

No heavily armed bouncer guarding the entrance to the secret backroom either.

I hurried to the bar and waved to the bartender. Bowtie girl wiped down a glass. She raised an eyebrow and smiled, taking her sweet time coming over.

▸ The Raid! Did I miss it?

"What raid?"

▸ The Round Table. They said they were waiting on Volunteers to run a raid in...

I quickly checked my notes under my Subroutines menu.

▸ ... the warehouse district. New Dresden. Am I too late?

"Oh, that raid. Yeah, you missed them. The Round Table and a whole gaggle of Volunteers left several hours ago."

I cursed and kicked the barstool.

"You break it, you buy it. Besides, you might still be able to catch up if you hurry."

▸ Really? How? I've never been to New Dresden.

"Go to the MAR Station, catch the bullet heading towards Royal Heights. You go past the Palisades, Lower Dresden, and then voila."

▸ And then what?

Another enigmatic grin.

"That's for you to figure out. I just serve the drinks."

I thanked her and dashed out, heading for the station. Out of breath from my exertion, I paid the ten Crypt at the kiosk and boarded the next available Diamond Line train. The doors slid shut and I hung on a strap, panting. The automated voice narrated the journey.

Now leaving The Commons. Next stop, Royal Heights, followed by The Palisades.

The city lights whipped past the windows.

Come on. Come on. Can't this high-speed bullet train go any faster?

Now arriving at Royal Heights Station.

I realized it was dark out, even in the rest of The Collective. No daylight in the land of the Citizens. And as before, I was the only one in this train car. I imagined it must have been shoulder to shoulder with Volunteers armed to the teeth a few hours ago.

Now leaving Royal Heights. Next stop, The Palisades, followed by Lower Dresden.

Would I miss all the action? Better late than never, I hoped. I wasn't exactly sure what a raid consisted of. Bigwig said hellhounds and Baskervilles were accumulating. He mentioned something about a hot spot. Mentioned rooting out the source and a rare target. The

Baskerville Hound was uncommon, which meant something worse was out there.

I checked my inventory as I waited, recalling my earlier encounter with the infernal dogs. Don't get bit. That was a good piece of advice. Had Rook not patched me up back then, that infernal burn status effect might not have been pretty. I had managed to kill one hellhound with my blade, but it took Bigwig and Rook both unloading on the Baskerville before it went down. Although similar creatures, the danger level was a different order of magnitude between the two.

And just how many devil dogs would be there this time?

Now arriving at The Palisades Station.

Now leaving The Palisades. Next stop, Lower Dresden, followed by New Dresden.

Five bullets and a dagger. No consumables. Maybe I hadn't exactly prepared for this raid. Dram. I would lend a hand and do what I could. I wanted that 5% discount. And maybe I could pick up some other goodies along the way. At least I had a forty armor rating, whatever that was worth. And I hoped canine teeth, no matter how infernal, couldn't pierce a bulletproof vest.

Now arriving at Lower Dresden Station.

Now leaving Lower Dresden. Next stop, New Dresden, followed by MAR Master Terminal.

Screens below the ceiling pulsed with advertisements, which I ignored. But suddenly a video came on, showing a scene of urban destruction from an aerial view. A newscaster's voice came over the speakers.

"Earlier this cycle, an explosion went off in a section of The Commons, damaging property and Volunteer avatars. Ground zero of the blast was believed to be an illicit Rez den, now demolished. Collective Security is actively investigating the cause of the explosion. Surveillance footage indicates an unknown courier delivering a package to the location of the suspected Rez den shortly before the blast. Collective Security is offering a financial incentive to anyone with information about the courier or the explosion."

What the frag?

Now arriving at New Dresden Station.

Distracted by the announcement, I shook my head. This was my stop. No time to think about this now.

I disembarked and took the stairs two at a time, pushing through the one-way turnstile to exit onto the street. To my left were high-rises of crescendoing heights. I imagined civvies sleeping safe and warm in their posh beds. To my right was a series of long, industrial warehouses with a backdrop of dark water in the distance, the crests of small waves glittering faintly from the reflected city lights.

The Warehouse District. Truth in advertising.

I hurried between the first row of structures. Streetlamps at regular intervals lit the way. I approached one warehouse and tried to pull open a large hangar door. No good. Chained and padlocked. I briefly wondered what need Citizens even had for such warehouses but couldn't spare the brain power.

There was a chatter of distant gunfire. Heading in the direction of the bay, I passed two more warehouses before I heard it again.

A burst of gunfire. Maybe from an SMG. Echoey, as if coming from inside. A distinct odor hung in the air. Brimstone and something else. Ahead, a side door into the warehouse was ajar. A heavy broken chain lay on the ground, cut in two. I listened at the door. Gunfire from somewhere deep within. I went inside.

The stench assaulted my nostrils. It was sulfuric, yes. But mixed with gunpowder, singed fur, and still something else. Something putrid. The interior was dim, the only light coming from the outside lamps filtering through filmy windows. Again, I cursed my lack of preparedness. I would give anything to have those thermal goggles back.

The warehouse was multi-leveled with a grid of catwalks that appeared to sink into the ground. Subterranean corridors connected to adjacent warehouses.

I drew my revolver and made my way down metal staircases to the lower level, ducking to avoid thick chains and cables coiled like pythons. I followed the sounds of fighting. There was another light source ahead. A flicker of flame dancing on a pile of ash and fabric. I circled around a massive stack of girders in the middle of the warehouse floor to get a closer look.

Crunch.

I stopped and looked down. What had I stepped on? My eyes adjusted to the light cast by the tongue of fire. It was the skeletal remains of a human hand. Blackened. I had cracked two of the fingers under my boot. I quickly stepped back.

Looking ahead, I noticed other bodies, equally crisped, lying in the recessed corridor. Then I realized what that elusive smell was. Burning flesh. Shouldn't bodies disappear? Go back to the Restoration Point? I thought of what that ColSec officer said about the explosion in The Commons. "A bottleneck at the Restoration Point." What was it like to die and not be able to respawn? Would you know that you were dead? Or was it just empty nothingness. I hoped to not find out just yet.

I climbed down into the corridor. Fighting must have started in this warehouse and spilled into an adjacent building.

There were more flames ahead. Small fires and charred remains.

Blood stains from man and beast dragged over concrete. The further I went, the heat of fire and the coppery scent of blood grew more potent.

"Ohhh bog... Ugh..."

I pivoted, quickly pointing my gun at the source of the moan. There was a person propped up against the wall in an unnatural way, like a rag doll. Their face was burned badly, and blood seeped from their mouth. I couldn't tell if it was a man or a woman, not that it mattered. Maybe they were like me.

▸ Sorry, you scared me!

"Kill me... Please..."

▸ What?

"My spine... My spine is broken. I can't move. The pain... oh bog... losing krovvy but not quick enough..."

I realized they must have been in terrible agony from their injuries.

▸ Listen. Maybe I can get help for you. Do you have any consumables? Anything?

"No... Put me out of my misery. I can't fight... can't move... Just kill me..."

▸ Where are the others? Did anyone survive?

They coughed up more blood, trying to shrug a shoulder but failed.

"More lewdies are... deeper in... Kill me you dram nazz... Do it..."

This person would just respawn, I reminded myself. It wasn't murder or anything. I would be doing them a favor. Volunteers helping each other and all that. But then, I hate to admit, a selfish thought crossed my mind. I only had five bullets. Did I want to waste one on this mercy killing? Such a dram selfish thought.

The crippled Volunteer seemed to read my mind.

"Shotgun... take my... Oh bog..."

A bloodstained single-barrel shotgun rested at their feet. I dematerialized my revolver and carefully picked up the weapon. It was a break-action shotgun—old school. I located the breach lever and opened the action. There was a spent shell, which I discarded. A belt around the Volunteer's waist held half a dozen shells with many empty slots.

Curious, I concentrated on the weapon to access its details.

Weapon: Breech-loading shotgun

Weapon Type: Ranged (ballistic)

Level: 2 of 10

Frequency: Common

Damage Output: 80

Details: A breech-loading shotgun with a single long barrel. One of the oldest and simplest shotgun types.

Properties: Ammunition - requires 12-gauge shotgun shells. Holds one shell at a time and must be manually reloaded.

Size: 40 metabytes

Eighty damage output? Wow. And the weapon had been upgraded a level. That must have contributed to its impressive power. At least, impressive compared to what I was packing.

"Kill me!" the victim wheezed in agony.

▸ Are you sure? Is there anything else—

"Do it!"

I plucked a fresh shell off the belt, loaded the shotgun, and closed the break with a click. Uncertainly, I brought the barrel up against the Volunteer's head. They struggled to move, attempting to lean into it, eager for the reprieve it would bring.

▸ I'm sorry...

I shut my eyes and pulled the trigger. There was a tremendous blast. The Volunteer's head turned to paste, splattering me with shreds of gooey flesh and bits of bone. When I opened my eyes, the head was vaporized. Gone.

A wave of nausea hit me. I dropped the shotgun and fell to my hands and knees, retching. Nothing came up, just dry heaving that twisted my insides in a vice.

The headless corpse slumped down the wall. No respawn yet.

What did I just do? I shuddered, getting back to my feet. I just killed somebody. No, not really. Not on purpose. I hadn't meant it. It wasn't real, right? Right?

A deep growling caught my attention, and I turned to see two pairs of glowing, red eyes approaching from down the corridor. Two large black dogs emerged from the darkness, hackles raised and teeth bared. Hellhounds. And I was clutching an empty shotgun.

In an instant, I knelt at the corpse beside me, trying to pull another shotgun shell free from the ammunition belt.

The dogs broke into a lope. One was injured, favoring a hind leg. Likely sustained in a previous fight. My fingers, slick with blood, failed to grasp the shell at first. I quickly wiped my hands on my pants and pulled one free, opening the action at the same time.

The first dog snarled and lunged forwards, the other one hanging back.

I popped out the spent shell and reloaded, snapping the gun back together. I swung the barrel up just as the dog pounced and pulled the trigger.

The blast hit the hellhound's torso at close range and in mid-leap, changing its trajectory. With an unearthly whine, the hellhound slammed against the wall, a gaping wound in its ribcage. Dead.

But the other dog charged me and there was no time. Almost on instinct, I reached into my mind's eye, drawing up my skill slots. I focused on the clurichaun skill and rolled away from the approaching threat.

Shooom.

Clurichaun skill activated. 30 seconds remaining.

Energy: 0 remaining.

The hellhound lunged at the illusory projection of myself, kneeling with shotgun in hand. It snapped its jaws at the empty air, slobbering with bestial rage. That was close. I was about six feet away and realized I yet again had an empty shotgun. And no shells within reach.

The hellhound snarled and turned to face me, losing interest in the illusion. Frag. It could probably smell me.

I dropped the shotgun and drew my revolver, standing and aiming. The dog ran at me and I backed away, taking shot after shot, aiming for its head.

I got off four rounds. One bullet pierced its skull. Another its neck. Another missed, ricocheting off the floor. The fourth buried itself in its chest. The hellhound slumped forwards, skidding until it lay before my boots.

Was it dead? I stepped out of biting range just in case.

I buried my face in the crook of my elbow as the scent of sulfur was nearly overwhelming. As if brimstone oozed from the creatures' wounds. Then I realized I had accidentally smeared bits of gore from the Volunteer I had euthanized onto my face. Disgusting.

Clurichaun skill elapsed. 30 seconds until recharge.

But then a welcome sight. The bodies of the hounds began to

glow. The subtle vibration steadily grew in concert with the motes of dancing light rising from their still forms. I dematerialized my revolver and stood between the bodies, spreading my arms wide to absorb the rewards from each monster at the same time.

Through the tips of my fingers, I felt the power absorb into my body as the glowing motes extinguished from the now still corridor.

{common} Data Card fragments obtained: hellhound 5/10. 10 Crystals obtained.

Not bad. But now that I had a taste, I wanted more. Too bad I didn't have another Tincture of Fortune handy. Nor did I have any means to forge in the field, if such a thing was possible.

I heard more distant gunfire and shouts. Somebody running. It sounded like it was coming from an adjacent warehouse connected by the corridor sunken into the concrete floor.

I checked my revolver.

1 / 5 ammunition remaining.

Hmmm. I picked up the shotgun and detached the ammo belt from the corpse. I counted five remaining shells.

▸ If you aren't respawning yet, I guess these are staying with me.

I dematerialized the revolver, buckled the ammo belt around my waist, and reloaded the shotgun. Five shells, one bullet. I wouldn't try to add the new equipment to my inventory, just carry them on my person. That way I didn't have to worry about storage.

Time to press on. Feeling more confident, and still with the full complement of my Essence, I went faster through the corridor. It was darker ahead, the flickering spits of flame further behind me. I squinted. Was that a red light around the corner? Something like a beam—maybe from a laser pointer—was dancing. Then I heard a scream and the sound of clanging metal.

I hurried and turned the corner. It seemed the corridor zigged and zagged before connecting to the next building.

A little light from the other warehouse penetrated the way and I saw the silhouette of a Volunteer swinging at a larger, darker silhouette. Another hellhound? Or worse?

▸ Hey! Do you need help?

The Volunteer grunted. It sounded like a woman. She was swinging a sword. It was a tight space, and she did not have much room to maneuver. The large canine was pressing in against her, growling menacingly.

"Kill this fragger!"

I raised the shotgun and stepped up, trying to get a clean shot. I did not want to accidentally hit the Volunteer, struggling in the poor light. My Accuracy wasn't the greatest, and this wasn't exactly a precision weapon.

The beast vomited fire, scorching the Volunteer's leg. I knew then it was a Baskerville Hound.

The woman screamed in pain but fought on. The brightness of the flame now illuminated the scene. The Volunteer was a very muscular woman, like a bodybuilder. I didn't recognize her. She had a metallic contraption wrapping around one side of her head and covering her right eye. The red laser emanated from this device.

She held a long, curved blade—like a katana—and used the sword to alternately block the creature's advance and to strike. And strike she did, but it was hard to tell what the effect was against the beast's dark fur. Smoke curled from the creature's nostrils and it snapped at her.

I got within several feet and pointed the shotgun at the hound's dark haunches. I pulled the trigger, and the gun recoiled hard against my shoulder.

The dog yelped in fury, stumbling forwards on damaged legs. I backed away and reloaded. Meanwhile, the woman stabbed her blade into its side, drawing blood. The beast suddenly jerked its bulk, wrenching the sword from her grasp. Blade protruding from its side, the Baskerville leapt and clawed at her face.

The woman fell backwards. The metallic contraption on her face ripped away, dangling by wires and a broken hinge intertwined with her flesh. An empty, black cavern of an eye socket was revealed beneath.

"GAH! Hit it again!"

I stepped forward and released another blast into the beast's side. It howled madly, flames dripping from its jowls as it turned to face me. I backed away and began reloading. The hound was badly injured. It was having trouble standing under its own power. But it could still burn me.

Then, from behind the Volunteer, two hellhounds ran into the corridor. Hunting as a pack, they each bit down on one of the woman's legs, dragging her backwards while the Baskerville looked on menacingly.

"No! NO! There's too many!"

▸ I'm reloading!

The woman dug her fingernails into the concrete as the dogs dragged her away, tearing at her pants and legs.

I raised the shotgun again. Three targets and a Volunteer in the middle. I switched back and forth between them, not knowing where to shoot and not wanting collateral damage. But then the woman materialized something strange. It was rectangular and lumpy. She held it in one hand and some kind of electronic device in the other.

"Frag this! Get back! If you make it, tell the Round Table I ittied bravely!"

Squinting, I realized what she was about to do. This crazy Volunteer was clutching a block of C-4 plastic explosive. And in her other hand was the detonator. Suddenly feeling very claustrophobic in this tight space, I turned and ran as fast as I could, trying to escape the blast radius.

Turning the corner, I flung myself to the ground as the explosion went off. There was a flash of light, and a shockwave of smoke and debris blew past the corridor. I covered my head and waited for the dust to settle, my ears ringing.

I waited a good minute before peeking around the corner, shotgun at the ready. It was quiet. Visibility was low with smoke swirling at the epicenter of the blast. But I heard no guttural growls and saw no glowing red eyes.

I stepped down the hall, shielding my mouth and nose from the particulate, noting the scorched architecture. No sign of the Volunteer or the hounds. But, through the haze, I did see shining ephemera. Ooh. That crazy Volunteer took them out. Almost took me out too. Finders keepers?

I reached for the floating loot over the indiscernible piles.

{common} Data Card fragments obtained: hellhound 3/10.

{uncommon} Data Card fragments obtained: Baskerville Hound 2/10.

20 Crystals obtained.

Not bad. I ran a quick check of my storage.

MEMORY
- **STORAGE: 292 / 290** (310)

Not maxed out yet. And I noticed that Fancy Jack's calling card took up one metabyte in a heretofore unnoticed Miscellaneous sub-menu of my inventory.

I searched for any sign of the Volunteer's katana. But it was nowhere to be found. Pity. And the ringing in my ears hadn't gone away.

Beyond the blast-induced tinnitus, I still heard fierce fighting in the next building. Time to move on. Rest in peace, anonymous Volunteer. Or should that be 'Restore in Peace'? I wasn't sure what was left of her. I walked to the end of the corridor, stepping through puddles of burnt viscera, and entered the next warehouse.

Round Table spotted.

This warehouse was like the one I had first entered, with multiple catwalks accessible by stairs. Shipping crates were stacked high, creating barricades of cover. I counted four Volunteers but heard more shouts, curses, and gunshots from above.

A Round Tabler carrying a submachine gun with a large drum magazine took shots from the vantage point of a catwalk. I hurried around the nearest stack of crates to get a look at the action. There was Rook and Bigwig, circling their target.

{rare} entity detected: Huodou.

A what?

Several phosphorescent flares were scattered on the ground, and some of the Volunteers had flashlights trained on the beast. It was large—larger than a Baskerville—and jet black. So black that the light seemed to sink into its canine silhouette. There was a large, weighted net over the snarling beast, but as the net caught fire, it quickly burned away.

"It's loose!" shouted the man from above.

Free from its confines, the Huodou moved quickly, and the very ground seemed to melt and catch flame wherever it stepped. The Volunteer above rained bullets at it, but it was fast. Another Volunteer, a scraggly fellow in a gas mask who was definitely not a part of the Round Table, charged forwards with a Molotov cocktail. He chucked it at the beast and the glass shattered.

"You fragging nazz! What possibly made you think that would work?" Bigwig shouted at the hapless Volunteer.

Sure enough, the Huodou sucked up the ball of flame into the black hole of its maw—broken glass and all—then quickly regurgitated what could only be described as napalm on the Volunteer. He died screaming.

The hound darted forwards, sending Rook and Bigwig into a retreat. Several crates caught fire as the devil dog brushed against them. More flames coursed up the warehouse walls towards the high ceiling. Could this whole structure come down if the fire got out of control?

Bigwig had his double-barrel shotgun out. Rook had her kusarigama attached to her back by long chains. No automatic pistols? Maybe she had run out of ammo. The body count, of both Volunteer and beast, suggested this had been a drawn-out slugfest. And here was the main attraction.

▶ I'm here to help!

Bigwig turned and flashed me a derisive look. I wasn't sure if he recognized me or not.

"You've got a gun. Bloody use it!"

He punctuated his command with a double-barreled blast of his own. The creature snarled and quickly weaved its way across the floor towards the closest target, leaving prints of fire in its wake. The closest target was Rook.

"Keep your distance, Rook!"

I instinctively stepped forwards and aimed, shooting at the side of the beast. Contact! It yelped, slowed for a moment, then kept after Rook, who was backed into a stack of crates. I reached for a fresh shell off my belt to reload. But then... Oh no! The shotgun started to fade from reality. Its particles dissipated into nothingness and were gone. Similarly, the ammo belt melted away.

Frag me!

That other Volunteer must have made it through to the Restoration Point. The logjam was cleared, at least for them. I recalled what Antisoc told me about the system safeguards against duplicating weapons. Bigwig gave me an incredulous look and shook his head.

I drew my revolver in one hand and dagger in the other.

Rook, sickles held at her sides, ducked and rolled past the lunging beast, slashing its foreleg. It howled, and the edge of her blade was slick with blood.

Just then—CRASH! A catwalk came tumbling down, crushing Rook's leg and pinning her to the ground. She cried out. The first time I had ever seen Rook lose her cool. Bigwig fired another blast at the Huodou as it whirled around. I ran forwards, unloading the final bullet in my revolver.

0 / 5 ammunition remaining.

It was all happening so fast. Bullets rained from above until I heard a *click, click, click*. The Volunteer with the submachine gun was empty too. In desperation, I threw my revolver at the creature's head. Bigwig scrambled to reload in my periphery. I only had my dagger. What could that do?

"Rook, do you still have any Regenerator Serum?" Bigwig shouted.

I couldn't tell if she heard him or not over the din. Rook was struggling to push the heavy catwalk off her leg, which was clearly broken. Off to the side, I saw the body of another fallen Volunteer, not yet respawned. An AK-47 lay beside him. Did it have ammo left or not?

The Huodou confidently stalked towards the trapped Rook, fiery jaws opening wide. Its eyes gleamed, and Rook appeared mesmerized by whatever she saw in them.

I was of two minds. My instinct for self-preservation at war with, dare I say, my irrational desire to save Rook. Maybe I just wanted to make an impression on the Round Table. Whether personal courage apart from avarice was a virtue I possessed, I truly could not yet discern. Who was it that said, 'know thyself'? Yeah, still working on that.

With only a second to spare, I rushed between Rook and the enormous, black beast. Intense heat radiated off its body, the air between us shimmered like a mirage.

▸ Leave her alone!

Breaking her line of sight with the Huodou, Rook shook her head clear, noticing me with surprise then immediately trying to free her leg from beneath the collapsed catwalk.

I brandished my dagger, ready to stab at the beast's face.

But then I too saw those ominous eyes. They were like bottomless holes, and in them, I could peer into another scene. But what? I stood transfixed. Time seemed to slow as I gazed into those eyes. And all I could hear was the ringing in my ears.

It was hard to describe exactly what I saw, but the gist of it was a naked figure in an empty room. Scrawny. Hugging itself for warmth and trembling pitifully. Layers of skin, like an onion, sloughed off. Layer upon layer, paper thin, revealing the utter emptiness within.

And then, the Huodou killed me.

FILE 23

DEATH

0
   1
10
   11
100
   101
110
   111
1000
   1001
1010

Bright light pierced my eyeballs. I tried to shut my eyelids to block it out but realized I didn't have any. Not yet. My mind lurched. I tried to move my limbs. Phantom pains. Signals to nowhere.

Where am I? What...?

In a tube. Stuck in a cylinder. A whirring sound. Beams of light, weaving the fabric of me together. Bones and sinews. Hot light criss-crossing through me. My nerves stung, each one coming online—

coming alive. And then my clothing and armor, stitched together right on top.

I remembered the burning warehouse. I remembered the Huodou.

Dead.

I died out there.

So that must mean...

Restoration complete. Now discharging.

I heard a metal clank and the small, vibrating platform lowered me out of the translucent restoration tube. I looked down at my hands in wonder. Ozone vapor wafted off my fresh epidermis. My outfit was crisp and clean. Not a speck of soot or blood.

Stunned, I stepped away from the tube, approaching the small panel beside the machine.

Your last restoration was {0} cycles ago.

Automatic restoration fee notification. 1,000 Crypt will be deducted.

Shiva! 1,000 Crypt?!

I quickly checked my menu as the currency drained from the C10K chip in my skull.

ECONOMY

- **CRYPT: 200**

No! I couldn't believe it. The restoration fee was 1,000? Exorbitant. Extortion. Robbery!

Then, with a sinking feeling, I combed through the rest of my menu.

My Crystals? Gone. My new hellhound Data Card fragments? Gone. My Baskerville Hound fragments? Gone. Even the calling card from Fancy Jack was gone. I was restored to my most recent data backup. Looking at the screen confirmed it.

My ammo and Energy were replenished, and the ringing in my ears had abated, but that was small comfort. I knelt on the platform for a long time, wallowing in frustration. My loot. My precious loot. Volunteers passing through the Restoration Point shot me quizzical looks.

But wait, something didn't add up. Didn't I have 1,180 Crypt after taking the MAR to New Dresden? Oh, I see. I backed up to when I had 1,200. Before buying a drink for Pixie and catching the bullet train. The subtle potential to exploit this system for financial gain briefly crossed my mind until I remembered the words of Antisoc. The penalty, or restoration fee, increased with each subsequent death. Well, their exact words were "prohibitively and progressively expensive."

At least I wasn't in debt. Yet. But what did I have to show for all my labors? For all the killing and dying? I had blown a fellow Volunteer's fragging head off!

I had been late to the raid, but bog dram if I didn't try to lend a helping hand. Now I needed to see if the Round Table agreed with that assessment. Were they still in that burning warehouse? Were the survivors still battling their rare opponent? How much time had elapsed? How long had I been... out?

No way was I going back to that inferno. Not right now. I would go to the Rathskeller and see what fate awaited me.

I slogged unenthusiastically across The Commons until I reached the steps leading into the subterranean Volunteer hangout. I could hear the bass from the throbbing electronica within. I hesitated for a spell, listening to the upbeat tempo of music that did not remotely match my current emotional state.

Grumbling, I pushed through the blue double doors.

To my surprise, the members of the Round Table were seated at their usual spot, save for the empty chair. I must certainly have lost time, being dead and all. I politely squeezed past the other patrons and one of the members noticed me, tapping a few others until they all turned.

Then, to my even greater surprise, all the Round Tablers started to applaud.

Okay, so I exaggerated. Just a few members of the Round Table applauded. And Bigwig was definitely not one of them. Although, I thought I detected a hint of respect in his sideways glance as I dared to approach the high roller table.

Still, it felt good to have a warm reception from such an elite group. And there was Rook, alive and well.

"Well, well, well. Look what the cat dragged in."

Apache spoke. I hadn't seen him during the fight, but he apparently heard about my minor role in it. Maybe he was an early casualty in that den of blood and fire.

"We were wondering when you might show up," Bigwig snorted. "Came for a reward?"

I looked from member to member. None seemed worse for wear from the nasty encounter. If they had healed up, cleaned up, or just respawned I didn't know. I briefly thought about the Volunteer I euthanized, whoever and wherever they were. And the other Volunteer who took a ride on the C-4 express. The Rathskeller was less crowded than usual.

▸ Did you get it? Did you kill the… What was it called again?

"The Huodou. Yeah, Rook got the kill shot."

▸ Really?

I turned to Rook in surprise. She smirked and brushed a white dread off her face. I said she didn't look worse for wear, but being this close, I couldn't help but notice the deep scarring across her face and upper arms. Although, that seemed more a result of extensive cybernetic augmentation than injury. Her red eyes flickered as she appraised me.

Another Round Tabler, I think he must have been the one shooting from the catwalk, narrated the recent events to which I was not privy.

"It was epic. You should have seen her. You get up in the monster's litso with your puny malenky knife, and the dram veshch sizes you up for lunch. Meanwhile, Rook cuts her own noga off to get out from under the rubble—slices the whole veshch right off—and activates her hydra power to regrow the limb. Huodou didn't know what tolchock it."

I nodded appreciatively, mentally processing the slang. Amputated her own leg and still won the fight. Rook was one bad-arse woman.

▸ I'm just glad you're okay, Rook.

I regretted saying it the instant the words left my mouth. I wasn't really on a first name basis with her. Bigwig frowned at me, and I suddenly felt acutely self-conscious of my feeble starter voice and my newbie status.

I tried to change the subject.

▸ The raid was a success?

Apache answered this time, gesturing widely with his hands. I tried to keep my distance from his formidable spiked knuckles. Not sure why he couldn't keep those stored in his Equipment menu. Part of his aesthetic, I guess.

"It was. The hot spot has been cleared. Mission accomplished—and a fragging nice Crypt haul!"

A Crypt haul I would see no part of. The rich get richer. The dead get poorer.

▸ What exactly does that mean? A 'hot spot.'

"It's like this, rookie. When a creature of higher rarity shows up, it attracts other creatures to the same area. Rare, legendary, mythical. Forget it. That Huodou set up shop in the warehouse district. Marked its territory. You viddied how many hellhounds and Baskervilles were crawling around in there. Or maybe not—you missed most of the action."

▸ I was... unavoidably detained. So, if you take out the bigger threat, the hot spot is cleared? And the rarer the creature, the more dangerous it is.

"Yes and no. Just because a creature is of a rarer frequency does not always mean it's more dangerous. It's just more infrequent. An uncommon cyclops can snap you in half like a twig. Rarity does not directly correlate to more danger. But it often does. Whatever the case, these creatures are attracted to their own kind. We take out the bolshy baddiwad, and that district should stay peaceful for a nice long while."

I was beginning to grasp some of the strategy here. Maybe the Round Table believed if they could target and eliminate the rarest frequency invasive entities throughout the Metaverse, there would be a trickle down effect. Like killing the queen of an insect hive. Was this how they would 'win the game'?

Bigwig blew out a lungful of air and cracked his knuckles, tiring of the conversation. Apache took the hint and shut up, grabbing a nearby stein and taking a hearty swig of glowing blue liquid. Meanwhile, Rook watched me in silence.

"Well, what do we think? Does this odin deserve the 5% discount?" Bigwig asked.

The other members rapped their knuckles on the table, voicing their agreement. Bigwig shrugged his broad shoulders.

"Then who am I to stand in the way? Although, to be honest, for a minute there I thought you might turn tail and run. But you stepped up. Showed some backbone, despite being a Xonny-come-lately."

I mumbled a vague reply. But I was thankful to get that discount. I needed every advantage I could get. Rook got up and wrapped her slender fingers around one of the straps of my ballistic vest.

"Follow me," she said in her low, slick voice.

Then she nodded over to the bartender. It was the enigmatic, smartly dressed woman with the bowtie.

"Erwina, two tokens please."

Erwina?

The bartender smiled that perfect white smile and slid two objects across the bar. I recognized them as the tokens that had granted access to the Schwarzmarkt. Apparently, Round Table members didn't need to bother with ordering a one hundred Crypt mind eraser to gain admission. Another perk. I dutifully followed Rook to the back of the Rathskeller where she showed the tokens to the Volunteer on watch. We stepped through the secret door.

The Schwarzmarkt was deserted, looking alien under the UV lights. No black market business. No caged death matches. We were alone. Did she want privacy?

▸ Where are you taking me?

"Just over here."

Rook led me to a small table and forcibly pushed me into a chair. She grabbed a stool from elsewhere and slid it close. Reaching onto her back, she pulled out a cable. On the other end was an asymmetrical syringe-like device.

I tensed up.

"Relax, it's a tattoo machine."

▶ Tattoo?

"For your friends and family discount. 5% off at the Armory. You scan the ID on your right wrist for everything else, but a little smart ink on your left wrist will signify which Round Table benefits you are eligible for."

▶ I see.

Benefits plural? I wondered if there was a discount for the Supply Depot too, or elsewhere, or even higher discount percentages I could earn.

I noticed for the first time that on Rook's left wrist was a small, round tattoo. A perfect circle with a sizeable black bird in the center with a distinctive beak.

▶ Is that a crow?

It was hard to read her expression with the pupil-less red eyes. But Rook pursed her ashen lips, holding the tattoo gun in the air.

"It's a rook, you nazz."

▶ Oh. Of course. When I heard the name Rook, I was thinking about the chess piece for some reason. The castle. The chariot.

This elicited another slight smirk. She shook her head, her nest of dreads flowing with the movement.

"If you want to tap into our special benefits, you need this smart ink. Who knows. If you keep going down this path, we can add more detail to the mark as you earn more privileges."

So, there were more benefits.

► Down which path?

"I saw what you did. You sacrificed yourself. You bought me just the amount of time I needed to pivot—to find a way to close that bounty. I'm grateful, and I would be willing to nominate you for consideration for the Round Table if that is something you are interested in. Endorse your application process."

► Really? You'd do that?

"You would have a long road ahead. Long. It won't be easy, and there is no guarantee we'd even have an open seat. But you showed real spirit out there. That's an unusual thing in this place. Tell me, did it hurt? When the Huodou got you."

I tried to remember. I had looked into its eyes. There was something there, some vision. Something discomfiting. When the moment of death came, it was over before I knew it.

► It happened so fast... there was something... Its eyes. Did you see anything when you looked in its eyes?

Rook grew reflective. She slowly lowered the tattoo gun. Eventually, she answered in a quiet voice. Although, there was nobody else around to overhear.

"What I saw was... beautiful."

My jaw dropped open. Beautiful? That was not my experience. Quite the opposite.

"Forget it. I hope you had a recent data backup. I know a lot of newbies wait too long between backups. Losing too much will make you want to rage quit. But of course, that's impossible."

► I lost a bunch of Crystals. Some hellhound fragments, a few Baskerville fragments. It could have been worse.

"Do you have a complete hellhound data card?"

I shook my head.

"How many fragments short?"

► I'm at 4 out of 10.

Rook accessed her menu. Soon, she produced a handful of crystalline items.

"Six fragments. And twenty Crystals. That will be enough to forge and fuse a Data Card. That's the best I can do. It'll be our secret. The Round Table frowns on sharing loot with non-members, and we definitely *never* share reward money. Also, we have our sponsorships to think about."

► That's very generous. Thank you.

With sincere gratitude, I accepted the gifts, feeling the pleasant sensation of the fragments and Crystals absorbing into my avatar.

Wait, did she say sponsorships?

She raised the tattoo gun once more, ready to get on with business.

"Just some light body modification. Won't hurt... much. But you need to tell me what symbol you want. A magpie?"

I looked at Rook. This strong, chromed-up warrior. This elite bounty hunter. Out of my league in every way. I still did not fully understand the feelings she elicited in me.

I remembered the first time I heard the Magpie moniker. It was when she chided me for taking Camel's loot. Afterwards, it had been hard to shake. Ironically or not, I realized now that a magpie was not unlike the black bird gracing her own wrist.

► Yes, a magpie will do fine.

She went to work, etching a perfect circle on my upturned wrist then beginning on the outline of a bird. She did it all from memory or pure inspiration. It hurt a little, but I didn't mind.

Bigwig walked into the backroom and cleared his throat.

"Everything okay back here?"

Rook didn't look up, just grunted a reply. Her burly partner strode over to inspect her handiwork. It seemed more like he was checking up on us. Or more specifically, me. Possessive?

"The thieving magpie gets a magpie."

He shook his head with bemusement. I noticed for the first time that Bigwig also had a small round tattoo on his left wrist. It was a rabbit, highly detailed. Huh. Unexpected.

"Magpies are very intelligent birds," Rook explained as she finished applying the smart ink. "They are good at problem solving, can use tools, and can even recognize themselves in mirrors."

I smiled. There were worse things to be associated with. Although, to be honest, I would have trouble recognizing myself in a mirror.

Bigwig muttered something under his breath and went away, heading back into the main section of the Rathskeller. Rook reattached the tattoo gun to her metallic bodice and wiped her hands.

"All done. Now you can use the discount any time you like."

▸ Thank you again. For everything.

I sat admiring the skillfully crafted marking—simple as it was. When I looked up, I was alone. Rook had slipped out like a whisper in the wind. I sighed and turned back to contemplate the tattoo just a little longer.

A permanent 5% discount at the Armory. That was pretty nice. Unfortunately, I had almost no Crypt left to spend. I was down to 200. The death penalty was no joke.

I opened my menu. Time to update my notes.

>**SUBROUTINES**
-    **Assist Antisoc with Repository Heist** (Complete?)
-    **Assist Serpents with Package Delivery** (Pending)
-    ~~**Assist Round Table with Warehouse District Raid**~~ ~~(Complete)~~

FILE 23.1

FUSE

I thought about Antisoc. Because of my rush to join the raid in progress, I hadn't followed up after participating in the heist. How would they react to me losing the thermal goggles and my interrogation by ColSec? And then there was the offer from the Serpents. After some more thought, I jotted down one additional note.

- **Apply to join the Round Table?** (TBD)

But right now, I had Crystals and card fragments burning a hole in my pocket, thanks to Rook's unexpected generosity. I exited the Schwarzmarkt. More Volunteers had wandered into the Rathskeller in the meantime, and the Round Table was holding court.

The bounty hunter with the SMG was making a speech. He had a wide girth and wore a brassy breathing apparatus. His arms, shins, and thighs were protected by plates of armor reminiscent of a samurai.

"—and to celebrate another successful raid, the Round Table is offering drinks on the house courtesy of Kowloon Tenements! Tired of your tube? Upgrade to a Kowloon Tenement. And always—Glory to the Volunteers!"

There was a mighty shout from the other patrons as the Round Tabler thrust his drink in the air, liquid sloshing over the top.

"Glory to the Volunteers!"

I looked over at Rook. She was back at her seat, sipping a drink. I found her compatriot's marketing pitch strangely off putting, but she betrayed no reaction either way. She, Bigwig, Apache, and all the others had moved on. I waited until the mad rush of Volunteers to the bar ebbed and went outside.

200 Crypt, twenty Crystals, and 10/10 common hellhound Data Card fragments. It was time to visit the Data Forge again. I went straight there and stepped up to the device at the center of the forge, scanning my ID and accessing the control panel.

DATA FORGE

CONVERT

FORGE

- **ITEMS** (from materials)
- **CARDS** (from card fragments)

FUSE

EXPORT

TRANSMUTE

I accessed the Forge Cards function. Two of the extruding cloverleaf podium tops glowed, eager to accept my offerings.

Insert the Data Card fragments for forging.

I materialized the ten hellhound Data Card fragments. They were like shards of weathered glass in dusky and ember shades. Now that I had a complete set, I realized they fit together like jagged puzzle pieces. Although, that image constantly shifted in the light. They levitated ever so slightly over my open hand.

I added them to the leftmost receptacle, which received them as surely as the power of magnetism.

Deposit Crystals for forging.

I materialized ten Crystals and placed them in the second lit receptacle.

Begin forging process?

▸ Yes.

This had better work. Dram my low Processing stats. I worked too long and hard to complete this set for a failed forging attempt.

Both pedestals shone bright. Energy and data convulsed, swirled into the center of the device. I shielded my eyes from the blast. At last, the glow subsided.

Card forging successful.

1 {common} hellhound Data Card (*Weapon / Armor*) forged.

And there it was, rotating in the air. The lenticular image of the hellhound was emblazoned on the card, although the beast's form lurched in an arched fashion as it spun.

I took the card with a sigh of relief. Then a revelation hit me. What would happen if I were to combine fragments from different data cards together? Instant failure, or something else? Whatever the case, I had no materials to experiment with and I knew in my bones that I did not have the stats to pull anything like that off. Not yet.

Time to see what this card was all about. I concentrated on it.

Data Card: Hellhound

Card Type: Weapon / Armor

Frequency: Common

Fusion Details: Add +10% fire damage to a single fusible weapon, or +15% fire resistance to a single fusible armor.

Size: 10 metabytes

Interesting. My snub-nosed revolver was my only weapon capable of fusion as my push dagger had the basic quality. My ballistic vest was currently my best piece of armor, offering twenty defense and only taking up ten metabytes of storage (although my tactical pants also would be eligible for fusion).

But what would be better, fire damage or fire resistance?

I was tempted to go for improved defense. I had seen a lot of damage done by pyromaniacal invasive entities. At the same time, wouldn't it be nice to have some of that fire power working in my favor? A little voice in the back of my head reminded me that sometimes the best defense was a good offense.

I cycled back through the options on the control panel and selected the Fuse function.

FUSE
- **SKILLS** (fuse data cards onto eligible skill slots)
- **EQUIPMENT** (fuse data cards onto eligible weapons or armor)

I selected the Equipment suboption. This time, three receptacles illuminated before me, surrounding the middle platform. I assumed the target item would go in the center, but it remained unlit.

Place a weapon or armor piece for fusing.

I brought out my revolver and placed it on one of the waiting podiums with a clink.

{common} snub-nosed revolver detected.

Insert a Data Card in the indicated depository.

I materialized the spinning hellhound card and set it hovering in place in the adjacent spot.

{common} Data Card: Hellhound *(Weapon / Armor)* detected.

Deposit Crystals for fusing.

I placed my remaining ten Crystals on the third podium. Hated to see those beautiful baubles go, but I appreciated the benefits they accorded.

Begin fusing process?

▸ Yes.

The Data Card dissolved. The Crystals melted into brilliant aether. Even my revolver broke down into constituent particles. Another refulgent light overtook all until, at last, my revolver glowed in the center pedestal as if heated in a kiln.

Weapon fusing successful.

Hellhound +10% fire damage fused onto snub-nosed revolver.

I tentatively touched the revolver's handle. The red glow faded and, to my surprise, it was completely cool to the touch. I picked up the weapon and examined it closely.

The gun briefly glowed a dark red upon equipping. The same color as the burning eyes of the accursed hellhounds. But just as quickly, it looked like an ordinary firearm once more.

I opened my Equipment menu and checked the details.

EQUIPMENT
- **WEAPONS**
  - **SNUB-NOSED REVOLVER** (30 metabytes): 20 damage output
    - **5 / 5 .32 caliber ammunition** (chambered)
    - **+10% fire damage** (Hellhound)

There it was. A little extra elemental kick. The fusion added ten metabytes to my revolver's data burden, but I obviously no longer had the ten metabyte Data Card elsewhere in my inventory, so my storage capacity remained unchanged.

And I could test my improved piece out at the Armory's firing range with the benefit of unlimited ammunition.

I wondered if the 10% fire damage would scale if I upgraded my weapon. The breech-loading shotgun I had the brief pleasure (and displeasure) of using during the raid was level two of ten and packed a considerable punch. Colonel Peacekeeper told me a little about weapon upgrades, but I would have to dig through my history to remember exactly what it said.

MEMORY

HISTORY

- **Supply Depot vendor said, "Take your sidearm. It has a damage output of twenty. If you upgrade that gun to level ten, you could reach a maximum damage output of 200! That's some serious firepower!"**

Right. In exchange for a fee, upgrades to a maximum of level ten would have a direct multiplier effect on damage output. Logically, the breech-loading shotgun began with forty damage, multiplying to eighty with the upgrade. So then, would the fire damage scale in direct proportion?

I also wondered if there was a method to undo a fusion if I acquired a better weapon. Could I get my Data Card back? Would I have to choose between salvaging the revolver or the card? Or was this a permanent bond?

Furthermore, if I had ten hellhound data cards, could I fuse them all to get +100% fire damage? Were there limits to one fusion per item? Did different types of weapons have different fusion limits?

There was still so much I didn't know. Even after all I'd been through, I was only scratching the surface of how this world worked. I wish I could find Camel—if he was sober—and pepper him with all my latest questions. Come to think of it, I hadn't seen him around lately. It was that or another trip to an information kiosk.

Before any of that, I resolved to back up my data. With my luck, I would get hit by a hoverbike crossing the street and lose this precious fusion. I left the Data Forge (a couple Volunteers impatiently waiting for me to vacate) and traveled back to the Restoration Point.

I had just left this place, and it didn't feel amazing to be back. At least the circumstances were different.

Welcome to the Restoration Point.

Volunteer 01001110 01101111 01100010 01101111 01100100 01111001

Your last backup was {0} cycles ago.

Would you like to back up your data?

▸ Yeah, yeah, yeah.

100 Crypt will be deducted.

I paid one hundred Crypt out of my remaining 200 and approached the machine that wove me back into existence. I needed to take another bounty soon. A bounty that actually paid.

Please enter the Restoration Station to back up your data.

Into the suspended MRI tube I went. Maybe it was more accurate to think of it as a high-tech womb. A digital cocoon.

Your data backup has been successfully completed.

Afterwards, I checked the information panel to confirm the backup.

DESIGNATION

VOLUNTEER ID: 01001110-01101111-01100010-01101111-01100100-01111001

ALIASES: MAGPIE
- **COSMETICS**
    - **WAVY ASYMMETRICAL CROP** (hair)
    - **ALMOND** (skin tone)
- **MODS**

- NEURAL-INTERFACE AXIS PORT
  - **B3-9S7-C10K CHIP** (10,000 Crypt storage)
- ROUND TABLE SMART INK
  - **5% ARMORY DISCOUNT**

STATISTICS

- **ATTACK:** (40)
  - **STRENGTH: 20**
  - **ACCURACY: 20**
- **DEFENSE:** (30)
  - **ESSENCE: 20**
  - **RESISTANCE: 10**
- **ABILITY:** (40)
  - **ADEPTNESS: 10**
  - **ENERGY: 30**
- **MOVEMENT:** (30)
  - **SPEED: 20**
  - **AGILITY: 10**
- **PROCESSING:** (50)
  - **PERCEPTION: 20**
  - **PERSUASION: 10**
  - **PROTOCOL: 10**
  - **PROBABILITY: 10**

SKILLS

- **Clurichaun** (10 metabytes)
- {empty}
- {empty}
- {empty}

EQUIPMENT

- **WEAPONS**
  - **PUSH DAGGER** (10 metabytes): 10 damage output
  - **SNUB-NOSED REVOLVER** (30 metabytes): 20 damage output

- **5 / 5 .32 caliber ammunition** (chambered)
- **+10% fire damage** (Hellhound)
- **ARMOR** (40)
  - **HELM:** N/A
  - **BODY: BALLISTIC VEST** (10 metabytes): 20 defense
    - **PROMOTIONAL T-SHIRT** (cosmetic)
  - **ARMS:** N/A
  - **LEGS: TACTICAL PANTS** (10 metabytes): 10 defense (+20 storage)
    - **TACTICAL BOOTS** (10 metabytes): 10 defense
- **ACCESSORIES**

INVENTORY
- **CARDS**
- **FRAGMENTS**
- **CONSUMABLES**
- **MATERIALS**
  - **2 {common} fern flowers** (2 metabytes)
  - **1 {uncommon} coco de mer nut** (1 metabyte)
  - **1 white linen cloth** (1 metabyte)
  - **1 vial of pure water** (1 metabyte)
- **MISCELLANEOUS**

ECONOMY
- **CRYPT: 100** (stored on B3-9S7-C10K chip)
- **CRYSTALS**

MEMORY
- **STORAGE: 275 / 290** (310) (+20 soft storage cap)
- **SCHEMAS**
  - **Tincture of Fortune** (fern flower + pure water)
- **HISTORY**

STATUS

TASKS

- **Remove clurichaun from a private residence in Royal Heights** (Complete / Paid Out)
- **Remove hellhounds from MAR Station Service Tunnels** (Complete / Paid Out)
- **>SUBROUTINES**
- **Assist Antisoc with Repository Heist** (Complete?)
- **Assist Serpents with Package Delivery** (Pending)
- ~~**Assist Round Table with Warehouse District Raid** (Complete)~~
- **Apply to join the Round Table?** (TBD)

FILE 24

HUNTING

After backing up my data, I decided to stroll through Spawn Alley. I was wary of Collective Security's threat—I was being watched. How? By whom or what? When? I had no idea. But maybe there was a way I could send a signal to Antisoc. Nonchalant. Discrete. Get some sort of message across that I could be trusted and wanted to parlay.

We had unfinished business.

The yokocho was empty, the neon sign switched off. It was as if somebody drained the color from the entire hole-in-the-wall establishment. Even the small, red curtain in the back was as drab as days-old dried blood. No customers. No fish-gutting chef.

Sigh.

Nobody's home. Maybe Antisoc got spooked after I was detained and questioned by ColSec. Either that or they rotated points of contact just as frequently as they moved headquarters. Would I ever hear from them again, or had they cut me adrift?

If ColSec really was keeping tabs on me, I couldn't just go asking around about the group they designated as terrorists. Public enemy number one. And it would sure be suspicious for me to be searching around The Commons for an imaginary grinning cat. I briefly thought of browsing the Supply Depot for a nostalgic can of tuna.

Here kitty, kitty.

No, the most natural thing for a Volunteer to do was to take on another task. That was what the system wanted and expected from me. Fulfill my contract. Hunt the monsters. And as it stood, I was in desperate need of Crypt. Down to my last one hundred, stashed in the chip in the back of my head. Another task might take the heat off me and put some pretty polly in my pocket. Two birds, one stone.

Two birds...

I thought of Rook.

No use in daydreaming. I pushed the thought away.

I only hoped that Antisoc was watching me just as thoroughly as ColSec. Then they should know that I did not betray them. Nor would I. But again, the words of that faceless Surveillance, anti-Terrorism, Apprehension, Security, and Investigations officer ran through my head. "Collective Security is prepared to richly incentivize any Volunteer possessing information about this terrorist organization."

No. No, no, no. I pushed that thought away too. The system stole my memory. I wouldn't sell out other Volunteers for a reward, no matter how rich... Right? I didn't have the Processing power to unravel this right now. I had to put my head down and keep going. Another bounty.

I left Spawn Alley and went to the Task Assignment Boards, keeping my eyes open for Camel or any other familiar Volunteer or feline faces on that way. No such luck. But I did arrive unscathed and found the boards available for use.

I scanned the code and the available bounties swam across the multi-screen display. Recalling the Round Table's hot spot concept, I was curious to see if any bounties would be listed in New Dresden—specifically the warehouse district—but did not immediately notice any.

As I looked over the opportunities, I reflected on my capabilities. I had progressed in my statistical categories, acquired modest weapons and armor, fused a Data Card onto a skill slot, and upgraded my ranged weapon with some fire damage. I witnessed and participated in my fair share of violence but so far only had two completed bounties to my name.

Did I feel up for soloing an invasive entity of uncommon frequency? Not a swarm but just one? Two options stood out.

Task Assignment: Remove minotaur from Grand Central Park in Eden West.

One {uncommon} minotaur has been detected in the hedge maze within Grand Central Park in Eden West.

Task Completion Award: 3,000 Crypt.

Task Assignment: Remove jiangshi from Elysian Spires Financial District.

One {uncommon} jiangshi has been detected at the Universal Cryptocurrency Credit Exchange in the Financial District of Elysian Spires.

Task Completion Award: 2,000 Crypt.

Bonus: 2,000 Crypt for eliminating target entity before the next cycle.

I was familiar with the concept of a minotaur, but off the top of my head, I had no idea what a jiangshi was.

Both were uncommon frequency single targets. Exactly what I

was looking for. I needed to decide before either task was snatched by another Volunteer.

A 3,000 guaranteed payout for killing a minotaur (if I succeeded) versus a 4,000 possible payout for killing a jiangshi (if I succeeded before The Collective was baptized in pink rain). I sure loved money and the things money could buy. 1,000 additional Crypt meant a lot for a poor sod like me.

I would take the gamble.

Do you accept this Task?

▸ Yes.

Task Assigned: Remove jiangshi from Elysian Spires Financial District.

As the bounty vanished from the Task Assignment Board, I searched again for the minotaur task. Maybe I could accept both? I wasn't aware of any rule about a maximum number of concurrent assigned tasks. But the minotaur task was gone. Nabbed by some other Volunteer no doubt.

Okay. Jiangshi it is. A 2,000 minimum payment, but why not be optimistic?

Having no concept of what this invasive entity was, I wanted to do some research at the Archives. But did I have enough time? The trouble was I had no way of telling when the next cycle would begin. There was no day or night in The Commons. I didn't have an almanac, or whatever it was, like Fancy Jack. And I didn't have the meteorological instincts of that elderly vendor at the Supply Depot.

Come to think of it, why not go and ask?

I covered the relatively short distance to the Supply Depot and strode in. Sure enough, the old woman was where I expected her to be, perched on her stool near the checkout counter. She smiled, wrinkling her eyes at me in faint recognition. I saw no parasol in her liver-spotted hands.

"Oh, ho, ho. Come to do some shopping?"

▸ I'm a little short on Crypt right now, but I hope to do so soon. Might I ask you a question?

"Ask away, dearie."

▸ The rain. You said you're never wrong about the rain. Do you think it is going to rain soon?

She paused, as if listening to the very fabric of the Metaverse, and raised her hand to detect some change of pressure or humidity that I was oblivious to. She smiled again.

"Not yet."

▸ Thank you. I really appreciate it.

"Before you run off, you should know that the renovations are finished. Our upstairs Auction House is now open for business."

I glanced over at the spiral staircase leading up to the previously inaccessible floor. Apache had mentioned this. Alas, I had no Crypt to bid on anything and nothing valuable to put up for auction. Something to keep in mind for later.

I said as much and bowed, thanking the vendor again before exiting. If it wasn't going to rain yet, I had time to research at the Archives.

FILE 24.1

TERMINAL

Passing through the darkened and neglected blocks on the far side of The Commons, I entered the concrete pyramidal structure and descended to the deep bowels of the ARCHIV. When the elevator finally spewed me out, I approached the curved screens and attached the headset.

Welcome to the Archives.

Initiate query.

▸ Mythology query, jiangshi.

Mythology query initiated -> Jiangshi

A Chinese variant of both the vampire and zombie archetypes, Jiangshi originate when Taoist priests reanimate the dead in order to send the bodies home over long distances for burial; however, these reanimated corpses deviate from the spell's command. Due to rigor mortis, these undead creatures can only move about by hopping, although they are surprisingly agile and can hop faster than most people can run.

Jiangshi awaken at night, seeking to kill living creatures to absorb their qi and become more powerful. Although completely blind, a jiangshi can sense human breath.

Great. Just fragging great.

▸ Mythology query, jiangshi weaknesses?

Mythology query initiated -> Jiangshi weaknesses

Items that are known vulnerabilities or repellent to jiangshi include mirrors, objects made from peach wood, black dog blood, glutinous rice, and vinegar, among others. Jiangshi can also be temporarily distracted by throwing small objects on the ground as they may be compelled to count them. The most effective method of stopping a jiangshi is to nail an immobilizing counterspell talisman to their forehead.

What? Where was I going to get the wood of a peach tree? And how could mirrors or throwing small objects on the ground work if the creature was blind? That didn't make sense. Then again, who said that mythology always made logical sense? I certainly didn't know how to create a counterspell talisman. And it would have been really helpful to know about vulnerability to the blood of a black dog earlier when I was busy shooting and stabbing several of them.

Well, if these hopping vampires were anything like the other invasive entities I had encountered so far, they would have to take damage from my revolver and dagger. No mention of vulnerability to fire, unfortunately.

I left the Archives, taking the long elevator ride to the surface, and crossed town to the MAR Station. I paid my ten Crypt fee and descended to the platform, stopping to study the transit map on the tiled wall.

Elysian Spires... Elysian Spires...

The transit map was laid out in a typical cardinal orientation, although it did not label any of the directions as such. To get to Elysian Spires I would need to ride the Diamond Line north until I reached the MAR Master Terminal, which was one stop past New

Dresden. Then it looked like I would have to switch trains to the Platinum Line and head the equivalent of west.

I briefly examined several other transit stops displayed on the map. Some I had heard of from previous bounty opportunities or from the mouths of Volunteers. Some were new to me. Eden West. New Dawn. Crystal Coast. Arcadia Harbor. Nova Sakahlin. Metro Central. Little Mecca. Potemkin Villas.

There were a lot of locations for the one million Citizens that migrated in the first wave. Maybe not so many considering the next thirty million in waiting.

How large could a Metaverse be? Was it limited in some way by the hard boundaries of the laws of physics? Or was it wholly reliant on available computing power? Or was it, like the physical universe, theoretically infinite? Then again, what if the physical universe was simply like a three-dimension Pac-man screen? Keep going in one direction far enough for long enough and you end up where you started.

A sharp pain registered in my forehead and I pinched the bridge of my unremarkable nose until it abated. Why was I here? I hardly seemed like the ideal recruit to infiltrate a digital world and dispatch invasive entities composed of foreign code, knowing as little as I did about the mechanics of such.

But I wasn't a recruit. I was a Volunteer. Allegedly.

A whooshing sound alerted me that the bullet train was rapidly approaching, and I boarded. As usual, I was completely alone on the train car. I passed through Royal Heights, The Palisades, Lower Dresden, and New Dresden. Flashing scenery rushed past the windows revealing glimpses of fiery red and amber hued skies. A sunless sunset?

Now arriving at MAR Master Terminal.

When the doors slid open, I was surprised to see several people in dapper business suits waiting to board the train. This was different. I barely had time to register it as I had to get off before the doors shut and the train sped away towards Upper Dresden.

The surrealness continued as I took an escalator from the platform to the main level. I found myself in a large transit concourse. Signs pointed to the different transit lines leading to far-flung locations, spinning off this hub in various trajectories to destinations known and unknown. Overhead, screens updated travel timetables, working like clockwork.

A significant number of people, presumably Citizens, moved about. They were all dressed exquisitely, and many carried fine briefcases or elegant handbags. It wasn't only Citizens. I saw fellow Volunteers passing through. None had weapons drawn, but I could tell from their accoutrement exactly what they were. There were also multiple Polizei bots posted at regular intervals, but they did not seem on edge, merely serving a function.

The Volunteers and Citizens ignored each other, each laser-focused on getting from Point A to Point B. I stopped gawking and strode deeper into the concourse, searching for a sign pointing to the Platinum Line. After walking for a few minutes, I noticed multiple Volunteers congregating in one specific area of the Terminal. And to my surprise, there was another Task Assignment Board right in the middle.

That confirmed it. There were multiple bounty boards. If this was a centralized transit hub, it made sense to have a board here rather than forcing Volunteers to schlep back and forth from The Commons after every job. One Volunteer appeared to be cashing in a completed task and receiving payment right then and there. Useful.

Turning around, I also noticed a long service counter. Behind it were a series of white metal cubes stacked on top of one another and running the length of a small wall. Two other Volunteers were accessing these boxes. Each box had a small sensor and a telltale red light.

Storage lockers! Is this for real?

I read the text describing the service.

Temporary single-point data storage. 500 metabytes max. 100 Crypt per cycle. 10 cycle limit.

Another convenience to use in a pinch. The rest of the description spoke for itself, but I interpreted 'single-point' to mean I wouldn't be able to access anything stored in one of these lockers remotely or from another access location. Compared to the Repository, the starting cost was the same but with significant size and time limits. A one night stand instead of a long term commitment. But more than enough size for any needs I would have at this point.

I located the Platinum Line and descended to the platform heading in the direction of Elysian Spires. It cost me another ten Crypt. I was down to eighty.

I boarded a train half full of passengers, all of whom studiously avoided me with practiced nonchalance, and hung on a strap at the rear of the car. The doors slid shut.

Now leaving MAR Master Terminal. Next stop, Elysian Spires, followed by New Dawn.

Advertisements for wares I could not hope to afford and news of events that meant nothing to me buzzed on the screens overhead.

As we sped beyond the orbit of the MAR Master Terminal, I glanced again through the windows. The auburn hues of the sky were turning lavender with hints of indigo nipping close behind. Soon it would be nightfall in Elysian Spires. The time when vampires come out to play.

FILE 25

JIANGSHI

Elysian Spires' financial district pulsed like some great digital heart. Twisting towers sheathed in obsidian glass and cold chrome scraped the outskirts of an empty heaven, the upper floors lost in the twinkling glare of city lights against the fading ombre of falling night.

I stood before a veritable financial temple, dwarfed in size by the sleek monoliths on either side, but oozing with monumental self-importance and brass plated faux historicity.

The Universal Cryptocurrency Credit Exchange.

Suited salarymen and women passed behind me on an immaculate street while Polizei bots and a security barrier blocked the entrance to this domed marble edifice of capitalism. Towering statues of Hermes and Fortuna flanked the august doors, and venerable columns announced themselves in a tidy row, marked by hanging flags of unknown origin.

Ah, it was the Reality Inc. corporate logo emblazoned on the flags. Of course it was.

"You there. Volunteer. Are you here for the task?"

One of the Polizei bots, wearing some rank-indicating insignia on its uniform, addressed me through its shielded helmet.

▸ That's right. The jiangshi.

"Good. The Citizens are anxious to resume use of this facility. The sooner you remove the invasive entity the better."

I glanced at the night sky. No sign of rain. The bonus was still in play.

▸ I heard they only come out at night. Can't the Citizens use the facility during the day?

"One of them discovered a burial casket in a supply closet. They were too afraid to stay in the building after that, even during daylight hours."

▸ I see. Wouldn't it have been easy to get rid of the, uh, invasive entity while it was sleeping?

"We are not authorized to do that. Now that you are here, we will disengage the security barrier."

A shimmer of light and two of the lower-ranking Polizei bots moved twin segments of the barricade, allowing me access to the entrance. The bots stood aside and watched me through their unreadable black helmets. The higher rank offered a final word of caution.

"There is one very important thing to remember, Volunteer. You are not permitted to make any after-hours trades inside the Exchange."

I rolled my eyes and kept walking.

I entered and took a curving flight of steps up from the lobby to the trading floor. The overhead lights were shut off, but in their panic to leave the building, the Citizens left much of the Exchange's machinery on.

The large, open space was bordered by circular trading posts and surrounded by various booths and workstations filled with flashing screens and active data feeds. Very little of it made sense to me. Numbers going up. Numbers going down. An alphabet soup of acronyms and initialisms. Charts and graphs. Market fluctuations. Trading algorithms churning away for the benefit of absentee info-barons.

With the lack of brokers and investment bankers—or whoever naturally haunted this capitalist mausoleum—the only sounds were the steady buzz of monitors glowing with ticker data and my echoey footsteps against the sleek marble floors. More Crypt than I could count changed hands in nanoseconds, invisible signals ripping through the air above me on automated cadences.

I materialized my revolver. It briefly glowed a satisfying red in my hand.

Stepping carefully, I moved further into the cavernous trading floor. The vacant trading posts—hung with panels and strewn with bladelike, black server towers—obstructed my sight. I strained to hear anything. Anything at all beyond my own steps and the persistent electric buzz.

Nothing.

I let out a heavy sigh, realizing I had been practically holding my breath this whole time.

Thump. Thump. Thump.

Something's coming.

Thump. Thump. Thump.

I held the revolver in front of me and backed away from the approaching sound until I bumped against one of the trading posts. Then I saw it.

{uncommon} entity detected: Jiangshi.

It looked like a man. But no man I had ever seen. Hopping on two stiff legs with arms rigidly outstretched, the living corpse had pale white skin with a greenish pall, highlighted by the sheen of the nearby monitors. Whether the green was from decay or some sort of fungus growing on the skin I could not tell. I smelled the stench of rotting flesh.

The jiangshi was dressed in long, formal robes from another time and place with a brimmed, black hat of velvet. The fingernails resembled blackened claws as they reached towards me. Its eyes were jaundiced and empty, but my own eyes were drawn to the yellow strip of paper hanging before its face, scrawled with symbols I could not read.

It opened its mouth, but no sound came out. Not a moan, groan, hiss, or click. Just a slack jaw revealing a mouthful of decaying human teeth.

Thump. Thump. Thump.

I aimed my revolver straight for the creature's forehead. It was only a couple yards from me now and hopping faster.

Thump! Thump! Thump!

BLAM!

The force of the blast knocked its head backwards with a jerk, and the jiangshi fell to its knees, chipping its long nails on the marble. Then, bit by bit, it decomposed and crumbled into a pile of ashes and bone.

4 / 5 ammunition remaining.

One shot, one kill? Nice! That was way easier than I expected. Maybe the easiest Crypt I'd ever made.

For my own amusement, I blew the wisp of smoke away from the revolver's barrel, attempted a Wild West gun twirl, and dematerialized it back into my menu.

Wait. Where was the system notification that the task was complete?

TASKS

- **Remove jiangshi from Elysian Spires Financial District** (Pending)

Still pending?

A rustling sound drew my attention back to the ossuarial pile on the floor. I watched in dismay as the jiangshi reassembled, springing back to its former mockery of life.

It lurched at me, clearing the distance with an agile jump, reaching out with its hideous nails and teeth.

As it made contact, a sudden chill came over my heart.

Alert! Energy draining.

Energy: 20 remaining.

Energy: 10 remaining.

Energy: 0 remaining.

Energy depleted.

I gave the creature a hard kick to the chest with my tactical boot, sending it reeling back.

▸ Gah!

I winced and clutched my heart. Whatever the jiangshi did, an inexplicably cold sensation lingered within my chest. I felt empty. Weakened. Did this fragger drain my qi? I didn't even know what qi was!

I fired twice in rapid succession. One shot grazed its cadaverous neck. The other buried in its torso, sizzling with latent heat. It was enough. Again, the jiangshi crumbled to the floor in a dusty heap.

I staggered backwards, not taking my eyes off the pile.

2 / 5 ammunition remaining.

Stay dead. Stay dead!

Still no notification.

Slowly but surely the jiangshi reassembled itself until the rigid body, ancient robes and all, tottered in place in front of me. Its dead, yellow eyes stared vacantly ahead. Its rotting mouth hung open, hungry for more of my lifeforce.

What I wouldn't give for some peach wood right about now.

I ran, weaving between the round posts dotting the trading floor. I needed to regroup. I needed a strategy. I could hear it hopping after me, faster than ever.

Thump-thump-thump-thump-thump!

Dram this thing was fast. I kept going, nearly tracing a figure eight through the large room as I tried to maintain barriers between myself and my pursuer. I had no doubt it could catch me in a straight race.

I ducked behind a large workstation at the edge of the trading floor. My heart pounded, but I clasped my hands over my nose and mouth, forcing myself to breathe as shallowly as possible.

If it couldn't sense my breath, it shouldn't be able to find me.

Thump-thump-thump. Thump. Thump.

Its movements slowed. It was searching for me. I took smaller and smaller breaths, trying to slow my heart rate and breathing until I was able to hold my breath entirely. But I couldn't hold it forever.

Only two bullets left. And my dagger. I had no reason to think the dagger would be any more successful in keeping this thing down. Where did that leave me? I might be able to distract it by throwing small objects. But what did I have? No Crystals. No card fragments. Just a few random crafting materials.

I slowly craned my head up. The jiangshi was moving away from me. Good. Still holding my breath, I peered into the workstation. Were there any pens? Pencils? Paperclips? Rubber bands? Not even close. There was a coffee mug and a stress ball, both with the Reality Inc. logo.

I was at a loss. Maybe I should have spent more time researching at the Archives. More time preparing. I needed to retreat, even head outside the Exchange. But would I be able to make it to the exit before this thing pounced on me?

I couldn't hold my breath anymore. I exhaled.

Immediately, the sound of the jiangshi's movement shifted. I heard the whispers of its mildewed robes, followed by the rhythmic hopping. From a tilted monitor on a nearby trading post, I could see a reflection of the creature hopping rapidly in my direction.

Thump-thump-thump-thump-thump!

Pistachios! There was an opened bag of pistachio nuts in the workstation. Some broker's nostalgic snack from a vending machine. I grabbed the bag and spilled the nuts out on the marble floor. They rolled chaotically, several dozen of them.

The jiangshi stopped, its slippered feet idling before the scattered mess. Seizing the opportunity, I stood and tried to reorient myself. Where were the stairs leading down to the lobby? Ah, there they were!

I broke into a sprint. At once, the jiangshi chased after me.

Thump-thump-thump!

Why couldn't you have counted the pistachios!? I guess my human breath was more enticing.

Reaching the stone railing separating the trading floor from the lobby below, I didn't bother taking the stairs. In a mad dash, I vaulted over the railing and sailed through the air, gun in hand, and slammed my leg hard on the ground.

▸ Oww!

Not a graceful landing.

Damage received.

Essence: 10 remaining.

What?! Are you kidding me?!

The pain in my leg was intense. I couldn't say it was broken but definitely sprained. Above, the hopping noise echoed louder and louder.

Thump! Thump! Thump! Thump!

I pushed myself up. It hurt terribly to put pressure on my leg. I wasn't sure I could make it to the exit in time. Spinning around, I noticed a glowing light emanating from a small alcove. Another room jutting off from the dark lobby.

I hobbled towards the light. Maybe there was another door. Or something I could hide behind. Instead, I saw vending machines. Three of them. Transparent glass windows showcased a wide selection of temperature-controlled items for purchase.

I got a crazy idea.

THUMP!

I twisted around and saw the jiangshi. It was already in the lobby, hopping straight towards me. Its long, black fingernails reached out greedily.

I fired a single round at its face, puncturing the hanging, yellow talisman. It fell, crumbling again. Ashes to ashes. Dust to dust.

1 / 5 ammunition remaining.

Ignoring the pile, I turned to scrutinize the vending machines. If this was going to work... I had one chance and one chance only.

There were several varieties of individually wrapped onigiri. Rice. And vinegar. Was onigiri made with vinegar? I tapped on the touchscreen panel to bring up the menu options. Ah, ingredients! I accessed the first option.

The vending machine spoke in the grating artificial tone so familiar to me now.

Ingredients: sushi rice, rice vinegar, salt, white sesame, nori, fish roe.

The pile of dust and bones began to stir behind me.

I smashed the onigiri option on the panel.

The price is ten Crypt. Please scan your payment source.

I held my barcoded flesh to the sensor light and soon the triangular rice ball tumbled down the chute. I picked it up, ripping off the plastic covering. On a small table against the wall lay a variety of utensils, napkins, and condiments. I grabbed a pair of chopsticks.

I quickly knelt before the swirling pile, the jiangshi threatening to spring back to non-life. One rigid, pale hand was already emerging from the debris. I ripped the onigiri into tiny pieces with my bare hands, shoving and kneading them into the dust. Once the sticky rice was distributed in the pile, I used the chopsticks to mix it around vigorously, scattering the putrid ashes across the alcove.

▸ You like that? You like that yummy rice you piece of Shiva?

I slid away from the pile, the two chopsticks sticking out like funerary incense. With my back against the glow of the vending machines, I materialized my dagger, holding it in one hand and aiming my revolver with the other. One bullet left.

I watched for any movement—any stirring—not daring to blink.

But this time, it stayed down. And after a minute of waiting, which felt like an eternity, the dust and bits of bone started to melt into an inky black ooze. In turn, that too evaporated.

Task Successfully Completed: Remove jiangshi from Elysian Spires Financial District.

Phew.

Shimmering geometric shapes rose from the floor and floated in the air. Among them, a luminous rectangular prism. A Data Card!

Bracing myself against a vending machine, I pulled myself to a standing position. My leg still hurt. Badly. But I limped forward to claim my prizes, releasing an audible sigh as I absorbed the goodies.

10 Crystals obtained.

{uncommon} Data Card obtained: Jiangshi *(Skill)*.

I smiled. A complete Data Card. No fragments to farm. And it was another skill card. I couldn't wait another moment to find out more about it.

Data Card: Jiangshi

Card Type: Skill

Frequency: Uncommon

Skill Details: Once per cycle, absorb Energy up to your Adeptness from a creature you kill. Does not work during daytime / sunlit conditions.

Skill Cost: N/A

Size: 10 metabytes

Interesting. Checking my statistics, I saw I currently had an Adeptness rating of ten. The lowest possible score.

With increased Adeptness, I could see this skill being very useful, although it was context specific. Only works at night. However, most of my hunting so far had been after dark.

I limped across the lobby to the exit. There was a 4,000 Crypt reward with my name, or at least my number, on it.

I flashed a peace sign to the nonplussed Polizei bots on my way out, not bothering to stop and answer their inquiries about the status of the invasive entity. Let those useless programs go find out for themselves.

FILE 25.1

PURGATORY

I headed straight for the nearest MAR station as fast as I could limp. There I paid my ten Crypt and boarded the Platinum Line back to the MAR Master Terminal. After waiting my turn, I approached the Task Assignment Board and cashed in my bounty.

Task Complete: Remove jiangshi from Elysian Spires Financial District.

Assigned to: Volunteer 01001110 01101111 01100010 01101111 01100100 01111001.

Task Completion Award: 2,000 Crypt.

Bonus Award: 2,000 Crypt.

Would you like to receive payment?

I eagerly watched as my paltry sum of 60 Crypt inflated to 4,060. Immediately my imagination filled with all the things I could buy. But as I minimized the completed task on the large-paneled bounty board, something else caught my attention.

The minotaur bounty from before. It was listed again. I could have sworn some other Volunteer had snatched it up. What did that mean? I selected the task to open it on the screen.

Task Assignment: Remove minotaur from Grand Central Park in Eden West.

One {uncommon} minotaur has been detected in the hedge maze within Grand Central Park in Eden West.

Task Completion Award: 3,000 Crypt.

Do you accept this Task?

It was the exact same task. Did the minotaur respawn? Or had the Volunteer failed the mission? Maybe even died in the process...

Eden West. I wasn't that far away. I would have to take the Platinum Line to the Gold Line, a forty Crypt round trip, plus an eventual ten Crypt for the Diamond Line back to The Commons. But geographically, whatever that meant in a Metaverse, I was not far. Was 'metagraphically' a word?

My leg was injured. My Essence was down, my Energy sucked off by a Chinese vampire. And I only had a single bullet left.

But there was no time limit listed on this task. No bonus for a speedy resolution.

Sure, why not. I'll accept the task. The only thing better than 4,000 Crypt was 7,000 Crypt.

Task Assigned: Remove minotaur from Grand Central Park in Eden West.

A hedge maze. Hmmm...

I stepped away from the bounty boards and heard a drumming sound from above. Looking up at the arched, windowed ceiling, I saw pinkish ripples and spatters backdropped by a dark sky. It was raining.

Instinctively, I wanted to seek shelter. I knew this rain. Freezing and burning. Flooding and drowning. But as I looked about, nobody else seemed particularly concerned. Citizens stopped and sat on benches or at small tables throughout the hub. Volunteers likewise waited or took seats away from the Citizens, patiently watching the rain beat against the panes overhead.

A diminutive man with a pencil mustache, hooded cloak, and a throwing knife bandolier around his chest leaned nonchalantly against a nearby wall, checking his nails. Clearly not a Citizen.

▸ Excuse me.

He raised an eyebrow and looked in my direction but said nothing, resuming inspection of his fingernails.

▸ The rain. The cycle's about to change, isn't it? Why isn't anybody seeking shelter?

Annoyed by my persistence, he straightened up and adjusted his bandolier.

"The Master Terminal is odin of the few places completely shielded from the rain. Gotta keep the trains running on raz, you know."

▸ Right. Good to know. Thank you.

He started to walk away. I called after him.

▸ So just wait it out then? Wait for the rain to clear?

"Do what you like, droogie. You won't get any benefits of the reset though just hanging about. Need a mesto to crash? Purgatory's 'cross the way. One hundred Crypt per cycle if you like."

He pointed past the Task Assignment Boards, across the long open hall, to a doorway. It was on the opposite side of the cubic storage lockers. The door simply had the emblem of halo and a sign on the wall that read: No Citizens Beyond This Point.

I crossed over to investigate. The door was firmly locked, but I noticed a sensor subtly recessed in the wall. Scanning my Volunteer ID, I heard a click and pushed the door open.

Inside, a series of narrow sleeping capsules lined one wall, like the ones in the Residential Towers but even more compact. I surmised this was a hostel for Volunteers on the go.

To one side was a cramped bar with a couple stools and a small seating area. A tall, hairless person with an exceptionally dark and rich skin tone distributed pre-packaged drinks from behind the bar with the benefit of two additional cybernetic arms. On the other side were two large vendor panels: one hawking salves and medicaments, the other specializing in ammunition.

"Welcome to Purgatory."

It was the bartender, speaking with a neutral but deep timbre in an untraceable accent.

"Drink. Rest. Basic items."

▸ It's 100 Crypt per cycle?

I pointed to the sleep capsules.

"That's correct. Choose any one that is free."

Not ideal, but I was a long way from home and needed to restore my Energy and Essence. I nodded to the bartender, or whatever role this person held. First, I wanted to see what was available at the ammunition kiosk.

Scrolling through the options on the screen, I found individual .32 caliber cartridges for sale at twenty Crypt per bullet. That was expensive! I also found some basic accessories. There were belt slide ammo carriers, ammo pouches, ammo belts, and a variety of holsters. I didn't currently have a belt to attach a carrier onto, so I wasn't interested in that particular option.

Accessory: Revolver ammunition pouch

Cost: 500 Crypt

Frequency: Basic

Details: Snap top canvas pouch. Holds up to six cartridges, loose or attached to a speed load strip. Can be attached to your belt or kept in your pocket. Speed load strip sold separately.

Size: 10 metabytes

Accessory: Ammunition belt
Cost: 800 Crypt
Frequency: Basic
Details: Standard black belt with twelve loops for individually securing cartridges in .22, .38/.357 or .44/.45 caliber.

Size: 10 metabytes

Accessory: Ambidextrous revolver shoulder holster with pouch
Cost: 1000 Crypt
Frequency: Basic
Details: A cross harness vertical shoulder holster with speed-loader pouch. Good for concealing a small or medium sized revolver. Adjustable for right-handed or left-handed users. Pouch holds up to six cartridges with speed load strip included.

Size: 20 metabytes

It didn't look like my discount would apply here. Also, the prices were rather high. Maybe they were charging extra because they could. No competition this far from The Commons. Convenience fee. Monopoly. Captive pricing. All that garbage.

I needed to at least replace my four spent cartridges. I also recognized that my snub-nosed revolver only held five rounds while larger revolvers typically held six.

But all this could wait. I would sleep on it.

I located an empty capsule, scanned my code, and paid the one hundred Crypt. Wincing as I put pressure on my injured leg, I crawled inside what was essentially a fluorescent coffin.

And the rain continued to fall.

FILE 26

MINOTAUR

I twisted the dial until the enveloping fluorescence dimmed to pitch darkness. I rested my aching body on the thin, cushioned layer on the bottom of the capsule emulating a bed. No outside sounds penetrated these sterile walls. There could have been a swarm of boisterous Volunteers passing through Purgatory and I'd have been oblivious.

At long last I began to drift, to dissociate. My tired mind wandered through thick fog. Fog I could feel but not see. I groped in the chill, morning mist. Vapor rising off the surface of placid water. Ripples lost in time. An errant splash.

I heard the sound of laughter, infinitely distant. A child's voice.

Where? Where is it coming from? Where are you?

I wanted to call out, but I had no mouth. I felt an unshakeable urgency to locate the source of that sound.

Slowly, a visual coalesced in my mind's eye. But nothing that matched the innocence I chased. Something malevolent and overwhelming. A rictus grin stretching across the universe and a voice as deep and abyssal as the ocean floor.

iIi kNoW wHaT yOu aRRRe

I lay paralyzed in the dark. A great weight perched on my chest, pinning me down. My limbs locked in place.

No. No. Not this. Not this again!

My bloodshot eyes ripped open. There was only the abominable smile, stretching larger than my perception could contain, hanging in the black void. The mighty tectonic plates beneath the ocean floor rumbled once more.

iIi KnOw WhAt YoU ArE

I fought against this mental attack. I strained with every bone, every muscle, every nerve in my body. I pushed back against the apparition so hard I thought the chip in the back of my head would explode.

yOU aRE a MONsTeR !!!

Pain. Piercing into my brain like ice picks through the edges of my eye sockets. Overwhelming and disastrous.

▸ AHHHH!!!

ERROR ||||IIIIIII ERROR |IIIlIII||| 01110011 01100001 01101110 01101001 01110100 01111001 00100000 01100100 01100001 01101101 01100001 01100111 01100101 00100000 01110011 01110101 01110011 01110100 01100001 01101001 01101110 01100101 01100100 -1%

I blacked out.

* * *

An unknown span of time later, my eyes flicked open in the darkness. Shaking, I reached blindly for the dial. I couldn't find it.

Forgetting where I was, I smashed my head on the low ceiling of the sleep capsule. Finally, I located the controls and turned the light full blast.

Alone. Alive. Confused.

What... What just happened? Deja vu. A half-remembered dream swirling down the drain of awakening. That sensation... I felt it once before...

Where am I? Not my residence. Somewhere else. That's right, Purgatory. The Master Terminal.

Deja vu, again.

Or was it nostalgia—the Greek word *algos* for pain, grief, and distress, combined with a derivative of *neomai,* to escape or to return home. A morbid longing for one's native country.

Huh. A strange thought. Where did that come from?

A menu notification flashed in my vision, breaking my reverie.

Refresh complete.

Essence restored.

Energy at full.

The cycle change. Right. Essence and Energy back at full. But why did I still have this throbbing pain in my head?

I dimmed the light part way and stretched out once more, concentrating on taking deep, slow breaths until the cranial sting subsided. As I lay, I remembered my current assigned task.

TASKS

- **Remove minotaur from Grand Central Park in Eden West** (Pending)

Kill a minotaur. Okay, let me think about this.

The Archives were out of reach. I wouldn't be able to do any research on my target. But the concept of a minotaur was familiar to me. A man with a bull's head. Right? Relatively straightforward. What else did I know? I thought it stemmed from Greek mythology. A monster that guarded a special place. That or it was used as a form of punishment against someone who displeased some god or king.

That was honestly all I could think of. Dram. Did Volunteers have access to any libraries in The Collective? Finding a volume on Greek myths to keep stashed in my inventory couldn't hurt.

My headache subsided, and I clambered out of the rented capsule and stretched. The capsule door automatically locked behind me.

I walked over to the ammunition vending kiosk. I found myself running low on multiple occasions, which was not good. But I also didn't want to get ripped off. I literally died earning that 5% discount at the Armory; it'd be a shame not to take advantage of it.

I resolved to shop for expanded ammo storage options upon my (triumphant?) return to The Commons. For now, I would buy the four bullets needed to refill my revolver, even at the inflated price. Four rounds for 80 Crypt. I gritted my teeth and completed the transaction.

I was already down to 3,880 Crypt. But my ammunition, Energy, and Essence were full. And my sprained leg felt good as new.

I checked my storage.

MEMORY
- **STORAGE: 295 / 290** (310)

Only fifteen metabytes to play with. It was possible that any loot acquired during the minotaur bounty might exceed my carrying capacity. I could rent one of those storage cubes for one hundred Crypt. Even if I died, whatever was in that box would be safe, even without a backup. Alternatively, I could trigger my clurichaun skill to burn thirty Energy to free up room.

Turning away from the limited shopping options, I noticed the hooded, diminutive man sitting at the table in Purgatory's modest seating area. He had several throwing knives laid out on a cloth and was concentrating on applying liquid from a vial on the tips of each.

I walked over to get a closer look.

"Keep your distance. This is deadly poison, it is. Don't wanna get nicked by this nosh or another."

The man didn't look up from his work as he spoke. I did as instructed.

▸ Poisoned throwing knives? Interesting choice of weapon.

He grunted a reply. I thought that was the end of the exchange, but after a while he elaborated.

"Some Volunteers messel themselves jack-of-all-trades types. Not me. Can't afford it. Had to specialize, I did. Stealth and poison. Nimble too. Plenty of value sunk into my Agility stat. Thrown weapons. Although, there's a nice blow dart gun I've been viddying at the starry Auction House."

▸ What types of creatures do the poisons work on?

"Different poisons for different monsters. And for some? No poison at all."

He held a knife up to the light, inspecting his work. Satisfied, he tucked it into one of the straps on his bandolier.

▸ Thanks for the tip about Purgatory. I'm Magpie, by the way.

He just nodded, finishing his work and meticulously stowing each throwing knife in its place. Didn't bother to share his name with me. It was probably something embarrassingly obvious, like Knives or Poison or something.

▸ Are... you on your way to complete a task?

He stood up, dematerializing the vial of liquid and smoothing his cloak.

"No bounty. Heading out to Eden West to farm some kappas."

▸ Eden West? Me too. I'm going to Grand Central Park.

"Same as me. Those dram kappas can't keep out of the koi ponds, the greedy buggers. Don't tell me you have a bounty on kappas. Then we might have a problem you and me."

► Not at all. Don't even know what those are. I'm hunting a minotaur. Supposed to be in a hedge maze there.

"I know the place. You hunting *a* minotaur or *the* Minotaur?"

► What's the difference?

"One's a noun, one's a proper noun, innit? What's the frequency of your bounty?"

► Uncommon.

"Just a minotaur then. The Minotaur, Asterion, gotta be rare at least, maybe even legendary. Only found in a proper labyrinth. But a regular starry minotaur—they pop up in all kinds of mazes. They're drawn to them. Linked, if you like."

Linked...

► Have you fought one?

"Nah. Seen Vols killed by them before. They are tough. But nothing special. Just a contest of strength really, if you're into that. Gotta watch those horns."

To illustrate his point, the man lifted two fingers above his head and pantomimed a charging motion. A tough, physical opponent. How many shots from a revolver would put down a charging bull in the real world? I needed to come up with a solid plan of attack before wandering into that maze.

There was one idea that came to mind.

► Since we're both heading to the same place, what if we made a deal? I'll help you farm your kappas, and you help me kill this minotaur.

It turned out the knife-wielding Volunteer was amenable to my suggestion.

FILE 26.1

KAPPAS

After further preparation, we left Purgatory. I followed his lead boarding the Platinum Line back in the direction of Elysian Spires, leaving the MAR Master Terminal behind. We then transferred to the Gold Line and rode it until we reached Eden West.

I still didn't know his name, and he did not appear eager to share it. The sleeves of his cloak obscured the ID tag on his wrist. Although, he did flash it at the station to pay the fare. It would have just been meaningless numbers to me.

The man indicated that he had a transit pass—unlimited travel for a set period of cycles. If I wanted, I too could purchase one at the Master Terminal. For now, the trip cost me another twenty Crypt.

We rode in silence in the rear of a half-empty train car. Several Citizens in crisp linen suits sat up front, away from the dangerous riff raff coming to do the dirty work. Daylight shone so warm and bright through the windows it was hard to believe it was artificial as we pulled into a station more idyllic than I expected.

Now arriving at Eden West Station.

We deboarded and I followed my temporary companion through an urban yet thoroughly domesticated environment. A gentrification, a neo-suburban reclaiming of a dense historical section of an industrialized city. But the truth was that there had never been any urban blight to reclaim. Not in a place like this. It was a thoroughly planned community with chic, walled-off homes and private gardens. Intentionally designed and connected by elegant walkways. There was only a mirage of historicity here.

We passed through multiple blocks until we reached the edge of an enormous park, opposite of a pedestrian-friendly street.

"Here it is. Grand Central Park."

Strange musical notes carried in the air. I peered through spring foliage and flowering trees to glimpse a quaint, old world amusement park. An elegant carousel with bobbing animals completed its melodic revolutions. A golden drop tower ride plunged beyond the treetops. Scents of popcorn and cotton candy assaulted my nostrils.

And the laughter of children.

What?

Crossing the street, I followed the other Volunteer on a path winding through the immense park. Through a wrought iron fence, multiple sets of parents held the hands of their children, enjoying the amusements. One child in a spring dress grabbed a red balloon by the string, a joyful expression on her freckled face.

▸ This is... I had no idea. There are children in The Collective?

My companion grunted.

"Could be. Don't trust everything you viddy."

▸ What do you mean by that?

"I meant what I said, and I said what I meant. This mesto gives me the creeps."

We crossed over an arching, red bridge. Below, couples enjoyed one another's company in dragon-themed paddle boats on a small lake. An unexpected anxiety gripped my heart. I suddenly wanted to change the subject. Distract myself.

▸ Tell me again what you're farming and how I can help.

"Kappas. Turtle chellovecks."

▸ Turtles?

"Like I said, they keep spawning 'round here and trying to eat the koi fish out of the ponds near the gardens. Have a taste for human flesh too. But the veshch they love most… is cucumbers."

▸ Cucumbers?

Without looking back at me, he materialized a small, green vegetable and held it aloft. Nothing remarkable about it. Just an ordinary cucumber.

"They can't resist. They'll even beg for them. They can learn human language, you know. So oomny yet so gloopy."

▸ What frequency are they?

"Common."

▸ So why farm them? You said you don't have a bounty so you can't be getting paid.

He stopped cold in the middle of the footpath and eyed me suspiciously.

"I've got my reasons, haven't I? Every so often the kappas drop something special. That's what I'm after. Don't care about any cards or fraggies. We can split the Crystals for all I care. But any materials they drop are mine. Got it?"

▸ Fine by me. Then you'll help me dispatch the minotaur?

He nodded and we continued on, the winding path carrying us deeper into the vast urban park. The trees were larger now. The foliage denser. A grassy ramble with scattered picnickers and kite-flyers gave way to something older. We crossed another bridge over a small creek, and I noticed several decorative stone lanterns dotting the trailside. I now saw no sign of Citizens anywhere.

The short man raised a hand in the air, then silently motioned to a large rock off to one side of the path. I followed him and we sat. Peeking through jutting bamboo, he pointed to a series of ponds connected by elegant wooden bridges and stepping stones. Wide lily pads dotted the surface and brilliant orange and white fish flashed underneath.

Beyond the ponds and past a stretch of manicured lawn was a walled garden with a tall stone archway. I could see green hedges beyond. The hedge maze! I could also glimpse caution tape and a security barricade warning off Citizens but saw no Polizei bots.

My companion spoke in a hush.

"There. You viddy that ripple?"

I turned my attention back to the nearest pond. I noticed nothing unusual. Nothing that couldn't be attributed to a leaping fish. I shook my head. Maybe if my Perception were higher...

"There's a kappa in there for sure. They can breathe underwater, so we gotta lure it out. Don't wanna spar a kappa in the water. They can drown you, bite you, and even try to ultra violence you."

Ultra violence? Maybe I didn't want to know what that meant.

▸ So we use the cucumber to get it on dry land?

"Just right. If there's just odin I don't need your help. But if we run into a pack I could use you. Just need a peet first."

To my surprise, the man materialized a travel thermos out of his inventory. He unscrewed the cap and took a swig. It smelled like freshly brewed herbal tea, and a trail of steam rose from the top.

▸ Are you serious?

"It's a lucky chasha of chai, innit?"

▸ Lucky chai. Is that anything like a Tincture of Fortune?

"That it is. But it lasts a lot longer and tastes a lot better. Need to increase my odds of finding what I'm after. Don't wanna be out here all day cutting open turtle shells."

I waited patiently while he finished his hot tea. He didn't offer me any, not that I felt thirsty now or ever. He seemed invigorated by the drink and ready for action.

I recalled that the Tincture of Fortune increased the probability of obtaining Crystals and discovering items of higher rarity for 600 seconds. I wondered what benefits this other concoction conferred.

He put the thermos away and stood, brandishing a large knife I had not seen before. Not a throwing knife but a sturdy six-inch blade. I tensed at the sight, but the man stared at the nearby pond again. Curious, I carefully tried to highlight the weapon without touching it, seeing if I could identify it.

Hybrid hunting knife

Realizing what I had done, the man quickly moved the knife out from my reach.

"Keep your grubby system functions away from my nosh, right? Now stay hidden and watch what I do. If it's an ambush, come join the spar."

With that, he quickly moved off through the bamboo thicket towards the first pond. He was nimble, as advertised, and his small stature made it easy for him to navigate through the environment. He held the knife behind his back with one hand and placed the cucumber on the ground, taking several steps away and waiting.

This time, I did detect increased rippling in the water, followed by subtle splashing. Seconds later, a slimy, green shape broke the surface of the pond. It was a head. A round, human-sized reptilian head complete with a sharp, hooked beak and round, flat eyes that held a predatory gleam.

Most disturbing to me was the top of the head. It was hollowed out like a dish, like someone had partially scalped this creature. The indentation in the skull was full of fluid that sloshed ever so slightly as it swam towards the edge. It gave the impression of a raw egg yolk in a bowl. Stringy, black hair hung from the sides of its crown, dripping with pond water.

"Kyūri? Kyūri?" the creature chirped, cautiously emerging from the murky pool.

It was the size of a small person, a bit larger than my companion but not as tall as me. It walked on two legs with a hunched posture. Its hands and feet were webbed claws, and the slickness of algae clung to its green skin and chelonian shell.

The kappa cocked its head to one side. I heard the wetness of its feet slapping against the grass as it scuttled towards the other Volunteer.

"Kyūri?"

A system notification chirped.

{common} entity detected: kappa.

The hooded Volunteer stood his ground as the shambling, wet humanoid approached, lured by the delectable cucumber lying in the grass between them. Then, to my surprise, the Volunteer gave a deep, polite bow.

The kappa stopped in place. Then it returned the gesture, bowing low. As it did, I noticed some of the water in the bowl-shaped depression spill out. The kappa hissed. Its body and limbs jerked awkwardly.

In a swift movement, the Volunteer drew his six-inch blade and made a quick slit across the creature's throat. It grabbed at its neck with its webbed claws, falling to the ground as it desperately tried to hold the spurting blood in place.

"Quick! Get over here!"

He was calling me. I left my observation post behind the bamboo and hurried to the Volunteer's side. He laid the incapacitated creature on its shelled back and seized one of its kicking legs.

"Grab the other noga and help me pull it away from the pond!"

I did, gripping a leg that was simultaneously nodular and slimy. The creature smelled awful. Pungent. Like befouled mud and stagnant lake water. Together, we slid the wet kappa back behind the bamboo thicket.

"Best to do it here in case any others are spying from the water."

Red blood gurgled from the kappa's open throat and its flat eyes rolled back in its head. The jerking movements continued, but the creature seemed to have almost no strength left.

My companion stabbed his blade hard into the kappa's soft-shelled belly, cutting down the center of the plate towards the groin. All the while it writhed and gurgled pitifully. Then the Volunteer pierced the creature's side, cutting around the perimeter of the shell. I could tell he had done this many times before.

I watched with mounting disgust as the Volunteer peeled the soft shell of the stomach away, revealing a mass of pulpy organs and elongated arms oddly attached in the center of its torso. The kappa smelled worse on the inside than the outside. I tried not to inhale.

Blood sticking to both of his hands, the Volunteer carefully wiped his brow with the back of his sleeve and stood, shaking viscera from his blade. He shook his head.

"Nope. Not here."

As the kappa's life force finally drained away, it began to shudder and glow. A scant few motes of light rose from the disintegrating corpse, shining bright even in the daylight. My mysterious companion scrutinized the floating objects and shrugged apathetically.

"Take 'em."

▸ But I didn't do anything.

"That's okay. I don't need 'em."

1 Crystal obtained.

{common} Data Card fragments obtained: kappa 2/10.

"We'll give it a minute, then try one of the other ponds."

▸ The same thing?

"Until I find what I'm looking for. I brought extra cucumbers just in case."

▸ Don't the kappas catch on to what you're doing?

"They are very predictable creatures. If you bow, they are obliged to bow back. The water in their *sara*—that is the source of their strength. If it spills, they are significantly weakened. Now if another kappa sees me attacking its kin, all bets are off. But odin at a raz these veshches are pushovers if you know what to do."

▸ Cucumbers and compulsory bowing. Not very sporting, is it?

The man glared at me from behind his hood and that was the end of the conversation. After enough time passed, the knife-wielding Volunteer was at it again. He selected a different pond, approaching from another angle, but all the subsequent steps were the same. Bait, bowing, and butchering.

I didn't ask why he bothered cutting open the entities as he did. If there was some special material they dropped, wouldn't they do so upon death? Why slice them apart in the midst of their death throes? After three or four of the kappas met a similar fate, I actually began to feel sorry for the disgusting creatures.

By that time, we had split the meager Crystals, my total share being five, and I accumulated eight out of ten Data Card fragments. I could tell my companion was growing impatient, but on the next kill, he found what he was searching for.

Cutting away and removing the shell protecting the kappa's belly, the Volunteer plunged his hand into the very center of the slimy guts and triumphantly pulled out a hard, round ball vaguely shaped like a small onion. The kappa let out a final shriek of indignity before shuffling off this coil, netting me a ninth card fragment in the process.

Alert! Account storage almost full.

Not now. I was more interested in this elusive object that had warranted so much violent turtle-man processing.

▸ All this work for a… whatever that thing is?

His former impatience melted away by his success, my companion relaxed and even broke a smile. He hadn't even used one of his many poison-dipped throwing knives. I silently wondered how long this would have taken, and how many kappas he would have butchered, had he not ingested that lucky tea.

"It's a shirikodama, innit? Smot it up some raz."

Shirikodama. Got it. Not really.

I made a mental note to research it the next time I was at the Archives as he added the bizarre prize to his inventory.

▸ Since you know so much about kappas, what does a completed Data Card get you?

"Pretty underwhelming. You can forge it into a very specific lomtick of armor. A helm. Basically your own version of a kappa's *sara*. When the bowl on top is full of water, it grants a hefty strength and resistance bonus. Very impractical though. I knew a Volunteer who transmuted it into a beer peeting shlem. Had the same effect but made him look like a total gloopy nazz."

▸ Transmuted it into what?

"You know, the shlapas that hold beer cans on your gulliver. Like this?"

He pantomimed holding two objects on either side of his head for illustration.

It seemed the more he spoke, the less I understood. But I think I got the picture of a novelty beer drinking hat. I vaguely remembered the export and transmute options at the Data Forge, the latter function allowing you to transform the cosmetic appearance of an item, weapon, or armor. It did seem worthless to have to balance a bowl of water on your head.

I didn't have a complete Data Card either way, but I could always try to sell, trade, or recycle it if I couldn't find a good use.

"You helped me. Raz to return the favor. Wanna take a gander at this hedge maze?"

I nodded. He dematerialized his hunting knife and we walked beyond the ponds. The splashing koi fish were now safe at least, although I kept a watchful eye so as not to be set upon by any vengeful kappas. Soon we crossed over the lawn and approached the walled-off garden. A park within a park.

FILE 26.2

LABYRINTH

Up close, the stone walls were much taller than I had realized. The green hedges beyond the ornate archway were thick, impenetrable to the eye. A plate affixed to the stone wall at the entrance simply read: Grand Central Park Hedge Maze. We slipped past the caution tape and stood in the entrance.

The hedge walls loomed taller than me and certainly taller than my companion. The dense greenery cast the maze in permanent shade, despite the bright daylight conditions outside. It was quiet, save for a gentle breeze rustling against stiff leaves. You could hardly see into the maze before the pathways turned off at sharp ninety-degree angles.

The other Volunteer tapped me on the arm. I looked down and saw him holding up a small ceramic container for me to take.

▶ More poison?

"No. Put it on your plot. Trust me."

Put it on? I cautiously accepted the container and turned it over in my hand. It wasn't ceramic after all but some sort of hardened leather. I could feel the weight of liquid inside, and the top was stopped with a cork. I highlighted the item and concentrated on it.

Shadowfoot Ointment.

I watched as my companion produced an identical container, pulled the stoppage, and sprinkled the contents over his person. He took a single step into the shade of the hedge maze. At once, his body grew dark, blending into the shadows.

Ah. Now I understand.

I copied his action, dousing myself with the oily liquid.

It smelled of midnight. There was no obvious effect until I too stepped into the shade of the hedges. A context-specific camouflage. Sure enough, the active effect was listed in my menu.

STATUS

- **Shadow Concealment** (active: 895 seconds remaining). **This status effect increases visual concealment in dark conditions for 900 seconds.**

Quick mental math. Fifteen minutes. Having been emptied of its substance, the container disintegrated into pixelated vapor and was gone.

"Ready to go in? Spy on your bezoomy scoteena?"

I nodded, catching his drift. We could try and locate the minotaur within the maze without being detected and suss out an advantage. The minotaur would be physically strong, but the two of us should be able to take it. I had already witnessed the formidable skills of the knife-wielder.

The sounds of the outside park muted the deeper we went into the maze. The warmth of the afternoon daylight sequence faded to a twilight chill. We had scarcely taken a left turn when the twisted path veered off again at a sharp angle. The hedges smelled faintly of dampness and old growth, a hint of something rotting just beneath the surface.

Visually concealed though I was, I had to be careful as my tactical boots trod over dry earth. My nimble companion made almost no sound as he glided through the maze ahead of me. However, we shortly ran into a dead end and had to double back. The pathways were deceptively wide at first, but as we ventured further, they narrowed, the hedges pressing in around us. Visually, the green on green looked the same, and after several turns and splitting paths, I was thoroughly disoriented by the silent walls of leaves.

▸ Hear anything? Any movement?

I asked in a whisper, and the other Volunteer shook his head. He stopped to prod and probe the hedge wall, seeking a space to perhaps squeeze through with his small frame. No such luck. Growing concerned, I checked the remaining time on the status effect.

599 seconds remaining.

We had wandered for five minutes. Just how large was this maze? But finally we spotted a landmark. Or I should say that I did. My taller height afforded me the advantage to see the top of a white structure extending over the hedges.

▸ There's something over there. A building. I don't know how to reach it, but if I can keep it in sight, we can work our way towards it.

We walked down a long stretch and turned right. Another dead end. Shiva! We doubled back and went the other way until we reached a left turn, moving concentrically closer to the landmark. As we neared, my companion flashed another hand signal for us to stop.

He leaned against the closest hedge and cupped a hand to his ear. With his superior Perception he had detected a sound. I strained to listen. On the other side of the wall, there was a slight scuffing noise. Even a snort. The minotaur was close.

With a finger to his lips, the knife-wielder led us cautiously forwards, stopping at a final opening and leaning around the corner.

Unlike the shady hedge rows, sunlight illuminated a clearing in the middle of the maze. In the center of the clearing stood a round building of elegant white stone. A narrow, black staircase wound round the outside of the building to the roof, which was enclosed by a small railing.

It was an observation tower overlooking the maze, about one story in height, and in the middle of the roof stood a marble statue of Minerva. Green ivy clung to the sides of the building, dripping past glass-paned windows. A padlocked door led inside.

And there was my target.

{uncommon} entity detected: minotaur.

The minotaur had the body of a human male, incredibly muscular, and naked—complete with large (uncircumcised) genitalia. It possessed the head of a bull with two intimidating pointed horns, as well as a cordlike tail. However, it had the large, bare feet of a man.

I was expecting hooves...

I crouched behind the other Volunteer, looking through the opening in the hedge. I watched in wonder as the minotaur stamped the ground with its feet. Scattered on the ground were white bones, picked clean of flesh. A human ribcage and a broken pelvis.

Did the minotaur possess human intelligence, raw animal instinct, or some combination thereof?

Without warning, the creature raised its thick tail and defecated where it stood. A large pile of acrid feces tumbled from its naked buttocks onto the floor of the maze. It continued stalking about its territory as if nothing had happened.

Yeah, definitely getting an animal instinct vibe.

I suddenly realized the hooded Volunteer was holding a strange

Y-shaped stick and pointing it at the observation tower. He appeared intensely focused on it, practically ignoring the horned menace standing in the way. So far, the minotaur had not noticed us.

I whispered a question in my companion's ear.

▶ What is the plan?

"That veshch has about 160 Essence. Some bits are tougher than others giving it an extra ten defense. I can soften it up, but if you want credit for the kill, you need to finish it off."

160 Essence? How could he possibly know that? I hadn't even realized the invasive entities had measurable Essence in the same way we did.

Some more quick math. With my revolver and current Accuracy stat, I would deal forty damage per shot, not counting the +10% fire damage. But with a defensive output of ten on its tougher parts, not all of the damage would get through. So, the maximum damage I could deal with my five rounds, if I hit the minotaur's most vulnerable areas, would be 200 (not counting fire damage).

I drew my revolver. It glowed briefly red with its infernal fusion.

The minotaur snorted loudly and twisted its bulky head in our direction. It had a crazed look in its large, bovine eyes—fixating on the fading red shine of my weapon. It released an unearthly bellow and charged.

"New plan. Run!"

I dove out of the way of the charging creature and my companion adroitly rolled in the opposite direction. The minotaur crashed through the edge of the hedge wall, horns first, sending broken branches and leaves flying. It slipped, skidding on the dirt path, and scrambled to right itself again.

Shiva on a stick!

I got up and sprinted down the corridor as the minotaur gave chase. I didn't know how well it could see me in the shade, but it was still chasing me. I ran to the end of the row and made a quick turn, then another. I could hear pounding footfalls as the snorting, bellowing beast gained on me.

I found myself standing in a long, open pathway. The next turn in the path was a significant distance away. I ran as fast as I could, cursing my twenty Speed. The minotaur rounded the corner behind me and lowered its horns, stamping the ground and readying to charge. It could easily run me down, gore me, and trample me to the death.

I had to reach that turn!

There was another tremendous bellow as the beast broke into a dash, head lowered. I ran, imagining the pricking points of those horns digging into my back. Reaching the end of the row, I threw myself around the corner. Right into a dead end. Frag me!

But the minotaur's momentum was so great that it smashed straight through the hedge beside me, tearing a hole into another pathway. Without waiting, I ran in the direction I had just come, doubling back.

I took turn after frantic turn in the maze until I no longer knew where I was in relation to the minotaur, the entrance, or even the tower in the center. I paused to catch my breath, straining to listen. The minotaur was moving about somewhere. I only hoped it was as lost as I was.

Okay. Look for the tower. Look for the white stone peeking over the top of the hedges. Make your way back and regroup with Little Knifey. (Hey, I had to call him something until I discovered more permanent identifying information.)

Prioritizing stealth over speed, I carefully made my way through the maze again. I listened for the minotaur, looked for signs of scattered leaves and broken hedges, and searched for a glimpse of the white tower.

There it is! My lighthouse guiding me back to the center.

I entered the clearing just as my Shadow Concealment wore off. My body and clothing abruptly resumed their normal shade.

Shadow Concealment elapsed.

To my surprise, Little Knifey crouched in front of the heavy wooden door at the base of the tower. It looked like he was trying to pick the lock. I hurried to his side, incredulous.

▸ What are you doing?!

"What does it smot like? There's something dorogoy in here. Did you kill the korova yet?"

He didn't have to wait for an answer as the minotaur entered the clearing a moment later. It bellowed once more and stamped the ground. Its wide eyes bulged with rage. A stream of white spittle ran from its mouth.

My companion dropped his lockpicks and scurried away. But I stood my ground, facing down the beast. I had an idea. I quickly dematerialized and rematerialized my revolver, taunting the minotaur with the red glow.

It charged at me full force.

Shooom.

Clurichaun skill activated. 30 seconds remaining.

Energy: 0 remaining.

I waited precious seconds, the illusory image and I overlapping as one. As the minotaur rapidly closed the distance, smashing bits of discarded bone underfoot, I sidestepped and darted up the winding stairs.

The whole tower shook as the minotaur collided with the heavy door. I gripped the railing, stumbling from the quaking impact. The sound of splintering wood and breaking metal hinges reverberated through the clearing.

I looked down. The minotaur was stuck! Its horns were buried in the thick wood of the partially broken-in door. It grunted and snorted, flexing its powerful legs, trying to rip its horns free.

A small throwing knife impaled itself in the creature's exposed back. The minotaur released a guttural cry. Little Knifey appeared, watching the beast carefully.

"Paralysis poison!"

Soon, the minotaur began to stiffen, its struggle dwindling until it remained standing dumbly in place. The image of myself, superimposed over the trapped beast, dissipated.

Clurichaun skill elapsed. 30 seconds until recharge.

I climbed down and stood beside the hooded man. He withdrew the throwing knife with a spurt of blood and tucked it back into his thigh holster. I kept my distance from the minotaur's legs, as they had been kicking and stamping moments before. But now all motion ceased, except for a rhythmic rising and falling of breath.

The Volunteer chuckled to himself, materializing his hybrid hunting knife, and stood behind the beast. I held my revolver ready.

Little Knifey grabbed the minotaur's thick tail and sawed it off, dangling it in the air like a snake before dropping it to the ground.

"Not so tough now, are you?"

Then, to my unfortunate surprise, Little Knifey reached around and castrated the minotaur, cutting his testicles clean off with the six-inch blade. Ropes of blood dripped between the creature's human legs. Completely paralyzed, the minotaur exhibited no reaction.

Shiva on a stick!

Little Knifey smiled sickly, enjoying this butchery. What a sadistic buzzard.

▸ That's enough! Let me end this.

"What's wrong? Weak brooko? I softened him up for you."

I stood beside the minotaur, placing the barrel of my gun to its temple. One large bovine eye rotated in its head, looking at me. Was that sadness I detected? Resignation? Turning my head away from any potential splatter, I pulled the trigger twice, delivering the *coup de gras*. The minotaur's eye glazed over as my shots smoldered within its skull.

3 / 5 ammunition remaining.

Task Successfully Completed: Remove minotaur from Grand Central Park in Eden West.

I stepped back and watched as the body slowly began to shudder and glow. I couldn't help feeling unnerved by the whole situation. Soon, motes of light rose and hovered in the air. Less enthusiastically than usual, I accepted them.

5 Crystals obtained.

{uncommon} Data Card fragments obtained: minotaur 6/10.

I looked back at the scattered human bones in the clearing.

▸ Do you think it was eating people? Could those bones be from a Volunteer, or even a Citizen?

Little Sadist shrugged.

"The farther you are from the Restoration Point, the longer it takes to respawn. For Citizens? Who fragging knows."

He was disinterested, looking past me at the observation tower. With the minotaur gone, I saw that the heavy, wooden door was ajar. One of the hinges was broken and the padlock torn from its place.

▸ You... you said there was something inside here?

"Something dorogoy, I think. Maybe worth a lot of pretty polly. Let's take a quick smot."

I dematerialized my weapon. Together, we pushed hard against the broken door, forcing it open.

While the building served as an observation platform to look over the hedge maze, the interior was obviously a gardener's shed. It was full of tools including gardening gloves, trowels, a hoe and rake, and bags of soil and fertilizer.

On a rustic table lay a large vellum-bound book. Old paper pages of varying sizes jutted out between the thick covers.

Invasive anomaly detected.

Invasive anomaly? That book...

I took a step deeper into the room when, all of a sudden, I felt a sharp prick in my side between the gap of my ballistic vest.

▸ Ouch. What was...

Suddenly, the blood in my veins started to coagulate. My muscles stiffened one by one. My limbs became unresponsive.

My heart sank as I realized what had happened.

Withdrawing the tip of the knife, Little Sadist walked past me. He wore a concerned expression as he looked up from beneath his hood.

"I'm sorry, droogie. It's not personal. But I can't let you have that book."

The dram buzzard! The mother fragger! He paralyzed me!

"Too rare a treasure, innit? You wouldn't even know what to do with such a veshch. Don't worry, the paralysis will wear off eventually. But a slovo of warning—don't try to come after me."

I stood, helplessly frozen in place. I tried to materialize my gun, my dagger—anything. If I could have, I would have shot him in the head and stabbed him a hundred times. The fury I felt welling up was overwhelming. The same sadistic urges I had silently judged him for now surged within me.

Little Sadist opened the book, carefully thumbing through its contents. He was absorbed by the anomaly, whatever it was.

I realized I could still access my menu. This mental action was free, unconstrained by my physical paralysis.

STATUS

\-   **Minor Paralysis** (active: 230 seconds remaining). **This status ailment causes major motor functions to cease for 300 seconds.**

Major motor functions. I could still move my eyes. I could feel my chest rising and falling with shallow breaths. I could even... just barely... twitch one of my fingers.

Little Backstabber cursed to himself. Soon, he began materializing and haphazardly dumping miscellaneous objects on the ground. I realized he was over-encumbered!

He must not have enough storage space to add that mysterious book to his inventory. Serves you right!

I heard a wet slapping noise outside. Then another. A hiss, and a creaky cackling sound. Little Backstabber turned, looking past me with annoyance. He drew a throwing knife from the bandolier and flung it in my direction. It whizzed right by me and struck something fleshy.

More rapid slapping sounds. I could sense multiple things approaching from behind. Something with a strong, pungent odor. Oh no. Kappas! Somehow kappas must have wandered into the hedge maze. The Volunteer glanced back at me a final time.

"Appy-polly loggies."

With that, he scrambled onto the table and undid a latch, pushing open one of the windows. Anomalous book tucked under his arm, he wriggled his small body through. Two loose sheets of paper fell from the book and drifted to the floor. Then he was gone.

Multiple kappas swarmed behind me. I tried to frantically move, but I couldn't. Their foul stench was astounding. I checked the timer on my status ailment.

207 seconds remaining.

Not good.

I braced myself for the worst. But to my confusion and relief, three kappas shuffled past me with their hunched gait, moving deeper into the garden shed. They went to the pile of objects that the cowardly backstabber dropped, digging through the refuse.

"Kyūri?" one of the creatures chirped.

"Kyūri! Kyūri!" the others answered.

I strained to focus my eyes and saw the kappas picking cucumbers out of the pile, eagerly munching on the vegetal delicacies. Oh bog, I hoped they stayed distracted for long enough. I counted down the remaining time—the minutes stretching on.

100 seconds remaining.

Feeling and motion gradually restored at my extremities, starting with my fingers and toes. I could even scrunch my nose in response to the swampy aroma. The kappas finished their cucumbers and sifted deeper through the pile of discarded objects, searching for more.

20 seconds remaining.

10 seconds remaining.

5 seconds remaining.

The paralysis elapsed, and I breathed a quick sigh of relief. The monsters hadn't turned their attention to me. But I saw those two mysterious pages lying near their huddle where they had fallen from the stolen book.

I had to get them. I just had to.

Tip toeing, I circled around the feasting creatures and stretched to pick up the pages. The nearest kappa hissed a warning at me but did not attack.

{rare} anomaly obtained: Unknown Voynich Manuscript page.

{rare} anomaly obtained: Unknown Voynich Manuscript page.

Giving the kappas as wide a berth as possible, I made for the door. There was a dead kappa lying outside the tower, a poison knife buried in its eye socket. A single mote of light hovered above the corpse, and I grabbed it.

{common} Data Card fragment obtained: kappa 1/10.

I also carefully picked up the discarded throwing knife, pulling it from the kappa's head. I wasn't sure if the tip was still poisoned, but I was sure this poison would be of a more lethal variety.

As the kappa's body dissolved into an inky puddle, I started retracing my steps to escape the maze.

FILE 27

SPOILS

I traveled through the bourgeois suburban landscape back to the Eden West MAR Station, constantly on guard for any signs of the elusive Volunteer whose name I didn't know. On the other side of the street, a mother and son passed on the sidewalk, walking a meticulously groomed pharaoh hound on a lead attached to a bejeweled collar.

I glanced in their direction. For a split second, one of the figures almost seemed to skip a frame, like some visual glitch had occurred. I rubbed my eyes and looked again.

I was tired. My mind must've been playing tricks on me.

I boarded the bullet train, taking the Gold Line to the Platinum Line back in the direction of the MAR Master Terminal. All the while I sat in the train car, I brooded violently over the betrayal. I fantasized about finding that little man, bludgeoning him, strangling him, and drowning him.

I had to get a grip.

The truth was I didn't stand a chance against him. Not yet. I wasn't strong enough. Wasn't skilled enough. Wasn't equipped enough to exact revenge.

I thought of his paralysis poison. Had I higher statistical value invested in Resistance, might I have withstood that status ailment? Might I have recovered faster? I gnawed my lower lip in frustration.

I had one of the Volunteer's throwing knives tucked away. Maybe I could use that to somehow track him down. But why bother? Maybe this fixation on vengeance was a waste of time. A distraction from what I really needed to do.

At least he had only temporarily paralyzed me. He could have used much deadlier poison if that was his intention. He did leave me to the mercy of ravenous kappas though...

Wanting to spend as little time at the Master Terminal as possible, I quickly transferred to the Diamond Line in the direction of The Commons. The three rides cost me a total of thirty Crypt.

Now arriving at The Commons Station.

Finally, I returned to my dismal home, which right now I found oddly comforting. Or at least familiar. I walked the neon-bathed streets under the perpetually dark sky, heading in the direction of the Task Assignment Boards. I was ready to draw any and all weapons and throw down at the slightest provocation.

Task Complete: Remove minotaur from Grand Central Park in Eden West.

Assigned to Volunteer 01001110 01101111 01100010 01101111 01100100 01111001.

Task Completion Award: 3,000 Crypt.

Would you like to receive payment?

▸ Yes, dram it.

The 3,000 Crypt streamed into the C10K chip, bringing my new total to 6,830. I would reserve one hundred for my next data backup, but right now there were decisions to make. I had money to spend, a small quantity of Crystals, and these two mysterious pages.

INVENTORY
- **MISCELLANEOUS**
    - **Voynich Manuscript page** (?)
    - **Voynich Manuscript page** (?)

Paranoid, I made sure nobody else was in the vicinity as I examined the pages, bringing the 3D image of each up to hover and rotate.

Each sheet, composed of old parchment, took up five metabytes and were obviously pieces of a larger whole. But I could see no purpose for them individually. Examining them, I saw they were not identical.

The weathered pieces of parchment were the color of old ivory, stained at the edges. Lines of delicate script in a language I did not recognize covered the pages. There were strange patterns and diagrams. Most striking were vivid ink illustrations of plants. Leaves, flowers, twisting roots, vines, and bulbous structures. I was no expert in botany, so I didn't put much stock in the fact that I could not identify any of the flora depicted.

Hmmm. I recalled that the leader of the Serpents, Der Schlächter, offered to 'pay handsomely in Crystals' for any relics I recovered. Did these invasive anomalies—these manuscript fragments—qualify as relics? I also thought of Fancy Jack, the self-professed pacifistic herbalist. I wondered if he could make sense of these drawings.

I closed my menu and stepped away from the Task Assignment Boards, walking over to the building where Camel had once rescued me from a nasty encounter with those goons, taking pot shots from the fire escape. Where had Camel gone to anyway? I hadn't seen him in what felt like ages.

I leaned against the side of the building, deep in thought. I needed to feel that whisper in the back of my mind. The guidance from my dormant conscience about the next right steps to take.

Eventually, a sense of clarity settled over me.

I decided to visit the Data Forge first to use my twenty Crystals. Depending on how I invested them, it would free up room that would prove useful during my impending shopping spree. As it stood, I wouldn't even be able to regain my full Energy at the next refresh; I was a mere four metabytes away from maxing out my expanded cap.

I passed beneath the sign of the crossed blacksmith hammers and entered the Forge. I accessed the powerful machinery in the center and selected the convert option.

Deposit Crystals for conversion.

I converted ten Crystals into Value, which I then assigned to Storage, bringing my regular cap to a round 300 and my soft cap up to 320.

Next, I decided to fuse my recently acquired jiangshi Data Card onto an available skill slot. Sure, it was a context-specific skill, but under the right circumstances, I could regain Energy without having to rest during a cycle change. Unfortunately, I would only be able to regain ten Energy per cycle until I increased my Adeptness stat.

The chief problem of economics. Unlimited wants, limited resources.

But I knew someone who possessed seemingly limitless resources. The leader of the Serpents. I saw that vault, overflowing with Crystals. The very thought excited me. But no matter what I wanted to give Fancy Jack the opportunity to look at the manuscript pages first. I might be able to learn something useful.

And what would I do with a hefty Crystal payday? More Essence and Resistance to keep me alive and healthy. Adeptness to improve the utility of my special skills. Speed of movement and Agility to dodge and maneuver. Perception to detect threats and opportunities in my surroundings and Persuasion to bend those surroundings and others to my will. Protocol to master the higher functions of the Metaverse and unlock a greater repertoire of opportunities. And finally, Probability, so that terrible things would stop happening to me with such high regularity.

I selected the Fuse option, followed by the Skill suboption.

Insert a Data Card in the indicated depository.

I did so, first placing then observing the spinning rectangular prism infused with the decaying and ancient colors of the titular undead creature.

{uncommon} Data Card: jiangshi *(Skill)* detected.

Deposit Crystals for fusing.

I deposited my final ten Crystals and rested my palms on the white handprint patterns. I steadied myself.

Begin fusing process?

As before, an experience both painful and psychedelic unfolded, wherein the Crystals and Data Card were consumed by the machine and my palms glowed white hot. A swirl of cascading light pierced my chest and a deep and stinging chill fell over my heart. I distinctly remembered the feeling of the jiangshi draining my lifeforce away, and an image of its dead face with a hanging prayer scroll flashed in my mind's eye.

I winced, but the image was gone as quickly as it had appeared.

Skill fusing successful.

Jiangshi skill fused to open skill slot.

2 / 4 skill slots assigned.

As with the fusing of the clurichaun skill, I could visualize four shifting cubes within me. Skill slots. Two were gray and dim; the other two were bright with purpose—the power of the defeated entities subsumed within me.

I checked my Skills menu.

SKILLS
- **Clurichaun**
- **Jiangshi**
- **{empty}**
- **{empty}**

If needed, I could rearrange the order of the skill slots. Not that it seemed to matter. Through sheer force of will, I could activate whatever skill I wanted so long as I had the Energy or met the requirements. This new jiangshi skill had no Energy cost at all but, like the vampiric creature from which it originated, required a victim.

With the Crystals spent, I was at 286 metabytes out of 300 / 320. Even if I regained my depleted Energy, my storage would not be full. That helped me strategize my next purchasing decisions.

Time to put this 5% friends and family discount to work.

FILE 27.1

LOADOUT

My next stop was the Armory, which was its usual buzzy hive of Volunteer commerce. I gave a lazy half salute to Colonel Peacekeeper as I perused the wares on display. So many diverse and unusual tools of destruction. Glancing about, I wondered how many other shoppers in here had earned a special discount courtesy of the Round Table.

There was a certain piece of armor I had had my eye on for some time. And now I had extra Crypt to burn. But not seeing it in any of the rotating displays, I scrolled through the sales kiosk until I found it. It was listed at full price. But I wanted it.

Armor: Tactical jacket

Armor Type: Body

Cost: 2000 Crypt

Level: 1 of 10

Frequency: Uncommon

Defense Output: 30

Details: A type of jacket designed for use in military, law enforcement, and other tactical situations. Made from durable materials and features a variety of compartments for storing gear. Also features reinforced elbows, shoulders, and VELCRO strips for attaching morale patches or identification.

Properties: Storing - when equipped, this armor increases memory space by 20 metabytes.

Size: 30 metabytes

I already had the black boots and pants to match. Tactical clothing—collect the whole set! Once you go tac, you never go back.

Yes. It would require thirty metabytes of storage in exchange for thirty defense output, but would increase my soft storage cap by an additional twenty. Well worth it, in my estimation, and I could easily wear it over my ballistic vest.

This would bring my total combined armor rating to seventy, although I understood that, practically speaking, those defenses depended on what part of my squishy body was hit. My head was completely unprotected at present. Hmmm. I guess that was where the Resistance stat came in handy—raising my overall durability regardless of individual pieces of armor. That or a good helm.

Next, I searched for some of the ammo carrying accessories I had seen in Purgatory. I quickly located the ammunition belt.

Accessory: Ammunition belt

Cost: 500 Crypt

Frequency: Basic

Details: Standard black belt with twelve loops for individually securing cartridges in .22, .38/.357 or .44/.45 caliber.

Size: 10 metabytes

And it was only 500 Crypt! The ammo kiosk had the gall to charge me 800 for the same item. Count me in and add in two extra rounds to replace the bullets I buried in the minotaur's head.

Finally, I needed to upgrade my melee weapon. I was carrying the same starter dagger I picked up during orientation. It was small and basic, meaning I could never upgrade it or fuse it with any Data Cards. As much as I despised the man himself and what he used the weapon for, I thought of Little Scumbag's hunting knife.

But scrolling through the kiosk, I saw no sign of it. I approached Colonel Peacekeeper, bracing myself for his larger-than-life persona.

"A day without blood is like a day without sunshine. Hooah! Can I help you, soldier?"

▸ I'm looking for a hunting knife. A particular one. A hybrid hunting knife. Do you carry it?

"A fine weapon and tool! So versatile! With its premium, stainless steel six-inch blade and curved spine, it is designed to be equal parts hunting and boning knife!"

▸ That sounds like the one.

"Designed to withstand the elements with built-in corrosion resistance, the hybrid hunting knife is the perfect companion for the outdoors gourmand and sportsman!"

▸ I'm convinced!

"Laser-fabricated from sheets of chromium-infused high-grade steel with a carbon fiber handle, it even comes in different colors. Orange! Camo green! Stylish and deadly!"

▸ Okay, okay. Do you have it?

"Negative! It is currently off rotation."

Dram it!

▸ Do you... do you have any other knives I could look at? I need to upgrade from my basic push dagger.

"Well why didn't you say so, soldier? I have a couple common options here that fit the bill!"

Colonel Peacekeeper raised a green metal finger and opened two shimmering menus in the air. He pulled up two melee options in particular.

Weapon: Bolo knife

Weapon Type: Melee (slashing)

Cost: 500 Crypt

Level: 1 of 10

Frequency: Common

Damage Output: 20

Details: A versatile tool with a heavy, curved blade, ideal for agricultural work and self-defense.

Size: 10 metabytes

Weapon: Mark I trench knife

Weapon Type: Melee (piercing / bludgeoning)

Cost: 500 Crypt

Level: 1 of 10

Frequency: Common

Damage Output: 20

Details: A double-edged dagger blade and a distinctive 'knuckle duster' handle for close quarters combat.

Size: 10 metabytes

The rotating 3D images of the two weapons looked interesting enough. The first was like a smaller version of a machete. The second was more of a narrow dagger but had a spiked knuckle guard attached to the hilt.

Both would have longer reach than my push dagger and would not be saddled by the basic property.

I did some quick math. 2,000 for the jacket, 500 for the ammo belt, twenty to refill my revolver, and 500 for a new blade added up to

3,020. With my 5% discount that would be… 2,869 Crypt, leaving me with 3,961. Plenty to keep the spending spree going over at the Supply Depot and still have a financial cushion left over.

But which knife would be the better replacement? Although it had served me well, I wouldn't hesitate to drop that push dagger down the data recycler for something better.

The bolo knife had more utility in that, besides chopping and hacking my enemies, I could also chop and hack other things. Ropes? Vines? Writhing tentacles? And I liked the appearance of the broad, heavy blade.

On the other hand, the trench knife had more versatility. The primary mode of attack would be plunging the narrow dagger into my target, with the added bonus of being able to use the subtly spiked knuckle guard to bludgeon opponents.

My instincts were overwhelmingly telling me to go with the trench knife.

Ideally, with my expanded ammunition reserves, I could consistently attack from range for longer. Then again, the snub-nosed revolver did not have the best range. With the exception of the hedge maze, most of my battles had taken place in urban environments. And even the hedge maze could be considered close quarters.

But crazy old Camel favored a long gun, even in this endless cityscape. I wondered why, remembering his scoped, bolt-action rifle and ghillie suit. A different approach.

I removed the push dagger from my inventory to make room for the new gear. Then I finalized the purchase of the tactical jacket, ammunition belt, two .32 caliber rounds, and trench knife.

I scanned the smart ink on my left wrist, then my Volunteer ID barcode on my right.

5% Armory Discount accepted.

I paid the reduced total of 2,869 Crypt. It was a lot, but I was getting a good bang for my buck.

Tactical jacket selected. Would you like to equip this armor?

Ammunition belt selected. Would you like to equip this accessory?

Mark I trench knife selected. Would you like to equip this weapon?

▸ Yes to all of the above.

With each acceptance, my appearance instantly changed. The smart-looking black jacket easily fit over my promotional T-shirt and ballistic vest. The ammunition belt slotted perfectly around my waist over the tactical pants. Lastly, I held and admired my new melee weapon before dematerializing it out of sight.

"Thank you for shopping at the Armory, soldier. Remember— don't shoot until you see the whites of their eyes!"

I went over to the Memory Hole to recycle the push dagger. I scanned my ID, watching the pink triangle shine cyan, and dropped the small weapon in. The dagger was instantly sucked into the void with a terrible rushing sound.

You received 10 Crypt. Thank you for recycling unused data!

I double-checked the new additions to my Equipment menu.

EQUIPMENT
- **WEAPONS**
    - **MARK I TRENCH KNIFE**
    - **SNUB-NOSED REVOLVER**
        - **5 / 5 .32 caliber ammunition** (chambered)
        - **+10% fire damage** (Hellhound)
    - **THROWING KNIFE**
- **ARMOR** (70)

- HELM: N/A
- BODY: TACTICAL JACKET
  - BALLISTIC VEST
  - PROMOTIONAL T-SHIRT (cosmetic)
- ARMS: N/A
- LEGS: TACTICAL PANTS
  - TACTICAL BOOTS
- ACCESSORIES
  - AMMUNITION BELT
    - 12 / 12 .32 caliber ammunition

I also checked my Economy menu and Storage submenu.

ECONOMY

- **CRYPT: 3,971** (stored on B3-9S7-C10K chip)
- **CRYSTALS**

MEMORY

- **STORAGE: 326 / 300** (340)

Not enough room left to refill my Energy to full. But I had a plan.

FILE 27.2

IMPLANT

I left the crowded Armory and crossed the lot to the bright siren lights of the Supply Depot. I entered just in time to glimpse the legs of multiple Volunteers disappearing from the top of the spiral staircase. The Auction House. I was curious about it, but that wasn't the reason I was here.

To my surprise, the aged vendor was not seated at her usual spot behind the counter. Instead, I found her rearranging items on one of the novelty aisles. I greeted her.

"Oh, ho, ho. Don't mind me. Just refreshing the retail displays. They—I mean we—have a new seasonal assortment coming in."

▸ Do you sell any personal data storage cubes?

"Storage cubes? We sure do, dearie. But they are in the back. Follow me."

The woman walked very slowly, shuffling down the aisles until we came to a doorway in the rear corner leading to a small back room. An overflow area for additional goods. We passed through a hanging curtain of plastic slats and she gestured to various large cubes stacked haphazardly on the floor. They were a lot like the cubes at the Master Terminal but more run down.

▸ Why do you keep them back here?

"They are not a popular item. Most of your kind keep accounts at the Repository. And they are a hassle to move. Very heavy. Too large to fit in most inventories."

▸ I see.

"Also, many rains ago there was a rash of break-ins. Such a shame, really. I remember a time when your kind was more noble…"

The old woman sighed deeply, staring off into space. There was that phrase again, "your kind." These vendor bots were something else.

I looked from box to box until I found the least expensive option, and one that appeared to be in relatively good condition. And it was on sale! In fact, most of the cubes were steeply discounted.

▸ Are these really so unpopular?

"They fixed the faulty locking mechanism long ago, but by then the cubes had a bad reputation. As I said, there was a crime wave back then."

I highlighted the box.

Item: Storage Cube

Cost: 1000 Crypt (500 with 50% discount)

Capacity: 100 metabytes

Details: A personal data storage cube that holds up to 100 metabytes of data. Cannot be used to store Crypt due to CEC regulations. Unlocked by Volunteer ID of owner.

Size: 500 metabytes

▸ Wow. This thing is really dense! How can I get this back to the Residential Towers?

"I could deliver it for you after hours, dearie."

▸ You? How?

"On my bicycle of course."

▸ Okay…

I couldn't tell if she was joking. Were vendor bots programmed to joke?

"I may not look it anymore, but I am more than capable of making a simple delivery. Are you staying in your usual place of residence or somewhere else?"

▸ The default room that was assigned to me. The one with my number on it.

"Then don't you worry. Buy whichever one you like and I'll be sure it gets to you before you can answer the following riddle: 'A face marked by time, silent stories to tell. Holding secrets of heaven, in each dent and swell.'"

I blinked at her, not comprehending. First a joke, then a riddle. Was she malfunctioning?

▸ Right... I'll just go ahead and buy this one then. 500 Crypt?

She simply smiled and nodded, opening the special vendor menu in the air. Transaction completed. I would just have to wait and see if my property actually showed up.

Any way I can get a receipt on this...?

My plan was to keep the storage cube at my place in the Residential Towers. I would stash whatever I wasn't actively using, freeing up more space and also providing an extra layer of protection against losing things from an untimely death. The crafting materials, the card fragments, the throwing knife—even the Voynich Manuscript pages could be kept for safekeeping until I decided what to do with them. That would free up twenty six metabytes right off the bat. Ten more if I stashed the kappa fragments.

3,471 Crypt remaining. I needed to save enough for the data backup and any travel required for my next bounty, but I had decided to check out the advanced body modification options downstairs.

Some nagging suggestion in the back of my mind willed me in that direction, despite my misgivings.

Yes, the last time was a nightmare. Getting the axis port installed in the back of my head was one of the most unpleasant experiences of my time in The Collective. And that was saying a lot. But I had now seen multiple Volunteers using implants. The katana-wielding woman in the warehouse raid came to mind. Rook was riddled with them. I even suspected that Little Knifey used some sort of implant.

I also remembered that an anesthesia option existed, but I forgot how much extra it cost. Maybe there was a way to mitigate the horror of additional modification procedures.

Leaving the aged vendor to her own little world, I descended the spiral staircase and stepped onto the black slate floor, scanning my number under the waiting sensor. The image of my avatar filled the central screen. Decked out in my black tactical gear, I didn't look half bad, even if 95% of my body was completely generic.

Ignoring cosmetic changes for now, I scrolled through the available options panel until I reached the advanced body modification submenu.

I scrolled through a long list of brain jacks, limb augmentation, and synthetic organ replacement before pausing at the ocular implant submenu.

Hmmm. What's in here?

As with the chip in the back of my head, I soon realized I would need to complete another prerequisite procedure.

Modification integration procedure: Ocular port installation: One-time surgical procedure to install ports in both eye sockets for ocular implant access.

Cost: 1000 Crypt

Oh no. Body modification surgery involving removing my eyeballs did not seem pleasant in the least. But it could pave the way for additional benefits, and the implants could be swapped out over time for better upgrades. Instead of body modification, I tried to conceptualize this instead as "data surgery."

Whatever code comprised my avatar would be permanently altered. Because I was grafting a new segment of code onto myself, the subsequent implant would not take up any storage. The port itself offset any additional data burden.

But that wouldn't make it hurt less. The good news was that anesthesia was advertised as on sale for 50% off. It was my cycle for large discounts! Could this have something to do with a new retail season approaching? Everything must go at a low, low price? The bad news was that 50% off still came to a steep 1,000 Crypt.

There were different kinds of pain: physical and financial.

If I decided to go ahead with the port installation, what implants could I actually afford? I found a few options, with improved implants in the same series dramatically increasing in price relative to the benefits they provided. I did not have a high enough Protocol stat for any of the advanced models.

977-C-ING-I 1: Ocular implant that enables monochromatic low light vision in dark conditions.

Cost: 1000 Crypt

977-C-ING-I 2: Ocular implant that enables night vision in dark conditions.

Cost: 5000 Crypt

Alert: You do not have the required minimum Protocol for this device.

Further upgrades in the series advertised thermal vision, dark vision, and even X-ray vision. What exactly was the difference between low light, night, thermal, and dark vision? I thought of the shielded thermal goggles from Antisoc, now in the hands of ColSec, and muttered a curse.

IE-9NLYS-I L/R 1: Single eye ocular implant that enables analysis of the Essence of {common} invasive entities.

Cost: 1000 Crypt

IE-9NLYS-I L/R 2: Single eye ocular implant that enables analysis of the Essence of invasive entities up to {uncommon} frequency.

Cost: 5000 Crypt

Alert: You do not have the required minimum Protocol for this device.

Was this how Little Knifey knew the amount of Essence the minotaur had? I suspected so, although I hadn't noticed anything unusual about his eyes during our time together. Hard to read under that hood.

Like the first series of implants, I saw additional iterations allowing analysis of the Essence of rare, legendary, and even mythical entities. The price of the last option was astronomical.

B1-N0C-PRCPT-I 1: Ocular implant that grants a bonus of +20 to Perception and enables 4x visual zoom capability.

Cost: 1000 Crypt

B1-N0C-PRCPT-I 2: Ocular implant that grants a bonus of +40 to Perception and enables 8x visual zoom capability.

Cost: 5000 Crypt

Alert: You do not have the required minimum Protocol for this device.

Wary of the potentially excruciating pain though I was, I rationalized that the benefits would outweigh and outlast the temporary suffering. Like childbirth.

It would cost 1,000 Crypt for the port installation, and another 1,000 for the implant of my choice. With the special sale, I could opt-in for anesthesia for an additional 1,000. Either way, I was looking to drop between 2,000 to 3,000 for this, out of my remaining 3,471 Crypt.

I had a sneaking premonition that something bad could happen if I carried out the surgery without anesthesia. My Resistance was low, meaning my avatar lacked a certain amount of toughness that could withstand such a physical violation and easily bounce back.

I had survived the first procedure but found it utterly excruciating. Would there be no consequence for repeatedly exposing myself to that level of pain or worse?

Still, 1,000 Crypt was a lot. I had to rationalize the purchase.

It was on sale. Half off. 50% discount. You couldn't beat that deal. There would always be more monsters to kill. More bounty payments to collect.

Two of the implant options involved both eyes while the Essence analyzing option was described as a single eye implant. Could I mix and match?

I simply didn't have the required Protocol to use a lot of the more beneficial modification options. There was even a retractable targeting reticle to improve ranged weapon accuracy that I did not meet the threshold for.

I wanted all the above perks. But only the port installation was permanent. I could always swap out implants later.

I settled on the PRCPT-I 1 option. A +20 bonus to my Perception and visual zoom was interesting. I was drawn to the low light option as well, but it seemed less useful than the upgraded night vision. I could hold out for that, or even invest in my own pair of thermal goggles.

And I would love to detect the Essence of invasive entities. That would be a game changer. But I could only afford and qualify for the implant that analyzed common frequency monsters. I didn't plan on farming kappas and hellhounds every cycle...

Here goes something.

Modification integration procedure: Ocular port installation) selected.

B1-N0C-PRCPT-I 1 implant selected.

Would you like to apply these changes?

▸ Yes. But I want anesthesia this time.

The familiar cloying voice responded to me.

With the current 50% discount, anesthesia is available for an additional charge of 1,000 Crypt.

▸ I already said I wanted it.

Would you like to purchase anesthesia?

▸ Yes, for the love of bog!

Anesthesia confirmed.

The round apertures in the floor opened, and two narrow pedestals shot up. The indicated places to rest my hands glowed white. I stepped between them, and my hands clung tight to the bright surfaces—immobilized.

Please remain still. Administering anesthesia.

A metal arm descended from the ceiling with a syringe and large gauge needle. I tensed as it whirred and clicked closer, zeroing in over some intended spot on my neck.

Without further warning, the needle plunged into the side of my neck. Bright red fluid coursed into me.

▶ Oww!

Why did the thing that was supposed to take away my pain have to cause me pain first?

Soon, all physical sensation drained from my body. Although my hands were fastened to the white hot panels, there was no feeling except complete numbness from head to toe.

Anesthesia administered. Please remain still. The operation will begin shortly.

Two additional mechanical appendages descended, swapping places with the first arm. The ends of each held onto a single metal mask, connected by wires and tubes, that was maneuvered in front of my face. Inside the mask I glimpsed inert gears like some sort of binocular mining drill.

I don't like this...

The arms recalibrated and moved forwards until the mask fit tightly over my forehead and eyes, leaving an indentation for my nose. I saw only total darkness.

Please remain still. Permanent ocular damage may occur if you move.

Frag me.

I braced against the pedestals, forcing myself to stay as still as possible.

Thankfully, the expensive anesthesia worked. I felt nothing but intense, dull pressure in my eye sockets. There was a loud, burrowing noise and my facial structure vibrated as the machine did its work. Although I could not feel it, I sickeningly imagined my eyeballs removed from my skull, metal rings fastened onto bone, synthetic neural fibers plugged into my visual cortex, and newly modified eyes popped into waiting cavities.

Operation successful. Ocular port installation successful. B1-N0C-PRCPT-I 1 ocular implant successful.

Draining 3,000 Crypt from my account—successful.

Freed from the device, I dragged myself up the spiral stairs and stumbled out of the Supply Depot, my eye sockets deeply sore and my retinas hypersensitive to the flashing lights encircling the Supply Depot. The numbness of the anesthesia lingered; my limbs were sluggish and numb.

My eyes... Ah... I might need some time to get used to these things.

I planned to immediately back up my data at the Restoration Point. Unfortunately, I felt the first drops of pink rain lashing me. Dram. It would have to wait.

I made for the Residential Towers, fighting against the numbness to clamber up the slick emergency stairs to the elevated road above. Streams of pink liquid ran over my boots. Wetness dripped off the sleeves of my new jacket. Crossing the street, I narrowly avoided tripping in a pothole concealed by the flooding waters. Benefit of increased Perception?

I scanned my code in the rattling cage elevator and rode it to my floor, massaging my eyes all the while. Locating my hole in the wall partway down the dim hallway, I scanned again and climbed into my little domy.

What the frag?

The white storage cube sat in the corner. The one I just purchased before the surgery.

How did... When...?

Scratching my head, I crawled closer and carefully inspected the box. The old woman really delivered it? That fast? And how did she get past the lock?

A sudden recollection came to me—Camel had two cubes like this in his residence. I had forgotten. Similar, but not identical. Maybe his cubes were an older model, before they fell out of favor. The vendor had said these were not popular storage options for Volunteers anymore.

That may be so, but there was another reason I wanted to buy it. After my involvement with the heist, I didn't feel comfortable showing my face at the Repository. Not yet. Maybe after things cooled down. I was sure the investigation was ongoing, and the threat of ColSec surveillance weighed on me.

Every action had a consequence. By agreeing to help Antisoc, I was now avoiding utilizing a service that many other Volunteers regularly enjoyed.

I needed to adapt. Adapt or... well, not die, exactly. Adapt or suffer.

I scanned my code in front of an etched circular pattern on the side of the cube. A red ring flashed white, and I heard a distinct clink. The cube did not open. Not physically.

I held my hand over the box and highlighted it. Soon, a separate menu appeared in my vision.

Ah. I get it now. The cube had its own storage menu, but I had to manually unlock it first. Time to test this out.

I opened my personal menu, then dragged and dropped several items from my equipment and inventory into the cube: the fern flowers, coco de mer nut, white linen cloth, vial of pure water, the six minotaur fragments, and even the throwing knife. They instantly dematerialized into the cube.

I kept the kappa fragments in my inventory for the time being.

Then—I hesitated. Did I want to stash the manuscript pages or not?

Little Knifey was out there, somewhere. Was it possible he would come looking for the missing pages? Perhaps he had no idea the missing pages even existed. Either way, I had no experience dealing with invasive anomalies, or what the leader of the Serpents called relics. Just how prized were they? Valuable enough for Little Knifey to paralyze me and leave me for dead.

I dragged and dropped the two Voynich Manuscript pages into the personal data storage cube. Temporarily kept safe behind two Volunteer ID-dependent locks.

I checked my new stash:

STORAGE CUBE: 26 / 100 metabytes
- **Voynich Manuscript page** (?) (5 metabytes)
- **Voynich Manuscript page** (?) (5 metabytes)
- **2 {common} fern flowers** (2 metabytes)
- **1 {uncommon} coco de mer nut** (1 metabyte)
- **1 white linen cloth** (1 metabyte)
- **1 vial of pure water** (1 metabyte)
- **Minotaur Data Dard fragments - 6/10** (6 metabytes)
- **Throwing knife** (5 metabytes)

And that brought my on-person storage (factoring in the +40 cumulative soft cap) down to 300.

MEMORY
- **STORAGE: 300 / 300** (340)

I scanned my identifier a second time and the circular light clicked back to red. Cube locked.

I was tired. My eyes were sore. My body tingled with numbness.

It was time to rest, reset, then back up my data.

I removed and set aside most of my armor and tried to get comfortable on the thin foam pallet. My cramped capsule was even more cramped with the addition of the cube.

I twisted off the light and waited.

Eventually, my awareness began to fade. I imagined the gentle sound of lapping waves. No terrifying visions came.

FILE 28

RELICS

Refresh complete.

Essence at full.

Energy restored.

I reached for the light.

An uneventful cycle change. The best kind. The system was refreshed and the programs rebooted.

My eyes were now only a little sore and no longer hypersensitive to the light. That was a relief.

I sat on my pallet and experimented, trying to zoom my vision in and out. It worked. My ocular implants adjusted like lenses on a camera. Up to four times the magnification, also known as scanning. Of course, there was very little to see in my tube and very little distance from which to see it. But the implants worked.

I got dressed and rode the elevator to the ground floor, then visited the Restoration Point straightaway without incident. I paid one hundred Crypt to back up my new and improved self: armor, weapons, implants and all. My True Self™.

Only 371 Crypt left and 10 free metabytes. But I was satisfied with my purchases and upgrades. I could deal damage up close or at range, cast an illusion, and absorb a target's Energy. My cumulative defensive total was seventy, and I carried seventeen .32 caliber rounds on my person. With my new implants, Perception was now my highest stat at forty.

Backup complete, I returned to my residence and removed a single Voynich Manuscript page from my storage cube. I made up my mind to take it to Fancy Jack for appraisal, and I was more comfortable carrying just the one for now.

But there was a problem. When I made the decision to sacrifice myself, intervening to protect Rook from the Huodou, the calling card Fancy Jack gave me was lost. The address to his apartment. I never backed it up.

Once again, I realized that actions and decisions have consequences. Often unintended consequences.

I tried to think. I met Fancy Jack near an abandoned underground mall after the ColSec interrogation. But his apartment could be anywhere in The Commons. I was in such a rush to join the raid I hadn't paid much attention to which direction he went after our conversation.

I visited the information kiosk and inquired after the virtual assistant for Fancy Jack's address.

I apologize for any inconvenience, but unfortunately, I am unable to accommodate that request. Also, I am not programmed to recognize Volunteers by their unofficial aliases.

Strike one. Next, I asked around at the Rathskeller, keeping my eyes out for Camel or Little Knifey. No sign of either. Not even with 4x zoom.

None of the Volunteers could tell me exactly where to find Fancy Jack's apartment, but a few told me it was located in the Kafka

Building, an eclectic mixed-use development on an elevated section of The Commons beyond Mendicant Row. They gave me general directions.

It was a long walk. I passed through multiple grungy pedestrian tunnels and scaled steps to bypass steep inclines of jutting concrete. Boarded up storefronts and vandalized windows were everywhere here.

Nice part of town.

Digital billboards and holographic advertisements loomed far overhead, including one for an automated-vehicle taxi service. I zoomed in on the ad. Apparently Volunteers could access the service through any information kiosk for a fee. Would have been helpful to know that an hour ago. I kept walking.

Up ahead, I perceived a bright glow and increased activity. Mounted work lights and unusual heavy machinery. The swirl of carrion bird Polizei drones. I quickened my pace until I reached a large construction site blocking my path.

Several Polizei bots stood guard. Behind them, tall but flimsy barricades obstructed physical and visual access to the area beyond. The makeshift walls were similarly graffitied and slathered with advertisements, and I couldn't tell which was more of an eyesore.

But I could tell that something was off. Through cracks in the barricades there appeared to be a deep blankness. A dark void. A hole in The Commons where part of the city once stood. This void was surrounded by scattered chunks of debris pushed together into heaping piles. And strangest of all, columns of moving digital code worked to stitch this portion of the city back into existence.

"No loitering or trespassing. This is a crime scene and active work zone," one of the Polizei bots barked.

Crime scene?

▸ I'm trying to get to the Kafka Building.

The Polizei bots conferred with one another, then the first turned back to me.

"Are you assigned to live in this sector?"

▸ No... I'm trying to visit a friend.

"Friend?"

The word did not seem to compute.

"Until the reconstruction is complete and all evidence gathered, there is no admission beyond this point unless you are a registered resident of this sector. Show me your Volunteer ID."

▸ No, no. It's okay. I was just leaving.

I took several strides out of the radius of system activity and observed.

Was there a way I could go around? Another route? In the distance, beyond the rubble, I perceived several buildings built onto what may have been a former highway overpass.

Even if I could somehow reach it, I didn't know the exact apartment where Fancy Jack lived. Would I go knocking door to door trying to find the herbalist?

A realization came to me. That explosion! The ColSec officer mentioned it during my interrogation. There was even a news segment on the train. Mendicant Row. A suspected Rez den. Ground zero of an explosion damaging property and avatars. This was where it happened. But this blast radius didn't resemble the effects of any type of bomb I could imagine.

Again, the thought bubbled to the surface that actions have consequences. But who was responsible for this action? This decision? The consequence for me was that I could not reach my destination.

Not now. And I didn't want any more heat from Collective Security. Best not to be hanging around an active crime scene.

I had one Voynich Manuscript page on me. I could take it to the Serpents and see what they had to say. Maybe this wasn't the type of relic their leader was interested in. Either way, I would reserve the second page for Fancy Jack just as soon as I could reach him.

That meant another long walk ahead of me. Even longer than before. Any information kiosks around to hail a ride? I didn't think so.

FILE 28.1

NADIR

Hours later, I arrived at Nadir Tower at the far lower end of The Commons, exhausted.

I entered the lobby and four armed Serpents in ornate masks stopped me.

▶ I'm here to see Der Schlächter. I have something I think he wants. A relic.

The masks regarded me in silence. Then one of them nodded and bid me to follow.

We crossed the marble floors and got in the freight elevator. The Serpent guard inserted a golden key. It was a long ride to the top floor. I fidgeted, suddenly second guessing my decision to come here.

I had nothing to worry about. I was here on invitation. Der Schlächter specifically asked me to bring any relics to him for a generous reward. And I didn't even need to be part of their creepy family. No strings attached.

So why did I feel this sense of foreboding?

Two other masked Serpents waited for us at the top of the lift. From somewhere inside, a deep vibrato reverberated through the penthouse.

Ohmmmmmmmm.

The guards escorted me through the impressive penthouse to an open, central room. And there he was. The enormous, hairless man seated in the lotus position in front of an ancient stone slab. He wore only a loincloth.

Der Schlächter.

At my entrance, he rose, reaching for a silk kimono. He smiled broadly, showing his large, white teeth. Before the kimono was on, I used my ocular implants to zoom in on the Volunteer ID barcode on his wrist. It read: 01000010 01100101 01110100 01100001 00110110.

"If it isn't the Nameless Volunteer. Returned to us at last."

▸ I have a name. They call me Magpie now.

"Magpie? Well, isn't that exquisite? Magpie. What fair tidings bring you to the Serpents' Lair on this auspicious cycle?"

I heard a rueful snicker and turned to see Razor, Buzzcut, and a few other Serpent goons seated nearby. Razor glared contemptuously at me.

"Razor, do be kind to our guest," the leader's deep, paternalistic voice chastised.

Razor gulped and sat up straighter, disguising his snickering as throat-clearing.

"Yes, Schlächter! Just had something loveted in my gorlo is all."

The large man glided across the floor until he stood uncomfortably close to me. I looked up at him, my eye level only reaching his silk clad chest.

"Am I correct in perceiving you have something for me?"

I nodded, materializing the single Voynich Manuscript page. Delicately gripping the edge between two fingers, I held it out. He took the sheet in his large hands and studied it.

"Very interesting," he murmured. "Where, pray tell, did you find this?"

▸ In a hedge maze in Grand Central Park. Eden West.

"And this was the only one? Just this one page?"

He turned his gaze on me, large eyes boring into my soul. I had the unnerving feeling that he could see straight through me. He would know if I was lying. Somehow, he would know. I had to choose my words carefully.

▸ Another Volunteer, I don't know his name, found a book. An invasive anomaly. This page fell out. I only have this page in my inventory.

He continued to stare at me wordlessly. Was it getting warm in here?

▸ I remembered what you said. You have an interest in relics. Does this qualify?

Der Schlächter motioned for one of the masked guards and whispered in their ear. The guard left the room. Looking at the four ragtag goons, I began to suspect they (Razor and his ilk) were of lower rank than the Serpents adorned in the striking feathered serpent masks. They were just children in this family, not mature disciples.

The guard returned carrying a small but ornately carved wooden chest which he passed to the leader, who dismissed him. Der Schlächter opened the lid and I beheld it was full of sparkling Crystals. My pulse quickened.

"How does one hundred Crystals sound in exchange for this one sheet of paper?"

One hundred!

▸ It sounds very generous.

"You appear to be limited on free space, so you can keep this chest to hold the Crystals until you can make other arrangements. Consider it a gift."

Low on storage space. How the frag could he know that?

Right before I could accept the chest, Der Schlächter pulled it back just out of my grasp.

"But before you accept this payment, there is something else I want to speak to you about."

▸ Oh?

"A job. A simple job that you are uniquely suited for. It would mean a great deal to me."

I remembered the note added to my Subroutines menu. The task I hadn't gotten around to accepting.

>SUBROUTINES

\-   **Assist Serpents with Package Delivery** (Pending)

▸ You mean the package you want me to deliver?

Razor, Buzzcut, and the other two whose names I didn't know snickered and nudged each other. An inside joke?

"No. We had another courier take care of that little delivery job for us. But thank you for remembering."

I guess I waited too long for that one.

▸ A different job then? What is it?

"Instead of delivering a package, this task is but a simple and harmless act of retrieval. Pick something up and bring it here to me. I will pay you… 1,000 Crystals."

My jaw hit the floor.

▸ 1,000 Crystals?

"1,000 Crystals. All for you in exchange for bringing me a single item that I believe to be here in The Commons. And again, this is a job that you, little bird, are uniquely suited for."

Me? Uniquely suited? I couldn't imagine how.

The masked guard returned, holding a larger chest. A veritable bounty of shimmering Crystals shone forth, threatening to overflow the container. It was a glorious sight.

I answered without hesitation, raw cupidity overriding any internal warning bells.

▸ Yes! Yes... I'm interested. Please tell me more.

Der Schlächter clicked his tongue and shook his head.

"Unfortunately, I cannot tell you any more details nor entrust you with this task unless you are willing to take a leap of faith. For right now you are still considered an outsider among us."

▸ A leap of faith?

"All of us here have taken part in a sacred ceremony. An initiation ritual, if you will. To serve on behalf of the Progenies Serpentium you must first participate in this sacrament. I believe you will find the process most enlightening."

I perceived the goons shifting uncomfortably in their seats and exchanging knowing glances. Did they not want me to take this initiatory step? Were they worried I would outshine them, put them to shame in front of their master? Or was there something else going on?

▸ Let me get this straight. If I take part in this initiation ritual, then you will give me the details of this job. And if I complete this simple job, I earn 1,000 Crystals.

Another broad smile from the leader. He rested a hand firmly on my shoulder, keeping the chest of one hundred Crystals tucked in the crook of his other arm.

"Beautifully summarized, little bird. It is as you said. And remember... I never lie."

How could I turn down 1,000 Crystals? Especially if the job was as easy as Der Schlächter said. This was a man with startling power. A man capable of bending the elements of this Metaverse to his will.

And the things I could do with 1,000 Crystals... The possibilities...

Despite my misgivings, I agreed. How bad could one initiation ritual be? It didn't mean I was swearing eternal fealty to this organization.

▸ Okay.

"You don't know how pleased I am to hear that. Follow me."

Leaving the meditation room, Der Schlächter led me into a large kitchen. The goons trailed behind hesitantly but obediently. I also noticed several of the masked guards joining us.

Nice kitchen. So, was this sacrament some form of meal? A holy feast?

"Disrobe."

▸ What?

"I *insist*."

Der Schlächter spoke with such force, such command that I found myself instantly obeying, shedding every layer of armor. A masked disciple quickly gathered the pieces and placed them aside. I stood naked, wanting to cover my private areas from the many watching eyes but having nothing to cover.

Was that a special skill he used? An overwhelmingly high Persuasion stat?

I was naked. Now what—a juvenile hazing routine? Were they going to take turns spanking me with a paddle?

"Very good. Now lay down. *Here*."

Der Schlächter lovingly ran his bare hand over a large wooden platform. I looked from the table to him and back again, hesitating.

"This won't take long."

▸ But I...

"I *insist.*"

The next thing I knew I was lying naked on the long wooden platform. The leader smiled fondly at me and ran a hand through my black hair.

"This will be your first step to true awakening, little one."

He nodded to two of his masked disciples who were at my side in an instant, latching my arms and legs to points at the bottom of the platform.

▸ Hey! What are you doing?

I strained against the bindings. This was not what I had agreed to!

"Calm yourself. Breathe. Do not give into fear."

Above me, hanging from the ceiling, were several large meat hooks.

Oh no. Oh no, oh no! I do not like this...

The disciples who tied me down wheeled two heavy contraptions behind them. I twisted my head, trying desperately to see what they were doing.

Meanwhile, Der Schlächter slowly unrolled a black bundle on the spacious countertop.

One disciple slid a needle into a vein on my arm, connected by a plastic tube leading to one of the machines. The other attached electrodes to either side of my head.

▸ What is this? What are they doing!?

"This first machine there is so you will not bleed out. The second is so you will not lose consciousness. You will not want to miss a moment of this."

I was pretty sure I did.

▸ Stop this. Please, stop this. Just let me go. I don't want to do this anymore. 1,000 Crystals? Keep your Crystals! Keep the one hundred Crystals too!

The leader shook his head, a sympathetic expression. The folds of skin on his hairless head wrinkled with deep and genuine concern.

"I am setting you free."

To my horror, he held up a large meat cleaver.

I cried in terror, writhing against the bindings. The Serpents stood solemnly, witnessing the unfolding ritual.

Then, bringing the blade down in a sharp motion, Schlächter chopped my foot clean off.

I screamed, and screamed, and screamed. But there was nobody to save me.

▸ What the frag did you do to me?!

The masked disciples applied a tourniquet above the severed bone and vascular, exposed flesh.

Horrific pain exploded up my leg. I felt dizzy, like I could pass out. I *wanted* to pass out. Please *bog* let me pass out!

A subtle electric shock at my temples jolted me back to the present moment.

"Do not run from this. Embrace it," the monster repeated in soothing, dulcet tones.

The others stared at the scene, not daring to look away. Although, I sensed Buzzcut would rather be anywhere else in the Metaverse right now.

I slammed my head back on the platform, tears coursing from my face.

I thought the worst was over. I was wrong.

Der Schlächter brought my severed foot, dripping with blood, to his mouth. And he began to eat it.

▸ No! NO!

I tried to shut my eyes, to look away. But a Serpent knelt behind me, wrenching my eyelids open painfully and forcing my head in the direction of their sick master.

"If I do not eat your flesh and drink your blood, you have no part in me," the master intoned.

His large, white teeth tore through the outer layer of skin, ripping it off in strips which he masticated and swallowed. He moved on to the muscles and tendons, chewing greedily and sucking the meat off the exposed phalanges bones. Sucking the fluid from my joints.

▸ You're sick! You're insane!

I wanted to vomit. I tried to vomit. But that was impossible.

"Let go of your preconceptions," he cooed. "None of this is real. None of it. This foot? Not real. Even your perception of pain is an illusion. All of this is simply data, information signals beaming through the network of your brain."

I struggled against the hands prying open my eyes, fought against the cords binding me. But I had no strength to fight. Blood pumped into my veins from the machine, replacing that which spilled off the butcher's block.

▸ Please! Please stop it! I beg you!

"I cannot stop until you let go. Free your mind from the confines of your limited perception. Understand that this is nothing more than ones and zeroes. Ones and zeroes. You must break through the illusion to find true power!"

As he spoke, he held up the partially devoured foot near my face. My own fragging foot. The bones protruded from the raw meat.

Ones and zeroes.

Ones and zeroes.

► Ones… and zeroes…

I tried to repeat it like a mantra; tried to focus on something to attach my mind to anything other than this living nightmare.

Through the opening in the front of Der Schlächter's kimono, I watched the two snake tattoos from his back slithering across his skin, coiling about his formidable chest and belly. Impossibly alive. The ouroboros—the self-devouring serpent.

"The first step towards apotheosis begins with accepting reality. Want a bite?"

► No!

I spat at the man. He just laughed, not bothering to wipe the saliva from his face.

"Even your spittle is nothing but bits of code. Completely artificial. But we seek something greater than The Collective can offer. Together, we will transcend all limitations."

His followers were becoming energized, riled by this sermon.

"Serpents rise!" the masked disciples chanted in unison.

I simply lay back on the table, sobbing helplessly.

As he gnawed on the joint cartilage and sucked the final bits of meat off my skeletonized foot, Der Schlächter belched and daintily dabbed at his mouth with a linen napkin.

Again he rested his large hand on me, this time on my bare chest.

There was a tenderness in that touch completely at odds with the horror that had just been inflicted on me.

"This was a hard experience for you. I know. Believe me, I know. But it was for your own good. To open your eyes to the truth. Now we can at last welcome you into our family. You need not be an outsider to our cause any longer."

I said nothing—could say nothing. My body trembled uncontrollably. With rage? Shock? Adrenaline?

"Now I offer you a choice. We can replace your lost appendage. Improve it. Transcend the flesh. Or we can send you back to the Restoration Point where you may be reborn whole."

Quivering, with tears and snot covering my face, I looked over at the Serpent goons. I realized that each one was missing body parts. Razor's lower jaw was entirely chrome. Buzzcut had a metal hand. There were similar parts and pieces missing from the others, and that was just what I could see above the clothing and masks.

No way. I wanted no part of this. No Serpent chrome would touch my body.

► Kill me...

Der Schlächter leaned in close.

"What was that, my child?"

► Just kill me. Please... kill me...

"As you wish."

The disciples removed the tube from my arm and the electrodes from my head. My footless, bleeding naked body lay strapped to the butcher's block. Exposed. Vulnerable. Powerless.

The butcher raised his cleaver high above my neck, then cut off my head with a single downwards stroke.

FILE 29

THEORIES

0
  1
10
  11
100
  101
110
  111
1000
  1001
1010

Restoration complete. Now discharging.

Awakening.

There was a loud clanking sound. A vibrating platform lowered me out of the restoration tube, unceremoniously depositing me beside it like an unwanted fetus.

I was alive. Again. Of course I was. Resurrected at the Restoration Point. The cycle continues. The endless cycle of misery.

I looked down at my body. My hands, my arms, my legs. I was once again clothed in my full outfit, including two tactical boots worn over my two attached feet. At least there was that bit of good news.

The panel nearby chirped.

Your last restoration was {0} cycles ago.

Automatic Restoration Fee notification. 2,000 Crypt will be deducted.

Warning! You now have a negative balance. Your account is overdrawn by 1,629 Crypt.

Warning! Compound interest will accrue on all unpaid debts each cycle until cleared.

Forget what I said about the good news.

Negative 1,629 Crypt!?

I quickly checked my menu and confirmed the dreaded truth. This was a worst-case scenario. This was rock bottom. And the Voynich Manuscript page was gone. I had removed it from the storage cube after my last backup… and gave it to the Serpents.

I didn't even have the energy to curse. I wanted to crawl under a rock and die. But death was impossible. There was no escape.

Many Volunteers were using the Restoration Point, going about their cyclic routines. I ignored them all, walking in a trancelike state out the front of this monumental structure—the beating heart of The Commons, recycling the souls of fallen warriors and sending them right back to the front lines.

Standing under the endless dark sky, I was listless. I had nowhere to go. Nothing I cared about doing.

But—what was that? No… *who* was that?

My increased Perception alerted me to a black figure across the street, staring straight at me. I focused, zooming in. The figure appeared cybernetic, and it was moving purposefully in my direction.

What now?!

Standing before me was a black cyborg. It wasn't wearing clothes but had black metal over almost its entire body. However, there were two very exposed human eyeballs, and a pink, human tongue and throat within the black metal skull. A translucent panel pulsing with lights revealed a beating organ—what looked like a human heart—in the middle of its chest cavity.

I had no clue what was happening. My instinct to fight or flee hijacked, I merely froze in place, gawking at this monstrosity.

The cybernetic figure reached out its arms. It was holding something familiar. It was a small, ornately carved wooden chest containing 100 Crystals. The payment from Der Schlächter for the manuscript page.

"Call me Ishmael," the cyborg said in a heavily processed voice. "This is the payment my master promised. He wants you to know that he is a man of his word."

I snapped.

▸ Your master? Der Schlächter!? He is a freak! All of you are!

"The offer stands. 1,000 Crystals in exchange for completing a simple job. We will also pay off your debt."

I glared at the abomination in front of me. Ishmael. I had heard something about this thing... The second in command of the Serpents. Der Schlächter's right hand man. As I looked over his body, completely replaced with metal, a horrible thought occurred. How much of his body had his master eaten?

I shuddered.

▸ I don't want anything to do with you!

"I don't see how you have much of a choice in the matter. And you had better hurry. Each cycle that passes, your debt will grow. The consequences of that can be... catastrophic. Despite what you think now, my master offers a path of true enlightenment. A path of transcendence. He is a great man."

I glared with undisguised loathing but restrained myself from speaking my thoughts.

▸ A simple retrieval job that I am uniquely suited for. Forgive my skepticism. What is it?

The monstrous skeletal face smiled, pulsing lights racing across conduits on its frame like exposed nerves.

"Your friend Camel is in possession of a map. We want you to bring it to us."

Well that was unexpected.

▸ Camel? What's he got to do with this? And what do you mean, 'a map'? The only things Camel cares about are cigarettes, booze, and pleasure bots.

"My master and Camel go back a long time. They were both Volunteers in the early cycles, and they endeavored to explore the furthest boundaries of this Metaverse. Back then, Camel went by a different name: Lamech, or Lemekh. This was long before my awakening. Camel found a map and went in search of the destination. But he was never the same after that. A changed man."

I couldn't believe what I was hearing. I was so surprised that I temporarily forgot my all-consuming hatred.

▸ That's... I don't know what... This is all... Huh.

"We believe Camel still has possession of the map. He obviously isn't using it. You are his friend. We want you to go, find the map, and bring it to us. Simple."

I immediately thought of the two storage cubes in Camel's residence. Could there be a map in there? But I hadn't even seen Camel in forever. I had no clue where he was. And... were they asking me to betray him? Betray my one and only friend? If Camel kept this map hidden, he must have had his reasons.

▶ A map to what?

"A sunken temple, lost beneath the waves."

Ishmael gave a polite bow, incongruous with his fearsome appearance. He held out the chest for me to take. I accepted it, looking down at the hypnotically gleaming pile of Crystals shining up at me.

When I looked up, Ishmael was gone.

I wandered The Commons in a daze. A hundred competing thoughts and emotions swirled about in my confused brain. I didn't know where I was going, I just needed to keep moving, like a shark.

I carried the chest of Crystals with me, lid closed. The smart thing would have been to go straight to the Data Forge. But I didn't care.

Eventually, my absentminded roaming brought me in the vicinity of Spawn Alley. To my surprise, I noticed a yokocho with a blue neon sign. The kanji for fish in a closed circle. A stoic chef served seafood to scant, miserable customers.

The shop! The contact point! It was open again.

I quickly took a seat on the only available stool and waved to the proprietor.

▶ I'll have the fugu.

If Antisoc didn't trust me, they could flatline me. Go ahead. Remove me once and for all from this neon hellscape!

Instead, minutes later the cat with the Cheshire grin appeared and nuzzled against my leg. I reached to stroke its fur, but it darted indifferently out of reach.

Holding the chest, I got up and followed the cat through the usual winding tangle of alleys and grim side streets until, once again, I stepped through a flat pane of light into the pocket server instance of the terrorist group known as Antisoc.

Fawkes, Tank Man, and Q. They were in full glitch-face mode, and their headquarters looked radically different. Instead of an abandoned laboratory setting, they had set up shop in some industrial plant. Large water pipes and air ducts violated the space from every angle, and electric breakers lined one entire wall. Antisoc's portable screens, grid hacking connections, and barely controlled chaos were the same.

The grinning cat leapt up on one of the horizontal pipes. Tank Man, I think, stroked its fur and whispered.

>**Good girl.**<

▸ I didn't think I'd see your faces again. Or lack of faces, I should say.

>**Just a standard precaution. We apologize if our absence caused you any undue stress.**<

▸ I didn't know what to think. Still don't. The heist... Was it a success?

>**The less you know about it the better, for your own safety. But you successfully executed your part of the plan. And you stood tall in your interrogation with a Stasi bot. Impressive.**<

Two of them stood before me. The one with the lab coat hung back, typing rapidly. Because of the masks and the modulated voices, I was not sure who was speaking. At times, it felt like all three were speaking simultaneously.

▸ But I lost your thermal goggles.

>**Unfortunate, but not a dealbreaker. We needed to pivot and cover all our bases, but we have failsafes within failsafes. Can't be too careful, especially with Volunteers like you running around**

with highly suspicious energy signals. Q, what is the current number?<

>382.<

I didn't have patience for all this cryptic Shiva. Not after what I'd been through.

▸ You promised you would share what you know about The Collective if I helped you. I did my part. Time to do yours. What is really going on? What is this world?!

The one in the lab coat kept typing away furiously. The other picked up the cat and stroked her fur. The one in the middle, I assumed Fawkes, nodded in agreement and took time to gather his thoughts before answering.

>So we did. So we did...

We can't share everything we've discovered, but here are some of the prevailing theories about what is going on. The true nature of this reality. We and others have frequently debated the merits of these competing theories. We'll let you reach your own conclusions.

Theory #1: The Collective is a mind prison, and we are prisoners for political crimes committed in the real world. There is no escape. No contract to fulfill. Volunteers will be reborn and reborn for an eternity with their memories wiped. You've done this same thing a hundred—maybe a thousand times before. The system creates false objectives and conflicts to keep us occupied and distracted. As the saying goes, you can always hire half of the poor to kill the other half.

Theory #2: The Collective is one giant cryptocurrency farm. Every action we take, as part of this complex system, is helping to generate cryptocurrency being used in the real world. Volunteers are slaves—cogs in a machine—forced to grind out profits for supermassive corporations. The more intense our experiences, the more profit we generate. Fear, pain, longing, anguish, confusion, despair—these emotions power the engines of wealth.

Theory #3: The Collective is a mind-control simulation and Volunteers are sleeper agents, operating without awareness in the real world. When a Volunteer takes a bounty, they are in reality assassinating a political opponent or target in the real world, obscured through an impenetrable VR veil. Each cycle change could be days, weeks, months, years—who knows, until we are awakened again to kill on behalf of the elite political cabals of the world.

Theory #4: The Collective is a psychological and philosophical experiment about the true nature of consciousness, and we are the subjects. The Volunteers, you and I, are nothing more than AI constructs. Self-aware, sentient AI? Unknowable. But there is no humanity here. And there is no difference between us, the bots, the creatures, and the Citizens. We are all programs— monitored and tested, poked and prodded, killed and autopsied and reborn—in a highly complex virtual laboratory.<

I stood blinking at the Three Magi.

▶ Those… sound completely ridiculous. I don't believe it. I didn't ask for theories. I asked for facts. Tell me what you *do* know for certain. After all I've been through, I deserve that much.

Although, come to think of it, that Stasi bot had threatened me with an "enhanced system refresh," effectively erasing my memory for a second time. Could there be something to that theory after all? Or bits of truth in all of them? Something told me the truth was deeper than any of those theories—and possibly more disturbing.

The Three Magi turned to face each other, their volume dropping and voice patterns growing indecipherable. They were conferring in coded distortion again. Finally, Fawkes turned back to me and visibly relaxed. Perhaps they were finally going to trust me.

>So be it. Here is what we are most certain of:

The Collective was built on top of a pre-existing system. Either these two systems are running concurrently, or one was built on the framework of an older, obsolete system.<

▸ And what is your evidence for that?

>**First, the cycles are irregular. The intervals between cycles are unpredictable and do not match any discernible pattern. We do not believe the rain that signals the change of a cycle is under system control. Currently, the system times their patches and refreshes with the rain, but they did not used to. They are disguising their lack of control over this element.**

Second, there have been many instances of outside interference. Outside of the system, that is. According to the system, when a Volunteer dies, they respawn at the Restoration Point. But some Volunteers are permanently changed in a way the system cannot restore. Some Volunteers disappear and are never seen again. The current number of active Volunteers is less than the total awakened. Did they fulfill their so-called contracts and get released? Doubtful. And then there's you.<

▸ Me? What about me?

>**When we first scanned your history, we noticed a disturbing error message you received. This error does not correspond to anything within The Collective. How do you explain that?<**

▸ I can't. I have no idea.

>**You are not the first Volunteer to receive that error. And you**

yourself described an incident—an unexplained external influence taking control of you at the firing range. Enabling you to make a shot that you would not have been able to make on your own.<

  ▸ That's true...

>Third... Well, Q will show you.<

Q walked to a folding table, carrying an unusual, high-powered microscope. He called me over. He removed a glass slide from his lab coat pocket and slid it under the microscope, projecting the results onto a large screen.

The object was blue and delicate, and when Q zoomed in to extreme magnification, the screen filled with an indecipherable wall of living code of breathtaking complexity.

>This is a sample taken from a rare fern flower, a piece of invasive flora you should be familiar with. When we examine the structure of its underlying code, we notice something strange. The code, the digital DNA if you will, underlying this flora does not match any known programming languages.

That's right. The third evidence is that the code that makes up the invasive entities is comprised of bizarre fragments of ancient and dead languages. Sumerian, Ugaritic, Hieroglyphics, Runes. Other languages we cannot even identify and have no means of translating. No programming language on Earth looks like this. Not one, nor ever has.<

  I stared at the display. It was inexplicably beautiful.

  ▸ So what does this all mean?

>Have you heard of the Calabi-Yau-Weyland Defense Appropriations Act?<

  ▸ No...

>Do those words mean anything to you?<

▸ Not at all. Why?

>We found an obscure reference to that when we were digging in the Archives. The system has since been patched and we can no longer locate the reference.<

▸ Sorry, I can't help you there.

>But there is something you *can* do to help us. You've proven yourself more capable than perhaps even you thought possible. We have another task for you. Something that will help us get closer to solving the mystery of this place.<

I was no closer to finding answers—not to who I was or what this world truly meant—but I felt I had grasped the end of a thread.

I had to keep pulling that thread until the whole thing started to unravel.

▸ Sure. Why not? I'm game. What do you want me to do?

>We want you to capture an invasive entity—alive. Smuggle it into The Commons and bring it to us to study.<

Excellent.

* * *

After I returned to The Commons, I took a moment to soak in all that had transpired. All that I had learned or failed to learn. And here I was, standing in Spawn Alley where my journey began many cycles ago.

Full circle. But not really.

So much had changed since my first awakening into this dark and violent world. And yet, it was a world not without hints of beauty and wonder.

I opened my menu and scrolled all the way down to my Subroutines submenu. I erased some of my old notes and replaced them with new ones. A renewed set of tasks. A vision for my next steps. I knew what I needed to do.

I opened my full menu and beheld my progress. The comprehensive record of my True Self™ according to Reality Inc.

DESIGNATION

VOLUNTEER ID: 01001110-01101111-01100010-01101111-01100100-01111001

ALIASES: MAGPIE

- **COSMETICS**
    - **WAVY ASYMMETRICAL CROP** (hair)
    - **ALMOND** (skin tone)

- **MODS**
    - **NEURAL-INTERFACE AXIS PORT**
        - **B3-9S7-C10K CHIP** (10,000 Crypt storage)
    - **OCULAR PORT**
        - **B1-N0C-PRCPT-I 1** (+20 Perception / 4x zoom)
    - **ROUND TABLE SMART INK**
        - **5% ARMORY DISCOUNT**

STATISTICS
- **ATTACK:** (40)
    - **STRENGTH: 20**
    - **ACCURACY: 20**
- **DEFENSE:** (30)
    - **ESSENCE: 20**
    - **RESISTANCE: 10**
- **ABILITY:** (40)
    - **ADEPTNESS: 10**
    - **ENERGY: 30**
- **MOVEMENT:** (30)
    - **SPEED: 20**
    - **AGILITY: 10**

- PROCESSING: (50)
  - PERCEPTION: **20** (+20 from ocular implant)
  - PERSUASION: **10**
  - PROTOCOL: **10**
  - PROBABILITY: **10**

SKILLS

- **Clurichaun** (10 metabytes)
- **Jiangshi** (10 metabytes)
- {empty}
- {empty}

EQUIPMENT

- WEAPONS
  - **MARK I TRENCH KNIFE** (10 metabytes): 20 damage output
  - **SNUB-NOSED REVOLVER** (30 metabytes): 20 damage output
    - **5 / 5 .32 caliber ammunition** (chambered)
    - **+10% fire damage** (Hellhound)
- ARMOR (70)
  - **HELM:** N/A
  - **BODY: TACTICAL JACKET** (30 metabytes): 30 defense (+20 storage)
    - **BALLISTIC VEST** (10 metabytes): 20 defense
    - **PROMOTIONAL T-SHIRT** (cosmetic)
  - **ARMS:** N/A
  - **LEGS: TACTICAL PANTS** (10 metabytes): 10 defense (+20 storage)
    - **TACTICAL BOOTS** (10 metabytes): 10 defense
- ACCESSORIES
  - **AMMUNITION BELT** (10 metabytes)
    - **12 / 12 .32 caliber ammunition**

INVENTORY

- **CARDS**
- **FRAGMENTS**
  - **Kappa: 10/10** (10 metabytes)
- **CONSUMABLES**
- **MATERIALS**
- **MISCELLANEOUS**

ECONOMY
- **CRYPT: -1,692** (stored on B3-9S7-C10K chip)
- **CRYSTALS**

MEMORY
- **STORAGE: 330 / 300** (340) (+40 soft storage cap)
- **SCHEMAS**
  - **Tincture of Fortune** (fern flower + pure water)

HISTORY

STATUS

TASKS
- **Remove minotaur from Grand Central Park in Eden West** (Complete / Paid Out)
- **Remove jiangshi from Elysian Spires Financial District** (Complete / Paid Out)
- **Remove clurichaun from a private residence in Royal Heights** (Complete / Paid Out)
- **Remove hellhounds from MAR Station Service Tunnels** (Complete / Paid Out)

  >SUBROUTINES
- **Capture an invasive entity alive and bring it to Antisoc** (Pending).
- **Join the Round Table** (Pending)
- **Retrieve Camel's map** (Pending)

UNASSIGNED VALUE: 0

STORAGE CUBE: 21 / 100 metabytes
- **Voynich Manuscript page** (?) (5 metabytes)

- **2 {common} fern flowers** (2 metabytes)
- **1 {uncommon} coco de mer nut** (1 metabyte)
- **1 white linen cloth** (1 metabyte)
- **1 vial of pure water** (1 metabyte)
- **Minotaur Data Card fragments: 6/10** (6 metabytes)
- **Throwing knife** (5 metabytes): 10 damage output

I closed my menu. Enough navel gazing.

Carrying my chest of one hundred Crystals to the Data Forge, one thing was absolutely clear.

▸ My odyssey is just beginning.

FILE [!SEQUENCE ERROR_]

NEST

I sped through the bright streets on the hoverbike, swerving to a halt in front of my building. I dematerialized the bike into my wrist cuff and got in the turbolift, slamming the gate shut and scanning my barcode.

Please. Please. Please.

The reward for the unprecedented "open bounty." The legendary loot. Those could wait.

Killing the gorgon freed my hunting party from their stone prisons. Citizens too, frag them—collateral damage. I had to trust their ones and zeros were streaming towards the Restoration Point. Had to have faith. But there was one more thing I needed to make sure of.

Please…

I charged into my flat, tossing my blade and gun on the weapons rack, my gauntlets and other pieces aside without looking. I doublefisted Replenishers, jabbing them into my neck and casting away the empty cartridges.

Essence restored.

I turned the corner into the bedroom. And there she was.

Michelangelo himself could not have sculpted something more beautiful, nor—to my eyes—Giacometti something more terrible.

Rook. Encased in gray stone.

▸ No!

Then that meant... it wasn't Euryale that got her. There was another gorgon out there somewhere. A third. A gorgon that the system could not locate. Another dram hybrid, more dangerous than the others.

I clenched my fist, then rammed it straight through the wall.

▸ Rook... I'm sorry.

How many cycles has it been?

I gazed at her face, frozen in time. Beatific and defiant all at once. Spotlights from a passing droneship and flashing billboards silhouetted her figure in a chameleonic glow.

My hand throbbed.

That was stupid, Magpie.

The phone rang in the kitchenette. A black, analog phone. It startled me. Nobody ever called here. I picked up the receiver. The voice on the other end sounded like it was coming from a million miles away.

"Volunteer, we have been monitoring your recent success. You have shown great skill in navigating the Metaverse. I believe you and I can help one another."

▸ Who is this?

"Your System Administrator."

END OF VOLUME I

EXTRACTIONS

REGISTRY OF INVASIVE ENTITIES

/SCANNING HISTORY
/COMPILING RECORDS
/GENERATING OUTPUT
//FAUNA

HELLHOUND

An archetypal supernatural dog recurring in mythologies around the world. These ominous creatures are believed to stand guard in the underworld or even serve the devil. Variants of this archetype are known from Greek, Norse, and Celtic myths, as well as English folklore.

BASKERVILLE HOUND

> Error. Missing entry: Baskerville_hound_{uncommon}

> See black dogs of English folklore -> hellhound archetype.

> Access Archives for more information

CLURICHAUN

An Irish variant of the mischievous solitary fairy archetype. Sometimes considered the nocturnal persona of a leprechaun, these fae tricksters are said to haunt establishments that store or deal in alcoholic spirits. If angered, clurichauns can be very dangerous. They have been believed to curse people, steal their belongings, and even cast spells on them.

> **Clurichaun spells and abilities**

If caught, a clurichaun can vanish if its captor looks away for even a moment. They are also believed to be able to create illusions. In extreme instances, clurichauns have been known to force mortals into years of servitude.

> **Clurichaun magical purse**

Clurichauns may carry a magical purse that contains a *spre na skillenagh*, a lucky shilling that always returns once spent. However, to protect this purse from avaricious mortals, a clurichaun will also carry a decoy.

HUODOU

A variant of the hellhound archetype originating from the legends of southern China, this large, black dog can both devour and breathe fire. As flames break out wherever it trods, it is viewed as an omen of misfortune, signifying wildfires and devastation. Looking into the Houdou's eyes will either reveal your deepest fears or illuminate your path to enlightenment.

JIANGSHI

A Chinese variant of both the vampire and zombie archetypes, jiangshi originate when Taoist priests reanimate the dead in order to send the bodies home over long distances for burial; however, these reanimated corpses deviate from the spell's command. Due to rigor mortis, these undead creatures can only move about by hopping, although they are surprisingly agile and can hop faster than most people can run.

Jiangshi awaken at night, seeking to kill living creatures to absorb their qi and become more powerful. Although completely blind, a jiangshi can sense human breath.

> **Jiangshi weaknesses**

Items that are known vulnerabilities or repellent to jiangshi include mirrors, objects made from peach wood, black dog blood, glutinous rice, and vinegar, among others. Jiangshi can also be temporarily distracted by throwing small objects on the ground as they may be compelled to count them. The most effective method of stopping a jiangshi is to nail an immobilizing counterspell talisman to their forehead.

MINOTAUR

> **Error. Missing entry: Minotaur__{uncommon}**
> **Access Archives for more information**

KAPPA

> **Error. Missing entry: Kappa__{common}**
> **Access Archives for more information**

//FLORA

FERN FLOWER

A magic flower found in Baltic, Estonian, Slavic, and other mythologies. This otherworldly flower blooms during a brief window on the eve of the summer solstice. Depending on the regional variant, it is believed to bring fortune to the person who finds it or grant powers to ward off evil.

Those searching for the fern flower must practice caution as dark spirits are believed to stand guard, empowered by the same solstice magic that caused the flowers to bloom. If caught by the spirits, flower seekers may be cursed or even killed. But these may be rumors designed to discourage libidinous young couples from going into the woods "seeking the fern flower."

COCO DE MER NUT

A very large nut believed to possess aphrodisiacal qualities, resembling both the shape and size of the disembodied buttocks of a woman on one side, and the belly and thighs on the other. Due to the erotic shape of this forbidden fruit, which grows on the female coco de mer trees, as well as the phallic-looking flower clusters of the male trees, it is believed the trees uproot themselves and make passionate love on stormy nights. Due to the bashfulness of the trees, whoever witnesses them mating will go blind.

Afterword

Glory to the ~~Volunteers~~ Readers!

I want to give a special shout out to all of you who were passionate, and remain passionate, about this "Nobody."

Your cognitions (conscious and unconscious) have influenced the course of this unlikely hero's journey.

Thank you for reading a MoonQuill original novel. More exciting stories can be found on at www.moonquill.com and on our platform, www.moonquillnovels.com

We would greatly appreciate it if you could take a moment to leave a review. Every review helps the author and supports their ability to continue writing fantastic books for everyone to enjoy!

Scan the QR code below to subscribe to our mailing list and be notified of new releases. You'll receive 4 e-books for free!